Dead Hands

Lorie Brink

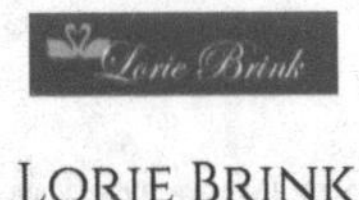

Lorie Brink

Printed in Australia

First printing: OCTOBER 2025

Paperback ISBN 978-1-7638145-6-1

eBook ISBN 978-1-7638145-4-7

Hardback ISBN 978-1-7638145-5-4

A catalogue record for this book is available from the National Library of Australia

COVER IMAGE BY PIXABAY

Thank you for your eternal support.
You know who you are.

Prologue

Beyond the rolling hills, closer to the sea, a tartan picnic blanket adorned with daisy petals, clover and nut grass was quite fitting for the alternate, tightly knit extended family. Tambourines and several bundles of legs for the silky oak easels they were constructing, lay about their feet. The gentle breeze whispered its message through the spindly leaves of the pepper tree, encouraging two young cousins—a boy and a girl—to drape themselves over their respective mothers' shoulders and hug them tightly.

'Mummy,' squealed the little girl, 'This is going to be the bestest art exhibition ever! The wind told us so.'

Idolising his cousin, the little boy gave her a toothy grin. 'Yeah!'

Swapping screws for tambourines, they sat cross-legged in a circle. The children either side of the mothers wriggled around until their knees touched. Swaying to the gentle count of three, their off-key harmony of a well-rehearsed folk song tumbled into the shade around them.

'The gypsy rover came over the hill, down through the valley so shady.'

Chapter 1

Flabbergasted at the volume of tears she had once kept at bay, Yasmin rubbed her bloodshot puffy eyes and admitted she had held onto the false hope of him visiting her and loving her like he used to, for far too long. Now, the only reminder she had of Rudy—or Ru, her nickname for him—was the sense of absolute disbelief and an untouched half-full carton of clothes in his side of the wardrobe.

'What's the point?' she whimpered and shifted it into the spare bedroom's oversized, floorless storage cupboard alongside the other boxes that belonged to his family. Yasmin stared at the accumulation. It wasn't the day to decide what to do with them all.

The tears fell again when she cradled the intricate Silky Oak carving, blindly tracing his flowing handwriting and murmured the quirky words etched into the love heart: *Yasmin loves Rudy and Rudy loves Yasmin forever, even if she loves solving puzzles more!*

The same age: except Rudy older by five months, they met at sixteen. By the time they were twenty, they admitted how very much in love they were, moved in together at twenty-two, then relocated to a new town at twenty-seven and started a new chapter in their lives. Reflecting on the years of fun and adventure they had shared while getting to know themselves; gave her little comfort. The inherited family cottage from her great aunt and uncle along with its deteriorating vineyard hobby farm in the South Australian foothills of the Mount Lofty Ranges, paved the way for the young couple to grow up quickly. It had taken a while to adjust to the major disparity from familiarity, yet individually they were on the road to success.

During the first five years, Yasmin reestablished the Pestel's name by growing and supplying edible flowers to the expanding boutique-restaurant market. Rudy, dedicated to the construction industry, followed the major projects landscape.

Then tragedy struck and turned their world upside down.

Morose, Yasmin dwelled on the devastating loss followed by the years of emotional isolation. It all stemmed from the longest snow season in history, flawed with the disastrous accident which instantly killed her best friend Emily, Rudy's paternal twin sister, and left their parents clinging to life. The shock extinguished his vim and vigour. Laying his parents to rest after turning off their life-support systems during the second year of hope and prayers sent him into a downward spiral.

Yasmin never fully comprehended why they had to die on the anniversary of his sister's death. The beautiful Emily, dead at thirty-one. Rudy an orphan at thirty-three. Yasmin had mourned the loss of her best friend and learnt to live with the void. Sorrow eroded Rudy's soul. He eventually quit his lucrative job and withdrew from everything and everyone around him.

The progressive detachment of her boyfriend became another constant in Yasmin's already lonely life, lending her existence to be trapped in his web of pitiful isolation. Without completely succumbing to the woeful situation, she threw herself into maintaining her thriving business. Her emotional support never wavered, but when Rudy moved into her late grandparents 1950s caravan in the shed and lived like a recluse the day after his thirty-fourth birthday, it tore at Yasmin's heart. Yet sheer determination drove her and eventually made the final payment of the inherited mortgage on her October birthday, three years later. And celebrated alone. Again.

Now, three days after her thirty-ninth birthday, Rudy was dead. The whole Craige family, dead. She slid down the wall and sat cross-legged on the floor in despair. Combo, her large, mixed-breed dog followed her progression with his intense eyes and sat beside her. With his brindle paw resting upon her knee, he lowered his rounded head and blunt nose into her chest anticipating the usual pretend-noisy kiss on the funny tuft of fur between his large ears. Except this time Yasmin bawled her eyes out drenching his multi-coloured fur and held her only friend close.

Chapter 2

C ombo's wet nose and the obnoxious clunk of the hour hand broke Yasmin's sombre reverie. Shuffling into the loungeroom, she bit back the tears at the memory of her mother's firm rebuke telling her to pick up her feet or her bottom lip. *One or the other, Yasmin Rose Pestel.* Plonking heavily onto the settee, the timeless classic black rotary telephone returned her stare. How could a machine be the only form of stability which participated in sad conversations?

Yasmin imagined her utterly devastated father sitting in the exact same chair bedside the exact same telephone table, thirteen years earlier. Great Aunt Rose, a widow and dove-like beautiful lady, one whom he treasured for his entire life had been taken unto the arms of an angel. How was a man, a father, to tell his youngest daughter that the woman she idolised was no longer on this earth?

Hearing her dad's voice in her head when she had asked him how he did it, Yasmin swiped at the fresh onset of tears. *It isn't easy and crying helps heal our heart. But the right people need to hear it from you directly. Remember that, should you ever be in this dreadful situation, my girl.*

Her slender index finger fitting in the hole snugly, pulled the corresponding digits on the dialler to contact the brotherhood. A fond term for Ru's three life-long mates, Timmy, Mike and Bob. Always in that order. Always together. Always there for Emily and Rudy.

Through trembling lips, Yasmin let out the breath she had been holding. Timmy answered after the first ring.

'Yasmin, are you okay?' he asked sincerely.

'I-I am,' Yasmin stammered, 'But Timmy, I am the bearer of sad news. It's—'

'Oh hell. Oh no, really sorry you have to deal with this on your own. Listen, Mike and I are here in the hospital with Bob. He fell off the stepladder the other day and is a bit dinged up, just come out of surgery so is a bit groggy. Nothing unusual there.'

'Sorry to hear that, please give him my best and for a speedy recovery.'

'Yep.'

'This is so hard ... have you guys got a sec?' she asked quietly, frowning at the edge that had crept into her voice.

'Sure thing,' he sniffled. 'I'll put you on speaker.'

Waiting for the echo, Yasmin steadied her breathing. 'My dear friends, so sorry to have to tell you this but our beloved Ru passed away yesterday. I'm sorry I haven't phoned earlier but it's been quite a dreadful time and there's going to be police involvement, hence the delay in letting you know. When I learn of his wishes, I'll let you know. I'm so sorry, Timmy, Mike and Bob, you have some beautiful memories ... draw-draw strength from th-them.'

Yasmin burst into tears and pressed the handset against her chest.

Timmy's demands finally reached her ears. 'How? How did he die, Yasmin?'

With her emotions in utter turmoil, she found comfort in smoothing the tuft of fur between Combo's ears. Feeling like her lungs were going to collapse described the last conversation the estranged couple held almost a year earlier. Rudy had told her the nasturtiums were tasty, and the lavender soil would eventually need turning. Shivering, she vividly recalled his lifeless eyes and the way he looked straight through her the whole time. Adding to the sad discovery in the cleared lavender paddock, he died on the anniversary of the death of his family. It had been such a bleak day too. The low clouds covered the tops of the nearby hills like a dull, drippy icing, yet the beds of blossoming French marigolds between the colourful snapdragons before the Queen Elizabeth rose garden reminded her of a lonely ray of sunshine bursting through a rainbow.

'But that's not how a rainbow works!' Timmy reminded her.

'You can see it, can't you?' She pleaded. No reply came. 'But why anywhere near the lavender? He hated the stuff with a passion.'

'So sorry.' Hushed, snivelling voices echoed through the phone.

'Ru lived like a hermit and avoided me after he moved into the caravan but left constant reminders of his presence by leaving the greenhouse door unlatched,' she sniffled quietly.

'We know that—'

Mike talked over the top of Timmy and encouraged her gently. 'Talk it out, Yas, we're listening.'

'Thanks Mike. Combo and I found him leaning up against the seventh row. He-he was facing the roses. His eyes were open but lifeless, just like-like the last time ...' She wailed. 'Why? Why did he leave me to discover his body in the cleared lavender paddock? That was just plain cruel. Why?'

'We're so sorry, Yasmin. Sorry you have to deal with this alone.' Timmy's voice trembled. 'But how? How did Rudy die? You have to tell us.'

The men's choked up voices and sniffles mingled with her own.

'They suspect a heart attack, but the police will be back here tomorrow morning. I am just so sorry for you all. You guys have lost the whole beautiful family.'

After a long pause, Timmy whispered, 'And our mother.'

Yasmin gasped. 'No! Oh no, oh my heart breaks for you guys. I am so sorry for your loss. When?'

This time Timmy's voice was distant. 'A little while after we came to see you pair earlier in the year.'

'Oh, that's so sad and so cruel because Ru never even made his presence known ... oh guys ... I am so sorry ... oh, that's so sad. But why didn't you tell me?'

'We couldn't. Uh ... not without Rudy there. Yasmin, we're going to have to have a longer chat at another time. The nurses need to do their checks.'

She quietly blew her nose and listened to the echoed sentiment.

'Yas, you'll be okay, I know you will be.'

'Oh, Mike.'

'Yeah, I know ... listen, we all caught up once a month since you guys left.'

Yasmin coughed and spluttered. 'You what? Even Emily?'

'Yes, it was a pact. Only sometimes with Emily. But all that's for a conversation at another time. Listen, Rudy sorted out a lot of the business affairs and paid for mother's funeral when he saw us. It's awfully sad about him and our hearts go out to you, but we need to tell you some things, actually a lot of things but not everything right now. And you have to do something.'

'What? You're confusing me. You just said you couldn't tell me about your mum because he wasn't here when you visited? I don't get it.' She paused and tried in vain to wave away the emotional fog. 'That's why you guys never took off your sunnies! At least that part makes sense now.'

Since she was met with silence, continued with the threads of her thought pattern. 'I'm glad he could help you guys out, don't get me wrong. I distinctly recall him securing a large project around the time of his parents' funeral, but afterwards he made me cut everything back in the paddocks, pay the rates in advance and go and see my family overseas, which left me with a few hundred bucks to my name and while I was away, he quit his job! He was so angry with the banks and the way they callously—'

'You have to listen to us, Yasmin. You have to play Rudy's game. You have to solve the clues. It's crucial for our business that you do. You need to understand that.'

'What game? What clues? Your business? Did-did you know he was going to die?'

'We can't do this now.'

'You have to! And why are you telling me what to do, Timmy? Why? I hate that and you know it!' reactively twisting the curly cord around her wrist.

He raised his voice for an instant. 'STOP it, Yasmin. Listen, we were never as good as you at solving riddles and stuff. We know there are hidden things you have to find before the police—'

'Hey? Illegal things?'

'No, no, his story, Emily's story, your inheritance, our connection. It-it's all hidden. We know it's so soon after and you're going to be riding the monster grief rollercoaster for a while but try and put your focus on this. It is so very important to all of us. We have to go. The nurses are getting really impatient. We'll phone you in a few days.'

Her mind was in a spin. 'Why didn't Emily write back to me?'

'She did. We have to go, Yasmin.'

The call was suddenly disconnected.

Numbly brewing a strong black coffee, the conversation birthed questions which bounced erratically in her head. *What inheritance? What story? Where are Emily's letters? How come they didn't seem surprised? What connection? They saw Ru regularly? What game? Why all the deception?* She clutched at her stomach. Bewildered grief constricted every organ in her body. Self-doubt formed hands and closed around her throat. *Why? What did I do to deserve this?*

She sat down heavily, head between her knees and drank in mouthfuls of air. Her mind drifted back to the threads of financial despair after the hospital costs for the years of care and the considerably expensive joint funeral. The only information Rudy had shared was his parents' last Will and Testament had bequeathed their meagre savings to their surviving son. He then expressed his disgust that the bank had foreclosed on the house and family business, thereby leaving no debt or proceeds. But from that date onward the subject of his family was taboo.

The long-buried question followed by the answers exploded through the denial barrier.

'Why? Because I was an outsider. Because I had taken him away from his home. THAT'S WHY!'

Chapter 3

The flashing light on the answering machine stabbed its way into Yasmin's subconscious. Rolling her eyes, it was no wonder she hadn't given the two-day-old message any thought and pressed the play button. A much older woman's voice had left a message for a *Rupert John Matson* requesting his presence at the usual get-together at Moojie Hill.

Only two people called Rudy, *Rupert*. Whether he was present or not. They were Leigh and Callum Jones. Not quite friends, but a married couple who called on them whenever they travelled through town. The last time they did, back in February, they and Rudy sheepishly transferred a cardboard carton from his caravan into the boot of their sedan. Yasmin distinctly recalled her bewilderment and confused anger after she innocently asked of the contents. The three of them denied all knowledge. Their blatant lie unsettled her for ages. Afterwards, Rudy became more aloof. The mutual dislike between Combo and this couple was pretty obvious, as was their obsession with her property. In particular the hundred-year-old Jacaranda tree in the front yard. Above all though, their fascination with Ru's depression.

But she had never heard of a *Rupert John Matson* and had no idea what went on at *Moojie Hill*. Or wherever the hell *Moojie Hill* was.

All of a sudden, the find-the-word puzzle in the local newspaper popped into her thoughts. Rubbing her forehead in exasperation snatched up the paper, added another word to her growing list but remained stumped at solving the nine-letter word. Yawning loudly, put a line through the word that didn't use the essential letter and tossed the paper onto the settee. Combo's ears pricked with anticipation then lowered in realisation. His grizzle mirrored Yasmin's mood, yet he never took his eyes off her.

<table>
<tr><td>Anise</td><td rowspan="5">

N	C	E
A	**I**	M
T	**S**	R

</td><td>~~Mace~~</td><td>Strain</td></tr>
<tr><td>Crime</td><td>Mice</td><td>Saint</td></tr>
<tr><td>Cairn</td><td>Mint</td><td>Satin</td></tr>
<tr><td>Cinema</td><td>Mince</td><td>Stain</td></tr>
<tr><td>Item   Resin</td><td>Merit</td><td>Trim</td></tr>
<tr><td></td><td>Nice</td><td>Train</td></tr>
</table>

Pulling an ugly face at the answering machine, Yasmin rewound and replayed the message. The voice was not familiar, but the recurring questions of who and why, were. After cross-referencing her calendar with the date and time of the phone call, she mocked her own foolishness.

Because the laundry door wasn't possible to be locked and the cottage was still his home, Rudy had free access whenever he wanted, thus leaving her delivery schedule open to the world. It dawned on her then that he received his messages when she wasn't at home, would delete them and she'd be none the wiser. Shaking her head forlornly, stared in the direction of the lavender paddock. *Not this time, hey Ru? Or Rupert? Did you lead another life?* Then, another thought crossed her mind. *Was it a coincidence? Just a wrong number and not you at all?*

Nearly jumping out of her skin when the telephone jangled then abruptly stopped mid-ring, glared angrily at it and promptly ignored its next noisy interference. The new string of questions compounded a headache, so she brewed another coffee and let the cold water from the kitchen tap drench her face. Her head hurt, her eyes ached and her nose was red-raw.

Moaning, gently dabbed at her face, 'Quickly running out of soft paper, Combo!'

For the fifth time in a row, the telephone stopped ringing half-way through the third ring. Yasmin scowled at the apparatus over the top of her coffee cup. Steam and tears blurring her eyes. Several minutes later, it rang again and didn't stop ringing until moments before it went to the answering machine.

She swooped onto the handset. Emotionless, said, 'Hello?'

'Yasmin, it's Leigh and Callum, we've got you on speaker. How are you, dear?' The woman's oily voice slid through the wire.

'Getting by thanks,' frowning at the unlisted telephone number. 'Leigh, you left a message for Rupert Jo—'

'Wasn't me.'

'Oh?' Thinking quickly, Yasmin asked, 'Are you coming to visit again?'

'No.'

'Aside from having a silent number, what's changed?'

'Um ... ah ... well—'

'I've got another question for you two. Do you usually phone Rupert?'

A delayed reply elevated her annoyance. 'Well? You always call him Rupert, so who do you know calls him Rupert John Matson?'

Leigh's breath caught in her throat. 'We only ever called him by his first name. Didn't dare call him anything else.'

Her blood turned cold. 'What? Why?'

In an unusually timid voice, Callum spoke swiftly. 'Are you alone?'

'I'm with my dog. Why?'

He groaned. 'Eugh, dislike dogs. Anyway, listen very carefully. Rupert, although depressed and bordering on deranged, wasn't who you thought he was.'

'Really, Callum? Why the past tense?'

This time, he was smug in his reply. 'Yep! Generous and clever too. Loved art, that's where Leigh and I met him, long before we met you actually ... we'll never forget his Monet collection. But going back to what we were talking about, the full name always brought about horrendous consequences and as time went on, we assumed your stepbrother was the boogey-man.'

Leigh's loud sob wasn't the only thing that instantly dried up Yasmin's tears. *My stepbrother?* In a choked whisper, asked, 'The what?' In the background, she heard the telltale signs of cigarettes being lit.

Leigh talked as she exhaled. 'We don't mean to scare you, Yasmin. But he changed. Sort of grew in size and aside from art, loved grey jackets and handlebar moustaches. Sorry, dear, we get that it's pretty raw.'

'Huh?'

Leigh sighed impatiently. 'His death.'

'How did you know?'

'Via the grapevine.'

'What grapevine?'

'His friends weren't yours. It happens sometimes. S'pose it doesn't matter anymore, does it?'

The volcano of emotions erupted. 'Is that all you've got? No condolences or any such thing? No can we do anything for you? Nothing?'

'We are trying to help you!' the woman exclaimed loudly. 'What did you expect to hear?'

'Something a lot nicer from people who have known us for so long. Instead, all I'm hearing are riddles! Lies even.'

'He really wasn't well. Surely you don't need us to tell you that,' Callum stated flatly. Leigh continued without so much as a pause. 'It's not our fault you couldn't see it.'

Yasmin spluttered. 'Back up a sec, are you accusing him of committing suicide?'

'Well, he was depressed ... probably his big heart just gave out. Stress and depression can take its toll you know.'

'Wait. You three were all lying when I sprung you loading that box into your car.'

Leigh spoke coyly. 'Guilty.'

'So? What was in it?'

'We haven't opened it yet. We had to wait.'

'For what?'

Leigh changed the subject harshly. 'Look, just let us know when you have thought about our offer.'

Yasmin scratched her head in confusion, then reached for her coffee. 'What offer?'

'To buy your joint.'

'*What?* You have got to be kidding me. I am not selling. How dare you?' She swore under her breath as coffee slopped onto her hand.

'How dare us what?' Leigh challenged. 'We're sorry for your loss. There. Is that better?'

Hot tears slipped down Yasmin's cheeks. Her downcast mouth stretched her eyes enough to make sure her mug was firmly on the table. 'No, not really.'

'Maybe you should take this opportunity to start your next chapter somewhere else. You'll soon realise there's nothing holding you back, except you.'

'Leigh!' Shocked, Yasmin held her face as if she had been slapped.

'Uh ... that didn't come out right. What I meant to say was—'

'You know something? I don't care to hear anymore.' Furiously swiping away the tears, stretched the telephone cord to its extent and paced back and forth. Yasmin raised her voice for the first time in an awfully long time. 'Leigh and Callum Jones, I DO NOT want to hear from you EVER AGAIN and DO NOT EVER, EVER come near me or my property. If you do, two things will happen. One, YOU WILL finally meet my dog and two, YOU WILL MOST CERTAINLY MEET THE POLICE.'

She slammed the receiver downwards, missed its target and promptly burst into angry tears all over again leaving the phone where it landed. Bawling loudly, Combo was instantly beside her. He cocked his head at each outburst.

'How dare they? How did they find out so quickly? My stepbrother? His Monet collection? Longer than ten years? And just how many times did they call in when I wasn't there? And why had they always insisted on calling him Rupert? Even to his face! Why?'

Yasmin stared at Combo while she reflected on the single occasion the Jones' did stay for light refreshments, and distinctly remembered Rudy didn't even correct them. *He never corrected them about anything.* Plonking herself onto the settee, she scratched her head. *The boogey-man? Grey suit? Moustache? STEP-BROTHER?*

Chapter 4

Leigh looked at Callum with a stoned grin. 'Jones? After all these years he never corrected her! At least the boogey-man's curse can't get us now ... still not gonna say his name but.'

'Nope.' Leaning over to his beloved, transferred the last of the putrid smoke during a kiss. Callum whispered and exhaled at the same time. 'We finally get to open this box.'

'Been waiting long enough. Hope it's money!' Leigh grinned.

'That'd be nice. We're running dry. Hey, the boys had better get their arse into gear for Moojie Hill.'

'Give them a call after.' Leigh tore the tape off the top slit of the packing box, ruffled through the packaging, then scoffed. 'Look Cal, five of the arrogant bastard's monogrammed plaques.'

He grunted, then lifted one out and gave her a toothy grin. 'Feel the weight, Leigh! This is better than money. Even if it's 14-Karat gold or as low as 9-Karat, they're worth a few bob!'

'But what about his initials?'

'We'll just melt these down!'

'Clive's furnace!' they spoke in unison, chuckled excitedly and rifled through the green sheets until the box was empty.

'Lousy bastard. Five? *Five?*' Leigh moaned and reached for a skinny cigar. 'My high has just crashed.'

She watched Callum retrieve the drug scales. Together they stared at the digits while he stacked the five plaques atop.

They both whispered, 'Three thousand, five hundred and eighty-five grams.'

Leigh inhaled heavily, pulled Callum's face into hers and exhaled into his open mouth. Relishing in the moment of the port flavoured smoke, they smiled sheepishly at each other.

'Here's to the boogey-man whose name shalt not be repeated,' Callum murmured.

'I feel real bad now. Poor Yasmin.'

He shrugged. 'Lucky Yasmin, more like it. She had no idea who he was! Let sleeping dogs lie ... eugh, hate dogs, let him not haunt us! Now, put on your laughing gear and pack your prettiest dress, Mrs Johns, we're going out for dinner. In Adelaide!'

'Adelaide? That's over two hours away!'

'Yep! You pack for two nights, I'll book!'

'You're the best thing that happened to me, Callum,' Leigh ran her tongue around her lips, and squirmed while crushing out her smoke.

'And I just love the way you do that!'

Chapter 5

Muttering under her breath, Yasmin refused to have the pair of horrible people consume any more of her mind. Instead, she reminded herself of the pending police visit the following morning. That and the information spilled from the recent telephone conversations raised her ire enough to start tying up loose ends. This time the phone's handle did find its mark. No sooner had it settled, it rang. her look would have turned it grey if it were a living organism.

'Yes?'

'Uh, Ms Pestel?'

'Who is this?'

'Stan, The Real Estate Man. Have I caught you at a bad time?'

A fresh onslaught of tears slipped down her face.

'Please excuse my abruptness, Stan. I had not long hung up from a particularly rude and distressing phone call.'

'Sorry to hear that, hopefully some good news will help. Congratulations! Settlement has been completed. You are the proud owner of both properties north and south of you. Your Pestel's Edible Petals will surely make an even prettier vista if you expand!'

Sniffing back the bittersweet tears, 'Thank you, Stan! Now to pay these off before I'm sixty, eh?'

He spoke philosophically. 'Look at it this way. We don't work for the banks, and they are a convenience. All conveniences cost money. However, we get one life and one life only, well, on this earth anyway! The land isn't going anywhere, meet the repayments until you can't then it's the bank's problem!'

'I like the way you think!' she murmured.

'Sadly, Title Deeds aren't a thing anymore, but I will e-mail through the entire suite of certified conveyancing documents. The fencing contractor has been paid out of the proceeds as agreed.'

'Speaking of which, I love the job he did. The white is a happy contrast, well, when we've had rain, but whitewashing it is going to be exhausting and expensive!'

'Not at all. It's a new trend which will easily withstand our climate. It's PVC here, or Vinyl in the U.S.'

'Nice! Please include his details. I might have a project coming up.'

'Will do. Oh! I almost forgot. As a show of goodwill given the late vendor was an employee of the Shire, they offset the family's rates with the overpayments held in Trust.'

'Oh, that is good news. May he rest in peace.'

'Yes, and his family are grateful his land has gone to someone local and not the land bank or a foreign developer. Thank you for keeping our landscape pleasing to the eye!'

She let out a shaky breath. 'And thank you for the good news.'

'Are you okay?' His genuine concern brought about another onslaught of sobbing.

Eventually, managed to answer. 'I will have to be, thank you for asking. Thanks for ringing, Stan. I appreciate your call.'

'Okay then. Congratulations on your amazing achievement. It does sound like you need to take care of yourself, so I'll ring off. Bye for now and thank you for supporting my business.'

She murmured her thanks again and gently replaced the handset. *Back on the mortgage merry-go-round!*

Her original jubilation of acquiring the adjoining properties disappeared over the tops of the rolling hills and her gaze settled in the direction of Rudy's little caravan. Groaning loudly, the disaster zone had filled her with unease when she first opened its door.

Even through blurry eyes, the scraps of blank notepaper torn into shapes or scrunched up and strewn everywhere was noticeable. The most peculiar thing was the rounded shapes of dolphins and whales. Even a mermaid! Rudy had never mentioned anything about the sea. But what was really macabre were the funeral notices covering the windows.

Clicking her tongue and reaching for Combo's treats, said. 'Come on, boy, it's not going to tidy itself up on its own.'

Chapter 6

The stepbrothers finished their regular arm wrestle with Giles letting his older and much stronger nemesis, Ivan, manipulate the outcome.

'I win, you loser. Again!'

'Yeah, yeah, whatever. What's the plan for Moojie?'

'You and Stu and not a cow named moo need to get pill-pressing, dude. Ha! Clever, eh? Eh?' Ivan puffed out his chest.

'Yeah, very clever. Any changes?'

'Heard the bloody Kraut sausage truck's gone gangbusters which may impact our customers again. Gotta be on our game. It's expected to be a massive event this year. '

Hating crowds, Giles rolled his eyes. 'Joyous.'

'Quit being the drama-queen. You've never been invited to the yarn in the barn.'

'Nor has your sprog!'

'That's right. It's not for soft cocks.' Ivan shadow-boxed him into the door of the fridge. 'Don't just stand there, get me a beer, then get together with Stu. The Johns are gonna be barking orders soon.'

Obediently, Giles wrapped his hand around the aluminium can failing to dent it.

'Speaking of the devils,' Ivan groaned and turned away to answer his mobile phone.

Seizing the opportunity, he violently shook the can and placed it on the counter.

'See ya later, mate!' he called out over his shoulder, scooped the keys off the table and raced out the door.

Ivan's abusively vile outburst was drowned out by the sound of Giles's laughter and revving engine. He reprimanded himself silently. *Idiot, he's going to make you pay for that.*

Chapter 7

Drawing in a steadying breath, Yasmin clipped open the caravan door. Desperately trying to slow down her thoughts while she collected up the pieces of paper lying nearby, she looked at the odd window covering and wondered how the man could have lived without fresh air. But it was the impeccably made bed that undid her resolve. For all his misgivings while they had shared an abode, Rudy had insisted on making the bed, only because she couldn't make it so neatly.

There was no trace of his aftershave or scent. Even Combo couldn't smell anything and went and laid outside the door. Taking her time, she folded the bed linen all the while looking at the paper patchwork, and noticed every corner was rounded. Peering closely, some of the letters and digits had been traced over, but only on certain funeral notices. *Letters in red ink, digits in black?*

She blinked a couple of times then glancing at nothing in particular noticed the colours actually depicted a type's mountain range. Pausing momentarily, she checked out the similarly morbid assortment covering the kitchenette window. To her astonishment, the colours created a similar outline but with more peaks and less valleys.

Peeling the curved corners from the window frame, Yasmin laid the flimsy paper over the little dining table and peered more closely. At first glance, the red letters made up Emily's name but paying more attention, several obits were in South Australian rural towns while others were as far away as Victoria, and a cluster in central New South Wales. She presumed the blackened digits were phone numbers but then noticed some of the capital letters had been blackened out. Mainly 'E' and 'S'. Shaking her head dejectedly; it was just too much so she went back to stripping the bed.

By the time the woollen underlay had been removed, Yasmin realised the mattress was brand new, and familiar. Then recognised the similarity to the ones they had bought twelve years earlier when they first moved into the cottage. Granted she had never stopped Rudy from going inside, with his whereabouts unknown except for the greenhouse left unlatched, but to have moved the mattress without her or Combo knowing about it, left her cold.

With the collage of funeral notices from the little bedroom window atop the one on the dining room table, the emptiness around her was harsh. Laying down on the bare mattress she closed her eyes and willed for sleep to take over her exhaustion. The overwhelming sensation of standing at the foot of a mountain, desperately searching for the steep path to climb so she could feel the sunshine again swept over her like an icy breeze. Combo's dejected sigh resonated deeply.

Awash with numbness, the lads' insistence rung loudly in her head. As did the thought of being a pawn. Although the urgency struck her as being odd, lying around feeling sorry for herself was not going to accomplish anything either. Gently wiping her eyes, she stared at the curved roof, and frowned. A yacht? Who would have drawn that? Why? Nobody had ever talked about being on water. The families had always been land lovers. Even in all the years of camping and exploring either with Emily and the lads or just themselves, they had never ventured anywhere near water. Ever. Taking a picture of the sketch, Yasmin shook her head in bewilderment. It kept moving from side to side when she slid open the drawers. Every compartment was empty. There wasn't even any dust.

Then she opened the simple wardrobe and stared, mouth agape. Hanging on a Silky Oak hanger, a long grey jacket shrouded a charcoal grey suit. Barely breathing, rested her hand against the lapel and turned it slightly. In addition to the emerald-green bow tie hanging around the hook, a fake handlebar moustache looked plain weird attached to the inside of the neck collar of the crisp white shirt. Yasmin shivered when she recalled the Jones' description. *The boogey-man?*

Completely perplexed, she closed the wardrobe silently, sat down heavily on the bed and banged the kick panels with her heels in frustration. Crying out in fright, the entire bedframe collapsed. Dazed, she found herself still on the mattress, on the floor. Combo was at her side in an instant and nosed excitedly around the edges. He kept trying to get underneath the whole configuration. Gently shooing him aside, she manhandled the mattress and leant it up against the window-wall. Combo sniffed frantically around a brown envelope. She watched in fascination and almost jumped out of her skin when he barked.

'That's a good boy,' she spoke firmly and picked up the envelope.

The folded corners weren't too dissimilar to every other piece of paper in the place. ONLY OPEN UPON MY DEATH was written in perfect capital letters.

'Oh Ru,' she sobbed.

Sliding out the folded piece of paper with trembling hands, Yasmin had no idea why she was so nervous. He had never physically hurt her. What damage could his written word do? With that thought in mind, she unfolded the shaped piece of paper and gasped. It too looked like a yacht. Taking a deep breath and exhaling noisily, fought back the tears when she saw his impeccable handwriting.

Yasmin,

I don't know if I should have thanked you for staying, or made you leave. I couldn't. I had nowhere to go. No family. The lads had their own lives. Just you in my space and sometimes in my face. I will thank you for the caravan.

I have to be burnt. Like Emily was. I felt her pain when I was forced to do that, so I have to suffer the same. Tell my three best friends, Timmy, Mike and Bob, I am glad we saw each other when we did. Thank them for the good times for me. I know you will, because that's who you are. Always doing what you're told.

You have to look everywhere. Even the floors.

I never told you the truth about my parents. They had a yacht that was in the family's name. The last I heard it'd had a facelift and was still moored at Emerald Bay. Anyway, it was a family thing. When Emily left this world, it automatically became mine. Fat lot of good that does me when I'll be dead, so you now own it but you have to share it with my three best friends. I know you will, because that's who you are.

Also, my parents left me some money. Some of that's yours now. It's just not all in a bank. Imagine me shrugging my shoulders the way I used to do it. You remember? Well, I've just done that now. Your love of word games and mysteries always did my head in, I just hope you enjoy my game.

You must listen to what Timmy says.

Yes, these are my wishes and lend to my Last Will and Testament. I want to be cremated.

I don't have any feelings of anything. I just don't want to live anymore. I made this choice. Now you will have to turn the soil in the lavender patch! I hated the stuff, but you grew it so well. You should have grown chillies too. It's time for you to have a break.

I did love you, but how could I have kept loving you when I didn't love myself or anything else? Go and have a good life, Yasmin. You can. I promise you that. You're young enough to fulfil nearly all your dreams.

Good bye. Rudy.

In the cruellest moment, everything suddenly made sense. Yasmin slowly read the letter again, searching for clues. Nothing stood out. Absolutely nothing. So, she read it out aloud and frowned at *'you have to look everywhere. Even the floors.'* Her frown deepened when she recalled Timmy and Mike instructing her to play Rudy's game.

By now, Combo was ready to pounce onto something in the far corner. His tail swished slowly. His one usually large floppy ear joined its mate on high alert. Stacking the kick panels underneath the dining table, she dragged the mattress across the doorway and shrieked when he barked. Fearing it was a snake she grabbed at his collar. Combo shook himself free, sat, shimmied backwards until he laid splot-like and pawed playfully at a circular piece of turquoise fabric stuck to the floor. Laying on her stomach beside him, she bit back a loud sob. A pink fabric letter 'Y' had been sewn on the top. The basketball stitch as neat as anything. Trying to slide it off the floor wasn't successful and eventually worked out it was attached to something. Sitting up, she pulled a length of PVC downpipe up through the floor, and peered into the void where it came from, recognising the aged concrete floor of the shed. She rotated the cylinder. It's length of 350 mm marked. Anything about Rudy incorporated perfection, precision and compartmentalisation. Turning the it upside down, the linoleum pattern on the end cap attached by tape matched the caravan floor. An uneducated eye wouldn't have been any the wiser. It was a perfect fit. *What an unbelievably calculated mind.*

Yasmin eventually worked out the order of timber planks to rebuild the bed frame. Sliding the mattress on top, nodded in self-satisfaction. Encouraging Combo to sniff the fabric on the container then commanding him to fetch, she watched as he thoroughly searched the inside of the little old abode before bounding over to the cottage. Wrapping the cylinder in the bundle of linen inside one pillowcase, she rolled up the collage of funeral notices tightly and stood them beside the tube with the envelope standing up behind them inside the other. Yasmin locked the caravan and slipped that key inside the bag of secrets. Catching up with Combo at the patio door, she glanced at the time as they entered the cottage. It was just gone noon. Sighing in relief that the day hadn't slipped away, locked the door behind her. It was the first time in her life she felt exposed and vulnerable to the elements. And nervous. The feeling compelling her to close the curtains, turn on the air-conditioning and activate the security alarms.

A small smile felt oddly rewarding when she read her e-mails. After several attempts, managed to compose a message to the fencing contractor requesting a quote. Yasmin's thoughts drifted back to the peculiar yet confronting warning about saying *the full name*. Then, just as swiftly, shoved the entire telephone conversation deep into her mind and slammed the door shut. When the image of Rudy's grey suit popped into her mind's eye, she did exactly the same thing.

Laying the pillowcase on the padded tablecloth atop the old Mahogany dining room table, Yasmin looked around and mocked herself for the state of affairs she found herself in. This time, reality struck her like a hammer. She had been living in the past for far too long. The furniture in the inherited cottage hadn't moved for as long as she could remember. Even the big old clock had been noisy since she was a kid. Her mind ticked over ideas of repositioning the furniture in the living area but it all got too hard. She slumped onto the settee and sighed heavily. Staring blankly at the newspaper puzzle, she flicked it onto the floor and laid down.

Combo's clicking toenails on the parquetry floor gave the usual sense of comfort as did the usual resting of his head on her knees. Instead, he lightly wrapped his jaw around her hand and pulled her gently while his tail wagged excitedly, leading them into the spare bedroom. For years they had walked past the room unsuspectingly. The only interior door Rudy permitted to be closed was the one that accessed the drab laundry with its horribly loud creaking door. But any attempt to address the matter had been quickly thwart. It was obvious Combo had had a lot of fun on the spare bed given the tousled-up edges of the dustcover. Traces of pink tissue poked out from holes in a makeshift mattress, bringing the tears to the forefront. It had been a very long time since she had seen so much of the stuff. The deeply buried memory surfaced, and the floodgates opened.

Rudy had always teased her about her love of Queen Elizabeth Roses, and at every opportunity would add to her horde of the same colour pink, except in tissue. Rudy's 28th birthday. The first time they had ever celebrated his birthday alone. She had wrapped herself in sheets of it as his gift. The embarrassment, humiliation and gutted feeling washed over her all over again. She could still see his look of utter disdain. The spat-words of wanting to be back home and completely disinterested in any intimacy tore through her like bear claws.

Gulping painfully, her shoulders sagged under the weight of the prolonged sadness. Turning to walk out the room, Combo blocked her path and nuzzled her wrist with his wet nose. She stared into his penetrating eyes and took comfort in the depths of the dark brown tenderness. They shifted from hers to the bed. Taking the hint, she ruffled the tuft of fur. He helped remove the dustcover in a gentle game of tug-o-war. A deflated sigh escaped at the mish-mash of curved overlapping shirts. *That's where your upper clothing got to!* With mouth agape and dustcover on the floor, several multi-sized white and brown rounded-cornered envelopes stared back at her. *Another yacht?* The white envelopes resembled the sail while the brown ones shaped the keel. Drying her eyes on the hem of her shirt, she reached for the largest of the lot. Lifting the flap and sliding out the manilla folder, scratched her head in bewilderment. Across the front was the family logo of their company. Their *transport* company? Combo whimpered at her strangled cry of frustration. She had always believed the family had been in the construction industry. Rudy could build things. Engineered things. Always.

The four initials curled around the C of their surname, Craige. The A and M of his parents' names—Adam and Milly—crested the top curve while the E and R of their adopted children—Emily and Rudy—were linked quite fancily around the bottom curve. The M and E linked with a flourish to represent their femininity. Underneath the monogram, was a simple yacht cut out of a newspaper.

CREAM?

She admonished herself for finding the letters of the family members amusing.

Alongside were clippings of dinky cars and an old-time pantechnicon. An actual black and white photograph of the entire family sitting on the bonnet of an unfamiliar truck had Yasmin scratching her head. Wiping at the sentimental tears, she realised she had never seen the family so young.

Cautiously opening the folder, a single envelope remained inside. The moment she removed it two emeralds fell out. Yasmin gasped. The last time she had seen the jewels was on a three-strand pearl bracelet attached to three other emeralds clasped around Mrs Craige's elegant left wrist. It didn't feel right touching them. Using a sheet of pink tissue, slid them back to where they came from and closed the folder.

Inside a smaller brown envelope, the last Will and Testament of his parents dated thirty years earlier. Yasmin didn't even want to open the last brown bulky envelope and gathered up the remaining white envelopes, which were all empty. She rolled her eyes in frustration and did a double-take. Sketched onto that ceiling was the exact same image as the one in the caravan. An exact replica of the picture on the folder. She took another photo on her personal mobile and burst into tears. *This was a horrible game.*

Combo barked when she shrieked. Her business mobile phone rang for the umpteenth time that day. Again, it was the funeral parlour's number and again, she ignored it. Burying her face into her companion's fur, wept.

'Leave me alone, Clive. I've got a feeling you don't want to order flowers!'

Chapter 8

Making sure he was out of camera view; Senior Constable Carl Ramond sent the long-awaited coded message to his undercover cousin.

Hey Cuz, your favourite test subject will be on point within 24-hours.

Her immediate reply made his eyes water.

Thanks Cuz, give Pooch my unwavering love. I know it'll be hard for you but make the most of this sad opportunity and enjoy your time with the K9s. Your efforts haven't gone unnoticed. Will make contact when the time is right. Out.

He studied the photo of the then three-year-old motley-coloured dog hanging proudly in his harness against the body of his favourite cousin. Their parachute floating above them like a billowing cloud. They had just commenced their tenth jump, and it was impossible to tell who had the happiest face.

Tears welled up again as he remembered how heart-wrenchingly difficult it was for them to leave Pooch with the former Special Ops pilot in the rolling hills on the outskirts of the neighbouring town. He on an entirely different mission, Pooch was left to follow a challenging trail, track a forever-changing scent and eventually walk into Pestel's Edible Petals shed. Although Pooch was monitored the whole time and it took nigh on two years, no human interfered with his progress.

'Amazing creatures,' he whispered and closed the lid of their encrypted laptop.

***

Meanwhile, on the other side of town Travis stared at the bleak interior of the Ford Transit van. The twins had been nagging him to clean it up ever since they rolled the boogey-man out of its rear doors. Just as they had nagged him to go after the dying man and remove his rucksack. He would have if the flower lady bitch hadn't turned up. Groaning loudly, he toyed with the hole in the carpet. It had been getting worse after each trip and was beginning to smell. He yanked at the loose edging and removed every bit of the mangy floor covering.

To his surprise, he found two small bags of green pills and several rolls of cash against the headboard. Stashing these into the front pocket of his denim overalls, followed a trail of round-shaped scraps of paper alongside the panel.

'What's this then?' he mumbled and tugged gently on a piece sticking out from where a pop rivet should be.

Smoothing out the creases, his voice shook as he read it aloud. 'Beware of the boogey-man.'

Eventually, the frown creasing Travis' forehead dissolved. In its place, an evil thought crossed his mind and slipped out his mouth. 'Hmm, maybe two can play this game after all.'

Chapter 9

Exhaustion smothered Yasmin like a heavy blanket. She flopped onto the recliner and prayed it was going to be the last of crying herself to sleep. Then argued with herself why she was crying. *Grief? Yes and no. She'd grieved Rudy for nigh on eight years! Shock? Perhaps. Feeling sorry for herself? No. Frustrated? Yes. Angry? Getting there!* Groaning loudly, the ringing bells of the landline dragged her out of her sad state. Laying there listening to it click over to the answering machine, she willed her eyes to close.

'Afternoon Ms Pestel, Sergeant Pyers calling to confirm our scheduled appointment with you, at your premises, nine o'clock tomorrow morning.' His serious tone softened. 'No need to ring me back, we acknowledge it is a difficult time. Rest and be kind to yourself, there is no right or wrong way to grieve. We'll see you in the morning.'

Yasmin swiped at the tears and tried to picture which of the policemen he was. Not giving it, or trying to sleep much more thought, brewed another strong black coffee. Mindlessly removing the PVC tube from the bag of linen and standing it upright on the padded tablecloth, ran her fingers over the perfectly stitched letter 'Y'.

Nodding slowly, muttered, 'Righto, Ru ... bring it on.'

Easing off the top cap, plaited cords hung down its centre which lifted a separate internal tube measuring exactly 300 mm long, covered in soft pink crushed velvet with its own lid. She sniffled softly. This time, the lid was like a mini hat box. It was beautiful. It had to be Emily's. Holding the tube between her knees, Yasmin unscrewed the covered lid and peered inside. It was like looking into a kaleidoscope, except the light fragments were thirty-one tightly rolled rolls of cash. She pried out and flattened out the notes of one roll consisting of every denomination and tallied up $1,605. *The twins' birth date.* Doing the multiplication, her hand flew to her mouth. That was $49,755 on the top row alone. A little bit nervous to see just how many rows the cylinder contained, she withdrew the entire inner tube and unscrewed the bottom velvet covered end cap.

Rudy was too consistent in his logic to combine items of different materials without a barrier. She had learnt that very early in their relationship. The plastic handled camping cutlery could not be in the same drawer as the stainless-steel. He had flipped his lid once too many times for her not to be more careful.

Removing a fairly heavy draw-string bag in the same fabric that matched the original lid, she peered inside the container to see that it had filled the lower void and let out the breath she'd been holding. Laying it beside the cylinder with her finger halfway, she guessed the top half held two rows of rolled up notes.

Gobsmacked, she quickly did the calculation. 'That's a lot of cold, hard cash.'

Way more than she had ever earnt in a single year and more than twice the amount she had in both bank accounts combined! Curiosity getting the better of her, carefully tipped the contents out of the fabric bag and stared in wide-eyed wonder. Unfamiliar heavy gold bangles, beautiful earrings, necklaces and pendants tumbled into a pile along with three smaller turquoise bags. Again, there was no compromise to the different material habit. Emptying the contents of each bag in their own space, Yasmin was staring at a pile of sparkling diamond rings and earrings, then three more emeralds. On its own, the three-strand pearl bracelet with five blank spaces and a broken gold clasp.

Trying to steady her trembling hands, she also tried to steady her erratic breathing. Recalling Rudy's letter, there was nothing to say whose was what and what was whose. Replacing the contents and the apparatus to its original condition, she prayed her knees wouldn't fail as she went into her ensuite and stashed the container alongside the PVC pipework inside the vanity cabinet. A perfect match aside from the vastly different size.

Combo met her outside the spare bedroom door and looked at her imploringly. He had been back on the bedframe and nosed around Rudy's clothing. Picking up the clothes that had fallen onto the floor, Yasmin added the apparel to his other box of meagre belongings and wrote the letter 'R' on it. Looking at the almost empty room, it was actually larger than what she initially perceived. *Perhaps this should be the office in future? It would certainly be cooler in summer but then I'd lose my view.* Yasmin groaned in dismay. *Not such a nice view now.*

Sighing heavily, she stacked the box atop the others in the storage cupboard, gathered up the envelopes and teased Combo with them as they raced back to the dining room table. Contemplating her future, she half-heartedly emptied the bulkiest brown envelope to see a myriad of notes, letters and journals drop out.

It wasn't light reading by any stretch of the imagination.

Ultimately, it would have been impossible for anyone to penetrate the tightly knit sibling unit. Rudy's lifelong mates, Timmy, Mike and Bob, were at the same adoption centre as him and Emily, and inseparable since they were three years old. Mr and Mrs Craige adopted the twins at the age of four. At the same time, arranged for Mr Craige's widowed sister-in-law to adopt the three boys. Until the boys all left home, they had lived beside each other; and Emily, so beautiful and well loved, was considered their sister too. The entire family, except the lads' mother, celebrated their birthdays in May. Hers was in April. The five children all received a sound inheritance at their coming-of-age party.

Yasmin had not been invited to their twenty-first birthday celebration and swiftly shoved the pained remnant back where it belonged. Her business phone rang just as she got up to boil the kettle. Recognising Timmy's number, rolled her eyes at the uncanny timing, scanned the ceiling cynically then reluctantly answered the call.

'Hi, Timmy.'

'Yasmin, just checking in. An update on Bob is he should make a full recovery. Just going to take time, patience and if he's a good boy, maybe a leave pass for a whole day!'

'That's a relief. I'm doing okay.'

He cleared his throat. 'Listen, you said something about the cops. Uh, when's that happening?'

'Tomorrow morning.'

'Have you found anything yet?'

'Yeah, some things,' she admitted coyly.

'How are you now?'

'Not sure.'

Coughing nervously, he replied, 'Oh, okay.'

'Timmy, what's your take on why Rudy chose the lavender paddock?'

He scoffed loudly. 'Probably the only clear paddock and he hated the stuff.'

Yasmin's breath exploded out of her like she had been punched in the guts.

'Sorry. Sorry, that was unkind.'

There was a scuffle with the phone, then Mike's calming voice. 'Yas, we all deal with grief differently and sometimes one's behaviour leaves a lot to be desired. That is no excuse for being *unkind* but sometimes anger, stress, frustration and hurt all get in the way of manners.'

'Yep, you can say that again. Lucky I'm the polite one, hey?' She sighed heavily. 'But sadly, he spoke the truth.'

'You said Rudy's last view was of your rose garden?'

'Yes Mike, but what's that got to do with anything?' she asked meekly.

Subdued voices filtered through the phone line.

'You remember that old knapsack you guys always had with you on the camping and hiking trips?'

'Hell yeah!' her watery smile must have come through her voice.

'That's our Yas!' Mike chuckled. 'Well, you have to find it. He slept with it when we last saw each other.'

'And when was that?'

'A couple of weeks ago.'

Yasmin gasped. 'Can you describe his eyes for me, Mike?'

'Empty.' He and Timmy spoke at the same time.

'Did you ever ask him what was going on?'

'Yeah, of course we did, Yasmin. He just said he had died inside.'

'Is that it? You didn't push the subject?'

'Oh, Yasmin, we have so much to talk about but not now. Find that knapsack. It never left his back all the times we saw him.'

She swiped angrily at the tears. 'Fine. Thanks for checking in. I'm eating well, and drinking far too much coffee.'

'Drink water too, young lady. We'll talk soon, Yas, we've got to go.'

'Yeah, me too.' Shook her head and lobbed a ball of scrunched-up paper towel into the wastepaper basket.

'Yeah, right-o. Okay, look, find that knapsack, Yasmin. Uh … please?'

Timmy disconnected the call before she did and failed to even smirk at their old game of who would hang up first. She was tired and her head hurt. Staring at her toes, she took in a deep, steadying breath. *Time for this pawn to start moving up the board.*

'Combo, we are entering level one of someone else's game, so we best be on ours, my boy!' His wet nose nuzzle on her hand was not the assurance she was seeking.

With almost three hours of daylight to play in before nature's curtains fell, being cooped up wasn't their style and only exacerbated the feeling of entrapment. Leaving the security alarms activated, she unhooked Combo's throw-ball toy and wriggled it excitedly. Within a split second he was at her feet, sitting with a raised paw and a happy grin. Securely locking the patio doors behind her, they raced over to the packing shed. The notification on her phone chimed and she double checked it was them that had activated the alarms. She chided herself for the security paranoia, but Rudy's death had also left her spooked.

Chapter 10

Sixty kilometres away, two men parted ways at the funeral parlour under a cloud of dispute. Closing the door, Clive threw dagger glances at the other bloke's broad back.

Fuming, he dialled the main office's number and voiced his complaint, only to be told by the secretary that it was in his best interest to comply with the on-boarding of a new employee.

'You could have at least warned me! The idiot who just left didn't even introduce himself or let me ask any questions, just told me what his expectations were, and had the audacity to wipe his fingers along the window frame. Pompous sod.' Clive seethed.

'Was he a solidly built man in a fancy suit?'

'Yeah.'

'Well, that was your new colleague.'

'Say what?'

'Yep.'

'This bloke didn't even indicate that! What training has he had? Where's his CV? Can you at least tell me his name?'

'Whoops. Sounds like you've both gotten off on the wrong foot. His name is also Clive, so it's going to be awkward, at least he'll sort himself out with accommodation. You will need to share the company vehicle though. Look, I'll send through his stuff soon ... sorry, but I have to run. The boss is really cranky today and on the warpath. Take care Clive, all the best.'

He hung up without uttering another word and set about straightening up his office.

Chapter 11

Pestel's Edible Petals numbering system of the rows continued with tradition. The furthest elevated bed from the patio being the first row. With the two-foot-high mounds travelling in a north-south direction, the florae simply grew better. It also followed the flow of the rolling hills, which, before the present day, made for a stunning vista when one stood on the patio or sat in the office and looked westwards.

Yasmin had taken Rudy's dislike for lavender into consideration and planted it in the first eleven rows, therefore the furthest away from the cottage. The next five rows consisted of alternating snapdragons and French marigolds, then six rows of Queen Elizabeth Roses. This year, the last six rows were alternating white and mauve African daisies and red dahlias. All edible, all beautiful, and her best year to date. Particularly for the lavender, except the plants were old, woody and tired. Not taking any risks, and clearing the field a fortnight earlier—being the latter half of September—she hadn't gotten around to levelling the mounds, turning the soil and replanting.

Any vehicular traffic on the property was strictly walking pace to minimise dust particles, and with the frequent watering and constant back and forth in the four-wheeler and carryall, all paths were well compacted. Arriving at the barren section, the only thought on her mind was to retrace Rudy's footsteps. It was easy to see where he had scrambled atop the first bed from the slightly overgrown grassy area beside the road and headed in the opposite direction, except his path resembled that of staggering. It was even easier to see where he stumbled before continuing on his wonky way. Then she remembered his bare feet. *Rudy hated not having anything on his feet.*

Following alongside his wayward tracks, Yasmin steered the four-wheeler one handed while sitting side-saddle. Dragging the extendable broad-headed rake over the mounds of soil at a slow speed, she repeated the usual process in the opposite direction. Each time, the soil toppled down the walls before settling near the drills. She then did the same with the sidewalls until the tyres of the four-wheeler had created a ridge of soft soil. Checking to see what remained, she was mildly happy to discover nothing but rich soil, healthy worms and fat, friendly grubs.

Combo followed behind the vehicle at a sensible distance; knowing only too well he'd get to play ball and enjoy the obligatory dried liver treats during the task. How he knew to do all the right things was another puzzle for another time.

At the bottom of the fifth row, she stood on the seat and scanned the top through to the eleventh. Rudy's footprints were more like shuffling steps by the end of the sixth bed and not as deep. Mimicking his shrug of the shoulders, she slowly raked the top, turned around at the row's end and levelled the soil. Again, nothing but fat worms, good grubs and rich soil. Shoving all emotional thoughts out of her head, threw caution to the wind and worked in the opposite of his delirious direction. Half-way through the row, whatever the rake got caught on nearly tore her arm off. Climbing down from the four-wheeler, Yasmin sat on the dirt against the mound facing the sun and said a little prayer. There was nothing obviously different with the top or side wall.

Crawling around, she carefully cleared away the soil and unhooked the rake. Instantly recognising the straps of the faded, dark green canvas knapsack; tears sprang to her eyes and remembered how Rudy took great pride in lugging the weight on their very first hike. Then, reality struck. *How could he have buried it so well?* She wrestled it out of the soil and was surprised to see only one buckle done up. The other housed a loosely fed loop with bits of pink tissue wrapping paper poking out of the holes as she shook the soil loose. The knapsack really had been well used. She could tell a story about each of the oldest holes. A lonely tear coursed down her dusty cheek. After undoing the flap, shook her head sadly at the sight of a haphazard yacht-shaped note sitting atop more pink tissues. Although it was still his handwriting, the grammarless and hastily written words filled the sail.

Yasmin time for me to go no more games I LOVED YOU I leave you with everything look everywhere not sorry feel bad too late hope am last this is so cruel they said it was kind to choose I believed them silly dangerous women be careful let

me go Emily needs me find Emerald Bay CREAM live goodbye my queen and her
*beautiful rose*s

'CREAM?'

Her cough-laugh dissolved into blubbering, replaced the note, did up the bulging knapsack and looked to the heavens. Slipping the straps around her shoulders, she felt warm and calm, then bawled uncontrollably. Through her swollen, tear-filled eyes and nonstop sniffling, finished levelling the row but left the seventh through to the eleventh untouched all the while trying to comprehend Rudy's rationalisation. He had been very particular in his mind, although delirious while scrawling his final note, and presumably wrote it where he buried it, which perhaps explained the half-closed knapsack. What she did know for sure, was his last view would have been the splendid pink blooms of her Queen Elizabeth Roses.

Until that moment, Yasmin had deliberately avoided the area. Very quietly, she sat next to where she had found him. The people who took his body had been so careful not to disturb the soil and she could still see the outline of his back. Gazing at what would have been his last view, gasped at the incredible picture and let more tears flow. She buried her hands into the soil and put her baby finger on where Rudy's hand imprint remained, imagining the thick gold band around his right index finger glinting in the sun. She frowned. *He was wearing it, wasn't he?*

Combo sniffed around the indentations and whimpered from the other side of Rudy's outline. Drawing her knees upwards, Yasmin snivelled and talked to him like he was sitting right beside her.

'You lied to me Rudy. Fly high. Be with your family. May God forgive you.'

Scooping up a handful of soil from the natural back rest in line where his heart would have been, she let the dust filter through her fingers and watched it get carried upwards. Yasmin wiped her tears and said another prayer. It was time to pick some roses for herself for the first time ever.

Leaving the beautiful blooms to fill her kitchen with their lingering perfume, the knapsack hugged her back. Sitting with Combo on the patio looking at the long shadows kissing the tops of the hills, raised a glass of whiskey to the heavens. Night fell quickly and the eeriness of knowing she was the only human on the property spooked her to no end. She let out the breath she was holding as soon as they were in the safety of the securely locked cottage.

Padding through to the lounge wearing her night attire and feeling a bit more alive, Yasmin hoped the instrumental music playing quietly in the background would quell her angst. With the tattered old knapsack on her lap while sitting cross-legged on the settee, the memories came flooding back of the good times. The buckles would outlast any of it, that was for sure. Something cold jabbed her thigh and gulping in fright, swiftly lifted up the knapsack. The music hadn't quelled anything.

Rudy's Parker Pen fell out of one of the holes in the bottom causing Yasmin to sob loudly into the back of her hand. She remembered how delighted he was when she gave it to him for his twenty-fifth birthday. Wriggling further backwards into the floral oversized settee and stretching her legs, muttered, 'You were a sentimental bloke.'

Painstakingly removing the folded layers of pink tissue wrapping paper, she counted twenty-eight sheets. Burying the urge to scoff, her hand rested on the edge of something hard, cold and round. In her mind's eye she imagined the old-fashioned Quality Streets chocolate tin. They had played a game of hide and seek with it when they first moved in together. Leaving each other love notes, shopping lists, wish lists and sometimes handmade trinkets in the tin, they would stash it somewhere in the places they had rented for the other to find. They never took anything out, just kept adding to it.

It had been her turn last, then they were thrown quickly into being adults and the game had stopped when they moved into the cottage. A lot of things had stopped when they moved into the cottage. The last time she recalled seeing the tin was in the back of the cupboard in the spare room, a long time ago. The tell-tale dent in the lid confirmed her suspicions. She didn't know if she should laugh or cry. The lid came off surprisingly easily for its age; then she burst into tears all over again. None of the contents had been taken out, but right on top wedged in the middle of the pink rose she had made for him, was his thick gold band.

She bawled into her cotton floral nightdress and took a trip down memory lane. The little bits and pieces dotting the mental landscape. The occasional giggle escaped her hoarse throat, a lot of watery smiles and more and more tears. Slowly replacing the contents in order, she fondled the jewellery then put it back to where she found it. Turning over the lid, discovered another torn yacht-shaped folded piece of notepaper stuck to the inside. Carefully removing it, she read the cramped writing in a whisper.

Oh Yasmin, what have I done? We had so many good times, I was remembering when we went on our first hike – we really didn't need all that stuff did we? Geez it was heavy, but there was no way I was letting you carry it. You looked so sporty, so pretty and when the sun shone behind that special ledge that we stood on, I very nearly proposed. Maybe I should have, maybe if we'd had our own family, maybe – maybe – maybe – just maybe. But I didn't. I detested being away from home, but then I saw how hard you worked and how you overcame the challenges. I was so jealous, but then I saw how much you loved what you did then I was so proud of you.

This knapsack has never left my back when I went out and nobody would know its secrets except you. The tin! How we had fun and your rose for me was just another thing you gave me that I treasured. I've left you some treasures too. Some people might look for things which don't belong to them, but I doubt they'll ever find the stuff. Only you must look for it. Thanks for not locking the cottage, but now you have to and sort out both those laundry doors. What an annoyance!

Just know I cannot undo what I got involved in. Some people didn't know where I lived. Some people didn't know you. Some people didn't know that you and I knew of each other. Some people thought I was the boogeyman. Some people got it wrong. Do not talk to strangers about me. Ever. Nevertheless, the more of my game you play, the more answers you'll get. You must play it all the way to the end.

I am going to die an extraordinarily slow death, but at times I'll be so bombed out of my mind I won't feel any pain. Know that, please Yasmin. I will not feel any pain. I don't. It's peculiar I am so coherent, but horseheads say that might wane as time goes on. They're masochists and sadists combined. Imagine a side profile of a fleeing mare. That's them.

A year after my parents died, I went and saw a Medium. She was so perplexed. All she could see was the company logo, emeralds and a yacht. I tried another one and all she got was a message from Emily pleading me not to give up, then in another voice begging me to join her. That's the one that I could hear all the time afterwards.

I went to several gatherings, somewhere far away. Quite a few of us met in the fields, in the valleys, in the gullies and over the hills and three of us got a lift back with the other horsehead and two other blokes. We all partook. It wasn't weed but it stunk awfully. Can only describe it as being of the earth. As time went on, I got totally addicted to something derived from the ground and blended with something else in the form of a small green tablet. I fought it for a long time but in the end Emily's voice penetrated my soul.

It feels so good to tell you all this, well, let you know anyway. Nothing will bring me back, but we did have some good times and you won't have to work so hard anymore. I fixed that up for you. Remember, do not talk to strangers about me. Do not even mention my name.

I might have time to write one more letter to you. This one has taken me ages and the yacht looks like it needed that facelift after all. Find it, share it, explore. Live, Yasmin, live at least one of those things you wrote on your wish list. My gift to you.

They say diamonds are a girl's best friend, but I can tell you those emeralds are worth a lot more.

Love from Rudy.

She didn't know how long her head had been shaking in bewilderment, but it was throbbing. Running her thumb over his last three words, there was a certain level of tenderness, kindness and honesty in this note. Yawning like a voiceless lion she continued to empty the knapsack of its layers upon layers of pink tissue. Almost at the bottom, wrapped in more of the tissue was a bulging envelope. It was the first time the corners hadn't been rounded, but the contents made that impossible. Lifting the flap, she gasped. Jammed packed with fifty-dollar notes and a whack of fives, a small, folded slip of paper protruded in between the denominations. She was about to remove it when she noticed it was a perfect rectangle. Using her eyebrow tweezers and a toothpick, carefully pried open the paper. The typed font was too small for her eyesight and for the first time in her possession, her great uncle's magnifying glass came in handy.

You have waited too long to be where you belong. Join us and together we'll help you. The seventh new moon at the intersection of Scaley's Valley and Broken Creek, then every third one after that. Or join us at the Moojie Hill exhibition. Soon, soon you can choose. So choose. We'll watch over you as you follow your chosen path which leads you to the long-lost voice. Join us and together we'll help you. You have waited too long.

A cult? Oh, Rudy, what did you do? Why? Yasmin flew into a rage, until her eyes fell upon the paragraph about him going somewhere far away. *The funeral notices!*

Sliding everything off her lap, she got the pillowcase and unrolled the larger collage onto the dining room table. *Peaks and valleys!*

Her heart went giddy-up and all of a sudden felt lightheaded. Reaching around for a dining chair, lowered herself into the nearest one and put her head between her knees. Breathing slowly, counted to five with each inhaled breath and seven as she exhaled. No time to have an anxiety attack, but it was the noise of her stomach that made her sit up and take notice. Even Combo raised his head curiously. *Food! We need food.*

The skillet was still on the stove, with the simplest thing to cook being another bacon and egg sandwich. Combo watched patiently as his auto-feeder trickled nighttime treats into his bowl. He would wait until she ate, always did.

Inhaling the aromatics, Yasmin set up her laptop on the coffee table and finished another bottle of water, idly scanning the cryptic clues. Thinking objectively with a healthy dose of logic; the pile of historical information on the dining table contained the family history. Did she really need to know all of it? But comprehending it would put her in better stead when she talked to the lads. Was it her business though?

Throwing her hands up in the air, muttered, 'Does any of it matter anymore?'

The police were going to pay her a visit regardless of what was tackled first, but she couldn't disclose any of the information, nor what Rudy had left her to find. Yasmin perused the paperwork devouring her sandwich, trying to quieten her busy mind. With one hand holding the last piece of bacon and the other the magnifying glass, she read the typed note again. Surmising Scaley's Valley and Broken Creek weren't going to register on a quick search on the Internet, she scanned the larger collage of funeral notices. After wiping her greasy hand on her dressing gown, she jotted down the coloured-in digits in order of discovery. There weren't enough zeros for mobile phone numbers. This time, the coloured capital letters made sense. When she followed the pattern of small zeros, single and double and inverted commas she smacked her forehead. *GPS co-ords!*

The only sets of coloured-in digits were *36* and *147*. The jumble of other digits was going to take more than one night to resolve, plus she needed a topographical map. A small smile teased the edges of her mouth at the fond memory. They all had loved orienteering and were good at it too. Changing tact, she studied the coloured letters on the smaller collage. All she could easily make out was Emily's name.

With a sore head and stinging eyes, Yasmin cleaned up after dinner, collated all the discoveries then stacked them neatly in her walk-through wardrobe. The knapsack went beside her bed. Making sure there was absolutely nothing lying around or out of place, she took Combo out for a quick walk and hurried back inside. Double checking every window was closed, tightly drawing the curtains and triple checking the doors, made sure the alarms were still activated, turned off the air conditioner, music, lights and inhaled the perfume of her beautiful roses before stumbling wearily down the hallway, closing all the interior doors on the way. Physically and mentally exhausted, prayed she would always find the energy to smile at Combo sitting on guard beside her bed.

Chapter 12

The inebriated couple strolled arm-in-arm towards their luxurious suite, supporting each other and laughing wildly when they tripped over their own feet. They hadn't noticed the man in the shadow of his unlit room lazily twirling his handle-bar moustache, with the long-grey jacket casually slung over his shoulder.

'Best you keep the noise down!'

His loud, nasally sing-song voice that of rattling corrugated iron stopped the pair in their tracks. Callum spun around and pulled Leigh behind him. Both stumbling backwards.

'You right mate? You look like you've seen a ghost?' the man asked as he pulled his door closed.

Callum allowed Leigh to reverse him inside their room. His eyes nearly popping out of his head when the man threw on his jacket.

'Uh, no-no, just had one too many.'

The second their door was shut, Leigh's legs gave way and gripped Callum tightly. Her face ashen. 'How-how did he know? How? They told us he was dead.'

Fighting back his own fear, he held his bride close and murmured into her head. 'It's not him, beloved! The boogey-man is dead, remember? The twins and Trav told us.'

'No, he didn't. Ivan did. But that moustache? The jacket?'

'You can't freak out every time you see a man with a handle-bar moustache or a long grey jacket! Come on, let's get back to where we were.'

Leigh mumbled and shrugged gently out of his embrace. 'I'll go and freshen up. You roll us a number.'

'Sure thing!' Callum let out the breath he was holding and crossed himself religiously. *Please let the boogey-man be dead. I swear I'll start praying again, Lord.*

The moment his wife stepped out of the bathroom, his promises evaporated into the sheerness of her negligee.

***

Meanwhile back at the local police station, a junior officer had just finished explaining to a city detective how their Branch processes forensic evidence, when his boss knocked.

'Doing overtime, Officer Ramond?'

'No, Sergeant Pyers, I'm making up the hours I took off earlier today. This is Forensic Detective Hillyer from City HQ.'

The men shook hands. 'You've caught us at a particularly busy time, Hill—'

'Chas, Chas Hillyer.'

'Owen Pyers. Righto, Chas. You've still caught us at a particularly busy time, and I won't be here tomorrow.'

'Day off?'

'Hardly! I'm interviewing a recently widowed local businesswoman. Ramond, you'll be riding with me.'

'Always a pleasure, Sir.'

'I might come along too, then! See how the country bumpkins do their thing.'

The junior officer shut the filing cabinet drawer loudly. 'Mr Hillyer, we are very professional—'

'It's okay, Carl, I'll take it from here. Off you go. I want to be on the road by nine o'clock sharp.'

'Yes Sir. Good night.' He nodded at the visitor and pulled the door when he strode out.

Pyers smirked. 'The lad's very proud to be a police officer and will probably defend us to his death. So, what brings you to our neck of the woods?'

'Feel like a bit of an errand boy actually but it's all part of the job. I'm gathering evidence on a spate of intrastate drug transactions, done the loop and you're the last post, for want of a better term. Only got here a couple of hours ago, met Ramond in the carpark and ended up here.'

Ushering his guest out of the room towards the exit, Owen said, 'Is it ever quiet down your end of town?'

'In this game? Hardly! With far too many damned cold cases. About tomorrow's chat ... is the death suspicious?'

'Too many of those bloody things in this State! One lives in hope the demise of someone is linked to easing someone else's pain.'

'Mind if I ride shotgun?'

'Yeah righto, Chas. We'll reconvene in the boardroom at zero eight thirty.'

'Do you provide the breakfast and a decent coffee?'

'Not tomorrow. Be prepared for a long day. You need a lift somewhere?'

'Nah, all good thanks.'

'Being late doesn't really cut it around here.'

Chas pushed through the main doors, 'Yep, night Sergeant Pyers.'

Scoffing quietly, Owen locked up and made his way towards the building's rear staff exit, calling out to the night duty officer. 'It's all yours, Jay. Be back in a little while!'

'Night Boss. Catchya on the roundabout.'

Chapter 13

The pre-dawn chorus rehearsed its symphony while Yasmin stared at nothing with eyes ringed like a raccoon's and bulging like a bullfrog. Her waking thought was of Rudy's repeated instruction to *look everywhere, including the floor*. The only part of the cottage she had been forbidden to touch was the oversized cupboard in the spare bedroom. Not that she had looked at its floor because she knew there wasn't one. Its old frame stood on the even older parquetry tiles. But she had found the hole in the floor of the caravan. Sighing heavily in frustration, decided a complete rearrangement of furniture would occupy her mind in a more creative way. The physical exertion would be quite therapeutic too.

Switching the lounge with the dining suite in the bay window alcoves, it made more sense to walk through the front door into the seating area than seeing the back of dining chairs. Collapsing the six-seater oval dining table into a four-seater round, also made the whole room look larger. She had never liked the tall dark, foreboding Mahogany bookcase against the wall between the bay windows, and sneezed with the removal of each ancient book.

Stomping on the tiles in the spare bedroom, which was never going to be fully utilised, she dismantled the bed frame and leant it against the drawn curtain. Yasmin also stomped on the parquetry tiles under the bed with none of them giving way. Shifting the now empty bookcase onto a rug and sliding it down the hallway, with determination and a few contortionists moves, pushed and shoved it into the room against the wall where the headboard remained. The books were returned to the shelves along with Combo's harmonised sneezes, and the two spare dining chairs sat with their backs against the old wooden bed frame.

Back in the living room, the coffee table went between the bay windows and after a thorough dust, polish and replenishment of linen doilies, sat the telephone, the caller identifier and answering machine, and writing pad. The Queen Elizabeth Roses looked even more beautiful in her treasured crystal vase and centred nicely. Alternating between both main entrance doors, Yasmin nodded in satisfaction. Picking up the newspaper off the floor, she added 'scream' and promptly scoffed and scribbled it out. *Don't cheat, Yasmin.* Stumped for the first time in a very long time, the correct nine-lettered word continued to elude her.

Combo's yapping from the spare room diverted her attention. She put her head around the door to see him sniffing along the bottom of the cupboard doors, scratching at the veneer. With his tail thumping the floor and both ears alert, he kept looking at her then back to the bottom of the cupboard. She opened its two doors. He was up on his feet with tail waggling eagerly. He pawed at her foot, looked imploringly up at her and whined.

Yasmin ruffled his head. 'Now? Really?'

His whined response encouraging her to systematically remove the boxes belonging to the dearly departed. Like an overseer, Combo stepped inside and investigated every square inch until he started scratching at the tile in the furthest corner. He wouldn't let up. Crawling in beside him, Yasmin gasped softly when her fingers played over the tile. Its hollow undertone and looseness heightening her own excitement. Almost in a stance of comfort, Combo leant into her shoulder as she easily lifted the peculiarly shaped tile and sobbed into the crook of her arm. Lying in a chipped-out crevice was an old-fashioned key. Its heavy ornate brass design captivated her attention like that of a child. Toying with the intricate fleur-de-lis design on the bow, she knew there was nothing in her cottage that it would open.

Praising her pooch, he forcibly sniffed it before pawing enthusiastically along the short wall. With his tail slapping her legs as rapidly as her heart pulsed, she shuffled several more tiles. Following their pattern, it was obvious the furthest one would be the first or the last to be positioned. Using the solid bit of the key, she pried the corner upwards and carefully removed the parquetry jigsaw puzzle. *The deception of this man!*

Lying face down in the recess, were three large natural-shaped envelopes with a broken solicitor's wax seal over each flap. Sliding out the documents of the closest one, Yasmin scan-read the official company paperwork formally declaring the three lads as the new directors of the Craige's transportation empire. Rudy's signature was on the bottom. Although he had admitted he had lied to her, she was flummoxed as to how big the lie was.

The Craige's were an extremely wealthy family and had ensured the lad's mother owned her own home. Her other assets were her business. Rudy and Emily inherited their parents' wealth, and there were no encumbered debts. Should any arise, they were to sell the Monet paintings. Emily had loved Monet. The two girls often had their girlie chats facing the gold framed 'Water Lilies'.

Yasmin then read the Last Will and Testaments of Mr and Mrs Craige written six weeks before the fateful holiday. It was simple and straight forward. They bequeathed each other their entire wealth. If they both should die, their twin children would inherit everything equally. If either or both of them should die, their own wishes would determine who gets what. Yasmin's breath caught in her throat.

She had to remind herself to inhale before opening the last envelope. It was Rudy's official Last Will and Testament. It was dated at the beginning of the current year. Although reiterating she was to have a good life and the rightful part-owner of CREAM, the helicopter was owned three-ways between the lads. Her jaw locked. *Helicopter? What helicopter?*

He had also opened up a bank account in her name and transferred his personal account balance into hers. The bank statement as at one month earlier was $4.2 million. Yasmin nearly passed out. Her hands shook. She read the document again. *What helicopter?*

Turning the page, she discovered that was just one bank account. An account had been opened up in each of the lads' names with the balance to be released to the account holders only. Said information was safely contained. His inherited fortune from the family would be shared between her and the lads equally, but only when whoever turned forty first. Under no circumstances were his instructions to be amended, altered, or ignored, and considered dead-hand control. The term deposit would reach its maturity date, and they would each evenly benefit from the $57.2 million initial investment six years prior. *Breathe. Breathe.*

Other wishes stated the families of the company's legal team as well as the accountants and financial adviser were to receive the envelopes marked to their attention. Said envelopes were also safely contained. The absolute final wish was to ensure his personal helicopter pilot and dear friend perform a thorough mechanical inspection and pay particular attention to the instrument panel.

'Somebody pinch me,' Yasmin murmured, re-read the third last paragraph and uttered, 'Dead hands more like it.'

Chapter 14

The melodic ringtone of her personal mobile phone rudely interrupted the concentrated effort in deciphering Rudy's deception. She stared at the documents laid out in front of her without paying any attention to the caller's details, and answered absentmindedly.

'Hello?'

'Ms Pestel, Sergeant Pyers calling.' His gravelly voice snapping her back to the present.

She replied shyly, 'Morning.'

'We're a bit behind schedule and heading out to see you now. Can we pick up anything for you?'

'For me? Like what?' she glanced at the clock.

'How about something from the bakery?' he asked kindly. 'It could be quite a long day.'

She replied automatically. 'Oh! Yes please, I'd love a pepper-steak pie, sausage roll, French vanilla slice and a ginger beer. I'll pay you when you get here.'

His deep chuckle rippled through the phone. 'Ms Pestel, it's on me.'

Feeling quite comforted, 'Okay, thank you, that's very kind of you. I hope you will join me in smoko?'

'Yes, that won't be a problem. There will be several of us including members of the K9 crew.'

'Appreciate the forewarning, I'll have mine on a leash. Incidentally, his vaccinations are all up-to-date if they're interacting.'

'Likewise. See you in a little while. Thank you. Good bye.'

Yasmin had fifty minutes to get herself and the living areas ready. She swiftly replaced the floor tiles, stacked the boxes, closed the cupboard doors, reopened them and stared at the accumulation. They were all sealed in a variety of methods, but one box in particular was so well sealed in clear tape it shone under the light. Bewildered that she hadn't noticed it earlier, hurriedly closed the doors, sat the spare chairs against them facing the drawn curtains and pulled the bedroom door shut. The unfamiliar key along with the envelopes got stashed amongst the growing piles of paperwork hidden in her clothes. Whipping around the cottage with the vacuum and after a record-breaking freshen up, the guest bathroom airing, opened up the main doors and windows with ten minutes to spare. Then and only then did she deactivate the alarms.

She couldn't sit still. After the myriad pots of Crown of Thorn underneath each window received a drink, the patio furniture and concrete got a whirlwind clean. Having the landscaper spread two metres of the river pebbles around the perimeter of her cottage was a blessing in disguise, given the abundant dog hair that had built up on the pleasant seating area. Overall, the predominantly white rocks always looked so pretty against the almost metre-high cobblestone verandah wall. Yasmin had always found the patio setting to be so calming. With its north-easterly aspect, the white slatted roof transcended her to somewhere in Greece or England. She hadn't been to either, but the magazine pictures had been the inspiration. The white wrought iron furniture was well cushioned. Their bold colours complimenting the brilliant red geraniums and bright array of gerberas growing in large white pots around the outer edges of the elevated concrete slab. Her usual sanctuary for calmness as absent as a waterfall.

Sighing heavily in the hope that admitting the last four years had been the loneliest, did not lighten the lead weight in her heart. But as far as she knew, Rudy's death was a suspected heart attack in the seventh row of the recently cleared lavender paddock, *of which she is responsible for*. There was no way they could blame her. *Was there?* No! She was still in mourning. She had lost someone of whom she had known for most of her life *who had lied to her*. Hushing up her mind harshly, Yasmin flinched when Combo barked loudly and sniffed the air furiously. Firmly restrained, his tail flicked slowly.

Paying heed to the speed sign, three vehicles approached while they descended the five concrete steps of the western side of the patio. Three men, two policemen and one in a light blue suit, in varying ages and stature alighted from the first vehicle, conferred with each other before striding towards the petite woman and her protector.

'We're sorry for your loss, Ms Pestel.' The younger and slimmest of the three walked ahead with his left hand extended downwards and a boyish grin on his face. 'Senior Constable Carl Ramond at your service but if you don't mind, I'll meet your pooch first. What's his name?'

'Combo.' She allowed herself a small smile and watched the interaction closely.

His voice instantly soothed any discomfort and bent down to shake Combo's raised paw. 'Good boy. That went exactly according to plan,' he said, stood and extended his right hand. 'Pleased to meet you, Ma'am. My colleagues, Sergeant Owen Pyers and Forensic Detective Chas Hillyer.'

The introductions were polite with gentle, yet firm handshakes while they expressed their words of comfort. Combo made a point of being in between her and the detective. His meaningful gaze, tall, lean build sent shivers racing up and down her spine.

'Ms Pestel,' Sergeant Pyers voice matched his mature, solid stature. 'Some of our K9 crew would like to take a stroll through the grassed area alongside the road, then at the end of your property. How would you like to play this?'

She looked at the four varied sized men and their matching dogs standing beside their vehicles, watching in anticipation.

'Perhaps allow Combo to familiarise himself with everyone's scent. It's his turf. I'm sure he'll let it be known where he'd rather be after the introductions,' Yasmin suggested calmly.

'We're going to get along just fine,' Sergeant Pyers grinned.

Senior Constable Ramond indicated for the K9 crew to approach. 'Ma'am, may I take control of Combo please?'

'If you think that's a good idea,' she simply replied and handed over the leash. In a softer voice, she talked to her pet. 'Combo, be a good boy. Gentle.'

The stance of her protector was not to be questioned, nor his intent stare at the two other men; before following the new set of verbal commands and allowed himself to be led by the young policeman.

'Wonders never cease!'

'The lad's a natural with animals, Ma'am,' Sergeant Pyers said reassuringly.

The five dogs sniffed each other enthusiastically before Combo sat and raised his paw under command of the one man. He instantly reminded Yasmin of Brutus from Popeye and felt safe standing five metres away. When he spoke, even the air around him paid attention. He looked up, grinned and led his crew towards her; Combo leading the pack.

'Ms Pestel,' his baritone voice naturally commanded respect. 'On behalf of everyone in my Unit, our condolences.'

'Thank you.' She looked at the men, nodded graciously and expressed a small smile acknowledging their respectful nods.

'I'm Sergeant Kohli, this is my partner, Zeus. When we're with colleagues I'm addressed by my rank, and Master when there are more dogs than humans!'

'Pleased to know you.' When her dainty hand disappeared in his grasp, they both chuckled. She liked him instantly.

'Your Combo is well behaved. Kudos to you. I can see the wonky ear of a Kelpie, Doberman eyes, a bit of Boxer, the who-knows-from-what splotches.'

Yasmin laughed. 'Wow! You really know your dogs. He's special, that's for sure!'

The big man grinned. 'What's his history?'

'I have no idea. He adopted me three years ago. The local vet, Stu Wilson, estimated him to be about five when he gave him a check up and see if he was micro-chipped. Nobody claimed him and he's been by my side since.'

'Well, he seems to be happy with all of us.' He smirked then. 'Should we see if he'll leave you?'

'I can guarantee you he won't if he knows there are treats from the bakery,' she chuckled softly and ruffled her dog's head.

'I bet five bucks the sausage roll wasn't for you!'

'You're a wise man,' Yasmin smirked.

'Ms Pestel, I extend an invitation to meet my crew on our turf in the near future under, dare I say, a more social atmosphere, hence the lack of introductions here.'

'I would like that, and Combo probably needs some dog company for a change, thank you. I acknowledge you're all on duty.'

He dipped his lid. 'Excellent. We've got work to do and you have things to talk about.'

Senior Constable Ramond dropped Combo's leash and joined the K9 handlers walking down the driveway. One bark and the dogs instantly sat. Yasmin stifled a laugh and looked at Sergeant Kohli enquiringly.

'Over to you,' he called out kindly.

Yasmin crouched down and immediately Combo sat in front of her and raised his paw. Shaking it and praising him accordingly, she interpreted his sideways glances as wanting to go with the rest of the pack.

Ruffling his head, she made him look at her and said quietly, 'Go. Be a good boy.'

After she stood, he ever so gently rested his front paws on her trim hips staring at her intently before turning his head, emitting a low growl at the two policemen and seriously eyeballed them. Then carrying his leash in his mouth, joined the crew.

'Amazing animals,' she whispered.

'Looks like the jealous type!' Forensic Detective Hillyer chuckled. 'Are you hungry, Ms Pestel?'

'Most of the time!' she responded automatically. 'There's a sanitising station just off the patio. I thought we could sit outside today being such a beautiful day.'

'I'll join you shortly with smoko, Boss,' he said.

Yasmin looked at Sergeant Pyers and murmured cheekily, 'I hope he was referring to you!'

'So do I,' he said with a deep gurgling laugh.

'That was a very kind invitation from Sergeant Kohli, is that normal or special treatment?'

'He's his own boss ... but we feel as if we've known you for years, from sight and reputation. Your Aunt Rose was a special woman.'

Wiping at her wet eyes, smiled and cleared her throat at the sound of approaching footsteps.

General chatter including more words of comfort were shared while they enjoyed the familiar bakery treats. The incessant ringing of her mobile phone interrupted the small talk. Excusing herself politely, she reached for the noisy necessity and rolled her eyes in recognition of the funeral parlour.

She put it on speaker as she answered. 'Hello?'

'Ms Pestel, it's Clive from Gentle Rest.'

'Yes, and you haven't stopped calling me. You know to send your flower orders to my e-mail.'

'Please pardon the intrusion ... but this isn't a business call ... um ... it is, but not for your flowers sorry. We need to confirm the final arrangements of your dearly departed.' He waited for several moments before continuing calmly. 'I know it's a sensitive time, but are you aware of any final wishes?'

'No, I do not. I have company with me at present and you are quite callous for not even passing on any condolences,' she replied coolly.

'Please forgive me.'

Curiosity got the better of her. 'What's the urgency, Clive?'

A long pause mixed with background sounds of paper rustling and muffled voices, before his voice came back to the phone.

'No urgency, Ms Pestel but we need to make arrangements depending on his religion and the type of funeral, that's all.' His voice a lullaby.

'Thanks for explaining that, I will contact you later on. Is there anything else?'

'Not at this time. Thank you, Ms Pestel. I will wait for your call. Good day.'

The call was ended and she drained her ginger beer.

'You guys are probably more familiar with this stuff, but don't you find it strange a funeral director would phone incessantly? I mean they are the only ones in town, and why so soon after a death?'

The men looked at each other wordlessly until Sergeant Pyers spoke up.

'It isn't unusual, however, there have been several suspicious deaths recently and we're trying to determine if there's a pattern.'

'Around here? Oh, that is so sad for the families. Surely you don't think they're connected?'

'Yes, it is very sad.'

Yasmin frowned at the ambiguous answer and raised her point of view in another way. 'But what's that got to do with the funeral parlour hassling me?'

The detective ran his long fingers through his surfer hairstyle, sandy-blonde hair. 'It is a little unnerving I agree. They mean well, are fastidious in their roles, just forget they deal with living people too.'

'Oh.'

Yasmin noticed the change in the men's facial expressions and waited patiently for one of them to speak. Eventually, Sergeant Pyers cleared his throat softly. 'Ms Pestel, we cannot discuss ongoing investigations. But what I can explain is usually the coroner has to perform an investigation on the deceased who died from perhaps unnatural causes in order for an official death certificate to be issued. This could take weeks.'

Looking from one man to the other, the questions exploded out of her mouth. 'Doesn't a doctor have to sign off on a death? Surely the next of kin would receive paperwork first?'

'All protocols are closely adhered to, and it is not uncommon for a funeral parlour to receive the death certificate first. Ultimately all this depends on the result of investigations,' Forensic Detective Hillyer said quietly.

Yasmin gulped back the forming anger and regained her composure. 'Look, I might be small and recently widowed for want of a better word, but I did not come down in the last shower. What is really going on here?'

'Before we discuss that, can we establish something please?' Sergeant Pyers asked firmly, encouraging the Detective to stand.

She sat back with her arms folded, studying the two men. 'Absolutely.'

'While it is just us having a conversation, would you mind if we referred to each other using our Christian names?'

Relieved, she said, 'Thank you. It would make it simpler,' and promptly extended her hand. 'Hi, I'm Yasmin.'

They all reintroduced themselves, shook hands and laughed nervously. She stood, dusted the crumbs off her lap and offered coffee.

'Please, we take it straight black, thanks,' Owen said politely.

'Superb!' she smirked and walked away.

***

'Surprisingly calm,' Chas stated quietly.

'Hmm, make a note of that will you.'

***

Putting the tray of coffees on the table, Yasmin waited patiently for someone to take the lead, until the Owen's look of expectation caught her attention.

'You have some questions for me?' she asked encouragingly, and blushed when the men sat after she did.

'Several in fact. I'm also going to talk openly and freely so take your time when answering, you've had quite a shock.'

She nodded her acknowledgement.

'Let's get started. After the discovery in the paddock did anything strike you as being odd?'

Lost in her own thoughts, she relived the bleak day and the brilliance of her beautiful flowers. The tears fell on their own accord. Dabbing at her eyes, she replied in a shaky voice, 'Aside from his bare feet and torso, from the moment I awoke I didn't feel right, and Combo, well, he was more clingy than usual.'

The men continued to take notes while she recollected the day's events. In a voice that flowed with the emotions, it was when she explained the pre-dawn checking for unfriendly bugs and cutting the orders for delivery, she sniggered at the detective's look of confusion. Proudly explaining her business supplied edible flowers for the boutique restaurants in the Stirling Valley area of the Adelaide Hills, her mood quickly sobered. She drained her coffee and began describing her return from doing the delivery run, then stopped mid-sentence and stood.

'Excuse me, I have to get something from my handbag, but write this down please. Uniform Whiskey, hyphen eight, Delta, two hyphen five, six, six, four,' and raced inside.

She rifled through her bag and pulled out several pieces of paper while rejoining her guests. 'Not the best filing system I know, but it works!' she laughed humour-lessly.

'Was that: six, six, four?' Chas asked.

'Yes.'

Flipping each one over, Yasmin eventually found the circled scrawl on the top right-hand corner on the back of a delivery docket and handed the piece of paper to Owen's outstretched hand

'UW-8D2-5664,' they spoke in unison.

'You memorised it?' Chas asked, astonished.

'Yes, a childhood game, as was the phonetic alphabet.' She smiled sadly, then stated, 'But this isn't a standard number plate, that's why it stuck. It's the first time I've thought about it since. It probably bears no relevance, but seeing as we're talking about that awful day, I felt it necessary to mention it.'

'Continue with your recollection of what happened,' he suggested politely.

Yasmin paced the patio, absentmindedly tipping the new shoots on a young basil plant.

'Combo was with me in my delivery van. He always is. I saw a yellow Tranny ... uh Ford Transit van, pulled over on the opposite side of the road with their hazard lights on. It was unusual for traffic to be this far up the road because I'm the last property. But what was more unusual was I had never seen a yellow Tranny before, and I do a lot of driving. Anyway, I slowed down, checked the number plate and pulled up alongside. Combo was on my lap barking aggressively at them out the driver's window.'

She rubbed her forehead and looked pleadingly at Owen. 'He has a bad habit of stepping on the seatbelt clip.'

'It happens,' Owen said kindly. 'Please continue.'

Yasmin pressed her lips together momentarily. 'The driver's window was open. A broad-shouldered, hairy, olive-skinned man wearing sunglasses was tapping on the steering-wheel like he was listening to music. All of a sudden, a woman with a long nose pops up from the seat beside him. Her mascara was all smudged and her grey-brown hair was in an extremely tight ponytail. I yelled above the incessant barking and asked if they were okay.' She rubbed her arms to dispel the sudden eruption of goosebumps.

Chas indicated the delivery docket, 'Can we have this?'

'No, I will take a photocopy of it. The other side relates to my business.'

'You were describing the couple in the vehicle; can you tell us more about their behaviour?' Owen prompted.

She hummed and hawed a bit, then flicked her fingers loudly. 'Yes! It was like Combo suddenly ran out of puff because he plonked himself down on my lap and yawned. Then what sounded like a toddler talking to itself made the man look away. His wiry black hair was all matted behind his neck. The woman scrambled over the back of the seat and made shushing noises. Anyway, I asked them again if they were okay. They spoke at the same time, then laughed together before saying quite clearly that they were twitchers. I also laughed at the weird description, then they explained that they were birders ... uh ... bird observers and were investigating new areas.'

'Do you recall any obvious identifications?' Chas asked directly.

'What? Like tattoos? Piercings?'

'Yes, that's what I mean.'

'No, I didn't notice anything like that but the dancing doll on the dash looked totally out of place. They didn't really look like throw-back hippies. But there was a weird stench that wafted between the vehicles. Not roadkill, but plain weird.'

Owen tapped the notepad and showed it to Chas, then looked at her. In a gentle voice, asked, 'Yasmin, we are going to have to talk about your discovery. You know that, don't you?'

She nodded her head. 'Yes. I feel I can talk about it.'

'Before we do, was there anything else about the vehicle and people you want to tell us about?' Chas asked firmly.

'I thought they drove away too quickly but as the day panned out, never gave them another thought until now. What I can tell you though, it was eighteen minutes past twelve because the 1812 Overture started playing at the exact time. I remember thinking it was a day of oddities. The uneasy feeling in my stomach hadn't eased up and Combo was either jittery or sluggish and regularly got under my feet.'

'You're doing well, Yasmin. Can you think of anything else?'

'Our eyes! They stung like crazy.'

The detective leant towards her and wrung his hands. 'Crying can do that, my dear.'

Yasmin couldn't stem the sudden torrent and excused herself. She took her handbag and photocopied the back of the delivery docket while drying her eyes. Locking everything away, she ensured all the internal doors were firmly closed and shut the front doors. Studying the photocopied scrawl with the last roll of paper towel tucked under her arm as she retook her seat, apologised for neglecting her hostess duties and explained where they could find the facilities. Chas excused himself immediately. Yasmin obligingly handed Owen the document. An aromatic-woody cologne trailed behind the detective forcing her to swiftly change the subject.

'Senior Constable Ramond ... look, I'm going to call him Carl ... it was Carl, wasn't it?' She ignored Owen's raised eyebrow. 'He seemed to be drawn to Combo. Did he lose a dog?'

Owen coughed quietly. 'Yes. A purebred King Charles Cavalier Spaniel worth a lot of money who got swiped as a puppy. I remember the situation well because he had just started at the Academy and it took a lot of encouragement for him not to change careers. He was blind with rage and made it his mission to track down the culprit. He never did.'

'Oh shame, how cruel.' More tears filled her eyes.

'Yasmin, you said the vet guessed Combo was about five?'

'Yes.'

'Do you see him regularly?'

'Not at all if I can help it,' she replied instantly and pulled an unpleasant face. 'Combo travels with me so we go to a vet out of town for his annuals.'

'Yeah,' was all Owen said and looked down at his notes.

Chas spoke loudly from behind. 'I'll close the door behind me, Yasmin.' Then made a show of adjusting his chair before sitting. 'Those roses, are they yours?'

She smiled coyly. 'Yes! Those are the Queen Elizabeth Roses.'

'And people eat them?'

She couldn't help but giggle. 'They could! I grow them and deliver them. It's up to the client what they do with them.'

'The smell is incredible.'

'It's perfume, Chas. Perfume.' Owen corrected him and rolled his eyes in mock annoyance.

The genuine laughter eased the building tension. Yasmin took a deep breath, let it out slowly and held the men's attention.

'I was putting my handbag away when an enquiry came through for a fundrais-ing gala dinner, with the theme being yellow. Four dozen bunches of French marigolds was the highest preference followed by several other suggestions of yellow or gold toned flowers. I was going to see if I would have sufficient supply. My greenhouse is on the way and I noticed the door was slightly ajar, again.'

She threw her hands up in frustration swiping at the build up of tears with her upper arms. 'I put it down to his constant absentmindedness and shrugged it off as an annoyance. I was momentarily surprised at the stunted growth but then remembered I had planted the dwarf stemmed seedlings. They have the largest blooms. Anyway, I was thinking I might just be able to pull it off as it was for a good cause. After latching the door behind me, Combo and I raced each other to the farm ... it's a daily activity.'

Shifting slightly in her chair, she frowned at the recollection of the stinging eyes and mild blood nose, then recalled Combo's breathlessness.

'Take your time.' Both men spoke at the same time.

Eyes cast downwards, Yasmin breathed deeply and slowly. 'I wandered between my roses,' paused, and looked at the men. 'Coffee?'

'Not yet thanks,' Owen said kindly.

Nodding her head, focussed on the geraniums and continued. 'I suddenly began to cry, looked upwards and around to see what caused the silly notion, but nothing out of the ordinary could explain it.'

Exhaling another deep breath, spoke and wrung her hands. 'I sobbed for a little while, then gathered my wits and paid closer attention to nature. The clouds were just starting to lift, and the birds were singing normally but Combo was so jittery. His shackles were up and staring towards the snapdragons. I bent down to his eye-level but couldn't make head nor tail of anything, so I kept on with my task.'

'I'm confused, where are what flowers?' Chas asked.

Yasmin closed her eyes forgetting nobody knew her hobby farm better than her. 'The furthest eleven rows were lavender, then alternatively snapdragons and French marigolds, then the Queen Elizabeth Roses—'

'*Were* lavender? Can you clarify that?'

'Sure, Chas. A little over two weeks ago I cleared the paddock of the old woody crop. Although it had been my best harvest, I was not prepared to take the risk and push them for another season.'

'Right, thank you. Please continue,' he said as he finished with his sketch.

'After the roses—'

'That's okay, I can see the rest from here. What happened then?' he asked brusquely.

She took a steadying breath and rubbed away another frown. 'I walked up and down each and every row of the flowers making my way to the snapdragons. I know my flowers and know the bright yellow ones had just budded. By the way, all my rows are elevated by almost two feet providing better water drainage—'

'You found him in the cleared lavender paddock?' Chas interrupted.

'Yes.'

'Did you have some sort of disagreement recently?'

Yasmin stared at him. 'No! We had a conversation ... well it wasn't really a conversation. Nor was it recent—'

She desperately wanted to talk about everything. Their estranged relationship. The devastating loss of his twin sister. How she had thought everything would be right again when he initiated the conversation. Instead, Yasmin wiped at her eyes and silently counted to ten. In measured tones, elaborated on the year-old memory of it being early in the morning and she had just finished harvesting the variegated Mother-of-all-herbs when he had spoken in monotone staring at her with empty eyes.

'So, you can remember what he said?' Chas asked while he scribbled something down in his notebook.

'Yes. All he said was that the nasturtiums were tasty and the lavender paddock would eventually need turning.'

The tears were cascading freely now. The hurt, indignation and bewilderment slowly changing the sadness of loss into anger at his selfishness.

She looked imploringly at the two men. 'Why leave me to discover his body in the lavender paddock? That was just cruel. He had said that soil would need turning, but really?'

'Yasmin,' Owen's firm, kind voice drew her attention away from dwelling too long on the sad memory. 'That was an awful thing to experience, how about we have that coffee? I would love to see these roses too.'

She smiled gratefully and stood, totally averting her eyes from the scrutinising gaze of the forensic detective. In true gentleman fashion, Owen opened the door for her and gently closed it behind him.

'Quaint!' he chuckled.

'Inherited when I was twenty-seven along with a mortgage. Not much has changed except the floral vista and I've paid off the debt!'

'Congrats! You should be proud of yourself.'

She watched him as he inhaled the perfume deeply. With eyes closed, the most beautiful smile lit up his stress-filled face.

He murmured, 'My wife would love to see these.'

'Well, I know of the best place to get them and you can have as many as you like.'

They chatted amiably about nothing in particular while she made a fresh round of coffees. Naturally the conversation returned to her edible flowers.

'Does anyone help you with your business?'

'No, I've always tended to my hobby farm alone.'

'That's a huge undertaking. Very admirable.'

'Thank you. I'll take our coffees out to the patio.'

Yasmin was relieved to see Chas walking around the front lawn and talking into his mobile phone. He was good looking in a rugged way and she almost melted under his gaze, but her conflicted feelings weren't going to pave the way for small talk at that particular moment. Standing on the opposite edge of the patio looking over the floral vista, she could make out the five men walking along the verge beyond her property. The dogs were nowhere in sight. She sensed Owen's presence before he said anything and turned to greet him with a small smile.

He returned hers and said quietly, 'My wife would also like to see this beautiful view, that I assure you.'

Nodding, said, 'Let's arrange that. In the meantime, perhaps you take some time to stop and smell the roses. While we're doing that, we can cut some. You're welcome to take some back with you.'

'It sounds like she's already been talking to you!'

They shared a genuine laugh and waited for Chas to join them. When he did, she talked freely about walking up and down the rows of snapdragons and marigolds with nothing appearing peculiar, except for little mounds of soil at the base of the elevated beds. Laying down on her stomach to investigate them closely was when Combo growled softly. She simply patted the soil to get his attention but was more interested in discovering if the earth worms had migrated to the other beds.

'But then Combo suddenly barked. It was a strangled sound. When I did look up, he wasn't in the same row. I panicked. He was in the empty lavender paddock and began howling to the heavens. His shackles were on end and his tail was straight out. No amount of shushing him would make him stop. I scrambled over the rows. That was when ... he ... w-was leaning up against the seventh row facing me. Like-like he was lounging against the bed of soil.'

'You scrambled over?' Chas asked incredulously.

'I'm only five foot three!' Yasmin swiped angrily at the spilling tears.

'Of course. Please continue.'

She continued to talk, looking only at Owen. 'I called out several times. He didn't move. His eyes were as lifeless as they were when we last spoke, but-but his hands were spread out in the dirt. I didn't move. I couldn't. I didn't realise Combo had moved until he wrapped his mouth around my hand and pulled me closer. I just sat down on the ground and bawled my eyes out, shouted at him, demanded answers from him while poor Combo just rested his paws on my knees, whimpering and whining.'

He leant over and patted her hand encouraging her to take deep, slow breaths.

'The really weird thing was he wasn't wearing a shirt or shoes of some sort. He never ever went anywhere without a shirt on and certainly never ever walked around barefoot. I can say that with confidence because I've known the man for a long time.'

Yasmin excused herself, went into the cottage and retrieved a floral handkerchief after washing her face. On her return, she flicked through the screenshots and explained in a soft voice that the time had been 14:38 and it was twenty-four degrees when the police were called. Yasmin had stayed with him until all sorts of strangers arrived at 17:34. She overheard the ones dressed in white saying it was a suspected heart attack on first observation.

'You're a very thorough person to have kept those details, Ms Pestel,' Chas commented formally without looking up.

Both men were writing furiously. She let out a deep shaky breath and said clearly, 'Sadly, I still don't know how he died.'

Owen and Chas paused, their pens resting on their notebooks, looked at each other, excused themselves and stood together. Yasmin watched them walk around the lawn presumably swapping thoughts and whatever else police do. Her mind was exhausted. Then she prayed they wouldn't consider the lavender paddock a crime scene. Instead of focusing on the possible, she concentrated on the known. The number plate. There was something peculiar about the number plate. *What about the nine-letter word?*

Groaning miserably, she put her head in her hands and begged for a silent mind.

***

Sitting either side of Bob's hospital bed, they listened to the faint blip of the heart monitor, watching for signs of the sleeping patient to awaken.

'How much do we tell Yasmin?' Mike asked Timmy.

'Nothing until Bob's back on deck.'

'That's pretty unfair. You reckon she's going to handle all the information on top of playing Rudy's game?'

'From the moment I laid eyes on her when he introduced us, I knew she had spunk. It was like she had an old head on young shoulders. Stop fretting, you big ol' softy, leave that for Bob!'

'Speaking of which, his eyes are open!' Mike grinned and squeezed the plump fellow's hand. 'Hey! You're awake, good to see you mate.'

Bob's cracked-lip smile made Timmy sniffle. 'Glad you weren't in a hurry to see Mother.'

In a hoarse voice, he replied, 'Who's the softy now?' His mates helped him sit up. 'Yas baby?'

'We'll talk again in a day or so, buddy. She's a strong woman. She'll be right,' Timmy replied. *As long as she doesn't talk out of school.*

***

Observing their faces and tense body language when the men sat, Yasmin kept hers neutral. Neither broached any of the pressing subjects, so she opened the channel of communication.

'Gentlemen, come clean with me. Has the most recent death brought you closer to an arrest?'

Owen pressed his fingers together like a tent. The deep frown and chewing of his bottom lip made it quite clear he was seriously considering how he was going to answer. She waited patiently. Silently. Eventually, he sat back and looked gravely at Chas whose indifferent expression gave nothing away, until the tiniest nod of his head.

'Yasmin, you're no fool and the evidence inadvertently collected by your prompt action will certainly be of benefit to our investigation.'

She remained quiet, hoping Owen would continue. When he didn't, she looked at him levelly and asked, 'How did he die?'

'We suspect toxins—'

'The toxins are akin to that of snake venom, Yasmin,' Chas said with authority.

She covered her mouth in horror and to quell the rising bile. Swallowing hard, shuddered at the thought of it. 'No way.'

Undisguised annoyance crept over Owen's face. 'We're unsure of the method. As in consumption or self-administration.'

'I don't get it.' she recoiled. 'Snake venom is injected into the bloodstream from its fangs so puncture wounds would be obvious. Right? The enzymes, toxic proteins and whatever other horrid things it contains breaks downs the cells. It's a terribly painful death from what I have read. But consuming it? How does that enter the bloodstream so swiftly?'

Chas cleared his throat. 'I will say your intelligence is quite refreshing given the circumstances. At present, we're still waiting for the toxicologist who is in the city with a growing backlog. But somehow or the other, the blood flow is restricted to the heart causing the organ to fail.'

'So, why is the funeral parlour being so persistent?'

'That's something else we'll talk about at another time,' Owen stated flatly.

She nodded absentmindedly and thought about the snake venom. With her eyes screwed up, she imagined the pain Rudy endured before he eventually died. Shaking her head, she wondered how on earth his state of mind could have slipped so low that he avoided any help. But to have the ability to be so calculating? That wasn't normal.

'Brainwashing!' she blurted out.

'Pardon?' The men asked in unison, then looked at each other frowning.

'It's like we share a brain,' Chas muttered.

Owen glared at him. 'We do not.' He then turned to Yasmin, 'What do you mean?'

'They must have been brainwashed. Hypnotised even.'

Chas dismissed her suggestion. 'Oh, come off it! Now, without thinking too hard about the answer, what was the most unusual thing about your sad discovery.'

Yasmin replied tersely, 'He wasn't wearing a shirt or shoes.'

'Duly noted,' Owen said watching Chas circle the previous entry in his pocketbook.

The tension in the air was getting rather unpleasant. Conversation had come to a complete standstill enabling her overactive mind to decode the number plate. With her smooth forehead creased into a deep frown and large eyes compressed into a tiny squint, she bobbed her head from side to side while letters juggled around in her mind's eye. Yasmin was looking at Owen but not really seeing him. Something tapped her foot. She shrieked with fright.

'Whoa, sorry Yasmin, but where the hell did you go off to?' Chas asked sharply.

She caught her breath and swallowed hard. 'Anybody ever tell you how damn blunt you can be?'

'You sure got a lot of spice in you for such a tiny piece of feminine! Just where did your mind adventure take you?'

Yasmin leant back with her arms folded and stared him down. With her mouth set in a tight line, turned to look at Owen. 'Right now, I am in no mood for rudeness so hear me out.'

Her face a light shade of crimson and voice not quite a hiss explained her knack for solving word puzzles. Owen frowned as he excused himself, got up to answer his mobile phone and walked towards the basil plant with his hand pressed against his ear.

'So, what did you come up with, Miss Brainiac?' Chas asked with a rather cute lopsided grin.

She barely caught herself from being drawn into it. 'You are intolerable, Forensic Detective.'

The grin transformed into a charming smile. 'And you are an incredible woman, so, please share.'

She blushed again and softened her tone. 'Do you know of an acronym for E.F.F.D?'

'Nothing polite, no.'

His quick reply caught her off guard and she laughed loudly. Owen looked at her with an eyebrow raised and immediately she pressed her lips together. Swinging her legs under her seat like a little girl, she studied Chas openly. His handsome face, almond shaped hazel eyes shrouded in thick long lashes, a deep pockmark beside the right side of his lips and gorgeous mop of hair was quite the bit of eye candy, but he sure had an air of conceitedness about him.

Owen sat back down, left his phone on the table and looked at her quizzically. 'Well?'

'We were discussing an acronym for a few letters. But to be honest, I don't want to think about anything else except this damned number plate.' She put her hands up to ward off interruptions. 'Hear me out please. When we separate the digits and letters, we can make words.'

The men looked at her incredulously.

'Oh, come on guys. We've all seen cheeky plates with numbers and letters being exchanged.'

They nodded slowly.

'Well, when we remove the hyphenations, UW8D could be interpreted as *you waited*, right?'

'Hmm, and?' Owen looked at Chas, who also had his left eyebrow raised, then quickly lowered it.

'Then we have the digit two'—she slapped her forehead—'Owen, what letters correlate to four, five and six on the keypad?'

He activated his phone. 'In that order: G, H, I, then J, K, L, then M, N, O.' To confirm his explanation, slid it towards her.

Yasmin's head bobbed from around like she was extracting information from all parts of her brain. 'UW8D ... 2 ... 5664 – L.ON.G. Long. *You waited too long.*'

'How on earth?' Owen whispered.

The colour drained from her face.

'Are you okay?' Chas insisted.

'No! No, I am not. What if it was them? The birders?'

The men fled from the patio. Their mobile phones glued to their ears and spare arms thrashing at invisible thoughts. Owen paced up and down the driveway while Chas jogged over the white pebbles from the front door and onto the grass. Yasmin stumbled into the cottage and flopped onto the settee. With her head in her hands, made a silent vow to Rudy. *I will help nail these cruel people.*

Following Combo's yap up the driveway, she flung open the patio door just as he landed on the mat and leapt into her arms. Yasmin hugged him tightly and cradled him like a big baby. He wriggled around until he was hugging her. Resting his head on her shoulder, he let out a huge puppy sigh dissolving her bravado. She carried him to the lounge, buried her face into his fur and burst into tears. His trembling and whimpering dragging her out of her self-pity. Wiping her face on the sleeve of her shirt, smoothed his coat and talked softly, reassuring him that everything was going to be fine. A solid knock on the patio door saw him bound off the furniture and stand guard.

Yasmin tried to disguise her sorrow by calling out, 'How many coffees?'

'Eight, if possible and all straight black, thanks,' Owen replied immediately. 'We've got water for the K9s.'

Chapter 15

Particles of white paint clung to the heavy plastic curtain behind the funeral parlour's incinerator. Giles swiftly applied the second coat, still mumbling his annoyance at the idiocy of Travis' decision. *Damn fool. Why be a witness?* Refilling the spray gun's canister, he looked up at the sound of his stepbrother swearing into the mobile phone before shoving it into his pocket.

'You nearly done on this closed-door respray, Bro?' Ivan called out, shadow boxing towards his stepbrother.

'Yep. She's a bodge-job, but that's what you wanted. Travis is gonna sink us if he keeps doing stupid things. What happens if the woman recognised him?'

'Don't get cocky, mate. I've just had it out with Callum who'll talk to the big T. Anyway, you need to pay her a visit.'

'What for?'

'The boogey-man forgot to pay his dues. Time to collect and time you stepped up to the plate.'

'What's the plan?'

'We know the sheds contained stuff all and the ancient caravan is a waste of time, so the rest is up to you. Do it when it's dark. Make it soon, like tonight. How much does Stu know?'

'Stuff all.'

'Good. Get Travis to drop you blokes off and tell him when to pick you up. I'll be waiting at our shed with one of the twins.' Ivan slapped Giles across his shoulder as he turned to walk away. 'You'll wanna finish up soon. Clive's getting antsy about us being here. I'll go and fix him up for the privilege.'

'With what?'

'Spondoolas out of Leigh and Callum's cut. They're too stoned to know any difference.'

'Careful man, she's plain evil.'

'Yep, with eyes on you, so I'll be right, then we'll be right.' He waved his steroid arms about like a magician. 'And make sure you tidy up properly.'

Giles flipped him the bird behind his back. *I always have to do the donkey work, you lazy bastard.*

Chapter 16

Yasmin opened the door for Combo at the same time Carl held it open for her.

'Ma'am,' his eyes full of concern and kindness. 'Here, I'll take the tray.'

'That'll be great, thank you, I'll be with you gentlemen shortly. Please don't wait.'

With a stern look, he commanded Combo to stay and protect, who immediately retreated and did as he was told.

I hope I didn't give anything away. She had just locked the main front door when Chas opened the patio door and stepped inside. Combo immediately bared his teeth.

'Ms Pestel, please join us.'

'Am I under suspicion?'

'No. We need your assistance in identifying something.'

She stared at him. 'Can you give me five more minutes please?'

'Yes, yes of course. Pardon me, Ma'am.' Embarrassed, made a hasty retreat.

She buried the urge to scoff and improved her appearance before ruffling Combo's head and praising him quietly. When she rejoined her guests, the dogs were lying at the feet of their handlers silently regarding the seated senior personnel. They all simultaneously stood to greet her.

She smiled, and sat. 'Such valour, thank you for being here. I see Combo has learnt a few more lessons!'

'He is a quick learner, Ms Pestel,' Sergeant Kohli said. 'My invitation stands about getting him to meet a few more of our squad.'

'Glad to see you have a bit more colour in your face.'

Owen's immediate comment prevented her from replying, giving both men a little smile indicating they should be comfortable. No sooner had the constabulary sat, their K9s did at a silent command from their respective handlers. Everyone spent far too much time focussing on their coffees or the concrete for her liking. She observed Owen's demeanour and instantly knew he was unimpressed. Chas' face was guarded but it was Sergeant Kohli who retained her attention. They cast an inquisitorial eye over each other, and both kept a poker face. Her lips twitched when he blinked first.

'Ms Pestel,' he nodded respectfully and asked, 'Do you recognise this shirt?' Using a stick, he held up a mauve paisley long-sleeve blouse.

'No, I do not.'

'Would your dearly departed have worn anything like this?' he asked gently.

'No. He never wore anything patterned and certainly not a woman's shirt.'

'What?' Chas exclaimed.

'It's a woman's shirt. The buttons are opposite to a man's shirt. See for yourself.'

'Is it yours then?' he asked.

'Hell no!' the words were out. 'I most certainly would not wear that.'

The smothered chuckles filtered around the patio. She had to concentrate on stifling her own giggles. Luckily Sergeant Kohli had the fortitude to command order.

'Can you confidently say you have never seen this shirt in your life, Ms Pestel?'

'Yes, Sergeant Kohli, I say with absolute confidence I have never seen that shirt in my life.'

'Have you ever seen anything like it?'

She had a flashback. 'Well, I had a trippy art teacher back in high school that would wear that sort of pattern that never matched the hippy style pants, but that was eons ago Sir.'

'Okay, we'll leave that one alone for the time being, but I have one question about half of the bare paddock.'

Yasmin looked steadily at the giant policeman and waited. *Breathe. Lower your shoulders. Breathe.*

'Who helped you level it?'

'Nobody,' she replied, praying her thumping heart wasn't heard. 'Nobody has ever helped me with my hobby farm. I do the lot, from the laying of the drills, building the beds, weeding, planting and cutting, setting up the irrigation and all repairs, right through to cleaning and replenishing the water dishes for Combo as well as the numerous bee and birdbaths.'

'The machinery?'

'Regular mechanical maintenance.'

'You?'

'Yes, that too.'

'Resourceful and independent,' Sergeant Kohli said kindly.

Yasmin showed her appreciation with a wry grin. 'I make do with what I have. Always have.'

He spoke to Owen. 'Boss, I have no further questions. We need to get back to HQ.'

It was like watching poetry in motion. His gorgeous fawn Belgium Malinois stood as soon as the massive man effortlessly did, and the rest of the K9 Unit followed suit. Combo automatically stood when Carl did. The handlers thanked her for the coffee and took their leave respectfully. Sergeant Kohli approached Yasmin and wrapped his bear-like hand around hers as she stood and shook it gently, His kind eyes spoke volumes.

'Ms Pestel, thanks for the coffee. Consider my offer but most importantly, take care of yourself. You have gone through a terrible ordeal.'

She blinked away the tears. 'You're quite persistent about Combo! Thank you, Sergeant Kohli.'

'And?' he asked with mock seriousness.

She blushed and whispered. 'And I will take care of myself too, thank you.'

'That's better.'

His wink was so fatherly it took Yasmin all her strength not to beg for a hug. He ruffled Combo's head, positively reassured him then commanded him to protect, who obediently stood beside Yasmin's left knee.

'Gents, see you there. No need to walk us to our vehicles.'

His colleagues including the detective, standing respectfully, semi-saluted the big man with only Owen speaking. 'See you then, Boss.'

The curt nod of heads symbolising a type's farewell, the rest of the Unit joined their boss. Carl made himself useful and gathered up the cups, rinsing them under the tap beside the washing line before stacking them on the tray. Yasmin thanked him, smiled at his and Combo's play, stifled a yawn, rubbed her eyes and frowned at the thought of the funeral parlour.

'Excuse me Sergeant Pyers, but when shall I make arrangements?'

'It's a little too early to say. Please bear with us while we assess the situation,' he said naturally.

Nodding in acknowledgement she glanced casually at the three men, each occupied with their own thoughts. She held their gazes but had difficulty in deciphering the guarded looks. Something was brewing, but it wasn't her place to ask questions, so she sat.

Following suit, Owen encouraged warmly. 'Tell us about your family.'

She chuckled good-naturedly. 'Oh, there really isn't much to tell. My great aunt and uncle bequeathed this beautiful cottage and derelict hobby farm to me along with my grandparents' old caravan and the mortgage. They grew grapes. About two years after they left this earth, my folks emigrated to Europe soon after my much older sister did.'

Chas sat. 'Do they know anything about the recent events?'

'Well, no … they don't know much about the last ten years actually. While we have had conversations, it's been hit and miss for long chats … you know … time differences, them being the social highflyers and the like,' Yasmin exaggeratedly rolled her eyes and laughed quietly.

'And you're okay with that?' Owen looked at her incredulously.

'Their parental love is unquestionable. You see, from a young age they encouraged me not to be solely reliant on it and to seek my own independence. I suppose I just took a leaf out of my older sister's book and well, I knew no different.'

'Is there anyone that can look out for you?' Owen asked gently.

'Not really. Perhaps you guys and the K9 crew would care to volunteer?' she smiled hopefully.

They all chuckled. Silence befell the patio except for Combo tarting between Carl and her for pats. Noticing the time, she announced that it was watering day and excused herself from their company.

'Mind if we come with you?' Chas asked politely.

'Not at all. It's not an elaborate setup but it's effective.'

Combo ran around crazily. Yasmin smirked. 'Yeah, you know what time it is! Sit.' He did.

Turning to her audience, she said, 'Gents, seeing as the formalities have stalled and it's midday, it's also play time so if you could please give us some room, we need to run and jump off the patio.'

'You what?' Owen asked, wide-eyed.

Chas stared at her, mouth agape. Carl's eyebrows shot up and came to a stop at the sharp line of a very, very short front, back and sides haircut.

'See, we R.A.C.E to the T.R.E.E and back,' she said with a wink, grinned and slid off her shoes. 'If you could please wait for us here, we won't be long.'

Carl easily read the play and encouraged his colleagues to move their chairs and stand against the table. Combo pranced around Yasmin's feet until they were standing beside each other at the far end of the patio. Knowing the drill, he waited for her commands.

'Wait. Stay. Race.'

No sooner had she murmured the final word; they bolted across the patio. Combo flew and landed sure pawed on the grass before racing away. Yasmin gracefully dived, tucked and rolled before springing back on her feet and sprinted after Combo. He waited for her at the base of the massive Jacaranda tree. No sooner had she reached him, he hightailed it back and sat on the grass, healthy pink tongue lolling and dripping happily while his tail thumped excitedly watching her race towards him.

Sucking in the big ones, Yasmin panted. 'I swear you get faster and faster each time, my boy.' She ruffled his head and pretend-kissed it noisily.

Looking towards the men at the patio, called out, 'Okay, let's go do some work.'

'My God, woman!' Chas exploded, 'Who the hell taught you to do that?'

She had desperately needed the adrenalin rush and burst out laughing. 'Gymnastics as a kid!'

'You ain't a kid,' he looked at her weirdly.

She tapped her heart and flashed them her bright sunshine smile. 'When you remain young at heart, you never get old.'

Owen and Carl stood there with huge grins and were still grinning when they walked either side of her and Combo towards the greenhouse. Chas' mobile rang just as he stepped off the patio, and swore under his breath. The frustrated tone of his voice when he answered made the others snicker quietly.

'He's from the city, so excuse his lack of manners,' Carl murmured.

As they approached the netted structure, a familiar peculiar feeling washed over Yasmin. *Oh no, not again.* She stopped and gripped the arms of the two policemen halting them mid-stride. Before she could say anything, Combo growled softly and leant into her legs. They all took a step backwards and covered their eyes immediately. Combo sneezed hard. He couldn't stop sneezing and began wheezing. Carl immediately scooped him up and raced him to the cottage.

'My eyes!' Owen groaned as they stumbled backwards. In an instant, his training kicked in and bellowed, 'Inside. Now!'

Yasmin grabbed onto Owen's shirt. 'It's the sixth time in the last fortnight, but it's worse today.'

'You withheld this information?' he stated flatly.

'I hadn't worked it out until now.'

'Someone's going to pay for this,' he growled.

Yeah, me. My business is ruined. Yasmin used her sleeve to wipe at her runny nose. 'Poor Combo.'

Carl had already requested Fire and Rescue E.R.T. assistance then swapped phones with Owen the minute they stepped inside. He apologetically handed them both a drenched tea-towel before dialling the local vet and dashed back to Combo's to dab his eyes. Chas simply got in everyone's way.

'What can I do?' he asked warily as he stepped around Carl's bustling.

Owen glared at him. 'Wet some towels and get a saline solution happening in the sink. Everyone else, blink rapidly.'

'Where are the paper towels?'

'I used them all,' Yasmin sobbed.

'Dammit Hillyer, use tea towels. Anything!'

Combo lay breathless on the couch. Weakly raising his paws, he kept trying to wipe his eyes. He didn't even try and raise his head.

'Have you got binoculars, Yasmin?' Owen asked through another wet towel.

'Yes.'

She stumbled into the office and stopped in her tracks. Only Rudy knew when she put the water on. Snatching them off the bookshelf, she was fuming by the time she handed Owen the set of WW2 Signal Corps Binoculars.

'My Great Uncle's pride and joy. I'm going to check on Combo.'

Yasmin sat, gently resting her best friend's furry head on her lap. 'Carl, go and do your job. I'll call you if there's a change. Did you tell the vet to come to the front door?'

'Okay. Yes, I did.' He stared at Combo. 'He has to be okay, Ma'am. He just has to be.'

'Go on,' she urged him calmly.

Chas approached holding out a dampened old tea towel and spoke softly. 'Ms Pestel, allow me to wipe your eyes for you.'

Combo's low growl prevented any interaction. Swiftly retreating, he winked. 'Real jealous type! Catch, you can wipe them yourself!'

Stifling a chortle, she dabbed at her eyes methodically recalling the events of the past fortnight. The occasional unusual blood noses coincided with Combo's sluggishness and they both suffered awfully sore, red, watery eyes. *Oh Rudy, what have you done now?*

The E.R.T. guys and the vet arrived at the same time. Carl flung open the front door and they hurried inside. No introductions were made, they just all got on with their jobs. The medics rolled up shortly thereafter and Yasmin's lounge instantly turned into a triage out of a movie scene. Furniture was re-arranged, monitoring equipment established and everyone with symptoms had a heart monitor attached to their arms. Swabs were taken from facial orifices while Chas took notes. Stu Wilson performed a routine check on his patient and kept touching Yasmin's hands.

'Concentrate on Combo and leave me alone please Stu.'

'People, I don't think this is poison,' he stated flatly and stepped away from the couch.

Owen glared at him. 'What do you think it is then?'

'Listen mate, we've never got on but let's put those differences aside for the time being, hey?' he challenged.

They faced off until Carl stepped in the middle and blocked their view. 'Say something constructive Stu, or don't say anything at all.'

He glared at him. 'My bet it's OC spray. You fellas ought to have realised that seeing as you use it more than anybody!'

Carl steered Stu to the door and hissed, 'What is the update on Combo?'

'He'll be right, dogs are more sensitive to things than us mere humans. You of all people should know that!'

'Well then, you can collect your things and leave.'

'I should take him with me, just in case. He can rest in my clinic. I'll monitor him closely.'

'YOU WILL DO NOTHING OF THE SORT,' Owen bellowed.

Stu's volcanic rage, tenfold in volume. 'OC SPRAY CAN BE HARMFUL.'

The E.R.T. guys covered in Hazmat suits had just stepped inside from the patio door and froze on the spot. Their appearance in conjunction with the shouting match sent Combo into an almighty burst of aggressive snarling. Yasmin called out to Carl to help restrain him. Nobody else moved. Owen and Stu resumed their stand-off. Both pairs of fists clenched and unclenched. They both cracked their knuckles. Chas eventually gathered up Stu's vet case and ushered him to the door.

'Best you take your leave. Here's my card. E-mail through the capsicum spray opinion along with your detailed report to Pyers and me.'

'You'll receive your bill in the mail, Ms Pestel. Just remember, I don't often do house-calls,' Stu flung harshly over his shoulder. Then spun around. His face red with embarrassment. 'I'm sorry, you didn't deserve that. I'll waive the call-out fee, please consider using my clinic again. It's really struggling.'

Yasmin stared at him dumbfounded.

Owen took a large step towards the vet. 'Get out of my sight.'

As soon as the front door closed, the E.R.T. guys talked calmly and removed their suits, slightly pacifying the crazed pet. Dave, the team leader, handed his face mask to Chas. 'Here mate, the vet's right but. The residue is similar to that of mace, but we'll see when it's dried. The DRIFTS method should prove it. We'll have to wait a little while though.'

The crew of five took turns using the kitchen, while conferring with the two policemen intermittently. Dave walked over to the couch, talking kindly the whole time and extended his hand downwards so that Combo could sniff him without feeling threatened. Eventually his tail thumped, but it was what Dave said after he'd introduced himself to Yasmin that nearly undid her resolve all over again.

'Ms Pestel, nice to meet finally you. Just sorry it's under these lousy circumstances. Most of my guys are familiar with your product too, and I really am sorry. I'm a hobby agronomist. What were you growing?'

'Dwarf stemmed French marigolds ... for larger flowers and mystic flavours.'

He frowned. 'From seed?'

She nodded.

'At a later date, give Sarge the receipt for your purchase. More importantly though, have you had any blood noses?'

Yasmin's gasp was audible. 'I have. Minor ones. Please don't tell me we've been poisoned.'

'Has Combo passed any blood? Lost an inexplicable amount of fur? You? Any clumps of hair?'

'No and no. Nor have I.'

'Monitor him closely for the next two months and yourself. Present to E.D. if you start losing clumps of hair. I doubt you have been poisoned but be mindful. From my investigation, the foliage damage is showing signs of being burnt from a chilli and oil spray. Now, I don't expect an answer, but I am willing to bet your eyes have been burning on occasions.'

His clinical tone prevented any emotions from erupting when she vigorously nodded.

'Look, I'm going to be honest with you. Pyers and I work closely together on all sorts of things. Anyway, stay upwind when you're burning the seedlings, it would be awful if your reputation for consistency was compromised. My cousin is going to be devastated though. You have supplied her restaurant for years!'

It took a long while for Yasmin to comprehend the message. Her shoulders sagged. 'Please allow me to break the news.'

'Of course. Before you pat your pooch, please go and wash your hands. I do suggest you give him a bath too.'

Nodding, she went to wipe her eyes and stopped when he ever so gently clasped her wrist and murmured, 'You don't want to do that.'

Her bottom lip quivered. 'Thanks for being here, Dave.'

His misty-grey eyes softened. 'You'll be okay, Ms Pestel. You're stronger than what you give yourself credit for.'

Chapter 17

Beyond the rolling hills, closer to the sea, a tartan picnic blanket adorned with daisy petals, clover and nut grass was quite fitting for the alternate, tightly-knit, extended family. Tambourines and several bundles of legs for the silky oak easels they were constructing, lay about their feet. The gentle breeze whispered its message through the spindly leaves of the pepper tree, encouraging two young cousins—a boy and a girl—to drape themselves over their respective mothers' shoulders and hug them tightly.

'Mummy,' squealed the little girl, 'This is going to be the bestest art exhibition ever! The wind told us so.'

Idolising his cousin, the little boy gave her a toothy grin. 'Yeah!'

Swapping screws for tambourines, they sat cross-legged in a circle. The children either side of the mothers wriggled around until all knees touched. Swaying to the gentle count of three, their off-key harmony of a well-rehearsed folk song tumbled into the shade around them.

'The gypsy rover came over the hill, down through the valley so shady.'

Chapter 18

With the pepper spray suspicion confirmed, Dave and his crew let themselves out with Carl and Chas following closely behind.

'Yasmin,' Owen spoke in a calmer tone while adjusting the lenses on the binoculars. 'How recently did you say you put in the overhead watering system?'

'I didn't. It's more like three, no four years ago. Why's that?'

'Any reason you'd have a spray head protruding away from the greenhouse?'

'No! That'd be just plain daft.'

Checking Combo's pulse and nose, she left him dozing on the settee. Yasmin took the offered set of binocs and joined Owen by the patio door. Adjusting the sights, she gasped softly at the same time shaking her head in disbelief. *You are kidding me!*

Failing to disguise her disappointment, muttered, 'Owen, the E.R.T. guys would have disabled the plumbing, I have to go and check this out.'

'Not yet. Wait until Carl gets back, he can sit with Combo, but I have to say something, Yasmin.' Owen looked at her intently, 'I mentioned before that Sergeant Kohli, myself and Carl feel as if we've known you for ages. Your distinguishable pink van and blooms have been a welcome sight for many years, you certainly brought a lot of smiles to a lot of people's faces, and you definitely grow delicious flowers, but we are trying to solve a possible murder case. We feel obligated to give you friendship and support.'

Yasmin pressed her trembling lips together and wiped away the small tears. 'Is that really why Sergeant Kohli insists Combo has some new friends?'

'Probably!'

'Is that normal?'

'I thought I'd answered that one. Anyway, I don't speak for the man when it comes to his forte.'

Accepting his reply, said, 'Well, I am grateful to you three for being so kind and although a victim of circumstance, you can talk to me as a friend. So, thank you, I graciously accept.'

'Good. Now, tell me about the greenhouse irrigation.'

Dutifully explaining the three-piece contraption prior to being installed in situ, its design simplified the 'nursery' watering system. Downward nozzles were spaced appropriately to irrigate the 400 seedlings sufficiently in two hours.

'I take it you don't like the vet?' Yasmin blurted out.

'I would like to hear your opinion of Clive at the funeral parlour.'

'You never answered that one! Well, I've never met the man. All flower deliveries are left at the unattended front office with the invoices, which are always paid on time. I just don't get the urgency unless they're hoping for a cremation to hide any evidence.' The last part of her thought process came out rushed. She clutched at his arm. 'Owen! How many other souls have died from snake venom, heart attack or suicides?'

He removed her hand firmly. 'I will not disclose that, Yasmin.'

'Aha! Then tell me how many have died in a six-hundred-kilometre radius, and where is the centre point?'

At that moment, Carl and Chas entered the cottage having quite the heated discussion and fell silent when they saw their boss and the grieving widow also having a serious tête-à-tête.

'Right, you blokes stay here and mind the pooch,' Sergeant Pyers commanded.

'Actually, I'm going to get a lift back to town,' Chas spoke bluntly.

'Copy that.'

'Ms Pestel,' the detective's voice softened, 'I will be in touch.'

She turned to look at him and did her best to keep her voice steady. 'Please go through Sergeant Pyers, Sergeant Kohli or Senior Constable Ramond.' *And don't look at me with those bedroom eyes!*

Owen opened the patio door. 'After you, Ms Pestel.'

They walked together towards the seedlings in brooding silence and slowed their pace the closer they got. Both tentatively sniffing, they looked at each other warily.

Yasmin smirked. 'Reckon it's safe, Boss?'

'You have a way with words; I'll give you that! About your question.'

'Yes?'

'You are too astute for your own good.'

'He needs to rest in peace, Sergeant Pyers.'

'Acknowledged.' He nodded towards the greenhouse. 'First things first. Dave's crew watered everything down and disconnected the power. Now you need to explain the plumbing and anything else you feel is relevant.'

'Fine. The protruding shower head is a new addition I know nothing about. And this ... this is the regularly unlatched pesky door which frequently did my head in.'

She unwound the wire latch then pulled open the door. Shaking her head, demonstrated how it could not possibly swing open by itself. Even if unlatched. Confidently entering the greenhouse gestured upwards and described the network of pipes overhead. Ducking under the nearest bench, Yasmin retrieved the four-step stepladder nimbly climbed to the second-top rung and scrutinised the pipework. She shook her head. Again.

'You have got to be kidding me,' she muttered. Then in a louder voice, 'Every nozzle has been changed and there's a new fitting in each corner pointing outwards.'

To prove her point, she went outside and looked up at all four corners. A normal glance would have missed them entirely because why the hell would she ever look upwards? But with the use of the binoculars and an unfamiliar eye, it was pretty damned obvious. Retrieving her mobile phone from her jean's pocket, took several photos at different angles. Back inside, dragged the ladder towards the furthest corner opposite the door and looked upwards as she scaled the rungs. Sure enough, an inline pump ran parallel to the main pipeline with an off-take connected to a large round shower head. She took several more photos and zoomed in on the label. The size of the pump would easily put out nine litres a minute.

'Bloody hell. If this isn't calculated, premeditated and every other 'ted there is, I don't know what is.'

'Hmm, some thought definitely went into this, that's for sure.' Owen agreed. 'Any idea who would want to sabotage your business?'

'No.' Staring forlornly at all the seedlings, Yasmin sighed heavily. 'Well, this just sucks. These are all compromised just like Dave said which means I need to withdraw from supply immediately. I think we should return to the cottage. You men haven't had lunch.'

'Very kind of you, but we need to make tracks.'

Retracing their steps, Owen asked Yasmin if she would participate in the current investigation on an anonymity and indemnity basis. She was to consider the suggestion and reply to his text message within five minutes at precisely 2200hrs that night. *Check in* for a favourable participation or *no worries* for a negative association.

'Why? What use can I be?'

'Any information may help solve cold cases.'

'Is it usual practice to involve civilians, victims, whatever I'm classified as?'

'It's not uncommon. For example, Dave. Our paths crossed many years ago and sometimes two heads are better than one. Any other questions?'

'Yes. Sergeant Kohli referred to you as his boss. Are you?'

Owen chuckled, 'We're both bosses, just not of each other so you could very well hear me calling him that too.'

'I'm not under suspicion?'

'Hardly. Well, not from where I'm standing … unless you should be?'

The tears fell. 'No.'

'Didn't think so. What security system do you have in place?'

Yasmin explained the alarms were set to audible at night and generally activated during the day, all controlled through the mobile phone application.

Carl and Combo met them still playing a gentle tug-o-war with the well-worn bath towel. 'Hope you don't mind, Ma'am?'

'Not at all! Thanks, Carl.'

'He's bouncing back pretty good, but I simply love that outdoor shower with the foot-pump! Combo knows how to use it too!'

Yasmin smiled. 'I can tell by your wet shirt!'

She looked up at Owen and held out her hand. 'Thank you very much for everything. I appreciate you being here and spending time with me today. Your company has been most welcome.'

With handshakes reciprocated Yasmin and Combo escorted the policemen to their vehicle.

'You know we'll be in touch very soon, don't you, Ms Pestel?' Owen asked firmly.

'Yes, thank you, Sergeant Pyers.'

Carl handed her a business card. 'Forensic Detective Hillyer requested I give you this on his behalf. He said to tell you that if you need clarification on funeral protocols, he could offer assistance.'

'Okay, thank you.' Yasmin stuffed it into her pocket.

She watched Carl bend down to eye level with Combo. There was a growing bond between the pair. It was quite touching seeing Combo rest his paw on Carl's hand and she bit back more tears when they put their foreheads together.

'Come on, lad,' Owen chuckled softly. 'He'll be here when we come back.'

Carl shook her hand, thanking her profusely for the pleasure of her acquaintance and Combo's company.

'Ms Pestel, we'll wait until you're inside before we leave.'

'Okay. Bye.'

At the click of her tongue, Combo was at her knee. Securing the cottage appropriately, they watched the vehicle drive slowly down the driveway. Trepidation covered her like a cobweb.

Chapter 19

Walking past the empty cages in the back of his clinic drumming the metal ruler along the bars to the rhythm of his footsteps on the sterilised floor, Stu grinned. *I'll win you over, Yasmin Pestel.* Arriving at the last cage, the moment the switch on the opaque glass was flicked to transparent the lights brightened instantly. At the sight of his young Shield-snouted Brown Snake rearing up defensively, the grin transformed into a broad smile.

'Come to Papa, my little Yasmin with the button nose and yellow-white belly. Milking time, precious-sss!' he sung.

Seizing it behind its neck, forcing its mouth over the vial, Stu felt himself harden as the liquid squirted into the container.

'Ooh, that's your record! Very good little one. Papa will feed you now.'

With the serpent coiling itself around the writhing shrew, it totally ignored the human's hands stroking its length. Stu positioned the vial beside the dried cane toad skins and set up the burner.

Instead of lighting it, he answered his phone glibly. 'Speak!'

'Hey, mate! What you up to?'

'Giles! Just prepping a brew. What's happening?

'Feel like an adventure?'

'Yeah. Been a weird day, mate.'

'Good. I'll swing by with some grub and thrash out a plan.'

'Righto. Bring beers too.'

'Heads up, it's gonna be a long night!'

'Got the best medicine for that. See ya.'

Chapter 20

After straightening up the household furniture and cleaning up the crockery, Yasmin removed a slice of rump steak from the freezer. Although ravenous, shared a reheated half sausage roll and the remaining bit of French vanilla slice with Combo.

With the Craige family paperwork covering the dining table, she got lost in the afternoon sun kissing the Jacaranda tree. Nothing like a cold, wet nose to get on with the task at hand! Putting the letters and journals in chronological order; the absence of reading material two weeks before the snow holiday to six months after the funeral of Mr and Mrs Craige, made sense. The three lads had written to Rudy constantly afterwards, sharing news about their lives, business challenges, and the sad decline of their mother's health. Not even reading between the lines did they give away what their business was!

Yasmin suddenly remembered about the helicopter. If Rudy had bequeathed it to the lads, obviously they would have known about it. Her ire rose swiftly. Pacing the cottage, Mike's gentle words of *having a lot to say at another time*, kept ringing in her head. Backtracking to much earlier in the piece, there had been an agreement between Mr Craige and the three lads which helped them out tremendously during particularly tough times in their own company. Annoyingly, still nobody disclosed *what* that company did!

She tried to remember when Rudy first started wearing the band of gold, but it eluded her. Yasmin just knew it never came off. That is until very recently. In life and the coinciding waning health, he had always referred to their boys-only click as Timmy, Rudy and the lads. Initially she found it odd that he referred to himself in the third person but that aside, Timmy was always mentioned first.

Pondering on what she had learnt didn't change the fact that the entire Craige family had passed away. She was the outsider yet now connected with the lads according to Rudy's wishes. There wasn't too much else she needed to know. But she did have a lot of questions.

Returning the latest archive box with its counterparts in the oversized storage cupboard, there was still the deepest void that needed answering. What happened with Emily? Her best friend. With her exemplary manners and etiquette, where exactly were her letters? Feeling utterly exhausted, Yasmin shooed Combo off the settee and rested her eyes briefly. Reflecting on the day's events, she sat bolt upright. *The seedlings!*

In full business mode, made the necessary but heart-breaking phone calls cancelling supply indefinitely due to a death in the family. The words of comfort from her clients were genuine and welcomed. Nothing reduced the taste of bitter disappointment. With the last of the Craige business packed away, emotional questions exploded like popcorn.

'Why deliberately sabotage my business? Huh, Rudy? Why be so vindictive then furnish me with wealth? And above all, why the hell tie me to the lads?'

Groaning loudly at the thought of phoning her family, it was a toss-up of catching them when they were just about to go out or to bed. At any time, her older sister, Candy, was nigh on impossible to talk to. The nine years age difference might as well have been twenty. Praying the boyfriend Lars was still in the picture, dialled his last known number and estimated it would be early in the morning in France. If he was still in France.

'Dis is Lars.'

'And dis is Yas,' she replied, angst morphing into nonsense.

His Danish accent with the French lilt a delight to listen to particularly when he yelled excitedly down the phone. 'Our beautiful Yas! Little sister, how are you? You've just missed Candice. Her and your mum have gone out for the day!'

'Lars, I'm well thanks. You sound ecstatic. What's going on?'

'We've done everything backwards!'

'You what? We're the ones down-under here!'

His laughter boomed the through phone. 'The last piece fell into place today! Can you phone really late next Wednesday night your time. Can you do that please?'

'I'll write it on the calendar while you're telling me everything about being backwards.'

'No! We're not backwards, we have *done* everything backwards, Yas. You still cheeky.'

'That's not about to change, Lars! Now come on, spill.'

'I sold my restaurant, we're both retired, we eloped and invested in some Saudi jewellery, you know like wedding and engagement rings and have adopted a baby.'

Yasmin was speechless.

'You there?'

'I … uh … yeah! Wow! A baby? A real baby?'

'Of course, a real baby. You ninny!'

'I mean a baby baby? As in a little boy baby or girl baby?'

'Of course! You think we adopt elephant baby?'

She burst out laughing. 'No. Wow! Hey, congratulations! That's awesome. So, you're a dad and our folks are grandparents, wow!'

'Der!'

'Der all right! Wow. When did this happen, Lars?'

'Just recently. The adoption on baby girl finally came through after waiting 13 months, so we decided to do everything else in the meantime. And we're moving.'

'To where?' she asked excitedly.

'Provence!'

'Oh wow! I remember Candy sent me a postcard when I was in my early twenties. The Lavender Fields … the inspiration … oh, Lars I am thrilled to bits for you both. Congratulations. That's awesome!'

His voice suddenly had a serious tone. 'How long has it been since we've actually had a decent telephone conversation?'

'A long while and long overdue.'

'Ouch. Your parents are now in their golden years. I will make sure they speak to you more often too. We'll all be living on the same Estate. Besides, you must be nearly forty, eh?'

'Yeah, getting there!' she chuckled lightly.

'Your turn to spill, what's been happening?'

'Oh, Lars, I don't want to put a dampener on your exciting news and the wonderful things you're experiencing!'

'Yasmin Rose Pestel, it is just you and I speaking. I have the house to myself for several hours then your dad and I play golf. Talk to me. It's always been easier for me to convey messages to your family to open the channel of conversation when you do all speak.'

'You're right about that.'

'Please talk to me, I can tell something wrong. Your nose ... it's blocked.'

She took a deep breath and crammed the last eight years into just under an hour. Taking a coffee and sitting beside the snoring Combo with Lars' kind words in the background, she realised she hadn't cried the whole time she had been talking. He suspected there was more to Rudy's death and accepted her abbreviated explanation of him dying of a broken heart with the funeral arrangements still to be finalised. He respected her enough not to push the subject and expressed his condolences. They did talk for a little while longer sharing stories, laughter and how much happier her folks were after living in a retirement village in the Alps, giving them free reign to travel between Italy and Switzerland. Yasmin wasn't even aware they had moved! *No wonder my letters hadn't been answered.*

'Do you ever think about the snow or visiting this neck of the woods?'

'Snow? No. A visit? Not in winter!' she laughed and shared a secret with him. 'Lars, when I was eighteen, I wrote on my wish list that I would spend six months of the year in the southern hemisphere for summer and six months in the northern hemisphere for spring and summer, that way I wouldn't ever be cold!'

His laughter was so comforting. 'Dreams don't cost anything beautiful girl, so keep that wish alive. You hear me?'

'Yes, I will. I promise.'

'Right, I will share your congratulatory messages and Yas, I will tell Candice and your folks about Rudy for you in such a fashion that they won't ask questions, okay?'

'Bless you. Thank you, Lars. You're a good man, great brother and will make a great dad!'

'Now that's what I've been wanting to hear for years!'

They shared several more good laughs before disconnecting the call.

Devouring a hearty serve of creamy garlic mashed potatoes and steamed beans, Yasmin reluctantly treated Combo to the rarest bits of the steak and explicitly instructed him not to want to go outside after 10:30pm. The pair played tug-o-war and other nightly games which they hadn't done for a little while. Washing away the day's woes and dramas, she lounged around on the settee with her head and heart hurting.

At 2201hrs, Yasmin responded positively to Owen's text message and promptly saved his contact details. The ritual of investigating the external perimeter of the cottage also returned, but at a much faster pace. She had just locked all the doors and set the alarms when her landline rang. It was Timmy. She let it go to the answering machine, then sent him a text requesting he phoned her on the mobile instead.

'Ah, hello Timmy, been thinking of you guys,' she said quietly about three seconds later.

'Hey, Yasmin, what'd you have for dinner?'

'Steak and vegetables.'

'Wow! Healthy.'

'Yeah, I finished the bacon and eggs. Hey, can you give me a sec?'

'Sure thing.'

She drew the curtains and closed all the interleading doors except her bedroom's. Sending Combo on a search and locate mission, he sniffed every square inch of the room, walk-through wardrobe and ensuite before trotting happily alongside her and decided the settee was suitably comfortable.

'Okay, I'm good to go. How's Bob?'

'He's awake, resting and just given you the thumbs up.'

'Nice! Blow him a kiss for me, will you?'

'No, I won't!' Timmy laughed a bit too loudly. 'But I am going to put you on speaker. Stand by.'

Hearing the echo and muffled voices, she greeted them all individually and was about to mention the jewellery when someone's cough drowned out her voice.

'Yas, it's Mike ... hi. To make this easier for everyone, I'm going to call you *Yas*, like always, Timmy's going to call you *Yasmin*, which will never change and Bob, well, he's always called you *Yas baby*, but tonight he's all ears because he really needs to rest his mouth. He'll thump the table, three for yes and one for no. Get it?'

'Got it.'

'Good.'

They shared a laugh and three thumps resonated through the phone.

'How'd you go with the cops, Yasmin?'

'Quite well thanks, they did what they had to do and I behaved appropriately.'

'Are you okay?'

'Yeah, yeah. They're just following due process.'

'Fair enough. Yas, is Rudy's death under investigation?'

'Not his specifically, nor can they say too much about an ongoing investigation.'

The silence was getting awkward so she broke the ice.

'As soon as I can make the funeral arrangements, I'll let you know. But how's this for a suggestion, Ru wanted a cremation so if I bring his ashes to you guys, we'll come up with a plan then? Does that sound okay to you all?'

Two positive responses and three thumps was the reply.

'Thank you. You see, I was under the impression we were destitute after Mr and Mrs Craige's funeral and distinctly recall Ru's absolute disgust at the bank for foreclosing on the house and business to nullify any debt. The surrounding circumstances of being an orphan and without his twin sent him into a perpetual downward spiral of despair. So, you can imagine my absolute shock when I recently learnt otherwise about the financial status.'

She was met with silence.

'You've got nothing to say, guys?'

'Yasmin, there is so much you don't know, and we don't know where to start, but tonight nor over the phone is going to be the time or the way.'

'Well, then I would like to read you some of Rudy's letter. You right if we do that now?'

'This is Timmy and on behalf of Mike and Bob, we concur.'

Yasmin unclenched her fists and calmly read out the snippets.

I have to be burnt, like Emily was. I felt her pain when we were forced to do that so I have to suffer the same. Tell my three best friends, Timmy, Mike and Bob that I am glad we saw each other when we did. Thank Timmy, Mike and Bob for all the good times for me, will you? I know you will, because that's who you are.'

She waited for assurance that they were listening before continuing.

'Still quoting Ru, *these are my wishes and lend to my Last Will and Testament. I want to be cremated.* In another sentence, he expressed his frustration of my pastime and hoped I would enjoy his game.' She wiped at a stray tear. 'And there you have it, guys, very similar to what you indicated the other night about playing by the rules. I think you know more about things than you're letting on and I don't believe that's very fair at all.'

She blew her nose and listened to the lads' stifled cursing and the clinking of mugs on a tabletop. She drained the last of her brew and did the same.

'Oh, Yas, we're sorry you have to go through all this alone. Are you safe in the cottage?'

'Yes thanks, I am safe. You've met Combo. Did I ever tell you that neither male accepted the other? Anyway, doesn't matter now. Listen, it's not easy but I'm gradually coming to accept Ru's decision. I know I tried every conceivable way to help or to ease the pain and suffering of loss, but only he could help himself.'

'You sure have a lot more intestinal fortitude than anybody we know, Yas.'

'Thanks.' She was hankering to talk about Emily, instead asked in a soft voice, 'Where are Emily's ashes?'

'Haven't you got them?'

'No. Well not as far as I know, but I haven't gone through any of the boxes that Rudy brought home. It was forbidden.'

'Have you been playing nicely, Yasmin?'

Playing nicely? She scratched her head while stifling a yawn. 'Yes, I have been.'

'Good.'

'Hey, what's the go with the helicopter?' she asked casually.

'Oh shite.'

The on-hold music came on without warning for several minutes.

Timmy's direct voice broke the age-old recording of Greensleeves. 'A subject to be revisited.'

'Okay, I can play this game. How about a small hat box?'

Muffled conversation filled her lounge room for several minutes.

'Yas, we can only think that box is the one that Emily's corsage came in for the combined thirtieth.'

'Hey?' she asked in a shocked voice, 'Did you all celebrate that together?'

'Yeah, of course!'

The on-hold music rudely interrupted what she was going to say, instead swiped at the hot angry tears that had sprung to her eyes. Mike's distressed voice made her feel a little better.

'Oh, double shite. Oh hell, oh Yas ... mother's sixtieth was in April and our birthdays are all in May. We celebrated it on the Tuesday after Easter. It made sense because we were all on holiday ... sorry babe, that sounded cruel. Timmy, Bob can you remember why Yas—'

'I remember,' she said dejectedly. 'I was told it was strictly a family affair for the girls and a camping trip with the boys.'

A domino of heavy sighs lapsed into a drawn-out silence. She suddenly remembered how she was going to start off the conversation.

'Well guys, it doesn't matter anymore. That was all in the past and I am going to uphold what Rudy has been trying to get through to me. I will share and work in with you. But you have to promise me that you'll allow me to contribute to the expenses because like a beautiful piece of fabric, I am the link that holds everything together. What belongs to you comes back to you.'

'Yep, sounds good, Yasmin.'

She scoffed silently. They hadn't been listening at all. 'Good chat guys and thanks so much for calling. I'm going to have to call it a night. I can't keep my eyes open.'

'Hey, too easy. You look after yourself. We'll chat in a couple of days, but you phone whenever you need to. Promise?'

'I promise. Thanks heaps.'

The mingled farewells and good wishes dragged on until someone yelled out, 'Race you,' before the line was disconnected.

Yasmin chortled smugly, double checked all the windows and doors again. With the cottage in comfortable darkness, she yawned and raced Combo down the passageway. Her phone chimed just as she put her head on her pillow with a message from Owen asking after if she was okay. She replied positively and felt around for Combo. He padded restlessly around her bed until eventually hopping up by her feet, sighing heavily. She was too tired to care why he did and how much room he took up.

Chapter 21

Combo's guttural growl woke Yasmin with a start. Sternly whispering for him to be silent, they crept out of bed and stood in the doorway listening intently to the muffled sounds from outside the lounge room window. It *was* shut and the curtains *were* drawn. *All the windows were shut and curtains drawn!* Quietly closing her bedroom door, then with a firm grip on Combo's collar waited in the hallway outside the spare bedroom door. It was horribly dark and eerily silent. *No electricity*. She gulped. *No alarms!* They heard the front door rattle. She immediately slid one hand down Combo's head and wrapped it around his muzzle. Fumbling for her mobile, sent an SOS to Owen. The phone clock read 03:13am before being slipped into the pocket of her floral dressing gown. They crept silently to the end of the hallway and froze when the other external door handle rattled. A man swore, then another. The crunch of two pairs of feet landing onto the decorative rocks made her hair stand on end.

She mentally followed the sounds of the rushing footsteps. The definitive crunch, grunt and thud landing on the concrete patio changed something in her demeanour. The next door would be the laundry door. The unlockable, noisy door. An absolute sod to budge, whether it was pulled from the inside or pushed from the outside. She remembered the trolley was up against it and for once hadn't been in a hurry to put away the laundered clothes. Swiftly and silently walking Combo by the collar to kitchen, in a very quiet and controlled voice she commanded him to sit and stay. He licked her left hand. In the blinding darkness, she felt around for the stove and lifted off the skillet. The pauses between the thumps against the weather-worn door were getting shorter. Creeping down the hallway gripping the heavy cast-iron fry pan in both hands, just as she snuck past the laundry the trolley crashed over. Hiding in the void between the laundry wall and guest bathroom, Yasmin stood soldier still. Listened. Waited. The interior door creaked. The slower it opened the noisier it got. She knew it, hated it, but tonight it worked to her advantage. A man swore, then opened the door quicker and swore again as he stepped into the hallway.

'Left or right?' he hissed.

Yasmin swung the skillet like a tennis racket. The intruder wore it, stumbled into the opposite wall and slid down to the floor. A calloused hand grabbed her wrist. She screamed. Combo growled and snarled.

'Stay!' she yelled.

A male voice hissed, 'Someone is going to kill him one day.'

Yasmin kicked out and was met with a grunt. She attempted a star-jump and let go of the skillet. The second man yelled out in pain and moved awkwardly out of the doorway. Taking advantage of the momentum, she used his vice like grip and pulled him further into the hallway. He lashed out. She felt a blow against her cheek then both her hands were suddenly clamped together with one of his and momentarily lifted off the ground. Yasmin screamed when his hand fumbled near her waist. Combo crashed into them. Snarling. Snapping. Then a loud yelp.

Rage exploded out of Yasmin like a violent storm. The tiles chilled her feet. She hopped, drove her right hip forward, swung her knee upwards with enough hope to split the burglar in two and collected with his groin. A sickening grunt filled the hallway. The instant his hands loosened she wrenched hers free. Clasped together like a human hammer, swung them upwards with all her might and connected with bone. A heavy lump pinned her feet to the floor. She called out Combo's name and tried to move. Fighting back the tears at the silence, she eventually got herself free. With shaking hands, Yasmin finally got the torch application to work and sobbed into the back of her hand when she saw the back of Combo's head. Hot tears streamed down her face. When she lit up the man who lay at her feet, she very nearly dropped the phone in shock. In an instant, the nine-letter word came to her.

'Miscreant!' She hurled at him and stomped on his exposed hand. 'You are dead to me, Stu Wilson.'

Squinting against the harsh reflection of the other man's sagging, polished bald head, she nimbly jumped over the bodies and raced towards Combo. Slipping on liquid and almost doing the splits while lunging for the kitchen bench, her phone smashed to the floor. Duck waddling, followed Combo's laboured breathing and sobbed and prayed while she stroked his head.

Several long moments later, Stu moaned. 'My nuts ... ohh my nose. You bitch, Yasmin. You and Combo had better watch your backs.'

'You really are a miscreant, Stu Wilson. Sums you up perfectly!'

'A what?'

'A lowlife, evil and unprincipled lousy excuse for a human. What did we ever do to you? You were here today. You bastard! How did you know it was pepper spray? Was it you?' Her voice rose hysterically.

'What did you hit me with?'

'My knee! My fist! You hurt Combo you cruel bastard.'

'I'm warning you, if we're not out of here soon, our mate's gonna come looking for us.'

'It'll be a party then, because the cops are on their way too.'

'Dammit woman. This bloke hates dogs more than his other mate, but he will hurt you.'

'Who? Why? What have we done?'

'Nothing. But you have got something that they want.' Stu hissed.

'Like what? And who are *they*?'

'Money. And I can't tell you anymore.'

'Money?' Yasmin scoffed. 'You have definitely got the wrong joint. I don't have any money! You think I'm this thin because I work hard? Flaming idiot.'

'Uh-uh, you're built for speed, not comfort.'

'As if. What did you do to Combo?'

'He'll be right. I never hurt animals.'

'But?'

'No buts ... except yours is hot.'

'Tacky.' *God help me please.*

Something rattled across the tiles.

'Just as well I brought a torch,' Stu muttered, and clicked it on. He shone the beam up his face and slowly stood holding his aches and pains as best he could with one hand. 'I'm going to trash this part of the house to make it look like you and I fought. Best you keep your mouth shut or else. Old mate coming up the road is not a nice person, believe me.'

'Yeah, you already mentioned that.'

Stu was apoplectic. He reefed open the top cutlery drawer sending its contents crashing to the floor. Skidded on the liquid en route to upending a couple of dining chairs. The answering machine smashed against the wall. He tore out the caller identifier, stopped long enough to place the antique telephone gently on the floor flipping the handset with his foot, then frisbee-d a few lounge cushions around. Spun the settee around. Threw Combo's bed against the dining room door. Then picked up the vase. Yasmin flinched when he shone the torchlight up his face.

'Is this crystal?' His blood-caked nostrils flared.

'Yes. P-please don't break it.'

'Mean something to you?'

'Yes.'

He smiled cruelly. Raised it above his head and instead of hurling it against the floor like he pretended, tipped it upside down. Her beautiful roses obscenely tumbled downwards, drowning at the same time. Ever so gently, he upended the vase onto the tile and glared at her.

'Rumour has it you're growing corpses?'

Too scared to squint at the bright light, tears sprung to her eyes.

'Hmm, dead men don't talk huh?'

Headlights turned into the driveway. Stu ducked down.

Instantly, his tone softened. 'Dammit, he's here. Pretend you're knocked out and make sure Combo doesn't move. I'll try and get this bloke away from here as quick as, but heed my warning, Yasmin. I always had the hots for you, but you have just snuffed that out. Somehow, we're involved in someone else's balls-up.' Stu talked even quieter and more hurriedly. 'Miscreant? Not I. Others? Yes. Listen hard. I'm gonna be saying some nasty stuff but I will kill him if he touches you. Hurry up. Or you will regret it.'

Without argument, laid with her back to the hallway, shoulders protecting Combo's head and her own head on the floor like she had passed out. Her breath as shallow as her opinion of the local vet who made sure her derriere was appropriately covered, patting it gently.

'That's a good girl.'

She voiced her contempt. 'You will regret that. Miscreant.'

Goosebumps erupted when Stu's cold chuckle and warm breath brushed over her ear.

'Be quiet.'

***

Killing the headlights as he swung the wheel, Travis waited for five minutes before opening the door.

'Stu? Giles?' he growled, sliding out of the vehicle.

'In here, Trav. She wasn't easy to put down, but her and that mutt won't be waking up anytime soon. Giles's out for the count.'

Cursing when he tripped over the toppled laundry basket, muttered, 'Didn't get very far did you?'

'Nope.'

'Did she talk?'

'Nope, just screeched about the dog. We gotta go. Help me move this big bastard.'

'What happened?'

'Skillet one, Giles zero.'

'And you?'

'Crushed nuts, bloody sore foot and what feels like a broken nose.'

'But you got her down?'

'Oh, yeah. Flower lady bitch and that fugly mutt won't be waking up soon. Come on, let's get outta here.'

'Give me your torch, mate. I wanna see her. I gotta do something.'

'Don't touch her. Don't wanna leave fingerprints mate,' Stu growled as Travis shoved passed him.

'Aww, pretty floral dressing gown. I'm going to get a piece of that hot arse for meself sometime—'

'We gotta go.'

'Yeah, yeah. Just got to do something.'

'Travis, hurry the hell up.'

Lighting up the floor with the torch, then his face, his lips curled into a leer when he saw her phone and smiled even more when his boot crushed it further into the tiles.

Stu's voice was dangerously low. 'Good one mate! We gotta get going.'

'Yeah, yeah. Quit ya nagging.'

Travis bent down and wrapped his free hand around Combo's neck. 'I will carve you up one day.'

Not quite touching Yasmin's body, he pretended to caress her shoulders and muttered evilly, 'We will be back. Again, and again, and again until we get what is ours.'

'Just get a bloody move on!'

'Shut the hell up, Stu!'

Then Travis saw the destroyed bunch of roses and sneered. He plucked the petals from the water-bruised blooms and scattered them over her.

'For your funeral, flower lady bitch. Better idea, your combined cremation. You and the mutt can join the boogey-man. Three for the price of one!'

His evil cackle clashed with Stu's forced guffaw.

'You're gonna have to leave your blue balls alone mate and gimme me a hand with this bloke.'

'Do we take him to the hospital?' Stu asked after they finally managed to get the unconscious body into the van.

'Nuh. The twins are back at the shed, one of them will sort him out. He's got a pulse and will probably have a bloody sore head. What did he tell ya?'

'That we had to collect some dosh. What's this about a boogey-man?' Stu asked, wide-eyed.

They both slammed their doors as Travis floored the accelerator pedal.

Yelling over the revving engine, 'None ya! Just hang on, this van can go sideways around a corner! Good that Giles dried some more skins before he came out with you, 'cos you're going to be busy leading up to Moojie Hill.' Then he laughed callously. 'No rooting for you for a while.'

'Yeah, bitch got me cods alright. Nice touch with the rose petals, Trav!'

They laughed, then fell silent for almost forty minutes. The highway traffic was typically truck and road-kill hopscotch at that time of the morning. Three cop cars, their sirens blaring, tore past them breaking the uncomfortable silence.

'Her?'

Stu crossed his fingers. 'Doubt it.'

***

Sitting cross-legged with Combo's head on her lap, his shaky breath barely reassuring. Yasmin stroked his furry face all the while replaying the threatening conversations. In the mix, a familiar question bounced around her head. *The boogey-man?*

After what seemed like an eternity, ear-piercing sirens bruised the darkest hour. She didn't move, not even when several vehicles raced up the driveway.

'Yasmin?' a deep voice called out urgently.

Elephant tears slipped down her cheeks, 'I'm okay. Combo's hurt. There's glass and liquid on the floor. No dogs allowed.'

She raised her head enough to see the tell-tale signs of torchlight approaching the laundry door. Several men and dogs were talking at the same time outside.

'What in the hell?' Owen stated and poked his lit-up face around the door frame. 'Carl, get in there now. Someone locate the bloody mains switch. NOW!'

'Yes Boss,' several replies called out.

With his headlamp switched to orange, Carl carefully picked his way over to Yasmin and suddenly stopped. He snapped on his gloves, bent down and held up a long needle attached to a syringe.

'Xylazine? That's a tranquilising drug.' His voice was filled with vengeance. 'Ma'am? What's a vet needle doing in your lounge room?'

'How about we get the local vet to do one more call out?' Yasmin asked icily.

Owen growled. 'Are you mad?'

'With rage and revulsion.'

He and Carl averted their eyes the minute someone flicked the mains, and respected her enough to turn their backs.

Owen's voice was barely audible. 'Yasmin, did he?'

'Nope. But they both came off second best.'

'Both? Ma'am?'

'Yes. Now, I am decent underneath my dressing gown but I cannot get up while carrying Combo, so would you mind?'

'Nobody comes inside until I give the word,' Owen commanded.

Doing their best not to make eye contact, Carl manoeuvred his hands under the sedated pooch and placed him gently on the unusually positioned couch.

'Did they leave with anything?' Owen asked and held out his hand.

Gripping it firmly, she nodded her thanks and spoke in a tone that sounded foreign to herself. 'Yeah. One will have a headache, the other will be walking awkwardly for a while and breathing through his mouth. Excuse me please gentlemen, I need to get dressed. Feel free to put the kettle on. There will only be one set of fingerprints on the cutlery drawer and whatever else is out of place in here.'

'And the skillet?' he called out behind her.

Yasmin spun around. Eyes unflinching in her cold reply. 'Probably contains the bald-headed bastard's DNA and my fingerprints.'

Owen's curt nod and suppressed smirk disappeared as quickly as the younger woman darted down the hallway.

The minute Yasmin closed her bedroom door the tears erupted in rivers. *Who else did you lie to, Rudy?* Dragging herself into the shower, she drowned the violation under a jet of icy cold water. Imagining herself to be a butterfly emerging out of a hideously suffocating cocoon, let all the suppressed emotional suffering right up to her latest traumatic experience swirl down the drain. By the time she dressed with strengthened resolve, she was more determined than ever to tie up loose ends.

Inhaling the brewed coffee aromatics, Yasmin confidently strode down the hallway ignoring the trashed laundry. But then she saw Combo being supported by Zeus and Carl so he could have a drink of water, and everything disintegrated. She burst into tears and sobbed even harder when Sergeant Kohli let her cry into his shirt.

'He'll be okay, Ms Pestel. It wasn't a large dose and it's like coming out of an anaesthetic, so a lot of rest is in order. No running and jumping off the patio for a while, for either of you. My colleagues enthusiastically described your midday fun!' He chuckled softly and lifted her chin. 'Hey, that's a hell of a shiner … how are you feeling?'

In between sniffles, she thanked him and told him she was fine, just horribly violated and extremely angry. Carl scooped up Combo and brought him over to her and the tears fell again. He whimpered and yawned. Sergeant Kohli excused himself and turned away.

Carl took the lead. 'Ma'am, I hope you don't mind, but I've pulled the settee cushions onto the floor for him. He mustn't jump around too much until he's totally conscious, which might only be later today. Tonight preferably, just to be on the safe side.'

She gave him a small smile and nodded her head. Frowning at the drawn lounge curtain she walked towards it.

'The window's smashed and so is your phone. The SIM is intact so looks like some retail therapy for you.' Carl gestured to the plastic bag on the dining table. 'When Combo's settled, how about I make you a coffee? I'll bring it over because the Bosses need to talk to you too. Sorry, but I can't tidy up until forensics arrive and I need not remind you, but I'm going to, he's from the city so who knows what time he'll get here.'

Yasmin nodded and stared blankly at what was her mobile phone. Then recalled the threats. Instinctively, she matched the cruel voice of Travis with the man in the van. *Was Stu scared? Why did he protect her instead of hurting her? Was he being honest? Who the hell was Giles?*

Shrieking loudly when Owen tapped the dining table, it took a while for her to regain her breath and for some colour to return to her face.

'Oh, my girl, you have had an awful fright,' he said gently. 'One of us will stay until your cottage is secure. Okay?'

Nodding rapidly, she bit back more tears.

'There's never a good time for an interview, but I would rather do this before forensics get here. Can you do that for me?'

She opened her mouth to speak and nothing came out. After several more attempts, she managed to squeak out a reply. 'Ye ... ahem, yes.'

'Good. Thanks Carl, when you're ready for the coffees.'

'Sure thing, Boss. The boys are happy to chill. Oh, good. Here's Sergeant Kohli now.'

'Sorry about your shirt,' her bottom lip quivered, 'but thanks for being here and for being my friends.' Chiding herself for sounding so feeble, she sat upright and pulled her shoulders back.

'That's more like it, Ma'am,' Carl said and deposited the tray of coffees in front of them. 'I'm going to be taking notes, but you just talk freely. This isn't an exam, but we are going to be doing this on a formal nature.'

'Okay. I'm ready,' subconsciously rubbing her sore hands.

After introducing himself to the interview, Sergeant Kohli spoke firmly. 'Ms Pestel, tell us about your security cameras.'

'Footage is saved onto a microSD card. When it's full, it records over itself.'

'Backed up to the cloud?'

'No.'

'That's a shame,' he muttered and wrote something down. When he looked up, his mouth was set in a tight line. 'Your business supplies edible flowers to the hospitality industry, is that correct?'

'Predominantly, yes.' She paused. 'Well, it did.'

'How many outstanding orders or future commitments do you have?'

'None. After recent events, I have had to cancel supply.'

His harsh look softened momentarily before he concentrated on his notepad.

'Do you recognise the burglars?'

'Only one of them. Stu Wilson, the local vet is the one who gave me the shiner. I think it was more reflex than intentional.'

When Sergeant Kohli grunted, Sergeant Pyers introduced himself.

'Do you recognise this, Ms Pestel?'

She automatically blushed. 'Yes. It's my skillet.'

'Can you explain why it was on the floor in the hallway please?'

'When I heard the laundry trolley topple over, I knew someone had entered my home. I feared for my safety and intended on using it as self-defence, so I took it off the stove and waited in the void. The inter-leading door creaks when it's being opened. I swung upwards and must have got lucky. Then I felt a hand clasp my wrist and I dropped it in fright.'

'Lucky it didn't land on your foot.'

'Indeed!'

'We'll have to take this as evidence.'

'That's okay, I have another one.'

They all suppressed their grins.

'Is that how you subdued the known burglar as Stu Morgan C. Wilson?' Sergeant Kohli asked with an eyebrow raised.

Yasmin shrugged. 'I guessed it landed on his foot because he swore and appeared to be unbalanced. He had my hands gripped in one of his, lifted me off my feet momentarily until Combo got a hold of him. I took advantage of the momentum. I don't know, it-it all happened so fast, but I know I got him a good one.' She failed to suppress a smile.

He sat back in his chair. 'Something you need to add, Ms Pestel?'

'Like I said, it all happened so fast. I hopped and aimed for his groin with my knee.'

'You hopped?' Both Sergeants asked simultaneously.

This time Yasmin let the smile bloom. 'Yes. It was a self-defence thing my best friend and I perfected many years ago. See, we both loved to dance and do gymnastics and practiced hopping on our weakest leg, then twisted and swung our other knee upwards with everything we had.'

'You practiced?' Sergeant Kohli leant forward as he asked the question.

'Constantly, and blindfolded, until we achieved the perfection that we both aimed for.' She giggled. 'How's that for a play on words!'

The men squirmed and looked around awkwardly.

'What happened in here?' Sergeant Kohli's waved his arm around.

'Therein lies a tale of a different kind.'

Formulating her thoughts while sipping on the very sweet, awfully strong black coffee, reiterated her comment about Stu not intentionally hurting her.

Crossing her legs and fingers, a silent plea of forgiveness momentarily consumed her thoughts. 'Oh, he could have, quite easily. I believe he's caught up in something he can't get out of and almost protected me against this man he called 'T'. Just like the letter.'

Yasmin explained the man's threats, then scoffed at their fanciful notions of her having money. *Don't blush. Don't even think about the stashed cash.* Coughing quietly, she described Stu's dramatic destruction of her roses and the gentle placement of the upturned crystal vase, along with the same tenderness to the antique telephone.

'Why would he have done that?'

'I suppose because he realised it had sentimental value,' she shrugged and frowned. 'It's weird ... I mean, he creeps me out and is a chemist and all, yet he was insistent this 'T' bloke wasn't to touch me.'

Sergeant Pyers announced himself to the interview before looking at her intently. 'Ms Pestel, do you think the destruction of your seedlings and this break-in are connected?'

'That's a good question. If Stu was doing a recce, he mustn't have given his partner-in-crime the layout of my cottage because when the bald one pulled open the squeaky laundry door, he asked for directions. That's when I clouted him, so, it's probably a question for Stu.'

'Noted. Are you on overly friendly terms with him?'

'Hardly.'

'Noted. You said he was a chemist? Can you clarify your statement please?'

'Yes! I only remembered it while I was waiting for you to arrive. His certificates were displayed in a back room. Today, that struck me as odd.'

'How did you get to see them then?'

Yasmin rubbed her eyes. 'When I first took Combo to him, he insisted on showing me around his revamped clinic. Guilty for being so observant!'

Sergeant Kohli continued with the questioning. 'Do you recognise the other man?'

'No, I do not.'

'Can you think of anything else that might help us in our investigation?'

'Yes, when the power came back on, the sensor lights and floodlights didn't. That's not normal.'

'Carl, make a side note to mention that to forensics please. Anything else, Ms Pestel?'

'Yes, there is. How do I go about taking out an A.V.O.?'

'You'll need to come by the Station.'

'Oh, okay. Thank you. I can't think of anything else right now.

'Thank you, Ms Pestel,' Sergeant Kohli spoke firmly.

She stifled a genuine yawn.

Chapter 22

The sun forced its way through the thick bank of clouds, casting dark shadows on the makeshift bed in the back of the van. The two men and women had almost given up hope and impatiently hassled Stu when he arrived with a bag of smelling salts.

'About time! His pulse is really faint. Reckon he needs a hospital but not the local one.' Trina ground her teeth anxiously.

'Here Ivan, wave this under his nose.' Stu stepped inside and handed him the bottle nervously.

'What's gotten in you?' Laqueel interrupted her own teeth grinding and stared at Stu.

'My clinic has been broken into. Youse wouldn't know about that would you?'

'Anything taken?' Travis asked, scratching his back against the edge of the van's rear swing-door.

'Yeah, the pill-press and some other stuff from my workbench. Just as well you didn't touch—'

'Whoa, wh-what happened?' Giles moaned, coughed and spluttered.

'You headbutted a skillet and I almost became a cripple with a broken nose,' Stu stated flatly.

'Stu? Where's Ivan?'

'Right here.'

'Hey Bro ... did we g-get the dosh?'

'She's as poor as a piccaninny, dude. You got the wrong intel and a headache to boot.'

'Me? But-but you said ... wait ... I-I can't see ...' Giles passed out.

'Stu, get him to a hospital. See you at Moojie Hill in three days.' Travis commanded.

'What about my clinic?'

'What about it?' Trina and Laqueel screeched their reply.

Travis wrapped his broad hand around Stu's arm and dragged him from the van.

'Time's up. Give me your phone. *Now.* If Giles carks it, it's on you.'

They wrestled each other angrily with Stu copping a box around the ears from each of the twins, losing one hearing aid in the process.

'Give him your phone. He wants your phone,' the twins chanted while gnashing their teeth.

Reluctantly, he handed it over just as a call came in from Sergeant Pyers.

'Hah! As if you're going to answer that.' Travis threw the phone and followed as it skidded on the gravel, jumped on it several times pummelling it into the ground.

Stu stared at the cheap, completely destroyed device. 'You owe me a new one, idiot.'

'No, no I don't. That's not your normal one. You left that in the top right-hand drawer of your desk. I'm onto you, lover boy. Now, you got somewhere to be. And then you got somewhere else to be. Don't let us down, Stu. The boogey-man—'

'Shh, don't speak of him,' the women shrieked and scurried away.

The two men faced off angrily. Neither retreated when Travis' phone rang.

Stabbing at the speaker icon, he spat out his question. 'What, Callum?'

'Leigh's a blithering mess! I thought you said the bastard was dead.'

'If that's what I said, that's what I said.'

'Yeah? How come we saw a man with a handle-bar moustache and a long grey jacket who spoke in the same nasally tone?'

'What? Like yours? Right now?'

'No!'

'Where did you see this bloke?'

'In Adelaide.'

'Hey? What the hell are you pair doing there?'

'None ya business. You sure the boogey-man is dead?'

'Say his name and find out, Callum.'

'You first, Travis.'

'Not likely. See you in Moojie Hill and bring Sal and her tribe with you. We won't have any room.'

'Yep.'

Stu challenged Travis the moment he pocketed his phone. 'Oi ... who, why and what the hell is going on?'

'None ya business.'

'This got something to do with that dumb-arse plan of Giles' or was it really yours?'

'Get out of my face Stu and mind ya business. I'm warning ya.'

'What's Yasmin Pestel got to do with all this anyway?

Travis' nostrils flared. 'Told you to get out of my face, lover boy. I wasn't going to touch the flower lady bitch while she was knocked out. What's the fun in that? But I will gut that mutt the next chance I get.'

'What about a new phone, huh?'

'Take it up with Ivan.'

They dodged each other's punch and hurled insults while they walked away from each other.

'Hey Stu, this is on you,' Ivan threatened him with his fist then slammed the van's rear doors shut.

'Don't suppose you're gonna tell me what's going on either?' Stu challenged.

'Correct. But all this is on you. Get going.'

Stu screwed up his eyes and clenched his fists, allowing himself to be pushed towards the open driver's door. His nose hurt when he tried to pull an angry face. *I'm so over this lot.* He glared at the bullying stepbrother of his mate groaning loudly in the back of the van and growled his demand. 'I'm gonna need some money and another phone, you lousy bastard.'

Gritting his teeth, Ivan tossed him a burner phone then counted out $500. 'Here, this'll have to do. Now clear off. You'll owe me more if my bro dies.'

'You bunch of yellow-bellied cowards,' Stu hurled over his shoulder and slammed the gearstick into first without using the clutch.

The moment the van was out sight Travis glared at Ivan. 'Have you been playing silly buggers in Adelaide?'

Ivan directed a mouthful of phlegm at his cohort's feet. 'Was about to ask you the same thing.'

'How can I be in two places at once, idiot?'

He cocked his head. 'Oh yeah. Stupid question huh.'

'Yep. To put it mildly.'

'Trav? You saw him die?'

'We didn't hang around after the bitch and noisy mutt returned.'

'Ah! So, he could still be alive then?'

'Dunno. But if you're game, say his name and find out.'

'You first.'

'Nope. Here come the twins.'

They watched the women saunter towards them.

Ivan muttered, 'Yeah. See you at Moojie if not before. I'm outta here.'

The twins' chant clashed with the sudden onset of tinnitus. 'Bye Ivan, be a good boy Ivan.'

***

Swearing under his breath, Stu threw several changes of clothes into a backpack along with his toiletry bag. His simple bedroom at the back of the clinic was the best deal for the bachelor. Nothing personal, just a bed. He never ate or entertained at the clinic. He used his nurses place for all that. Any of them. Whenever it suited. Whether they were there or not.

The second last cage in the back room had stood empty the longest, nor had it been cleaned. Aged skeletons and the excrement of long-forgotten food for his pet snake evident. The fact that he hadn't had any animals in the clinic for a long time, except for the venom donor, wasn't public knowledge. The drug orders had kept him gainfully employed. The on-repeat recording of barking dogs, squawking cockatoo and occasional cry of a tom cat hadn't raised any eyebrows with the try-hard sole-trader neighbourhood.

Wearing disposable gloves, he moved the deliberately dried scat-covered newspaper and slid out the tray. *They didn't know about this!* He fanned the stolen $80K, flinched when he tried to screw up his nose at the mustiness then shoved the wad to the base of his backpack. Cussing when he noticed the drawer open, dropped his 'emergency only' phone alongside the cash.

Flicking the switch on his pet snake's cage, Stu thumped the glass repeatedly in horror. His agonised cry echoed through the empty room. His Shield-snouted Brown snake had been skinned. He had incubated the snake egg himself and had watched it emerge from its shell with incredible determination despite its size. In the beauty of the moment, named it Yasmin. The first time in his life he had taken on a pet. Angrily swiping at the sudden onslaught of tears Stu made a vow to the dead serpent.

'The bastards are going to pay for this. Big time.'

Vengeance inspired him to make a phone call to Leigh. Their love-hate relationship a peculiar recipe for keeping each other's secrets. Propping the clinic's portable phone under his right ear with his shoulder then switching to the left, he solemnly wrapped what was left of the lifeless pet in its own floral sheet.

'How's it going?' he asked when she finally answered.

'Stu! This is a nice surprise,' cooing softly, 'I look forward to seeing you at Moojie Hill.'

'Yeah right. Hey, got a question for you.'

'Anything! You know that.'

'What's the panic about the boogey-man if he's dead?'

Leigh's breath shuddered through the phone. 'Damn! Was hoping you'd never have to learn of him. Times are a changing in this thing we've got going. Sally's thrown a wobbly, the men are all testy, suppose it's time you ought to know but you're gonna have to wait, my smoke's gone out.'

'Care to hurry up? I've got things to do.'

'Yeah, yeah. You are our main man with supplies. Okay, here goes. The boogey-man is a scary, scary mo-fo. Never say his name, else he'll find out and will kill you. Ivan and Giles saw it happen and ever since, nobody dares mention it.'

'It's not Travis? Do you really trust Ivan?'

Her cackle made his skin crawl.

'Nah, Travis drove the hearse, and Ivan, whilst the strongman, only smells that way. Anyway, meester busy man, someone Callum and I knew recently died and left us some spondoolas ... which we blew.'

'How unusual!'

They shared a quiet chuckle.

'Exactly! Hang on, I'm just going to light up again.' After several attempts, she finally spoke. 'Anyway, the boogey-man always wore a handle-bar moustache and a long, grey jacket. Callum knew about all this before me.'

'So, it's Callum then?'

'Hell no! I can vouch for that. Anyway ... um ... well, he was in the same hotel as us. Stu ... Stu, I nearly died of fright.'

'What? Who? This boogey-man?'

'Yeah! Sort of put a dampener on our night if you get my drift.'

'Hmm, that scary huh?'

'You have no idea.'

'Who else knows about him?'

'Everyone but you. Sorry bub, was hoping you'd never learn of him. Always tried to protect you from it.'

'Or is it you?'

Cringing at Leigh's shrieking laugh, he adjusted the volume on his hearing aid the moment she spoke. 'All you need to know is I reckon you're a nice guy who grows the best weed in town!'

'That's all you like me for, Leigh!'

'Aww, come now, we had some good times in the early days.'

Stu recoiled at the horrid memories. 'You swore you would leave my snake alone.'

'I did.'

'Someone didn't.'

Stu sniffled at Leigh's crude description of the suspects. Eventually he said, 'This boogey-man? He's not really dead?'

'I'm not gonna take any chances, man. Promise me one thing but.'

'What?'

'Never ever say his name if you ever learn of it.'

'I promise. Bye Leigh.'

'What exactly is your hurry, Stu?'

'Giles needs medical attention.'

'Don't let me hold you up, he makes the best pills!'

'You're a cold-hearted bitch.'

'Yeah, whatever. Just don't talk about—'

'See ya, Leigh.'

Gently laying the remains of his pet in the shallow pit, Stu fired up the small incinerator, opened up the gas jets on the burners, set the timer for two hours, upended the container of Isopropylamine and closed the door of his veterinary clinic forever. Silently thanking Leigh, Stu watered the revenge seed.

Without removing the gloves, he changed the number plates of the now-white van to the stolen ones from a white BMW, hung a saline drip from the hook in the van's roof-lining and inserted a cannula into a vein in Giles's forearm. Eventually. *Dehydrated fool.*

Taking the back roads through the vineyards, he hummed along to Radiohead and made a beeline for Adelaide. With his partner-in-crime moaning and groaning in the back Stu circled the hospital twice.

'Hang in there, Giles, got too many uniforms at the moment. Stay with us buddy,' he spoke over his shoulder.

'Where ... taking me?'

'To a friend.'

'Moojie. Get m-me to Moo-Moojie ...'

'Yeah, you be right, keep talking.'

'Tired.'

Stu drove until he found an empty church carpark, climbed over the headboard barricade and bent down beside Giles.

'Here, wet your mouth and lips. Did you take any of the stuff we made?'

'Huh.'

'The pills?'

'Weed.'

'Good.'

Giles groaned when Stu helped him sit up and slurped noisily on the water bottle before his eyes closed.

Slapping his lolled head, 'Hey, mate, can you tell me who traffics the pills?'

'B-b ... tired ... head hurts,' he muttered, feebly swiping at a globule of saliva.

'Okay mate. Getting you some help. I'll be back.'

'Like Arnie?'

Stu chuckled softly and wrestled with the backpack straps. 'Yeah, mate. Just like your hero.'

He then slipped on a pair of black-framed reading glasses and tied a bandana around his head. Ignoring the three missed calls from Leigh on the burner phone, Stu made one phone call.

'Ambulance. I am reporting a man in the back of a white van by the church on Main. I heard a gunshot.'

Flicking out the SIM card, he snapped it in half and threw the useless phone underneath the passenger seat. Dragging the pieces of SIM along the length of the outside wall of the church, Stu scampered through the rear carpark and jogged along the easement between two rows of houses, dropping a glove and bits of the card several blocks apart. *My rules now.*

Chapter 23

'It's still not ringing, Boss!' Carl threw up his hands in exasperation.

'Great ... and here comes the city slicker.'

Yasmin groaned. 'Do Combo and I need to be around?'

Sergeant Kohli looked at her with a wry grin. 'No, you could both do with fresh air.'

She smiled her gratitude. 'But nobody needs to go past the laundry.'

'Nobody will because Zeus will be standing guard.'

Carl was at her side in an instant and scooped up Combo. 'Which door?'

'The dining room! It leads onto the verandah away from the front of the house. Mind the last step, it's not a normal width. Go on the grass, the decorative rock makes a horrid noise when walked on. Quickly, let's go behind the patio, against its wall. We'll be in the shade.'

Like two naughty kids with a stolen cookie, they scarpered through the door.

Making sure his newfound friends were safe and comfortable, Carl murmured, 'I'll be back with something to drink.'

'Thanks. Hey ... who can't you reach on the phone?'

'The vet.'

'Oh.'

Yasmin didn't even notice Carl leave. The magnificent vista of the grazing paddock and its rolling hills in the background captivated her attention albeit mindful of Combo chasing rabbits in his dream. Absent-mindedly stroking his head, she gave a fleeting thought for Stu.

Owen spoke as he walked towards them. 'Yasmin, we're getting ready to leave soon. Carl will be here until later this afternoon. We have organised our maintenance contractors and anticipate having your cottage secure by sundown. Also, you will need to set your own code to the combination lock we have put on your switch box.'

She absorbed the information with a neutral expression subconsciously rubbing her fat cheek.

'It's not that bad, Ma'am,' Carl said reassuringly and handed her a bottle of iced tea.

Nodding slowly and with a small smile, Yasmin said, 'Guys, I appreciate you, and everything, and more. Thank you so much for getting here when you did. Sergeant Pyers, if you have time, perhaps you would like to accompany me as far as the rose garden and pick some for your wife?'

His chuckle developed into a deep belly laugh. 'You know something? I would like that very much.'

Carl jumped at the opportunity to dog-sit and be security. She quietly pretend-kissed Combo's sleeping head and left the two men to discuss police business while she retrieved the four-wheeler and its carry-all. Adding two stainless-steel buckets to the trolley, as well as gloves and secateurs before wrapping a raincoat around her waist, her trusty four-wheeler started on first go. She pulled alongside Owen and hopped off.

'Here you go. I'll meet you at the ninth row from the cottage. Carl, you and Combo can make sure nobody enters my cottage from the front. I have to put the water on the remaining flowers.'

They looked at her, reluctant to move.

'Suit yourselves.'

Without waiting for a response, she spun on her heels and walked briskly towards the greenhouse shrugging into the raincoat as she went. Deftly unlatching the door, she didn't hesitate and closed it behind her before pushing through the rear door to the maze of pipework. The pipes with the green paint were strictly for the seedlings. She had let Rudy know that right from the outset. The remaining maze either led to the house and garden beds, or the hobby farm and the underground spare tanks as emergency fire suppression but mainly used when they were drought stricken. Turning the lever to point in the direction of the hobby farm she unwound the valve handle and watched the pressure needle reach optimum level. Nothing else appeared out of the ordinary. Rolling back her shoulders she also rolled her eyes to the heavens. Hearing the four-wheeler chugging along slowly, while removing the raincoat Yasmin jogged over to where Owen was pulling up.

'You just don't stop do you?' Owen stated in admiration.

'Oh, I stop to smell the roses every day!' she replied, forcing herself to sound light-hearted. 'But thanks for the compliment.'

'Why the Queen Elizabeth Rose?'

Yasmin's passion for the particular flowers poured out of her like a waterfall. 'Their perfume so exquisite. The pink so feminine. Their cluster of blooms so elegant and regal. Totally fit for a queen! Plus, the species being hardy and fairly disease resistant makes life a lot easier, but it's the smiles they bring to people's faces which makes the effort worthwhile. These beautiful plants known as the very first Grandiflora were bred to mark the Queen's Coronation in 1953, but most of all I have always loved the thornless, long stemmed, four-inch beauties.'

They automatically drew in several deep breaths of the moderate perfume filling the air. The rose splendour could make the saddest person happy. Being planted on elevated beds, the growth height was almost five feet with abundant pink blooms. You felt like you were walking through an avenue of roses. The butterflies flitted above, and Yasmin let Owen in on her secret of how she'd lie on the dirt in between the beds and simply gaze upwards. The prettiest shade of pink against any coloured sky was breathtaking.

'Wow! I should have listened to my wife earlier in the piece,' Owen chuckled. 'Now I am going to have to tell her she was right all along!' He was still laughing as he checked for bees before burying his nose into a bloom inhaling deeply, going from one to another in amazement. 'There are a few people who would love to partake in this amazing experience, would you mind?' he asked through a face of petals.

'That would be my absolute pleasure. I was thinking these and my other flowers should go to the funeral parlour, but now I would much prefer them to only go to the hospital, old people's homes and people I like. Do you think we can make that happen?'

'If I take my wife some, I reckon we could move mountains!'

They shared a long laugh and it felt so good.

Still smiling, Yasmin said, 'You take as many as you like. Cut them quite long down their stem and carefully put them in the bucket. We'll swap them into the other bucket for transport, then secure them appropriately in your vehicle so they'll arrive in the condition they look now. I'm going to sort out the birdbaths.'

'I'm meeting her for a late lunch at the hospital cafeteria. This is going to get the old girls' talking!'

'They'll be saying a lot more if you didn't take some for them too,' she winked.

About half an hour later, both buckets were full of the exquisite blooms and Owen's eyes were as bright as his smile. 'That was quite therapeutic, thank you! Hop on, let's go and get these beauties ready for travel. We've both got things to get on with.'

With the roses secured in the patrol car, they returned Owen's wave as he drove out the driveway. Carl's radio crackled to life announcing a suspected arson. He snapped it off instantly. Sensing Yasmin was preoccupied, insisted he return to his duty of Combo-watch.

'Ma'am?'

'Sure, thanks Carl.'

She was not about to deny him that. Mongrels had violated her home and Rudy had intentionally ruined her business, and she was not going to be pleasant company to be around. Grabbing the shovel and rake, Yasmin angrily snapped on a pair of gardening gloves and systematically tidied up the long overdue mess around the pipework. Then she started on the seedling shed. Wheeling the empty burning-pile bin closer, emptied all 400 ruined seedlings into it. The plastic containers went into the recycling bin. Furiously swiping at the perspiration beading on her brow, she winced when she brushed her cheek. When she gingerly washed her face cursed Rudy for the first time in her life. And Stu. And Giles, with his ridiculously polished bald head. And Travis. He was going get his somehow.

Incensed, she proceeded to wipe down the dirt covered benches then methodically disassembled and stacked them one on top of the other. After savagely shovelling and raking the dirt floor, Yasmin dragged the long step ladder into the enclosure and stabilised its footings before climbing three quarters of the way up. Determined to remove all the overhead pipework, she started with the shower heads in the corners and worked backwards until the very last sprinkler nozzle ended up in the recycling bin along with the inline pump. Knowing the configuration intimately, the deliberately loud clanging on the ground was extremely satisfying. Dragging the step ladder back into the packing shed and laying it under the bench, she pointed to the loft. *You are next.*

Returning to the rose garden, a gentle breath of wind caressed her right cheek as she laid on the dirt, and stared into the clear blue sky. Large tears trickled down the sides of her face, plopping softly into the soil. Closing her eyes, she concentrated on her breathing and listened to nature's melody until the sound of distant yapping dragged her out of her semi-consciousness. Realising that Combo would be looking for her, she sat up at the same time he and Zeus turned into the row.

'Stay. Sit.'

Zeus didn't, but Combo did. She raced to him; his happy face bringing tears to her eyes.

'You found me!' she exclaimed with the same enthusiasm his tail was thumping the ground which she could feel in her head.

'Are you okay, Ms Pestel?' Sergeant Kohli called out.

'Foolishly thirsty, but yes thanks, on my way to you now,' she sang out confidently but watched Combo's every step.

Hearing a chuckle, she looked up to see Sergeant Kohli halfway down the next row burying his nose into the blooms, one after the other. Her smile must have been dazzling because he pushed his broad face in between a bunch and grinned back at her.

'Now, that's the smile we've been waiting to see!' he said kindly, walked towards her and handed her a bottle of water.

The 500 ml was gone in a flash. Wiping her mouth with the back of her wrist, then over her forehead, said, 'Thank you! I definitely needed that.'

'Thought as much. My staff will be on another assignment effective immediately and I have limited resources for a couple of days. We've brought you some groceries and more paper towels on the presumption you won't have any intentions of leaving your property unattended in the near future. I have brought my wife, Owen's wife and Carl's mother—'

Yasmin shook her head. 'Pardon me, Sir, I only heard something about limited resources and paper towels?'

He smirked and repeated what he had said about the visitors.

'When?'

'They're here now.'

She gasped. 'Oh, that's lovely, but I must look a fright!'

His look of compassion brought tears to her eyes and she pressed her lips together to stifle the sob.

'Ms Pestel,' he drew her into his huge arms and hugged her like a father would embrace a child; rocking her while her heartache poured out her eyes.

Eventually she nodded and murmured her thanks. He held her at arm's length and teased her lightly. 'Now you look like a fright!'

She smiled a little and wiped her face on the bottom of her shirt. Combo and Zeus set the pace by walking slowly in front of them. They strolled to the bottom of that row, then up the next, giving Yasmin time to compose herself and share her knowledge of the roses. Stopping at the watering station, she washed her hands and face, wet her hair and was surprised to see the two dogs drink from the same bowl by her feet at the same time.

'Yep, looks like you've just come back from a run. Clever girl,' the big man winked. 'Combo's recovering well. He's young and fit, but will be very hungry by tonight.'

'He won't be the only one! You're awfully kind to bring the ladies and some groceries, thank you. Please tell me how much I owe you.'

'We'll work out an arrangement. These boys seem to have clicked, but you do need to socialise yours a bit more.'

'Now you're insisting! Perhaps yours can discover some new scents out here or utilise the lawn out the front sometime, only on the condition there's temporary fencing setup. I don't think mine's traffic smart.'

'He isn't. But he is incredibly fast, agile and trainable.'

Yasmin looked at him quizzically and partook in small talk on the way to the patio. Zeus and Combo trotted alongside happily, when they weren't playing tug-o-war with each other's collars.

'Ah, I see the ladies are enjoying their stroll around the lawn under Carl's protection. See you in about twenty-five minutes?' Sergeant Kohli suggested.

Yasmin hesitated and looked at him with wide eyes. 'Am I safe inside?'

He smiled reassuringly. 'The window has been repaired, and all the external locks have been changed out. The noises you hear from the laundry are under observation so you needn't worry about that. Nobody has been inside without supervision and certainly not past the laundry. Run along. Now you've only got twenty-three minutes!'

'Thank you so much, I don't know how to repay you,' she whispered.

'Twenty-two minutes.'

She chuckled and ran inside.

Exactly twenty minutes later, wearing a pretty blue sundress with her hair simply styled and swept into a ponytail, Yasmin cautiously opened her bedroom door. Only Combo was waiting for her patiently. He sniffed her dress, legs and feet then gently stood on his hind legs and hugged her. She realised he had never seen her in a dress. It then dawned on her that she hadn't worn a dress since Mr and Mrs Craige's funeral. At that precise moment with Combo beside her, she decided it was the first page of a new chapter in her life.

The confidence wobbled. 'Pity it feels like everyone else is turning my pages!'

Combo nuzzled her knee with his wet nose. Much to her relief, the inter-leading door of the laundry was still shut. At the sight of the sparkling clean new window in the living room, Yasmin smiled. The whole area looked tidier, brighter and smelled fresher. Then she realised all the other windows had been cleaned. Someone very thoughtfully had put a new linen doily underneath the vase of freshly cut roses that were now sitting on the table. Resting beside another filled vase on the kitchen bench was a note with a smiley face drawn beside the writing: *Come join us on the patio!*

Combo impatiently resumed brushing his wet nose against her legs. Not wanting to give in to the nagging questions, accepted the emotional rollercoaster would be her ride for a while. *I have suddenly got my own friends.* Forcing herself to take a steadying breath, kept a smile on her face and breezed onto the patio. Carl swiftly came over and gently clasped her wrist at the same time settling Combo.

'Ma'am, I'd like to introduce you to my dearest friends which means they are yours too,' he said with flair. 'You already know my Bosses. This lovely young lady is Sergeant Kohli's wife, Pam, and this lovely young lady is Helen, wife to Sergeant Pyers who will join us soon.' Carl paused, wrapped his arm around the oldest lady and said, 'and this wonderful woman raised me, so I call her Mum.'

'Oh, please call me Nanna. Everyone else does!' the dear lady grinned.

The hugs were very welcome.

Helen held her the longest. 'Owen was quite coy about this latest incident, my dear. But as soon as I saw the roses, I knew it was you! Although we have never met, I feel as if I've known you for the last ten years! I am sorry for your loss. Remember, there's no right or wrong way to grieve,' she whispered and hugged Yasmin again. Then in a brighter voice, 'You do grow the most exquisite roses I have ever seen in my life, thank you for being so kind.'

The women fussed over Yasmin like mother hens. She blinked away the tears and smirked at Sergeant Kohli who winked and grinned knowingly. Combo sat at her feet obediently, his tail swooshing happily. She smiled down at him then turned to her guests.

With a light chuckle, said, 'Thank you all so much for your company and your thoughtfulness. Please come back anytime!'

Her wit dissolved any awkwardness, with conversation and laughter flowing easily. Carl offered around the platter of homemade shortbread biscuits and poured glasses of iced tea. Owen arrived just in time to polish off the delicious morsels, barely concealing his beaming smile.

'Afternoon all!' he chirped happily.

His natural air of authority and calm nature captivated everyone while he shared several light-hearted tales of the treasured friendships,

'Yasmin, we welcome you into the fold,' he said gently, 'Before it gets too late, would you mind if Carl escorts these lovely ladies to your Queen Elizabeth's?'

She knew her grin was answer enough, but nodded her head enthusiastically and said, 'Of course I wouldn't mind! That's such a lovely suggestion. Carl, the buckets and sterilised secateurs are in the carry-all behind the four-wheeler. Please help yourselves.'

Watching the group meander away, Yasmin collected up the crockery from afternoon tea. Combo and Zeus stayed with their respective owners until Sergeant Kohli gracefully waved his arm. Combo read the play and trotted alongside Zeus. Yasmin watched in astonishment.

'Gentlemen, again, thank you for everything. Please ensure I have the invoices for the tradesmen and I'm confident you didn't suggest a floral stroll for nothing.' Smirking, she looked Owen straight in the eye.

He nodded. 'You're right. We haven't had any luck with locating the van and the number plate isn't real. Have you thought about anything else that may be of use to our original investigation?'

'Yes. Having long hair tied so tightly is a script for a headache, but the woman … yeah, her features were taut, but she didn't seem in any discomfort. Drugs maybe? And why would someone have a toddler in a windowless van?'

'Good point.'

'I reckon the woman is the one you need to look for. Either she's the weakest link or the controller.'

'Why do you say that?' Sergeant Kohli asked bluntly.

Shrugging casually, 'Just a gut feeling.'

'And the man?'

'He was here this morning. He came to pick up Stu and his mate. His cold, callous voice fitted my memory of the creature in the van.'

'How can you be so sure?'

Yasmin fidgeted and scratched her head.

'What aren't you telling us?' Sergeant Kohli persisted.

She wrung her hands. 'He said something about our funeral or cremation, but Stu interrupted him.'

'By saying what?'

'That they had to leave.'

'Which would explain the scattered petals?'

'Possibly. I thought we were going to have a chat with Stu, what happened there?' Yasmin asked innocently.

The little muscle in Owen's taut neck twitched. 'M.I.A.'

She grimaced and averted her eyes.

Sergeant Kohli coughed. 'Will you pay a visit to the funeral parlour and see what events occur while you're discussing Rudy's arrangements?'

His question caught Yasmin completely off guard. She stared at him. Her breath slowly normalising.

Indicating himself and Owen, said, 'At this point in time, only us two know his name. We intend keeping it that way.'

'Thank you, I appreciate that and no media,' she replied quietly. 'Yes, I will pay a visit to the funeral parlour. I've got a few questions of my own.'

Owen coughed. 'It'd be appreciated if you reported back to us.'

'Of course. Is there a suspicion around Clive too?' she asked calmly.

'We have nothing to go on with recent events that involve you.'

'And I'm the connection without being under investigation?'

'Something like that,' Sergeant Kohli said quietly. 'Would you be seeking answers to your questions soon, Ms Pestel?'

She looked at both men levelly. 'I'm not going to deny my anxiety about leaving my property unattended, but I know I have to at some stage. Let's make it Saturday. So, yes. Quite soon! Combo and I will come into town on Saturday. I need to collect my mail and will tee up an appointment for then. After I've filled you in with whatever I have discovered, if anything, I need to go about obtaining an A.V.O.'

Her confidence level was rising the more she thought about being in control, nailing the bastards culpable of hurting Combo, Rudy's death, and the pain they had caused several other families. *And for breaking into my home.*

'Good,' Sergeant Kohli clasped his hands around hers. 'Thank you.'

Owen discretely put his phone away and patted her on the shoulder. They joined the returning happy group with Carl proudly displaying the perfectly cut roses. The ladies hugged Yasmin again and insisted on helping her in the kitchen before they went back to town. Knowing not to argue with such a gracious suggestion, they nattered together on the way back inside. No sooner were they; Nanna took the lead.

'Young lady, we are going to swap phone numbers. Please consider coming to lunch with us when you're next in town and coordinate everything through Pam.'

'Yes, Nanna,' Yasmin replied dutifully but with a smile that would challenge the sun's brightness.

'This calls for a group hug,' she said loudly with a mischievous laugh and tucked the tea towel neatly over the oven door handle.

A knock on the door was met with her saying cheekily, 'Come in if you're good looking!'

She was mischief this old bird, and great value. Owen opened the door as Sergeant Kohli pulled him back and in a split-second Carl scooted through the gap. These was Yasmin's kind of people. They duly shared their contact details and laughed uproariously at the message-tone jam session.

'Righto, lovely ladies, we need to head back,' Owen said gently. 'We will all stay in touch.'

After Yasmin and Carl secured the buckets in the back of Sergeant Kohli's vehicle, the women hugged again. She bit back her tears and fears and thanked everyone. The two Sergeants made a point of being the last ones to get into their personal cars after Carl had opened the doors for the ladies and secured Zeus in his seat.

Owen spoke in a no-nonsense tone. 'Yasmin, same deal as last night with checking in.'

'Yes Boss,' she replied falsely confident.

'Then you'll inform me, won't you, Boss?' Sergeant Kohli insisted.

The two men spoke in low voices before nodding formally at Yasmin.

'We'll watch you leave from the patio. Thanks again. Bye.'

Chapter 24

After much wet-nose nudging, Yasmin set the combination lock to the switch box, then went to investigate the new external locks. Flummoxed as to the location of the keys, was about to make a phone call when her eyes fell on the smiley faced envelope against the vase. The contained note explained the doors were keyed-alike, including the laundry doors.

Changing into a pair of gardening clothes, she swapped out the age-old keys for the new ones. Loving the weight difference of having only two keys for the whole cottage hanging off her hip, scooped up the clothes for washing. The laundry! She hadn't even given it a thought and immediately felt bad. Adding to her relief of the silent door swing, was the vintage style peacock design wallpaper covering the old fibro walls. Delighted with the addition of shelves either side of the top-loading washing machine, and a brand spanking new security screen door as well as a timber door. Even her busted old trolley and baskets had been replaced. She peeked inside the washing machine tub to see where all her clothes ended up and giggled, sent a text to Owen thanking him for her stylish new laundry.

Her mobile chimed with a text message within a minute. Thinking it to be from him, was surprised to see it was from Bob asking about the colour of the fabric similar to a chain that held everything together? She burst out laughing. Good old caring, sensitive Bob. The best listener out of the three. Her one worded reply of *turquoise* resulted in an immediate response with the emoticon of two hands clasped together.

Combo's inspection duly completed, hassled her to be outside. Securing the cottage and setting the alarms to notification only, the pair raced each other into the packing shed. It was time to tackle the loft. Waiting for the four halogen lights to warm up, she exhaled loudly, dragged the long stepladder and secured it against its floor. Nimbly reaching the top rung, the landscape in front of her evoked childlike excitement and didn't resist the temptation of exploring. There were old buckets with dents and corrosion, rusty tools, plastic seedling starter boxes, of which should all go straight into the bin. Concertina folders on the dilapidated rusty bookshelf of old business records brought back a flood of emotional memories. Kicking at several rake handles, she paused mid strike. Scratching her head then shaking it, she was convinced she had never stacked nine archive boxes three high, set away from the others.

Preparing herself to shift something heavy, Yasmin nearly flung herself off her feet. The top box empty. So was the next. They were all empty! But they sat in front of a large old metal trunk. One she had never seen before. No lock, just a solid metal slide latch.

'Secrets or questions, which one has more?' she muttered.

Her happy disposition quickly slipped towards despondency. Still muttering about the deceptiveness, slid back the bolt and wrestled with the heavy lid until it stayed propped up against the corrugated back wall of the shed. Underneath an unfamiliar green bed sheet lay a bundle of light pink envelopes tied with pink string, and the unmistakable scent of old lavender. In between several other unfamiliar bed sheets and some fairly new camphor blocks, Yasmin bit back the tears at the sight of Emily's ballet shoes and her childhood ballerina bedspread, followed by sealed packets of new linen. Underneath lay a bundle wrapped in calico with a pink and blue intertwined satin bow. With the clues slowly being exposed, she guessed Rudy and the lads would have used the helicopter.

Nodding defiantly, not one of them had ever beaten her in a hand of Poker nor a game of stare-down, and wasn't about to let them start. With shoulders back and chin lifted, lined an old bucket with one of the sheets and filled it with the calico bundle and letters. The rest of the contents in the trunk would remain where they were until after the funeral. She had enough things to go through. Trying to get her head around the mysteries that surrounded the man of whom she had lived with and loved for so long was a challenge in itself. Concealing the trunk in its pre-discovered condition, Yasmin descended the ladder with the handle of the bucket hooked through her arm. Combo was at her feet in an instant, running around in circles. If he was as hungry as her stomach was growling, she understood his urgency to eat. Swiftly folding the ladder and laying it down where it belonged, turned off the big lights and reigned in her over enthusiastic furry mate.

Still spooked, Combo enjoyed play time, dinner and treats inside the tidy cottage before taking over the entire settee. His bed lying forgotten in the corner. Having complete confidence with the locked switch box, the entire security system was activated with audible alarms. Wolfing down a delicious beef stir-fry with the ginger and sweet chilli dressing, Yasmin willed herself to dissect Rudy's behaviour while she cleaned up. By the time the dish rack was clear, a single word summed it up.

'Controlling,' she muttered, then in a lighter tone called out, 'You and your puppy-sigh is all I need, Combo!'

His ears pricked up at his name and emitted his special verbal hug. With only the outer patio door open, light jazz music playing in the background and all the curtains drawn, Yasmin sat at the dining room table with two piles in front of her. The calico bundle, and the pretty pink envelopes. Playing her typical decision-making game of Eeny, Meeny, Miny, Moe, it was pretty obvious the letters would be the winner.

Not wanting to tear the earliest post-marked envelope she pried open the flap, considering the years the seal was impressive. Yet, she didn't know if she should be angry or simply cry. The watermark on the stationery of a delicate hummingbird taking nectar from soft pink and purple flowers enlarged the lump in her throat. Emily's impeccably neat handwriting flowed lightly over the grey writing lines.

My Dear Yasmin,

I write to wish you a very happy birthday with many happy returns and hope to see you soon. You are so good for that dear brother of mine, although I must say his possessiveness can be a tad smothering. We both know he means well.

Exciting ideas are afoot for the celebration of our 30th birthday! Aunt Polly's 60th is the month earlier so we're hoping to have a combined do. Although it is a few years away, time has passed very quickly of late. So far, the ideas are a fancy dinner, a cruise, a night at the theatre or a trip overseas, but with the lads' businesses, the latter may be deferred. I personally would love to wear a beautiful gown with sparkly shoes and have a beau on my arm dancing the night away after a juicy steak!

Perhaps you could entrap my dear brother for a while so I can have a night or several without his constant overarching protection. He calls on me regularly which is so lovely, but I would prefer if he announced his pending arrival.

Do you know he caught me with a man in the piano bar of the Sheridan? How he found me was anyone's guess! Anyway, we were not doing anything frightfully naughty, but by golly it could have led to an extraordinary experience, of that, I am sure. Alas, it was not to be! I saw the funny side of it afterwards, particularly when I wondered if it would have been different if I were with a girl. I so wish I could have told you this in person, we would have giggled long and hard. I miss you and our girly chats. Sitting in front of the 'Water Lilies' just isn't the same.

That is enough of me, I am so excited about your business venture and am pleased you embraced the spreading of your wings. I do not believe I am quite ready, but you will be the first to know when I am. Please write soon.

Love and miss you,

Emily xoxo

Yasmin dabbed gently at her eyes just like she remembered Emily doing when they shared their secrets, their dreams, and their fears. Yasmin herself had written religiously every three months and sent birthday cards, but it was clear her correspondence hadn't been received either. Sighing heavily, reached for the second letter and carefully slit open the envelope. This time the decorative writing paper was of two red-backed fairy wrens fluttering above a daffodil on a soft blue and white background. The writing lines were an even fainter grey and Emily had used a pink pen. Her complete, articulate manner of speaking evident in her writing.

My Dear Yasmin,

Happy Birthday to you! I miss you and I have not heard from you but Happy Birthday to you!

I was so sad I missed your phone call the other day and why from a public telephone? I hope you are okay but did ask Rudy the question. He says you do not have a phone number which I find most strange because you run a business. I did get your letter before Christmas and thank you so much for such a thoughtful gift. You sound well, but lonely. I miss you too and the fun we had. We sure did have some great times. I love the scent of the Charlie Red! It is now my favourite. Even Dad says it is dainty and most suitable. I do declare, how wonderfully different is its bottle!

How is business? I do not get told too much information as everyone is so busy. I took up art classes, continued with my dancing, but dear brother did not think it appropriate I wear tights or outfits akin to dancing. Imagine if I had seriously pursued gymnastics! Heavens, I fear he is getting worse as he ages. Goodness knows what he will be like when he is as old as Dad! Even he was saying he held grave concerns about the lack of stretch of the apron strings that us twins share.

Mum and Dad have been tremendous with everything all our lives. They are doing well with their business and were talking about retiring but still keen to have a family trip. Oh yes! I almost forgot. We will be having a joint party, a formal dinner at a fancy restaurant. You must come please Yasmin, you must. I miss you so.

Rudy promised me us three would go on another camping trip afterwards for a few days, do some more orienteering by exploring some hills where there are waterfalls and a whole bunch of different plants and birdlife to see. A holiday! I cannot wait and you deserve one as well. He has promised me, so he has to do it and gee am I reminding him every time I see him! I cannot wait for you to tell us some jokes around the fire. It has been so long since we all had fun together. Of course we have grown up, and of course we all work but I must share a secret with you. His business has been busy which is good for him and me, because I get to have a little breathing room when he goes away. I worry about your safety though. He seems to be away an awful lot.

I managed to get away for a weekend with a group of friends from a drama group I helped establish for simple children. Poor dear things, they had a delightful time performing at the aged care facility, but somehow Rudy found out and insisted he drove me home and not catch the bus with my friends. I think that was our first real squabble and it lasted the whole two-hour journey. Gosh, I was so angry. But we are twins so it was hard to stay cross with each other for long. I do feel I am the stronger and more flexible. When my dear brother has his mind made up though, there is no turning it.

I do so hope to hear from you soon, my only true best friend. I love you and miss you awfully. Please write soon.

Love and miss you,

Emily xoxo

Yasmin was so disappointed in herself for not making more of an effort to keep in touch with Emily by phone. Pouring herself a shot of whiskey, her mind churned over the annoyance of Rudy withholding her mail from being received on both counts! He was away a lot but that was no excuse for Yasmin not to contact Emily. *But the lies!*

Reaching for the next letter she double checked the date stamps. This would have been the year of the big birthday bash. Tears sprung to her eyes. Adorning the simple light blue writing paper was a swan in the process of taking off from a calm lake. Typically, Emily's pink handwriting flowed elegantly across the pages.

My Dear Yasmin,

Where were you? I missed you and I so badly have to see you. I have not heard from you. Oh, please excuse me – Happy Birthday my beautiful friend. I am 30! We are 30! I am guessing you did not celebrate yours in style. How very sad.

It has been so long now since you went to live in your little cottage and I have never been able to come and see you. I do not even know your business name! Do you know your own name is not listed in the telephone directory? Well, I have finally put two and two together and know it is not you preventing me, but my dear brother. I suspect your letters have been intercepted as well.

The lads are quite concerned with this stranglehold. That was their term. And I overheard quite the argument. Naturally they all shook hands and carried on like nothing happened afterwards. But my word! Yasmin the cussing would rot the sails off a tall ship. I was fascinated and would not dare use any of them but by golly, they obviously use them frequently. The string of expletives was very clever.

Dad almost made me wash my mouth out with soap just for listening! The cheek of him and I told him so because he had been listening too! He and Mum send their love. They also miss you, your nonsense and quick wit and the last time they asked after you, Rudy stated outright that you were too busy with your business and to not ask again. We were quite taken aback with his attitude. I am now very worried about you and your social life.

I have maintained my agility with gymnastics discretely and can now do the splits just like you did when you were a youngster and tried to teach me. Gosh! The fun we had back then! I am leading a double life now. The lads are really worried about Rudy and his controlling nature particularly as he explicitly told them to keep an eye on me. ME! The lads have been my sanity savers!

I do thank you so much for the beautiful bracelet you had engraved especially for me. It was our little secret that I preferred White Gold. I wore it at the party and Rudy was so inquisitive, particularly when he saw the magnificent roses! I actually think he was quite miffed that this parcel had slipped through his eagle eyes. You are so dear to me, my beautiful friend.

I know Rudy means well, but gosh, he is taking the brotherly responsibility just a bit too far. Dad and him had serious words. Even Aunt Polly took him under her wing for a while and had a good old heart-to-heart. Then he came and saw me and explained he was terrified something would happen and he was not around to protect or save me. I assured him that he would always be with me, in my heart and probably my head considering we are the type of twins we are. He laughed so hard he cried which set me off like a Giggling Gertie. It was the best laugh we had shared since we were early teenagers.

He invited the lads around, then he went on a business trip somewhere, came back more loaded than what he already was. You do know you do not have to work? All the same, us kids got together again and had an absolute blast. Really wish you had been here to see the laughing lad you fell in love with.

Yasmin, I must tell this to you. Dad, Mum and me have been talking about going on a skiing holiday. Snow, not water! I jumped at the opportunity, anything to have some freedom.

Now, this is important to you. The family solicitor urged me to write a Will. It is the <u>adult</u> thing to do. Have you got one? It is quite a difficult document to write but all those emotions must get put aside, my beautiful friend. I will sum it up. You and Rudy get everything. If Rudy dies, you get everything. If you die, he gets everything. Super simple but there is a lot. The certified copy is with the family solicitor and the original is in my very own personal safety deposit box. I organised that all by myself! How very grown up of me (and sneaky). Outside of the nice old man at our bank nobody else knows about it.

I mentioned before: you do not have to work. I respect you are quite independent and extremely proud, but with Rudy's self-made wealth and any inheritance, you really do not have any financial worries. I hope he has told you this and you are loving what you do because you are doing it for love and not making ends meet. You are very sensible with money and switched on, but my beautiful friend, live life – you really can! Oh, how I miss you.

Dad and Mum showed both us kids their instructions, they are really quite well-to-do. I had not ever thought of it in great detail because I did not have to. But Yasmin, you have always worked that gorgeous butt off to make ends meet and get ahead. I admired your drive and took inspiration from you by excelling at everything I do.

I know Rudy left everything to me because he made me read what he wrote last week. He adamantly insisted it was his first and final unless things changed, and we know Rudy, if that is what he says that is what it is.

One day you will see my letters, of that, I am sure. I will keep writing as I know you will, and perhaps either one or hopefully both will be able to read them to each other. Can you imagine the party we will have! Just you and me! Oh! I must tell you; I have developed quite a penchant for whiskey. Strange for a lady I know, not saying you are not a lady because you always drank it, but me; The Lady. Sherry is too sweet, and I would not dare put rum to my lips. Beer has to be icy cold in the same temperature tall glass, but no fluffy, not on my lips.

I told a beau that one time and he thought it was hilarious. Me and my naivety, Aunt Polly explained certain things to me. She is quite well versed in the birds and the bees. I often wonder what her life story is but she is tight lipped and super rich. Us five kids are super blessed to have been adopted and welcomed into such a loving, down-to-earth family. They are generous too! Did you know they organised quite the fundraising gala for a large orphanage in the city? It was glorious and very successful.

My beautiful friend, I must sign off else this will never reach the mail box. I will be writing again as I suspect you will be too.

Look after yourself, dear Yasmin. I miss you so much.

Love and miss you,

Emily xoxo

Yasmin was so absorbed in the letter she jumped out of her skin when Owen's text message came through. After sending a positive reply, read the letters again. It felt like her head was going to explode from the restless emotions. Anger. Regret. Loneliness. Deceit. They all coursed through her veins like a volcanic river. Big hot tears traced their downward path and plopped onto her lap. Emily had been screaming for help *and* for her best friend. It was too long ago to remember what Yasmin wrote, but she did recall writing Emily with her concerns of Rudy's controlling nature. *Emily wasn't the naïve one at all.* Yasmin slapped her forehead in self-annoyance.

The fourth letter was dated Boxing Day and although Emily's writing was incredibly neat, the note was hastily written. A delicate sprinkling of gold glitter on the faintly silhouetted Christmas Bells being the only colour on the ivory writing paper. It was so simple and beautiful. Yasmin's mouth quivered and the tears momentarily blurred her vision.

My dear Yasmin,

Merry Christmas! Ours was busy and joyous as I hope yours was too. Only short and sweet, bit like us. The key is wrapped up in a calico bundle tied with a blue and pink ribbon which is in the bottom of my glory box.

Missing you like crazy! I'm sneaking off to celebrate the New Year on a houseboat. Girls only! Except the Captain. He is MY dreamboat. I so wish you could be here too. The lads will be occupying Rudy. Where are you? What are you doing? If you are all alone, that is so cruel. I know your Family were talking about going overseas, have they come to see you yet? Can you try and get away? Rudy told us you had a pretty pink van, and you grow the most amazing Queen Elizabeth Roses. We knew that already! I do not share his distaste for Lavender. I have it in all my drawers. Oh! What a great deterrent, how very naughty of me!

Love and miss you,

Emily xoxo

Yasmin's eyes darted to the bundle and for the first time in a very long time carried Great Aunt Rose's blue, yellow and white crocheted blanket off her bed into the lounge. It was going to be a late night. Transferring Emily's correspondence and the calico bundle onto the recliner, Combo didn't budge from the settee. Just watched with one eye open as she brewed a coffee, then sat guard when the bathroom door closed.

Fresh in appearance but not in mind, she summarised Emily's letters and mentally removed Rudy's deceptiveness while robotically stirring the enamel off the mug. Totally baffled at the notion of thinking she actually knew him, took her coffee to the lounge and spent a long while trying to dissect the lives of the twins. Arriving at no particular logical answer, the date stamp on Emily's fifth letter summoned her attention. *Two months* before the fateful trip. The amazing choice of writing paper was a statement in its own right. On a light green background

with snow-capped mountains and a winding road, a suitcase stood at the foot of
the notepaper.

My dear Yasmin,

I am so excited! Mum, Dad and I are going skiing. Rudy was not at all happy, and my dear friend, you <u>will</u> get the blame should something untoward happen. He kept saying you were needing him to do things around the house, but I assure you, us three know different. For starters, it has always been the cottage, not the house! Nevertheless, you would never be held accountable for anything that happened to us, if ever anything should. Heavens! We are going skiing in this land, not overseas. I made the error of suggesting you and him join us. Whoopsies.

I need you to meet MY dreamboat.

I digress. I fear Rudy's possessiveness, jealousy and controlling nature is getting the better of him. Not even Aunt Polly could rationalise with him this time, and again the lads gave him what for as only best friends can. I do worry for you. We all do. We love you and miss you terribly, me more so. I have not had a girly chat since you left and I am older now and things change as we get older. By the way, I hope Water Lilies is hanging on your wall?

I fear I will be an old maid too because although Dad has encouraged me to find a suitor, alas, dear brother squashes any flame. You will learn one day about MY dreamboat. I had a chat with Aunt Polly and suggested I become a Madam, that way I know people do actually have it off and either pay for it or get paid! I would just make a cut off the top without my virtue being soiled. She laughed hysterically and recommended I put all such notion out of my mind. She is very wise!

I will write from the ski resort. I have booked my own room; and every room – even the bathroom with a spa in it, has the most exquisite view. I am so excited. I have always wanted to fly through the air and have a snow fight. Dad, Mum and me are looking forward to this trip so much. I will build a snowman for you, my beautiful friend. One with a big carrot. Tee hee. Oh, how very, very naughty of me!

I so wish you were coming and I pray you will be able to surprise me, but I will not get my hopes up. Rudy has made so many false promises of late, I have learnt to quell my expectations. Gosh, how that hurts from kin. I am sorry if he has done that to you as well. I abhor cruelty to anything. Perhaps you should get a dog. They are loyal and love unconditionally from what I have seen.

Oh, I have cleaned out my room in case I decide to stay at the resort! They have a variety of seasonal jobs there. I am sure I will adapt swiftly. I am so excited! I would have told you that several times.

I love and miss you, my beautiful friend. You look after yourself, always listen to yourself and do not change, just get wiser.

Love and miss you,

Emily xoxo

Toying with the last pretty pink envelope, it was post marked two days before the awful life-taking accident. Uncontrolled tears erupted. Pre-empting the excitement and enthusiasm of the holiday, the snow adventures and the fun, she was reluctant to read the letter. Finishing the almost untouched cup of coffee in one long drink, leant against the headrest and shut her eyes. Emily, such a beautiful woman, so much love to give, so kind and thoughtful, and simply gone far too soon.

Yasmin slid her finger under the flap and frowned at how easily it opened in comparison to the others. Shaking her head, she unfolded the lavender-coloured writing paper with its picture of a snow-white owl sitting on a lonely timber post in the bottom right corner. A tear had been drawn on its face in black ink. It stood out like a deformed petal on a perfect blossom.

More large, hot tears chased those that flooded her cheeks. 'Oh Rudy. Why?'

My dear Yasmin,

Wow! This place is extraordinarily beautiful, and the snow bunnies are especially handsome. The first twelve days were incredible. We tobogganed, felt like I was flying when we went on the chair lift and fell on my bottom several times while trying to balance on the silly narrow skis. I had it down pat by the third day and had the most amazing, kind, thoughtful snowman to teach me the art. MY dreamboat. MY snow man. We are inseparable. I told him I would be staying and looking for a job. He taught me how to make the best snowballs for the snow fight! MY snow man has joined us for dinner most nights and has invited a select few VIPs to go on a scenic tour in a motorised snow vehicle soon. One couple about to retire have just acquired a winery and have extended an invitation. Another couple are a bit reclusive. I think he maybe high up in the police (well, Dad thinks so.) But another couple has an animal refuge farm on the other side of the Alpines, they too extended an invitation. So jolly exciting! MY dreamboat and me are the youngest by almost a generation!

My beautiful friend, the look in MY snow man's eyes is something I have never seen from anybody else before and my body has never felt such a tingle. Everything goes gooey. Is this what true love is? Is this how it feels? I have decided it is.

THEN RUDY ARRIVED

It was a surprise visit and we were all so sad you could not make it. He told quite the fabricated lie which we all saw through, then he made a point of telling MY snow man that if ever something should happen to me, he would hunt the man down. Well! The men, Dad included, had quite the conversation in the soft snow that was falling outside the restaurant at lunch time. Mum and I changed tables so we could not see the interaction and had quite the special conversation. It was like we got to know each other over a fine beef lasagne and tossed salad. Oh, and several glasses of some delightful red wine and mouth-watering garlic bread. It is true that a mother and daughter relationship is especially special and a different kind of special to that of a father – daughter relationship.

MY snow man paid me a visit last night and said he did not believe in ultimatums and certainly would not tolerate one in our relationship. Rudy made it quite clear that MY snow man was not good enough for me and he would make our lives or relationship very difficult. It was so cruel, oh, Yasmin, I have not stopped crying. Dad insisted I should live my life the way I wanted, and him and Mum would keep trying to encourage Rudy to grow up and let me spread my wings. You came into the conversation my beautiful friend. They are so worried about you, they wished they had visited you earlier but have said that us three will take a trip to see you when we get home.

MY snow man promised he would wait for me, but would make his presence scarce while the meddlesome brother was in the airspace. Well, Rudy is leaving this morning after breakfast. Did you know he had his own aircraft? Actually, it is a helicopter big enough to take six people plus his very own pilot. He proudly told us that he had achieved this under his own steam. Dad and Mum and me genuinely congratulated him and offered to charter it when we go and see CREAM.

Shortly, I will dutifully wave my dear brother off, finish my letter to you then do my utmost to find MY snow man. MY dreamboat. Yes, I have claimed him, but I swear on this letter I write to you that I will not smother him.

Right! That wasn't half as bad as I thought it would be. I did not even cry. Rudy accepted my decision to extend my holiday – those were the words I used, and Dad and Mum are thrilled. I deliberately sought MY snow man. We hugged and kissed in the firewood barn. Oh, Yasmin! I have found true love. Him, Dad, Mum and me have just had a delicious Devonshire tea and we are joining other distinguished guests on a private tour. Oh! I have already written about that. I am so excited, I cannot wait. MY snow man and I get to sit up the front together. I love it when he holds my hand.

We then have a picnic lunch and return back to the Resort in time to get ready for an impromptu fancy dress. The costumes are all provided and because we will not be there during the day of, we get to choose early!

MY snow man gave me inside information as to what was available. As soon as he said Snow White, I claimed the costume. He said I would look the part with my ebony hair, blue eyes and...and he told me repeatedly I had the fullest, most kissable lips he had ever seen in his life. My beautiful friend, I feel like I'm floating. Cloud Nine. Yes. MY snow man, MY dreamboat, MY instant family and I will sail away into the sunset.

Dreams cost nothing, my beautiful friend. Remember that.

I do miss you and wish you were here so we could celebrate your Birthday together. Happy Birthday to you! I must get this in the mail tonight else it will be another week. I wanted you to read the latest at the earliest opportunity and share with me the longest snow season in history!

Love and miss you,

Emily xoxo

With Combo now resting his head on her knee, she smoothed the furry tuft and closed her eyes. They flew open at the screaming message from her mind: *it's not too late, set the alarm!*

Chapter 25

The loud clunk of the bronze hands on the wall clock awoke her with a start. *Four o'clock?* Stretching to ease the stiffness in her back which compounded a thumping headache and sore neck, she took her time in getting her bearings. *Emily.* Immediately, Yasmin's eyes fell upon the letters lying on her lap. Tracing her index finger over the beautiful handwriting, the choking sigh forced fresh tears to well up, stinging her still-tender eyes.

Opening the curtains, the early morning darkness gradually gave way to a painted twilight. Soft flecks of pink and orange highlighted the scattered fluffy clouds. The dawn chorus rehearsed its repertoire and the resident little willy wagtail twittered happily nearby. *So much unfinished business.* Glad to have her own company for a few days, silently gave thanks for seeing another daybreak and got ready to meet it head on.

Combo enthusiastically hung around her in the kitchen while she knocked up a toasted bacon and egg sandwich with melted cheese and barbecue sauce, and a bottle of coke on the side. Thanking her newfound friends for their thoughtfulness, presumed they knew of the same remedy for what felt like a minor hangover.

Pushing Rudy's deception aside, Emily's letters gave Yasmin a new purpose. With their daily routine of smelling the roses and a solid half hour play completed, she set about getting some work done. Except this time, it wasn't floral work. It was all about Emily.

Laying the calico bundle gently on the dining room table, Yasmin untied the impeccable bows. The waft of lavender potpourri made her grin broadly which turned into a loud gasp. The sheerest of lingerie and other negligees folded in between the lightest of tissues with their tags intact was astonishing. Emily sure had a fantastic eye for classy, sexy fashion! There was no question about that. With utmost care, Yasmin laid the delicate fabrics beside each other until she found a white box. Lifting its lid, a stark white bulging envelope and two very different keys concealed another form of correspondence. The feel of the old flimsy typewriter paper was as evocative as the memorable clack and ding of the carriage return.

Dear Yasmin,

I type this formal letter to convey my sincerest regret that I did not make more of an effort to contact you and I know you will share the same regret. Let us not burden ourselves as such. Instead, let us celebrate our eternal friendship. I hope that you will enjoy wearing these delicate pieces of fabric some time in your life, even if it is for self-loving. I bought them when I was under the impression you were to be married. Nevertheless, they are yours.

Now, my true, beautiful friend; down to business. One key in particular will unlock a whole new world for you, and that is the long one. The old heavy one? Rudy has got the other somewhere and the lads are going to need it. In the cellar of their home is an old Silky Oak sideboard. Rudy and I discovered it when we were little, and Aunt Polly let us use it as our hiding place when we felt scared. It was our secret and we stashed a lot of things in there. A lot of incidentals which meant something to only him and I. When I reflect on the matter, it was actually quite selfish of us not to share the hiding place with the lads. I know they will forgive me. I owe them so much for their help in giving me opportunities to have fun. If I should not be here, please give them my key. Rudy and the lads would have had a secret pact; they had so many which were none of my business.

This letter will sound awfully final but Rudy has planted the tragedy seed.

Now it is all about you.

I have mentioned previously about my very own safety deposit box. Now you are going to learn about my secret. I became awfully lonely and volunteered at an orphanage after you left. I overcame most of my childhood traumas and thanked the good Lord those establishments had improved their business practices. Anyway, I helped a couple adopt a little boy. They were perfectly matched with their incredible looks, endearing natures, common sense, and aptitude. The little boy had a premature birth and born with a crippled hand, but that did not deter their insistence that he was the child they wanted to be known as their son.

We, that is, Dean, Julie and Herbie—the little boy—became very close friends and frequently met in private. That was the most beautiful thing about Julie and Dean's relationship. Their honesty with their adopted son as soon as he could comprehend what they explained. It was so sweet when he called Julie, Mummy-two!

I think the lads may have worked out I was doing something out of the ordinary because several times they saw me return home in different clothes to what I left in. I love those lads with all my heart; they never judged me and they covered for me aplenty.

Rudy never found out. Until he called on me unexpectedly and saw me wearing funeral clothes and utterly distraught. Julie had been killed in an accident and we had just laid her to rest. Rudy was furious. I can only describe it as blind with jealousy. They were MY friends.

Afterwards, I continued to secretly meet with Dean and Herbie, and we became extremely close to the point where Dean and I fell madly in love. Dad and Mum approved. Herbie looks at me as his third surrogate mother. Poor little spot, so much pain and loss and so young. Remarkable at sketching mind you. I introduced him to Monet and he showed me his beautiful interpretation of Water Lilies. Yasmin, he included a dog! Sadly, I know not what became of the picture.

Dean took a job in the snowfields, that is why we have decided to have a holiday there. I have not told a lie. It was the only way I could spread my wings. You will understand; of that, I know.

In a compartment in the bank box will be an address and telephone number. Dean of course is MY snow man. MY dreamboat. His home is where Julie grew up. Her ashes were scattered there and us three made a pact that the house would stay in his family forever. Herbie is going to need ongoing attention on his crippled hand, and I swore I would continue helping in any way I could. It is not in town, so be prepared to travel away.

You are my sole heiress. I need you to continue fulfilling my oath and deliver some mail. My beautiful friend, I know you will. My legal Will and Testament will broadly cover these instructions. The irreparable hurt which has been inflicted upon those who I love, by a twin, is breaking my heart. In the manner Rudy has been behaving, I suspect he has implemented dead-hand control. I will do the same. Nevertheless, I pray that only you will finish what I started if my demise should come about.

Your eternal friend,

Emily Craige

Yasmin sat in shock. Mouth agape. Overjoyed that her dear friend had lived and loved, the magnitude of sorrow of her snow man's life, hit hard. To have lost two loved women in such a short period of time would be mortifying. Like whizzing vehicles, thoughts raced at her and shot past. *Action Emily's request. Visit the old bank. Cut flowers. Arrange funeral. Deliver mail. Urgent. Urgent. Urgent.* There were so many things she had to do. Her eye's blurred. She teetered forwards. Her chest tightened.

***

Leaning casually against the fridge in the staffroom, the Station's receptionist, Ruth, was animatedly describing the delicacies consumed at an administrative seminar held in Adelaide the previous week.

'Sergeant Pyers, I couldn't believe how sweet the dahlias tasted!'

'What? The actual flower?'

'No, no! Those adorned the table in spectacular fashion. Its tuber was roasted with other vegetables. But what was truly special was they came from Pestel's Edible Petals! A local!'

'Have you met the lady who runs it?'

'No. Just know she's got a large dog and a pink van. I'm glad I got to finally taste some of her proceeds because I know her roses are exquisite. It's just so sad she's had to shut up shop.'

'Oh?'

Ruth looked at her boss sideways. 'As if you didn't know.'

'Know what?' he asked innocently.

She looked around and lowered her voice. 'Rumour has it her stepbrother suicided. I saw my old hairdresser while I was away and she reckons there's a spate of these incidents around the Moojie Hill get together.'

'The what?'

A junior officer walked into the room. 'Hey Sarge. Ruth! We've been looking everywhere for you. There's a problem with the photocopier.'

'Okay, I'm there now.' She looked at her boss and winked. 'Duty calls,' and ushered her colleagues out of the room.

Staring at the floor, a deep-set frown transformed his face and muttered. 'Stepbrother?'

'You makin' the coffee, Pyers?'

His head flew upwards resulting in a crick in the neck. 'You still here, Hillyer?' he growled, slapping on the kettle.

'Yeah, I'll be heading back to City HQ tomorrow. There's been a breakthrough in the case I was working on—'

'Which one?'

'My biggest yet and a cold case. About six years ago, a drive-by shooting took out a bank johnny. Initially we believed the victim to be in the wrong place at the wrong time, but we've been barking up the wrong tree the whole time! The neighbour's son, a minor at the time of the incident, has come forward with a box of old photos discovered in the attic.'

Handing Chas a mug of straight black coffee and raising his own, Owen said, 'Here's to a satisfying result. God knows we need more of 'em.'

'Cheers! Yep.' He inhaled the bold aroma. 'Nice brew. Anyway, mate, I've dispatched the items from Ms Pestel's place to forensics and will keep you posted.'

Pyers was halfway through the doorway, turned and said, 'Either myself or Kohli. See ya, mate.'

***

Yasmin couldn't get away from the hot breath. Blindly feeling for the restriction realised Combo's paws were steadying her, leant backwards breathing through her mouth and finally managed to open her eyes.

'Thanks boy, I'm okay,' and sniffled wiping his tear streaks.

Feeling like she had just short-circuited, took a long while to process the chain of events impacting her life. Running her hands over the tuft of hair between Combo's ears soothed them both to the point where they sighed at the same time. Her mouth slowly lifted at the edges with the sneaking suspicion she knew where Emily's ashes were hidden, much the same time the travel bug began to gnaw. She was just about to go into the office when her landline rang. Answering it, her voice sounded lighter than how she felt.

'Good morning?'

A quiet chortle came through the speakers. 'Yasmin, dear child. You sound awfully happy after losing someone you've known most of your life,' her mother admonished.

'Hi Mum, I'm just doing my best to hold things together. This is a lovely surprise! How are you? Dad? Sis? Lars? Niece?'

'We're all here, pet,' her father called out. 'We couldn't wait another day. So sorry to hear about Ru, Lars filled us in on the whole family's demise. Awfully sorry, hon, are you okay?'

'It's been an arduous rollercoaster to ride, but I'm getting stronger each day thanks Dad. I've got plenty of good memories to reflect on.'

'That's my girl.'

'Hey is Candy there too?'

'Where else would I be?' she jested lightly.

'Congratulations big sis to you and Lars. I love your style!'

'Yeah, crazy hey, but wow! Life is for living so spill. What are your plans?'

'Just getting my head around things at the moment. It's taking a while but the fog is clearing. I'll probably go and reconnect with some old friends then have a holiday.'

'Fly here!'

'Too cold! Fly here.'

'Too hot!'

The laughter was genuine, and the banter continued without an in-depth conversation being held. In typical international Pestel family style, the conversation revolved around the Europe-based members and how their lives were now taking on a different challenge with the excitement of a new addition to the family and another White Christmas on the cards. They kept telling her to join them but dropped the subject quickly when Yasmin reminded them about Combo. They weren't keen on dogs and complained bitterly about their noisy barks, butt sniffing and all the fur. Yasmin smothered the giggles when she looked at the accumulated dog hair on the settee. She knew full well her mother and sister would have the biggest fit, but her dad would smile knowingly at his little girl. With everyone sending their love and good wishes, the call ended as suddenly as it begun.

The spring in her step improved instantly and after a thorough clean and the alarms still activated, Yasmin aired out the cottage and sat at the dining table. Her inherited ceramic drink coasters weighed down the corners of the unrolled collage of funeral notices, while her eagle-eye scanned the array of numerals. Two sets of digits far outweighed any other. Squeezing her eyes tightly, the pattern of these numbers represented peaks and valleys. *Snowfields?* Convinced they were GPS coordinates; the first thing she did was compare the latitude and longitude digits to that of the cottage. Her sigh of relief fluttered the paper. She surmised the digits suggested Emily's place of death. *So, her snow man and son live around there?*

Leaning backwards and stretching loudly, the sedentary lifestyle wasn't normal practice and her body complained bitterly. The moment she was on her feet, Combo was ready for action. He followed her movements and raced around excitedly when she retrieved his box of liver treats. Standing on the concrete verandah outside the dining room door she took in the view. It had been many years since she had actually taken the time to appreciate it. She just loved the soft, springy grass though. Racing each other around the cottage and onto the patio, stretched, played tug-o-war, stretched some more before taking the flying leap and played tiggy on the lawn.

Half an hour later, both puffing and panting lying side by side, Yasmin stared at the deep blue sky and smiled. *We will find your snow man, Emily.*

Throwing several ideas around in her head about the quest, she knew she wouldn't be able to concentrate on anything until the arrangements had been made at the funeral home. Contemplating her options while sharing several bottles of water, reluctantly phoned the funeral home and hung up before it rang. Frustrated at the fluctuating emotions reminded herself that Rudy had to be laid to rest so Emily's quest could begin, redialled.

'Gentle Rest Funeral Home, this is Clive.' His soft voice weirdly soothing her nerves.

'Hello Clive, this is Yasmin Pestel.'

Interrupting his expressive repeated condolences, she informed him that a cremation would meet final wishes and asked when a service could be held.

'Tell me, are you having many guests joining you?'

'Well, that's just it. I will be the only person in attendance and ... well ... I actually feel quite inadequate.'

In a melodic tone he explained, 'It's quite common to feel like that in these situations, believe me. Perhaps you ought to consider a private service, Ms Pestel ... hmm? This Monday at ten o'clock is available. It's a nice alternative and I'll ensure the chapel and priest is available to say prayers, and I can help you select a couple of hymns. There will be a coffin adorned appropriately with a gilded name plate bearing the soul's name and timeline, ordinarily. In due course, this is generally removed before his vessel continues on its journey, then affixed to the urn of ashes which will then be available for collection. Or, I can arrange to have them delivered.'

Yasmin cleared her throat and wiped the sudden onset of tears with the back of her hand. 'I haven't selected a coffin or urn.'

'Ah, Ms Pestel, it must have slipped your kin's mind. He came to see us several years ago and selected his own with the details already etched onto a plaque.'

'He what?'

'I acknowledge your astonishment, but some men do this to save their loved ones the anguish. It isn't uncommon.'

'Really? What does it say?'

'Ms Pestel, you ought to know your step-brother's details.'

She coughed and spluttered. 'Now just you wait one minute, Clive. You hassled me to no end very soon after he died and you're just telling me this now?'

'Ms Pestel, you sound emotionally exhausted and I'm sorry. It's quite natural to forget information when one is grieving. You did tell me it was going to be a cremation, so on Monday, I will greet you and escort you as I do with all mourners. On the day, there is no rush, so please don't think you're imposing on anybody else's grief. The priest will escort you to your vehicle. Perhaps you consider getting someone to drive you home?'

Her mind was exhausted. *Had he already told me about the arrangements? Did I already mention a cremation to him? No. That was to the lads. Stepbrother? What the hell?*

'Are you still there?'

With her head in her hand, whispered, 'Yes. And then?'

'Sometimes the scattering of ashes is either declared in their final wishes, or the loved ones make the decision as to what they all agree would suit the deceased. Ms Pestel, grief is a slow journey and there are no time restraints to do this.'

She sniffled quietly. 'I plan on being in town on Saturday, can I come and see you?'

'That's quite normal. How about 9:30am?'

'Um, yes, okay. Yes. That will be fine, thank you.'

'Okay, Ms Pestel, see you then. Thank you. Good bye.'

'Good bye.'

Yasmin had no idea how long she'd sat in a daze, but it was obvious it had been for far too long. Groaning loudly at the numbness of her backside, pulled her knees up to her chest hugging them morosely. Combo lazily yawned and nuzzled her bare feet.

She played with his soft ears. 'Come on boy, let's go inside. I can't think straight.'

In an attempt to soothe her troubled thoughts, the vocals of her dad's favoured Irish crooners—The Clancy Brothers—played while she took a catnap long enough to unclutter her mind. Adamant she had only spoken with the funeral parlour once and not been aware of Rudy's decision when she did, definitely knew it was the second time someone had mentioned he was her stepbrother. The more she thought about things, the more she believed she was being played a fool. By absolutely everybody.

'No more.'

With Emily's quest taking priority of her thoughts, Yasmin dialled the bank where she had her Girl-Friday work experience, which led to her very first paying job, and meeting the Craige family. Knowing full well who the dear old man was, she prayed he hadn't retired. He was old back then! Listening to the receptionist's spiel, Yasmin finally got the chance to speak.

'Mr Taylor, please,' her voice very formal.

'Personal or business?' the voice stapled its way through the phone line.

'Business. Private and confidential business.'

Suddenly the voice had some warmth about it. 'One moment, please.'

The distinguished old man's voice boomed through the phone, 'This is Mr Taylor. To whom do I have the pleasure of speaking with?'

'My dear Mr Taylor, I am so relieved to hear your voice. Yasmin Pestel calling.'

'Ms Pestel!' he exclaimed, 'This is a surprise, I've got time to have a chat, have you?'

'Yes, I certainly do. Thank you!'

They spent the next forty minutes catching up on twelve years of absence, the changes in the local community and how Yasmin's business had commanded her attention with deliveries in the opposite direction. They shared respective condolences about the massive void in the volunteering community with the recent loss of his wife and the earlier losses of the three family members.

'You have some business to attend to in town?'

'Yes. Long overdue, but my mail had been intercepted. Until recently that is.'

'Oh. Oh, I see ... how is my favourite stray?'

'Not yet at peace. I am sorry to be the bearer of sad news, Mr Taylor, but he passed away. It's quite recent and not common knowledge given the circumstances.'

She dabbed at her eyes while listening to the older man's quiet sniffles, words of sympathy and melodic nose blowing. Eventually he composed himself and shared several amusing stories of Rudy's ruthless business strategies and his Midas touch gambles.

'Those are lovely memories, thank you,' sighing heavily. 'Did he confide in you?'

'Yes, yes he did.'

'That's good. I am glad he talked to someone.'

They got lost in their own thoughts before an old-man-cough dispelled the silence. 'What can I do for you?'

The words tumbled out. 'I need to withdraw a safe keeping box and plan on making a quick trip up and back tomorrow. Are you available?'

'I can be. Let's make it for 11:30am. From memory you're about four hours away. We'll complete our business giving you enough time to be home before sundown, but I will ask you to please consider having a meal with me sometime.'

'Absolutely! Thank you very much Mr Taylor, I look forward to seeing you in the morning.'

'Indeed, see you then Ms Pestel. Good bye.'

'Bye. Thank you.'

Running her hands through her hair, gasped at its dry, knotty condition. Easily convincing herself that anonymity was crucial for a longer road trip, let her fingers do the walking and secured an early—pay for the convenience—appointment with a hairdresser ninety minutes up the road. After listening to a rather long-winded, one-sided debate about synthetic and real human-hair wigs, settled on the latter.

'You wouldn't know of a dog groomer, would you?' Yasmin asked hopefully.

'Right next door, luv! Run by me daughter's family. Made sense given some dogs get pampered more often than their owners!'

'I'll pay the early fee if mine can be done at the same time please.'

'He'll be ready to go when you are! Discount for cash. See you tomorrow.'

'Thanks. Bye.'

Combo nudged the patio door. They took a steady jog around the yard finishing inside the packing shed. Waiting for the lights in the loft to warm up she looked across the floral abundance through watery eyes. Pam's incoming call caught her by surprise, but by the time she heard the chirpy voice the tears were gone.

'We were just talking about you Yasmin, and Nanna suggested we called. You're on speaker.'

'Hello lovely ladies,' she replied with an easy laugh.

'Do share! What are your plans?'

'I'll have a whack of cut flowers early Saturday morning which I want to donate to the hospital for appropriate distribution, then I've an appointment at 9:30am at the funeral parlour ... that sounds awful doesn't it? Anyway, about the flowers, do you think we can make it happen?'

'My word!' Nanna's jubilant voice was the loudest. 'Meet us at the canteen dock behind the hospital at eight o'clock. By the way, do you need a hand?'

'Thanks, but I should be okay.'

Her refusal was met with doubt until Helen steered the conversation towards joining them for a few hours afterwards, which she graciously accepted.

'By the way, have you heard about Carl?' Nanna asked bluntly.

'No, I do hope he is alright?'

'In health yes, abode no.' Her mischievous chuckle was contagious.

The older woman went on to explain that the house he had been renting had been sold a while back, but the new owners now wanted to move in before Christmas instead of afterwards. Therefore, the verbal agreement was no longer applicable.

'You're not letting him move back home then?' Yasmin asked cheekily.

The exaggerated coughs, splutters and chortles were entertaining in their own right. 'No, but if you need an independent security guard for a few weeks, he's available.'

Teasing the older woman about accentuating her son's independence but momma makes his arrangements, was also met with hilarity. The old dear went on to explain that Carl had taken annual leave so he could sort himself out.

'How independent is independent?'

'Completely! He's hiring a motorhome and staying at the local caravan park, although he did threaten to drop off his laundry.'

Her laughter peeled out loudly. Everyone joined in for several minutes adding their own bit of nonsense. For the first time in what felt like a long time, Yasmin could see a faint light at the end of the dark, cruel tunnel.

Feeling quite buoyed, she grinned at Combo's happy face. 'Nanna, please have Carl phone me tonight between seven and eight o'clock.'

'Thank you, dear, I look forward to seeing you on Saturday,' she said most appreciatively.

'You're welcome, thanks ladies, see you then. Oh, what can I bring?'

'The flowers!' came the resounding, unanimous reply.

They rung off after more shared laughter and nonsense. Playing tiggy with Combo between the rows released some of her pent-up anxiety, but breathing in the scented air lying on the cool soil gave way to a feeling of taking charge of her life.

Chapter 26

Giles waited solemnly outside the hospital for a taxi and gingerly patted the bandage around his head. The old, white-bearded man with the bulging shopping bag by his feet making small talk to pass the time, didn't help his mood.

'Which direction ya headin'?'

Giles grunted. 'East. Not that it's any of your business.'

'Mind if we share the ride?'

'Nuh. How far you going?'

'All the way to Moojie Hill.'

His eyebrows shot up. 'By taxi?'

'Yeah!'

'The cabbie will love you. Shouldn't go bragging about your wealth.' Giles flinched when he got jabbed in the ribs and grumbled, 'Easy, old timer.'

'It's me, you stupid prick!'

Giles shook his head in confusion. 'Stu? You hairy bastard! What the hell? I got KO'd and you're playing games! And I been interviewed by the city cops.'

'Did you spill?'

'Nuh. Stuck to our age-old plan and eventually remembered my name as Stewart Morgan, that's with an E and a W, whose wallet got nicked. Reckon I've got temporary am-amnesia.' He rubbed his head.

'Are you right to be discharged?'

'Yeah, been cleared of serious concussion and they needed a bed. Anyway, the government has donated fifty-five bucks to my taxi fare, just gotta convince the cabbie he'll be paid at the other end!'

'You gonna keep your mouth shut?'

'What you and I have done together, mate, I ain't about to divulge any secrets. But Ivan and Trav will be wanting your blood. The thought of Kohli freezes *my* blood and I sure as sitting here don't wanna think about Callum and definitely not Leigh. But will bet my life the twins will be grinding out a curse!'

'Tough titties, I ditched the burner phone. Listen mate, they've all got complacent and greedy and I'm tapping out. Reckon whoever carked it at the flower joint is going to be the beginning of the end, and I don't want to be caught up in any of it. Trying to help you if you're interested.'

'Can't. They've got me by the short and curlies.'

'They swiped the gear out of my clinic. Bastards killed my snake too.'

Giles simply nodded his head. 'Not surprised, bet you're relieved you didn't have any four-legged animals.'

They fell silent and watched a one-legged man confidently manoeuvre himself from a wheelchair into a waiting vehicle.

Giles eventually cleared his throat. 'How much did I tell you?'

'Not enough.' His mate's desperate look made Stu check himself. 'Mate, all you told me was someone forgot to pay his dues, and the flower lady had it stashed. Anything else you care to reveal?'

Giles sighed heavily. 'I can't.'

'Ivan scares the crap out of you, don't he?'

'Yep.' *And we've got a truckload of cash stashed for a rainy day.*

Stu checked his watch. Stood and held out his hand. 'Well, mate. I wish you all the best. I'm not going down with any of youse.'

'What about Moojie Hill?'

'I know where you all hang out.'

Here's a test for you, mate. Giles winked lazily. 'And the boogey-man?'

Stu grinned evilly. 'What boogey-man?'

Bet Leigh blabbed. 'Can I get a message to ya?'

'Nah.'

A silver-service taxi pulled up alongside. Stu peeled several green-backs and slipped them into Giles' hand when he helped him stand. Over his shoulder, he watched a nurse weave her way through the growing throng of patients and visitors, and grinned.

'Here's a couple of hunjies. You go on ahead.'

'Cheers mate! Dunno when I can pay you back.'

Stu shrugged, 'Wasn't mine in the first place. Catch ya later, mate.'

Once the door was shut, Giles leant over the front seat and dropped a one-hundred dollar note. 'Hey mate, can you do a loop? I wanna check something out.'

The driver pocketed the cash. 'You're the boss.'

From behind the hospital's concrete pillar, Stu waited until the taxi was out of sight then walked into the foyer and entered the men's facilities. Removing the white beard and applying a moustache, he slicked back his hair and pulled a cap down over his eyes. Unrolling the long grey jacket, slung it casually over his shoulder and stuffed the brown paper bag into the rubbish bin outside the main doors. At the nearest public phone box, he dialled the number committed to memory.

'Hey Trav ... yeah ... settle down and listen up. Giles is out of hospital and in a cab. Tell Ivan I slung him a few hunjies. Ciao!'

He dropped the hand piece and jogged over to a nurse with bright purple hair hailing a taxi.

The cab idled at the pedestrian crossing. Its meter ticking over with the ever-slow footfall of a family crossing in front of them.

'Hospitals, the great leveller,' the driver murmured.

With a clear view ahead, a man and a woman conversing beside another taxi drew their attention away from the flow of pedestrians. Giles leant forwards and chuckled.

'Hey mate, check out the colour of that nurse's hair!'

'I am! Would wolf-whistle if it were permitted these days, but the dude with the handlebar moustache looks positively evil.'

Giles covered his grin with his hand. 'Yeah.' *He's going to be.*

'Hope she knows what she's doing,' the driver muttered and accelerated slowly.

Catching a glimpse of the woman as they drove past, Giles bit back his gasp. *Penny?*

Chapter 27

Lining the three wheelie bins within throwing distance from the loft, Yasmin scaled the ladder and set about disposing the superfluous accumulation while deliberately averting her eyes away from Emily's trunk.

Working methodically with growing satisfaction of her progress, moved a bundle of new tarps still in plastic bags, revealing a bundle of timber legs nestled in another green sheet. Her stomach sunk. Crouching down to inspect them closer, Yasmin discovered they were Silky Oak, turned and varnished. The foam-lined box beside them contained gold-coloured hinges with matching screws, and a diagram on how to erect easels. Underneath them was a similar cardboard box containing monogrammed ovals with the letters R.J.M. in gold-paint. Just thinking about this *Rupert John Matson* turned her guts. The sheer weight of the box sent the last dregs of achievement plummeting to the ground.

The notion of spreading the foreign stuff around was completely opposite to Rudy's clinical compartmentalisation. One pile would have been so much kinder instead of cruelly chaining her to the emotional rollercoaster. Leaving the negative thoughts and the latest discovery where they were, continued with her task. Two more piles of old buckets and an unusual stack of polystyrene boxes standing on their ends to go, then she was done. With the rubbish being collected the following morning, it was going to be the start of a very long yet extremely successful day.

Frowning at the boxes, she automatically accused Rudy of more deception. Shaking her head, hit them all with her long stick before going anywhere near them. Three fell over completely. The others tipped at an angle. With the empty ones cleared out of the way, a single, unsealed, unmarked old packing box begged for her attention.

'What now?' she grumbled.

Sliding the carton under the light, unfolded the flaps and choked back a loud sob. Staring back at her with mesmerising blue eyes, a baby photo of a girl wrapped up in a pink paisley blanket. She looked like Emily, except her little nose was pointed.

After the box got kicked back to where it came from, clumsy robotic movements bounced off the numbness of Yasmin's hands and mind in her descent from the loft. Feeling as used and neglected as her plough-disc firepit, established a fire with the discarded items. Hungry flames curled old bits of cardboard before eating its way through the bundles of stale paper. Smoky tendrils reached for Yasmin no matter where she stood. Combo barked. She turned to see him silhouetted against the shed, larger than life.

'Yeah, I know you don't like the smoke. Well, I'm not liking much at the moment, but we do what we have to do.'

Standing further away from the pit, unceremoniously tossed the last of the dead seedlings into the smouldering embers. Combo rounded her up after she'd laid the long stepladder underneath the bench, ran to the caravan and jumped at its door. His patience dwindled while Yasmin fumbled for the spare key behind the tyre, and crawled underneath the caravan instead. He yapped excitedly. Seeing his tail swish from side to side, laid on her back and shuffled in beside him. Taped beside the faux covering, an envelope. A plain, normal envelope.

With the key now in her pocket and envelope in the tips of her fingers stormed towards the patio. Deep breaths barely abated the volatile emotions simmering like a bath of acid. Flicking her latest mail onto the table, ruffled Combo's head.

'We'll put the rubbish out first, boy.'

At the gate, she made him sit and wait while she jogged backwards for a bit then spun around.

'Race!'

They reached the patio at the same time.

With her back to the flower paddock and chest heaving, peeled open the envelope and slid out a solitary piece of A4 paper. No yacht. No rounded corners. Just a handwritten note centred perfectly on the page.

I am sorry Yasmin. One thing led to another under a new moon. The father's name
was never recorded at birth.
There will never be any claim to anything because it will be impossible to prove.
Believe me when I tell you I went by a completely different name for a very long
time. Then someone else took it.
None of them ever knew my real name, not even my surname.
It's not even engraved onto my death plaque.
I'm glad you finally stopped correcting the Johns' pair. Johns, not Jones, Yasmin.
Remember that.
She is not who she says she is. Nor is he. Remember that too.
I beg of you, please forgive me.
Rudy

Yasmin returned the note to the envelope, stalked inside with it and fully secured the cottage. Combo held her gaze until the bathroom door closed. Under a fall-blast cold shower, shards of a broken heart tore through her tear ducts.

Back in the lounge with pruney skin, Combo's head rested on her lap while she morosely smoothed the tuft of fur between his ears and thought long and hard about Rudy's funeral. Realistically it was an absolute waste of money to pay for a private service if he had already paid for the cremation and urn. Expectedly, she should attend the meeting on Saturday morning and dutifully report her findings afterwards. Scoffing at the clandestine investigation, her current frame of mind would not stand for anymore deception. Silence, except for the clunking clock stoic in its precision as comforting as a pianist's metronome.

Feeling liberated after letting Timmy's mobile phone calls go unanswered, her and Combo played chasey through the house before eating dinner. Cleaning up afterwards took longer than listening to the noncommittal messages. When the telephone rang at a quarter to eight, Yasmin made a mental note to get herself a new answering machine and picked up the handset hoping it would be Carl.

'Hello?'

'Ma'am! It's Carl Ramond.'

Her shoulders dropped in relief. 'Hey, hi! Can you give me a sec? I've just remembered something.'

She raced into the laundry, rifled through the dirty clothes pile and pulled out the crumpled business card. Combo, loving the idea of doing hallway zoomies, raced her back to the lounge and nestled back into the settee like he owned the world. She quietly pretend-kissed his head.

Stretching the phone's curly cord, positioned her laptop alongside on the recliner and got comfortable. 'Okay, I'm back. You sound nervous?'

'That's because I am.'

'Good, but please talk to me as a friend. I've got a question for you first.'

'Righto,' he replied affably.

'Hey, what's Forensic Detective Hillyer's story?'

'Huh? Oh, him. A city slicker casting an eye on how us country bumpkins do our job apparently.'

'Oh, how fun!' Yasmin slid the business card into the laptop's sleeve.

Carl chortled. 'Not really. I think you ought to know he was called back to the city which might delay what we've been working on.'

'Oh, work's work I suppose. Tell me, did you ever get hold of Stu?'

'Uh no, Ma'am. I can't say anymore so please don't ask me any questions.'

Yasmin smirked. 'Best you do the talking then.'

Carl stumbled over a few words before confirming what Nanna had explained. While he was describing his predicament in lengthy detail, Yasmin took the opportunity to catch up on e-mails. Delighted to have received the fencing quote and the discounted bottom line, simply loved the idea of the scalloped design along the length of the front lawn and clean lines along the hobby farm. The contractors could have the entire project completed in four weeks if she could commit within 48 hours and make a decision on the several driveway gate and shed security options in the same timeframe.

'What sort of motorhome do you have then, Carl?'

'A large, fully self-contained one. If I may utilise your washing line, all I need is power and water and I will pay for the privilege. I would be needing a place for several weeks leading to two months at this stage ... if that's not being too forward.'

'You don't think my property is too far out of town for conveniences and the like?'

'No way, Ma'am. I love space and my own company. I'll make sure I have ample supplies and will promise not to get under your feet. Although I suspect I'll have plenty of people willing to drop off food who will obviously want to see you!'

Yasmin smiled. 'Of course. What about company?'

'Can I have a dog? Please?'

'He would need to meet Combo first.'

'That's an easy fix.'

Carl's raw and honest enthusiasm buoyed her mood and explained the projects that required overseeing.

'I will pay you a retainer for the duration.'

'Um ... are you going somewhere?'

'Yes.'

After an awkward silence, they agreed to weigh up the options and discuss things in greater detail over the telephone the following evening.

Chapter 28

'Come here, handsome,' the expensive escort swaggered towards her long-standing, dashing client. 'Looks like you've had a hard day!'

Chas grinned slowly, 'Reckon you're gonna make it even harder.'

'Your wish is my command,' she cooed.

'I'm sure your price will meet my expectation.'

Slowly unbuttoning his shirt, she murmured seductively, 'When hasn't it?'

'Hmm, we'll be here for a while.'

'I'm happy to play housey, Mr Detective.'

He admired her nakedness and followed her into the sauna.

Chapter 29

Now sporting a wavy, shoulder length feminine hairstyle, her long-forgotten natural curls instantly resurrected, she could also competently smooth them down enough to wear the flowing auburn wig. For the first time since she was a kid, she had a fringe. For the first time in her life, she didn't have to be a blonde. Combo strutted in and balked.

'Haha! He did the Scooby-Doo thing!' the hairdresser burst out laughing.

The interaction between and him her French Poodle pup softened the icy edges of Yasmin's heart, more so when he had leaned into her after returning to her natural appearance.

Yet, the closer they got to her old stomping grounds, the more her jaw ached. Glad to have worn her navy blue and white collared dress with matching handbag and stilettos, she was also relieved she could still walk and drive in them! Praying the bank would accept the bandana around Combo's neck as an indicator of him being a comfort dog, they pushed through the tall, heavy timber doors and stepped inside the historic building. Absolutely nothing had changed. A young woman strutted towards them with a look of derision and spoke impolitely from a distance. Her words studded with the abrupt click of her stilettos on the polish tiled floor.

'Ma'am, this is not a park. No dogs allowed in here.'

If Combo could talk, he might have told her something different. *A dog?* How could this aromatic, handsome, pristine, protective bundle of fur, be *a dog?* Yasmin buried the urge to laugh. The stance of her pooch was a combination of absolute indignation and pride.

Following suit, she replied, 'I am a long-term customer of this bank and I have an appointment at 11:30am.' She looked at the grand old clock on the wall. 'Which is right now.'

No sooner had she said that, Mr Taylor purposely strode towards them with his hand outstretched and a welcoming smile.

Wrapping his hands around Yasmin's, he greeted her warmly. 'Ma'am, welcome. It is good to see you again. You're right on time, come with me please.'

Ushering them to his office, he stood aside. Speaking in a subdued voice, 'Won't be a moment, Ms Pestel, please take a seat.'

It was none of her business what he was going to say to the staff member, so she did and suddenly realised her face ache was from the clenched teeth. Combo stood in the doorway and sighed when Mr Taylor coughed and closed the door behind him.

'You are a handsome fella! And a very warm hello to you, my dear!' He clasped Yasmin's hand and drew her upwards into a hug.

'Mr Taylor, it is so good to see you. Please excuse me, I didn't mention I'd be bringing Combo with me.'

He hushed her gently and encouraged her to be comfortable. 'It's quite okay! Rudy had told me all about your shadow. And I love dogs.'

His look of compassion almost undid her steely resolve but the moment he handed her his handkerchief; she failed to withhold the flow of tears. Patting her hand, he talked at great length about her own parents and the nonsense the long-term friends had gotten up to in their younger days. The tales swiftly curtailed any further waterworks.

'It's high time you knew that you got that job on your own accord all those years ago!'

Yasmin thanked him for his kindness, then steered the conversation back to the topic at hand. 'What else did Ru share with you, Mr Taylor?'

'His aliases, adultery, guilt and absolutely everything in between including his passion for gold, timber, art, travel and helicopters.'

Yasmin opened and closed her mouth like a fish out of water.

'I was his confidant and it's too early to talk about all this, Ms Pestel. Let's talk about it at another time.'

'Please pardon any unintended petulance but it is definitely not too early to talk about all of this. Yes, Emily is my priority, but before we chat more about her brother, I do have a question.'

'Only one,' he looked at her sternly.

She returned his look. 'You said aliases, plural. Let's start with Rupert—'

The old man aged ten years in front of her. 'Never ever speak his full name.'

Yasmin released her breath slowly.

'Dash it all.' Mr Taylor's heavy sigh took a long time to dispel. 'I concede. You need to know some things which are not going to be easy to hear. I take it you have learnt about the offspring?'

'Yes.'

His aging voice and hands shook a little, while explaining that he and Rudy spoke every day even the morning of his passing.

'You did? How?' Yasmin exclaimed.

His look of compassion instantly blurred when the answers dawned on her. *The landline. I wasn't at home.*

The dear man's slightest nod confirmed the wordless statement. He then explained that two women only knew Rudy by the tri-name alias, and he knew he was playing a very dangerous game of ménage à trois. That aside, both were pregnant at the same time. An unfamiliar man had come into the meld much the same time but got particularly friendly with the daughter of the older women upsetting Rudy awfully, until he discovered some things about the man's sordid past and devised a plan. The man morphed into the new R.J.M. Apparently, both women were so addicted to something they didn't know who was what, when or where. As the pregnancies developed, Rudy was on to the conman's shenanigans and avoided all interaction to the best of his ability and left him with the women and offspring.

Yasmin subconsciously rubbed her arms to smooth the goosebumps.

'You may recall he didn't want much to do with a Leigh and Callum Johns?'

'I'm not so sure about that. But I sure as heck want nothing to do with them.'

'Good.'

'But the name? Why?'

'I asked the very same question. Regularly.'

'And?'

Mr Taylor wiped his eyes. 'At first, he wanted to know how it felt to play games. To remember how to have fun. Comprehend why you enjoyed them so much. He did admit he had fun coming up with the name. Anyway, time marched on and he got caught up in his own dimension. Sorry, dear, but you became an unsuspecting player in the most important game of your life.'

She coughed. 'Is that it?'

With raised eyebrows and peering over his glasses, he simply stated, 'For now.' Then, leant across the table and patted her hand. 'You are here for Emily today. How about we focus on her, hmm? She was such a darling girl,'

She squeezed his gently and nodded politely. 'Yes, she was. My only true friend. My best friend.' Combo's noisy utterance made them both smile. 'Now this four-legged blessing is my best friend!'

Ears pricked, he stood with front paws resting on Mr Taylor's desk, who grinned and said, 'Perhaps her spirit lives within!'

'Scary that he knows so much English!'

Combo settled and the light-hearted interlude disappeared into the memory banks.

'I am sorry you have to tie up the loose ends after all these years, more so because we saw the parents' coffins lowered ... now they're cremated.'

Yasmin's eyes bulged. 'Pardon?'

Shaking his head and tutting in concern, 'Goodness child, you look as pale as anything. Oh dear, another secret. You recall I laid my wife to rest?'

'Yes, I am so sorry. How are you coping, Mr Taylor?'

He dabbed at his eyes. 'My grip has only marginally lessened on the edges of that emotional rollercoaster.'

She sympathised with a knowing smile.

'Anyway, I visit my bride every Sunday with her favourite flowers and tell her about my days ... old habits ... but five months ago, I noticed an exhumation being conducted behind a hessian barricade six rows down. I'm never in a hurry to leave and often say prayers to all the souls around her and encourage them to party the way we used to.'

Yasmin scratched her head. 'Five months ago?'

'Ms Pestel, the caretaker is ... never mind, I'm going to cut a long story short. The caretaker told me that it was Mr and Mrs Craige's exhumation. There had been a mix up in their wishes and it was overdue.'

'Where are the ashes?'

'Rudy collected them the Sunday afterwards.'

'A quick turnaround?'

'Money talks. Nevertheless, I watched him weave his way through the cemetery until he stood in front of me and said he was sorry. But it was his eyes. They were worse than I'd ever seen them before.'

Yasmin got up and poured a glass of water, then stood beside him while he gripped her hand. He explained how Rudy had looked like a dead man walking. Void of expression, pallid complexion and hugging the urns like no tomorrow.

'Oh, Mr Taylor, I am so sorry you had to see that. I truly am.'

'I will find a younger photo of the whole family as a reminder of who they were in their prime and share it with you. That is the image we need to remember them by, Ms Pestel,' he said and patted her hand in his comforting grandfatherly manner.

She smiled at him tenderly and dabbed at her own eyes. 'I would like that very much, thank you.'

'Come along, let's get down to business.'

At the fourth row of the vault, Yasmin handed him the key.

'I'm glad it is you fulfilling this quest, my dear.'

'I'm not sure how I'm supposed to feel, yet here I be!'

Mr Taylor presented her a long stainless-steel box before escorting her to a matching bench, laid a bank bag on it and told Combo to *stay* – who did by sitting on Yasmin's foot.

'Ring the bell when you're ready, I'll be waiting out here.'

With the lid removed, scoffed lightly at Emily's typical style of everything being neatly packed. Eleven jewellery boxes including two navy blue ones, her lacy makeup bag, treasured mother-of-pearl manicure set and a set of seven miniature French perfume bottles sat atop six brown envelopes and a white one with Yasmin's name neatly printed on its face. Underneath everything sat an impervious vacuum-packed bag. Emily's beautiful handwriting covered a small lavender-coloured note. *Aunt Polly always said a lady needed her own independence, so here's $200K just for you. XOXO*

Biting back a surprised gasp, Yasmin's eyes fell upon the lacy makeup bag and nibbled at her bottom lip. She wound back the years to when they shared girly secrets of where they would hide messages or emergency money. The memory came flooding back. Unclipping the delicate mother-of-pearl makeup compact and using the tip of the matching tweezers, out popped the mirror. A short, sudden laugh combined with a sob echoed when she discovered the multi-folded Kit Kat wrapper. Wiping at the tears, remembered how the gorgeous woman loved her Kit Kats and would never share them. To prevent anyone asking for a chocolate strip, she bit right across all of them. In her handwritten note slightly larger than a postage stamp, were Dean's contact details. Yasmin sniffled then grinned and ruffled Combo's head. They were definitely going on an independent road trip. Making sure there was absolutely nothing left in the box, she put all the contents in the bank bag and held it close to her chest.

At the sound of the ringing bell, Mr Taylor arose from the chair with his hands clasped together. 'Are you okay?'

Clearing her throat softly, 'Yes, thank you. Would it be inappropriate to sit in your office and read some correspondence?'

'Not at all. Will you allow me to take Combo for a walk? I'll come back with coffee and perhaps a treat,' he said kindly.

'Of course! We would love that.'

The moment the door closed, Yasmin opened her envelope. There was no doubt about the instructions. Her eyes almost popping out of their sockets by the time she had finished reading the last of Emily's informative, incontestable document. While being the soul heiress to Emily's fortune, she certainly had some wishes to fulfill. Two bank accounts were to be established with $5.25 million bequeathed to Dean and Herbie, along with Emily's chalet in the Austrian Alps. A separate bank account purely for Herbie's medical costs earning interest on its $900,000 original balance.

Yasmin inherited Emily's leased penthouse suite in Koloa, Hawaii. She giggled then sobbed when she read the note in the margin, *summer all year round, just for you*. A birthday account had been established in her full name with an opening balance of $300,000, nine years earlier. Her own inherited amount was a staggering $36.45 million. What she did with the jewellery was entirely her decision.

Paperclipped to the bottom of the last page, a folded note.

Dear Yasmin,

Yes, my parents are extremely well off, clever with money and associated investments. I learnt a lot from Aunt Polly as you have discovered. She already has her envelope. Art can be challenging. I do suggest you learn about real estate. It is so easy, and so much fun, and you get to travel! The lease will run out, so do something for yourself for a change. Even if you don't get to see the penthouse, it truly is an amazing part of the world. There is a gentle giant who is fairly high up with the locals; he is the man to see.

Anyway, I had no idea how wealthy Mum and Dad were until they sat with me one week before I turned 30 and explained my pending wealth. I was astonished. How I wish I could have told you this in person. So sad. All that aside, Mum and Dad inherited their fortunes from several family members as they each were the only living offspring to very large families. Like you, did what they loved and loved what they did and their wealth increased. Clearly, they did not have to work as hard as they did and very few people are aware of their actual fortune. I am privileged and honoured to be able to share mine with you. As you have read, I have successfully done that, and happily!

Although you ought not need to know the contents of the mail that does not concern you, please be assured there shall not be any claim to theirs or yours.

Should I be unable to, I implore you to action the bank accounts for MY snow man and son at your earliest opportunity, then find him or at least phone him. If you are reading this, I know you found our girly hiding spot and probably laughed then sobbed when you saw the wrapper. By the way, I will always eat Kit Kats like that! You never liked anybody touching your pillows, well nobody gets to touch my Kit Kats.

Thank you for being in my life and for being a part of my life. Gosh, this sounds so formal but there is never a bad time to say that to someone. I love you like a sister and you are my only true best friend, plus I miss you like crazy.

Emily xoxo

P.S. If this is not Yasmin Rose Pestel reading my correspondence, hand everything over to the manager of the bank immediately and hang your head in shame.

Yasmin jumped when Combo woofed softly. She could taste the coffee from its aromatics alone, and stood to close the door.

'He loved his puppy-cino!' Mr Taylor grinned.

'No doubt he'll love you more if that's a Vanilla Slice in there,' she dabbed at her eyes gently.

'It is. After all these years, their slices are still better than their cakes!' he chuckled softly. 'Where are we up to?'

'Some pressing business matters to address.'

'Under direct instruction from the late Miss Emily Craige only, I presume?'

'The one and only!'

Aged hands drifted lightly over the keyboard.

After confirming the surname of the account holders, Mr Taylor paused and looked at her sternly. 'Thank you. One moment while I familiarise myself with the details.'

'Okay.' Bewildered, Yasmin scratched her head.

The coffees and sweet treat were consumed in silence while absorbing themselves with their respective tasks at hand. Yasmin silently promising Emily her wishes would be fulfilled one way or another.

The dear old man smiled broadly. 'I will not disclose how these were established prior; however, I formerly announce your accounts are active. Additionally, you have successfully activated the other accounts with a statement needed to be delivered to the account holders. Are you able to action this directive, Ms Pestel?'

'Yes, Mr Taylor, I most certainly will be! I may even be able to fulfil the obligations by this time next week.' Yasmin twitched her lips at the sound of the printer working its magic.

He looked at her with tenderness and twinkling eyes. 'Emily would be thrilled, bless her beautiful soul, particularly as it'll be the son's birthday.'

'What shall I tell them?' Yasmin whispered.

'The truth,' he suggested matter-of-factly and put the documents into an envelope, handed it over along with a brown paper grocery bag. 'Would rather you put the bank bag into a more inconspicuous one.'

Polite small talk and well-meant paternal advice was received graciously while she filled the bag appropriately. Thanking him for everything and promising to stay in touch, also assured him it would be a privilege to join him for a more substantial meal. They clasped hands firmly before dabbing at their eyes respectively. She watched his broad smile further crease his soft, aging skin while he ruffled Combo's fur and shook his paw.

Proudly escorting his visitors towards the main doors of the bank, held them open as any gentleman would expect a lady to accept, smiled and murmured, 'Thank you for doing what you are going to do.'

Yasmin smiled and nodded, not trusting herself to speak at that moment.

'Go well, dear lady, and have a wonderful time. Thank you for your business.'

She stood there for several minutes before whispering, 'Thank you, kind sir. All the best to you too. Talk soon.'

Taking a different route home and well over an hour into the trip, she was famished. Discovering that travelling with a comfort dog actually had its perks, they were able to enjoy their hearty truck stop meal without too much attention.

Eat where the truckies eat is the golden rule for good food. Yasmin had read the quip somewhere, and again, it proved to be accurate. Stretching their legs with a quick walk through the well-established town, they happened upon a recognised RV motorhome hire company. Considering Carl's excitement about his hired one, she made a decision instantly. Having a large map of Australia on the wall nearest to the enquiries counter made it so much easier to plan her adventure, particularly as there was another agency en route to Victoria.

Discussing the various options with the pimply lad behind the counter, Combo kept pressing into her legs. Yasmin turned around and noticed an athletic man studying a large map on the wall behind them. With his right hip dropped and hands-on-hips stance, reminded her of a revoltingly crude bully from high school. She automatically turned her nose up in disgust at the exact moment he turned around. His look of amusement made her blush.

'Do I remind you of someone?' he asked.

His small voice caught her by surprise. 'Only until you spoke. Don't mind us. Have a good day.' Yasmin clicked her tongue to get Combo's attention, turned away and flashed a dazzling smile at the shop assistant. 'Can I have my comfort dog in any of these?' she asked quietly.

He draped himself over the counter to be met with Combo looking directly at him.

'Aww he's smiling! Sorry miss, but not from us. There is an independent one near the Bridge ... here's their card. I think they do. I can phone them for you?'

'Thanks all the same. We need to get going.'

'Righteo. It's a great day to have a great day!'

'Thanks! I like that one.'

Combo flatly refused to go near the passenger side the van. He sat at the driver's door, one paw raised, ears rigid. Yasmin opened her door, scoffing quietly when he bounded straight over to his seat. 'You have been spoilt today, mister!'

Behaving himself while he got clipped in, she smothered a giggle at her own inability to contain her emotions. Ignoring the chime on the mobile phone, drove away without a backward glance. Ten minutes into the trip, she rolled her eyes and answered the unidentified incoming call.

'Hello?'

'Don't believe everything you hear or see—'

'Who is this?' she demanded of the muffled male voice.

'I know who you are and where you live—'

'Stu? Is that you?'

'Stop bloody-well interrupting me, woman!'

'Give it up, Stu. All you're doing is pinging me off. And if you're stalking me, I'll sic the cops onto you which will make them happy because they are looking for you.'

'I am not Stu. I am the boogey-man.'

'Well, you can just boogey off.' Yasmin stabbed at the disconnect icon.

The phone rang instantly. She declined the call. After the third occasion, pulled off the road, switched off the mobile phone and took several deep breaths.

'No. I call the shots from here on.'

Instead of pondering, or hanging around, Yasmin told Combo exactly what she was planning to do. The closer they got to their cottage, the more he relaxed and the greater her excitement built. Parking inside the packing shed as the shadows lengthened across the property, Combo investigated his domain while Yasmin set up the watering system before securing the valuable documents. Disabling her ID, she dialled the number to the independent motorhome company and had changed into her gardening clothes by the time the call was answered.

'This is Duke.'

'Hi, this is Ms Rose, do you hire dog-friendly motorhomes?'

The man laughed. 'Sure do, it's me bread and butter. A lot of ex-servicemen need a get-away with their best mates.'

'That's sweet. Do I have to pre-arrange or can I just pitch up? Like really early next week?'

'Depends on your choice of vehicle. Discount for cash.'

'Nice!'

Yasmin described the 4-berth motorhome she had instantly liked. Confirming he had a similar one available with a larger water tank, he was ecstatic to hire it to her and her dog for four weeks.

'Lady, I'll even throw in a bottle of wine in the fridge for ya! Red or white?'

'White, please.'

'Done.'

'Nice!'

'Do you smoke?'

'No.'

'Too easy. Got one here with your name on it.'

'Lovely, thank you. Oh, can you stash my little van somewhere out of the weather please? I'll pay you extra for the convenience or inconvenience and intend on arriving early in the morning.'

Duke's booming laugh punctuated his reply. 'Cash is king! Gates open at six o'clock. Speed safely!'

For the first time in a very, very long time, Yasmin did her and Emily's twirling happy jive and sang their silly little ditty when they eventually got their licenses, on the same day. *Yay! Today is the first day of the rest of my life, and I know how to drive!*

In the fast fading dance of daylight, racing Combo through the last six rows and down the driveway to retrieve the bins Yasmin had an epiphany. Five cartons of hastily bought mixed acrylic vases were finally going to a new home! As soon as they were stacked neatly into her van and the shed lights extinguished, Combo initiated another race. This time to the rose garden and back. He came to a skidding stop near the fire pit and sniffed the air furiously. Yasmin caught up to him. Together they followed a delicate fragrance around the back of the sheds, among the irrigation pipework, then a merry dance towards the little caravan and back to the fire pit where a light breeze took the scent away.

Bewildered, the pair walked around the cottage before standing on the patio. Listening. Inhaling deeply. They were surrounded by silence and a ceiling of stars. Yasmin was just about to unlock the patio door when something drifted across her right cheek, almost like a warm breath. A sense of calm swept over her. It felt like her best friend's ghost had let her know she was doing the right thing. Combo sat quietly at her feet looking around swishing his tail. Yasmin couldn't stop smiling. Locking the doors behind them, he automatically raced around conducting a search-and-find mission while she drew the curtains in the living area.

It was five minutes to eight when the landline rang.

With Combo leaning against her legs, she answered cautiously. 'Hello?'

'Hi Ma'am! It's me, Carl. Have I caught you at a good time?'

Yasmin smiled and ruffled Combo's head and pointed towards the couch.

'Yes. Let's thrash out the nitty gritty while I get myself something to eat.'

'Sure thing. Um, how are you going to do that while you're on the phone?'

'Easily. The curly cord reaches the kitchen!'

'So cool! What are you having?'

'An egg cooked in a sauteed ring of capsicum, grilled tomato, bacon of course, all sprinkled with parsley on a slice of toasted Turkish bread.'

'Oh yum! Do you deliver?'

After sharing a hearty laugh and an hour later with her appetite dealt with accordingly, they reached an agreement.

'Can I let my bosses know, please?'

'Yeah okay. Hey Carl, I will not be talked out of anything. You hear me?'

'Wouldn't dream of it.'

'Good. And Combo needs to meet your dog.'

'Yes, he does. Have you bought yourself a new phone?' he asked candidly.

'No, not yet. I'll have my business phone with me. Anybody who wants to get in touch with me has that number as well.'

'Yeah, but you haven't got a back-up and you're travelling. I reckon you should get yourself another phone.'

'What's your dog's name?'

'You just changed the subject!' His voice sounded like Kermit. When Yasmin didn't respond, he said normally, 'Radar. It's Radar, Ma'am. As good as Radar on M.A.S.H.'

'Cool name! Make a plan and while you're speaking with the sergeants, please ask one of them to contact me in order to make arrangements for when I am in town this Saturday.'

'Certainly. Night Ma'am and thank you so much. I won't let you down.'

They eventually rung off after a thousand more thanks.

Yasmin sent an e-mail to the fencing contractor and requested the bank details for a forty percent deposit. They would be expected to commence the project on Monday. She received the response from the contractor at the same time she completed reviewing the paid company extract of their business. There weren't any familiar names, but the document went into the project folder along with the scope and quote. They didn't need to know the profession of the site supervisor!

When the telephone jangled a little while later, she suspected it would be from one of the sergeants. Answering it pleasantly, she smiled at Sergeant Kohli's deep voice.

'Evening, Ms Pestel.'

'Good evening, Sir, all's well in this neck of the woods.'

'Excellent. Carl has jubilantly shared the good news, uh, thanks for giving him the opportunity.'

'It's a win-win, Sergeant Kohli. Can I take you up on your offer of socialising Combo with your K9s, please?'

'Definitely. The A.V.O. paperwork will be ready for your signature and I'll be at HQ by ten hundred hours. Does that suit?'

Yasmin confirmed it did, then explained her schedule for the day and went on to describe the morning tea kindness from earlier in the week and offered to return the favour if he thought it appropriate. Accompanying his rumbling chuckle, the suggestion of either a chocolate cake or a dozen chocolate eclairs was warm and encouraging.

'Sir, were you able to apprehend the culprits who broke in?'

His pause lasted just a fraction too long. Eventually, he cleared his throat. 'Not yet. Has the local vet contacted you?'

Yasmin answered a little bit too loudly. 'No! Why? Why do you ask?'

'Should he do so, would you tell him it is in his best interest to make contact with us, please?'

'Of course.' Combo jumped up and put his paws on her hips. 'Um, how do I go about getting an official harness for Combo as a comfort dog?'

'Leave that with me, Ms Pestel,' he offered, then asked firmly, 'What are your plans?'

'A road trip.'

'Hmm, you would make for a strong opponent in a game of poker!'

'Oh, that I do.'

'All I ask is you check in regularly,' he said quietly.

'Thank you for caring, Sergeant Kohli.'

They disconnected the call simultaneously. Yasmin squealed delightedly and hugged Combo. A quick game of zoomies outside was halted by the peculiar fragrance and again, a warm, gentle breath of wind caressed her cheek. Combo stood on his hind legs and buried his head into her tummy in true sooky-doll fashion. While soothing his fur, Yasmin hoped everything was going to work out and noisily pretend-kissed her treasured pooch.

Chapter 30

With his lips pressed together, Sergeant Kohli looked across his desk at the undercover agent.

'Me thinks Ms Pestel has got a guilty conscience,' Penny said quietly.

'Yeah. My instincts are telling me the same. You already have her tailed?'

Penny's smirk was answer enough.

He shook his head knowingly. 'It's high time your boss knew about this thing you've got going, young lady.'

'Yeah, I know. It's getting harder every year! Although, this is my annual holiday and a great cover. By the way, what do you reckon about my hair?'

A broad grin lit up his meaty face. 'Very purple, Penny!'

'Turn around until I say when.'

'Okay, you're on!' Sergeant Kohli had become accustomed to his friend and colleague's game over the years and was always amazed at how her appearance could change so swiftly.

After a couple of minutes, she asked her question again. 'By the way, what do you reckon about my hair?'

This time, his breath caught in his throat. 'My God. I didn't know black could be so black! But what the hell have you done with your eyes?'

'Yeah, it took a long time but I'm really happy with it. It's real hair you know!'

'Your eyes?'

'All part of the gig. Time me for me to be somewhere else. Keep your ears on!'

He caught her blown kiss and put it in his top pocket. 'Be careful, Penny.'

Her typical reply was to curtsy, giggle and walk out backwards. She didn't let him down. Rubbing his forehead, he shook his head again and prayed under his breath. The same one he had said for the last thirteen years.

***

The red glow of a flicked cigarette caught Penny's eye when she stepped out of her car. Groaning inwardly, tucked a strand of hair from the black wig behind her ear, forced a smile on her face and approached the man as he pushed himself away from her pottery-art façade.

'What are you up to, Callum?'

'Aw pretty Penny, how'd you know it was me?'

'Just a lucky guess! What are you doing here anyway?'

'Just came to make sure you're joining us again at Moojie?'

'Haven't let you down so far. What's the goss?'

'Trav and Ivan are at each other's throats. Giles and Stu … well, they've been very silly boys. Leigh is beyond testy. Say, Pen, what's your take on the boogey-man?'

She took a staggered step. 'Geez, Callum! What the hell?'

'Just wanted your view.'

Her voice came out as a shrill. 'The same as it's always been. I don't want to know!'

'Okay, okay, keep it down. I'll let the crew know to expect the Goth chick. Hope you and Stu finally tie the knot. He's been hanging on your love for a long time!'

'Just have to wait and see. Night Callum. Don't visit me again please. You still creep me out when you wear that silly suit when it's not even winter!'

Keeping to the shadows, his hearty laugh echoed off the tin-walled path. 'Still keepin' our secret. See ya at Moojie pretty Penny with her pottery.'

'I'll be seeing you,' Penny called after him.

Slipping inside the concealed door before the alarms activated, the anticipated message on the encrypted laptop set her plan in concrete.

| Parcel located | Track and trace successful | Green light | Out ||

Chapter 31

A vehicle spun its wheels not far from the gateway startling them knee deep in the pruned snapdragons. Yasmin issued the 'Race' command but by the time they reached the roadside, there was nothing to see. Nothing, except a burnt caramel glow splitting the horizon and heaven. With Combo on high alert attached to a retractable leash, by the time daylight graced their world only the Queen Elizabeth Roses remained. And a lingering suspicion of who would be snooping around.

Dowsed in ambrosial perfume, not even gazing through nature's wallpaper into the tinted cotton-wool ball clouds with Combo's silhouetted head like a weird umbrella subdued the persistent goosebumps. When her best friend sat with both ears pricked, eyes scanning and nostrils deciphering the abundant scents, he was not to be disturbed. After several prayers and less tears, she swiftly finished the task at hand.

Combining years of experience with her proficient technique, the sight of the van's rear interior had the desired therapeutic effect. After several wardrobe failures, she finally settled on a yellow and white polka dot dress with capped sleeves. It, like the rest of her pretty things, was practically brand new although having hung in the wardrobe for over nine years. Feeling quite brave, alarms set to audible, Yasmin took on the day.

By the time they reached the town's outer limits, her nerves had put Combo on edge who snapped at every oncoming vehicle. Pulling alongside the dock behind the hospital, her angst radiated as brightly as her face. Nanna's grounding advice combined with genuine friendly nonsense when she told them the next stop was the bakery helped stabilise her confidence and Combo's agitation. With the cardboard cake box concealing the ganache covered chocolate sponge secured in the back, she lowered the temperature-control and interpreted Combo's penetrating look and raspberry-sigh as an expression of indignation.

'I'm sure you'll have plenty of doggy-treats today, my boy.'

Perfectly manicured lawns beside the curved decorative driveway of the Gentle Rest Funeral Home didn't ease her angst. The beds of daisies and variety of lilies surrounding a massive fig tree left her feeling confused. If the place didn't overflow with grief, the garden would be wonderful to walk through and that tree would be awesome to climb.

Combo strained to get out the driver's side of the car and shivered and panted. Straightening his bandana and gently cupping his head, she held his gaze and whispered that he had to be a good, quiet boy. It was when she straightened her dress she noticed the tremble in her hands. His soft growl brought her attention to an older, tall, yet stocky man dressed in an ill-fitting black suit and rapidly tied tie. He approached them with a peculiarly happy gait. She got the heebie-jeebies straight away. It wasn't just his build that appeared unusual for someone who worked in the funeral industry. His grey toupee didn't sit right. His blotchy knuckles looked painful when he adjusted the starched collar of the whitest-of-white shirt.

He stopped short and called out softly, 'Ms Pestel, I'm Clive. I'm a dog person more than a cat person and would be happy to meet your boy if he'll allow me.'

Combo's leant harder into her legs. His tail didn't wag. They took a step backwards when he stepped forwards.

'Hello Clive. No, he isn't friendly today,' she replied firmly.

'Okay.' His voice changed to that of an animated boy, and patted his quads, 'But gosh you are a handsome boy! Come puppy, shake? Puppy, puppy, here boy!'

With teeth bared and shackles upright, Combo kept turning his head away from the man's extended hands who eventually stood and focussed on her. Behind his large square glasses, the googly eyes conveyed comfort when he spoke, yet the hypnotic rhythm of his voice made her own fill with tears. She cleared her throat, accepted the pressed and neatly folded handkerchief he presented, and dabbed gently at her eyes.

She smiled as best as she could. 'If troubles are halved when they're shared, perhaps sharing grief with strangers provides greater comfort to our own souls.'

His eyes never left her face. 'That's very profound and Rupert's not suffering anymore. But you have a good dog here and are watched over.'

Her stomach tightened.

'I would like to see the official paperwork.'

'Oh, I am surprised you haven't received it,' a slight edge had crept into his voice.

Making a show of adjusting her handbag, looked at him squarely. 'I presume you were paid when the casket and urn were chosen?'

'Yes.'

'Was a funeral service paid for?'

'No.'

Shrugging, 'I don't want a private ceremony or service. Would you please go ahead with the cremation per his wishes? And I would still like to see the plaque.'

A strange veil fell across Clive's face. The look of comfort turned to steel for a split second, then in the repetitive hypnotic voice said, 'That wouldn't be very fitting, Ms Pestel, not fitting at all.'

'Why?'

'It's a most unusual request. I will have to ask my superiors when we're next scheduled to use the incinerator.'

'The what?'

'Bones need an extremely high temperature to return to ashes, Ms Pestel,' he casually explained.

'You do several bodies at once?'

'Goodness, no!'

Annoyance, discomfort and distrust swirled through her bloodstream.

'Your body language is practically shouting at me! Relax, I'm not going to bite you or your dog!'

She hadn't remembered folding her arms across her chest. 'Let me get this straight. We have the funeral service, with a priest, hymns, the private chapel for one kin and her dog, then wait how long for the ashes of a poor soul for a cost of how much?'

'Let's go inside, we can talk better there,' Clive went to usher her inside.

He swiftly withdrew when Combo growled his warning.

'You really must refrain from approaching either of us. We prefer the out-doors.'

They eyeballed each other steadily until he broke the gaze and looked over her shoulder. His voice lacked emotion. 'Of course. An account will be sent if there are additional costs.'

'When will the ashes be available?'

'Seven to ten days is normal, but it could also be up to three weeks,' his voice alternated between calm and shaky.

'Can you tell me what type of urn I am to expect?'

'A stainless-steel one.'

Her breath stuck in her throat. 'And the plaque?'

Clive looked at her quizzically. 'The same.'

She pinched the bridge of her nose. 'I am going to have to get my head around all this. Cancel the service. This is just all too much,' and bit back a sob.

Combo whined and blocked her path at the same time Clive took a step forward. Then a larger one backwards. 'It's okay to cry. You're still grieving. We can talk again next week.'

'I'll get your handkerchief back to you when it's laundered. Good bye.' Yasmin dabbed her eyes, screwed them up squeezing out as many tears as possible.

Combo sneezed, snarled loudly and balked at Clive who had moved closer. Yasmin shook her head angrily and retreated to the driver's side. Whatever Combo said worked a treat because Clive was nowhere to be seen by the time they were on their way. Only securing her beloved companion halfway down the driveway, drove to the K9 headquarters with stinging eyes. Combo, abnormally quiet with head turned away, sneezed frequently and messily. Trying to console him talked softly the entire time, but still he ignored her.

Once she had straightened up her reversed parking attempt, her eyes felt almost normal, wrapped her hands around her pooch's face firmly having to turn his head to look at her. He sneezed violently. Using the borrowed handkerchief, wiped her own face and reached for the box of tissues for Combo. It was only then that Yasmin noticed the tear tracks down his furry face. Sobbing, she wiped them away apologising the whole time. He eventually put his paw on her thigh and rested his head on her shoulders, making her cry louder. His thumping tail against the door panel encouraged her to look up. Carl was striding towards them. Combo wriggled free and stood on the auto window controls, doing his utmost to scramble outwards barking madly.

Grabbing at his harness, Yasmin yelled, 'Combo! Enough!' He ignored her and kept barking.

Carl barked back. Silence fell over the carpark.

'Sorry. Glad he's happy to see you. I'm a bit of a mess and made him sad too.'

'Allow me to take him for a walk to have a sniff around. We'll be within view. Take your time.'

She unlocked the doors. 'Hey, I thought you were on holidays!'

'I am!'

No sooner was Combo out of the car, he vomited. Yasmin shrieked, grabbed her water bottle and dashed out to comfort him.

'Ma'am, it's bile? How come he's been crying?'

While pouring some water onto the hem of her dress, wiped his face again and described Combo's reaction each time Clive approached them.

Yasmin gasped. 'He leant me his hanky! My eyes!'

'Have you still got it?' he blinked as rapidly as he spoke.

'Yes ... oh Combo, I'm so sorry boy.' Her bottom lip quivered, blinked away the brimming tears and emptied the bottle over her hands.

'Hey, hey, stop punishing yourself. Their senses are a thousand times better than ours, that's all,' Carl said reassuringly. 'Hey! You've got a new hairdo. Looks great, Ma'am.'

At that moment, they all stared at the impenetrable tinted windows of a cream-coloured sedan driving slowly through the carpark before it disappeared around the back of the building. Combo sniffed the air furiously. Yasmin frowned at the obscured number plate and lack of mudflaps, then found a resealable bag in the glove box and handed it to Carl. He looked at her like she was insane. Shrugging her shoulders, dropped in the semi-sodden handkerchief.

'I only dabbed at my eyes! Oh, and wiped my face from Combo's sneeze.' Yasmin said almost sarcastically, 'I didn't blow my nose.'

His look of disdain melted into relief.

'As if I'd hand you a ... oh, never mind,' she flinched when Combo barked twice and wagged his tail.

'Come inside, Ma'am, you can freshen up before your next appointment. I'll take that bag and look after Combo while you're doing so.' Carl suggested as he saluted the approaching senior officer.

'Coffee?' Sergeant Kohli asked, sporting a broad grin.

'Yes please, with cake!' she replied immediately and used the back of her hand to wipe the tears.

'Sergeant Pyers will join us shortly.'

With Combo at his heels, Carl did the honours of retrieving smoko. On their way to the staff entrance, duly brought Kohli up to speed who grunted in acknowledgement. Yasmin disappeared down the hallway to the facilities and made herself as respectable as she possibly could.

Waiting for her in the office overlooking a lovely, grassed area with shelters, was a very welcome cup of coffee and the chocolate cake already sliced. She didn't need to say anything, her grin spoke volumes. Combo stood on his hind legs and gently laid across her lap when she sat down. Praising him gently nodded her thanks to Carl who encouraged her pooch to hop down.

'Nice to see you again, Ms Pestel. How'd you go at the funeral home?' Sergeant Pyers asked when he walked into the room.

'Likewise, Sir. On first impression he's a creepy man. Plus, I think his handkerchief is laced with something.' Yasmin did not miss the peculiar look the three main men exchanged. 'You see, my eyes were stinging, just like the other day. Combo had been crying too. I couldn't reach the mirror; do they look red?'

Carl shuffled his feet. 'They're not as bad they have been'—held up the bag—'I'll get this to forensics.'

'The funeral home?' Sergeant Kohli asked.

Yasmin exhaled defeatedly. 'Apparently everything had been paid for years ago except for the actual funeral service and as the official paperwork has supposedly been filed, I didn't see any reason why there should be a private service with just me and my dog in attendance. I told him as much and cancelled the service.'

'No official paperwork has been issued, Ms Pestel,' he stated quietly.

'Surprise, surprise. This whole thing is beginning to smell. Anyway, I don't care to return there. Only you three have my permission to collect the ashes or receive them if they're to be delivered.'

'You sure?' Sergeant Pyers asked.

'Absolutely.'

Yasmin didn't miss his twitch. She busied herself with the coffee and cake, leaving the men to talk amongst themselves, all the while her mind mulled over the conversations, Rudy's clues, the deception, the different names – when suddenly she had a thought.

'Excuse me, but what is Clive's surname?'

Carl immediately replied. 'Smith. Why?'

The astonished look on her face forced him to explain, without hesitation, that the town's third assistant funeral director in five years had made a point of introducing himself to the local constabularies when he arrived in town. Her slow, contemplative nod didn't convince anybody with only a brief smirk breaking her poker face.

'Oh, I just thought it might be Wilson!'

They shared a good laugh before Sergeant Pyers gestured towards the door and spoke loudly, 'That'd be too easy, Ms Pestel!'

Carl escorted Yasmin and Combo along the covered walkway and stalled beside the nursery. Abundant fluff-ball, fat-bellied puppies either suckling or exploring took Yasmin back to being a little girl. She had sat in the middle of the animal fair and let the young clamber all over her, much to her mother's horror and father's delight.

'Oh, Carl,' she whispered, 'This is cuteness overload and a welcome sight for a pair of very sore eyes!'

The new momma dogs raised their heads, studied her briefly, focussed on Combo, tapped their tails in recognition of Carl then went back to resting and nurturing. The older females supervised the mischievously curious little bundles. Combo crept slowly downwards, rested his head on his front paws and looked at all the puppies and momma dogs. He whimpered softly. His eyes roamed over every square inch. The happy little yaps and occasional maternal growl appealed to his ever-twitching ears until one stretched as she stood and shook. Eyeballing him relentlessly, the closer she got, the louder his whining. He rolled onto his side, then his back, flipped onto his feet, shook, sat and raised his paw.

'Well, I never! It's as if they know each other.' Yasmin gasped, 'That's not possible, is it?'

He chuckled. 'Couldn't tell you, but Ma'am, you don't have to whisper.'

'I feel I have to!' Yasmin then spoke normally. 'What's going on at the funeral parlour?'

He coughed. 'I don't know what you're talking about.'

'You three are either onto something or are using me.'

This time, Carl ran his hands through his short-back-and-sides. 'Neither. None of us men are used to a woman who blurts out questions.' He smirked at Yasmin's beetroot-red face. 'Good. Time for the introduction with the bigger ones now. You ready?'

'It's now or never.'

Sergeant Kohli called for Combo by command to which he responded instantly. He sat by the big man's feet but did not follow him or move until Yasmin had ruffled the tuft of fur between his ears. He looked up at her expectantly and she noisily pretend-kissed his head.

'Sook,' the big man mumbled trying to hide his grin. 'Senior Constable Ramond will walk with you and we'll follow so your dog can see you're in safe hands, while at the same time, mingling with unfamiliar ones. By the way, why his name?'

She chuckled. 'Because he's too handsome to be called Bitsa and his Boxer type head looks like the front end of a Combi.'

'Very clever!' He returned her grin and gestured for them to proceed. 'We'll be right behind you and Combo will be watching closely. Just relax. Oh, one more thing, the big boy is called The Intimidator. Do not run.'

They walked into the enclosure with all the dogs sitting to attention at the command of the Master.

'Time for you to leave us lads be, Ms Pestel. I've got my money on Combo breaking first,' Sergeant Pyers spoke gently.

Yasmin's chuckle froze in her throat. A huge, muscular Rottweiler ambled out of the shadows. Even with a greying muzzle, The Intimidator's penetrating yellow eyes bore through to her soul. His attention swung to Combo who stood his ground. The other K9s dropped to their haunches.

'Looks like we're about to see who's going to win the bet.'

'Looks like there could be a mess too.'

The Master's deep belly laugh echoed through the enclosure. 'We'll see you sometime this afternoon, young lady. Have a great time.'

Combo sat in the middle and looked from one to the other. Poor puppy didn't know which way to go until she patted her thigh. He wiggle-waggled his way into her hands cupping either side of his head. Holding his gaze, smiled then noisily pretend-kissing him on his head, again.

'Love you, Combo. See you later, be a good boy and play nicely.'

He ever so gently hugged her waist. Pushing him down, ruffled his funny tuft of fur and sniffled softly. Biting back the tears, looked at Sergeant Kohli with a watery smile.

'Yeah, I had my money on you!' he chuckled heartily. 'Sergeant Pyers will escort you to your vehicle.'

Watching on in fascination, the huge man effortlessly control his K9s with a simple command, click of the fingers or movement of his arm. Combo followed the lesson with his eyes and ears pricked. Yasmin turned when she heard the gate open and didn't look back, almost blubbering when Owen wrapped his hand gently around her wrist.

'You, young lady, are a blessing in disguise,' he said sternly. 'Now go and enjoy yourself.'

In true chivalry, he opened the driver's door for her and closed it gently as soon as she was settled.

'Where are you having lunch anyway?'

Wiping at her eyes, said, 'I wouldn't have a clue!'

He out-fumbled her and was speaking with his wife before Yasmin had activated her phone. He scribbled something down in his notepad and tore out the sheet. Grinning broadly, pressed it into her hands, stepped backwards and sent her on her way with a flourish.

Chapter 32

With his massive hand splayed across his stepbrother's chest, Ivan had him pinned against the wall of their shed.

'For the last time, did you rat me out?'

'I never would, Ivan! I stick with you. I always have.'

'Good boy.' He bunched up Giles's shirt, pulled him into his embrace and slapped him hard on the back. 'Glad you're alive, bro. But Stu's a dead man, you know that don't you.'

'I reckon we're better off without him.' *And he's better off without us.*

Forcing him to sit on the chair and indicating for a smoke to be rolled, said. 'We need supply for Moojie Hill. Who's going to do that?'

'The same mug that's always done it. I believe the pill press is somewhere else, but all the patrons have to do is choose ... so no biggie hey?'

'Choose. It's not too late to choose!' Ivan chanted cruelly. 'Hurry up and roll us that smoke. Trav and twins are calling in on their way up to the farm and I need to be off my face before the women speak.'

'I'm hearing ya.'

Chapter 33

Why does twenty minutes down an unfamiliar road without cars or buildings feel like an endless journey? Why does a scratchy radio transmission heighten anxiety? Yasmin navigated the sweeper to the right over the concrete causeway with eyes peeled for a driveway marked by a bright blue painted tractor tyre,

'At long last!'

She loosened her glue-like grip on the steering wheel and drove through the entrance, instantly transported into a fairy tale setting. Graded winding road, grand old easy-climbable trees, lush green grass, but it was the white picket fences decorating the length of the driveway that left her with a ghost of a smile.

Parking alongside the perfumed flowering orange tree and in front of five bright beach umbrellas laying on their sides, Yasmin shrieked when the three ladies noisily swung around from behind the shady structures.

***

Slapping the bite sleeve against the grass stain on his trousers, Carl looked at the visitor snuggling up to an oversized stuffed toy.

'Can dogs have split personalities, Master?'

'Couldn't say, but you need to make it more challenging else he'll get you every time.'

'He's so fast!'

'Ready to go again?'

Carl chuckled. 'Yeah, but this time give me a head start!'

'Kit up and get going.'

The moment Carl stepped out of the shade, the command was issued. Master's laughter got drowned out by Combo's barking chase and Carl's animated cries of help as he changed direction and ran along the swing bridge.

***

Three and a half hours later with an up-styled even more feminine hairstyle and the softest of skin, Yasmin had stepped into a whole new world of pampering. With the ladies all sporting new looks and outfits, the thoroughly enjoyable summer clothing party, pampering and High Tea made more special by sharing in each other's company. Not only did she have a full stomach, but it ached from the laughter.

Speaking over the top of Pam and Helen, Nanna persisted with her suggestion. 'You should stay longer, my dear.'

'I really can't, thank you. I do have a lot to do.'

The women hugged each other warmly with those heartfelt sentiments following her back into town. After a successful shopping spree of several things for Combo, including two new frisbees, and for herself an elaborate digital camera, a new mobile phone, fashionable spectacles, several pairs of sunglasses and probably far too much food for the road, she battled to hold back the growing excitement.

Emptying her post office box, the bundle of junk mail and window-faced envelopes was normal yet was astonished to see there was a parcel to collect. Appreciating the compliments from the friendly assistant who handed over a large box, they both commented on the sheer size, lightness and the amount of packing tape.

'There's no return address, Ms Pestel, but it's definitely for you!'

The handwriting wasn't familiar. It was was postmarked one week before her birthday, but the pink coloured string sent her elevated mood into a flat spin. Nodding her thanks, her frown felt like it had been hammered in place. Before stashing the carton in the back of the van, she shook it roughly. Something thumped against the bottom. Venting silently, shoved it in between the shopping bags and made her way to K9 Headquarters. It was only then did she allow herself to admit how much she missed Combo. Following protocol, her first attempt at reverse parking was successful. Taking a deep breath, smoothed down her fresh white floral fit and flare dress, exhaled slowly, threw her shoulders back and stepped it out towards the office door. *I've got this.*

Carl must have been playing cockatoo and met her halfway across the carpark. 'Wow! You look a million bucks, Ma'am.'

She couldn't help the loud laugh that escaped, 'Thanks Carl!'

He enthusiastically described the dogs play, and how Combo had fitted in well with the games, enjoyed the light agility class and only ate after the others. Between him and his new friends, including The Intimidator and Zeus, they initiated a lot of the misbehaviour driving the Master crazy between hysterics and outright frustration. Combo had been adopted by a Beagle and Carl's chocolate Labrador Retriever, Radar. The other two Belgian Malinois brothers hung together but had extended their familiarity when they saw the growing bond with Zeus.

'It's almost as if they all knew each other!' his braying laugh, contagious.

Carl opened the door allowing Yasmin to enter the office and was met with a wall of men in blue, gawking appreciatively. She recognised a couple, but it was the two sergeants who expressed their obvious reaction.

'Holy smokes! That should be illegal shouldn't it, Boss?'

'Sergeant Kohli, I couldn't agree more!' Sergeant Pyers chuckled loudly. 'Ms Pestel, you are a sight for sore eyes.'

Her face was crimson. 'Thank you, gentlemen. My mouth hasn't been this way up for a long time! Sergeants, you really have a way with words and it's comforting to know you recognised me, just hope my Combo does too!'

Genuine laughter filled the room before the K9 handlers took their leave respectfully.

'I'm going to ask again. Please tell me who and how much I owe for the groceries plus the fantastic repair work on my cottage,' Yasmin looked at each one as seriously as she could.

Owen spoke up. 'You don't owe anybody for anything. If it makes you feel better, we'll come to an agreement where we hire your property until the balance is nil. Would that be acceptable?'

By the time he had finished speaking, her grin almost met her ear lobes. 'What a splendid idea! Feel free to use the defunct greenhouse as a storage shelter.'

Carl handed her a kit bag containing a guidebook, new harness, blue bandana, squeezy ball and two collapsible dishes. He explained with pride that Combo had successfully graduated the first stage of being a service dog. Getting her to repeat the word *service*.

'It just sounds better, Ma'am! Oh, here's the document you wanted. Have a read a bit later, we can deal with it then.'

Sergeant Kohli led the way into the playground where The Intimidator behaved like a puppy juggling a chew toy.

'He was awesome in his day,' Sergeant Kohli said proudly.

Yasmin chuckled softly. 'Appropriately named too.'

His other pals doing dog things, except for Combo, Radar and the beagle who were playing a three-way tug-o-war. The Intimidator barked once and rolled onto his feet with ease. That was the cue. As soon as Combo realised who was with the men, he dropped the toy, did zoomies and tried to encourage his new buddies to do something. Anything! Combo and a couple of others sniffed around Yasmin and instantly dropped to their haunches when Master commanded them. She ruffled her pooch's head before taking a couple of steps backwards. He did the same and sat with his tail swishing excitedly. Completely disobeying Master, The Intimidator ambled towards the group, gently shouldered Combo on the way past and stood in front of Yasmin. That's when he eventually sat, looked at her intently and raised his paw. She shook it gently and lightly rubbed his shoulders talking to him softly. He ever so slowly laid down on his side and lifted his head as if to say, *'well woman, scratch my tummy.'* Yasmin giggled, sat cross-legged on the ground and rubbed his tummy. When Combo whined, the old boy's docked tail thumped the ground abruptly silencing him. He eventually got himself on his paws. Face to face, she barely breathed. He shook a bit unsteadily and in a flash Combo and Zeus were either side of him.

'Unbelievable,' Sergeant Pyers murmured.

Master spoke firmly, but his large face was alive with joy when he helped her stand. 'Ms Pestel, call your dog please. It's time you pair went home before they all want their stomachs scratched and heads noisily kissed!'

'You can! I only pretend!' She clicked her tongue.

Combo walked towards her while she walked backwards, singing out her goodbyes to the other pooches and telling them they were all very good boys. Zeus approached Combo. They nosed each other and stood with their heads' millimetres apart. Combo repeated the same action with The Intimidator, yapped, then loped to stand beside Yasmin. The three men escorted the pair in an orderly fashion towards the large metal sliding gate before he turned around, looked up at Yasmin then whined.

She indicated with her head. 'Go on, be quick.'

Amazed, Combo went to every single dog and either nuzzled or butt-sniffed them. When he approached Zeus and the Intimidator, he laid down on his belly, hind legs splayed in true splot-style and crawled towards them, making it clear he understood the pecking order while enjoying the full-length grassy scratch. Athletically flipping to a standing position, barked several times over his shoulder and trotted towards the four humans. His final barking session encouraged them to all respond and were still doing so when the gate slid shut. Yasmin commanded him to be quiet, clipped the leash onto his new harness and everything went back to being normal. They were escorted to the vehicle in a way friends reluctantly farewell special visitors.

'Gentlemen, saying thank you doesn't seem sufficient for what I have experienced today, as well as the patience and kindness you have shown to me these last few days.'

'Ms Pestel,' Sergeant Pyers clasped her free hand firmly. 'It is us who thank you. We'll be in touch soon.'

She shook each of their hands solidly and grinned. 'I will always look forward to that. Thanks again.'

Combo happily hopped in from the passenger side and sniffed the air. A big globule of drool landed on his canvas seat cover. Ruffling his head, double checked his seat belt connection and closed his door quietly. Carl opened her door and stood aside. She sat and swung her legs in like a lady. It's a great way to show off shapely calves, even with short legs! He perved openly, firmly closed her door with a blushing grin and they all said goodbye to each other again with enthusiastic waves.

The last of the sun's golden rays cast a beautiful hue over the Jacaranda tree whose colours almost blended in with the soft lavender coloured sky. Giving her four-legged protector the opportunity to re-establish boundaries outside, automatically went to play back telephone messages and slapped her forehead at her forgetfulness.

'Oh well, they'll just have to ring back!'

Chapter 34

With Combo scratching at the door to be let in, Yasmin activated the suite of alarms and closed up the cottage. The large box sat ambiguously in the middle of the lounge room floor. He had a good sniff around it, nosed it towards the wall and promptly walked away. Their interest levels matched. Besides, other matters had higher priorities, like cash. Her eyes nearly popped out of her head. Feeling excitably nervous, she decided eight thousand would be enough as travel money and stashed the rest throughout her wardrobe. Collating the ambiguous clues in one pile on the foot of her bed, the mail for Emily's snow man and son in another, Yasmin wandered what on earth Rudy had gotten her into. Then the tri-named nemesis poked her puzzle-solving brain.

'And where the hell did Rupert come from?'

Combo padded around her bed and blocked the doorway to the passage. For too long her one and only old suitcase had waited underneath the bed. Frowning at the unexpected weight, she put her back into it and managed to lift the old thing across the middle of the bed. Unclipping the straps, and relieved the zips still worked, flipped open the lid and gasped loudly. Combo was beside her in a flash sniffing enthusiastically at the foreign odour. Lying in the void and partly wrapped in pink tissue an exposed familiar ornate gold gilded frame. Her head shook on its own accord. *Water Lilies.* Holding the picture upright, a laminated certificate of authenticity slipped out of the first layer of paper. Tucked in between another layer was one large, rounded envelope with her name written neatly across the face of it.

Emptying the contents impatiently, a sealed, unaddressed normal-shaped envelope plus a folded rounded note landed on her bed.

Dear Yasmin,

I had several faults, but the largest and most tragic was my jealousy. I cannot undo the hurt it caused or the lifelong pain kinder people will endure. The story of why you ended up with this Monet painting is too convoluted to explain. Just accept this original as the one it is, the one you remember and the one you and Emily favoured. It is yours and yours alone. The rest of the collection is with our dear old friend. By now, I'm sure you will have realised your wealth. I know it wouldn't change a single cell in your body. Because that is who you are.

Please deliver this envelope to Emily's snow man. You will discover where he lives, and I know you will meet him. Emily would have left instructions like I have. Be assured, him and his little boy can have an adventurous life if they accept what is enclosed.

Don't be sad when you read my plaque. I know you will complete the last piece of the puzzle.

Go and have a good life.

Love from Rudy.

Looking towards the heavens, she silently begged God to bless Rudy's soul then help him to rest in peace. Wrapping the prized piece of artwork and certificate in a spare doona cover, tucked it away in the wardrobe.

Dusting her hands together, uttered, 'Yep, another matter for another time.'

Combo settled himself back in the doorway, sighing heavily. Laying all the game pieces at the bottom of the suitcase, she packed according to destination. Deciding that Emily would also be going on a road trip, her lacy makeup bag and manicure set went into Yasmin's handbag. Eyeing off the jewellery boxes, curiosity got the better of her. Tears welled recalling the delicate earrings the beautiful woman wore. Guessing the two unopened navy-blue velvet boxes were for the snow man and his son, they went into Yasmin's handbag as well. *Gonna need a bigger handbag, girl.*

Another historic purchase came to the forefront. This time in an oversized Italian designed shoulder-bag she had bought on a whim with her sister. Scrounging around in the bottom drawer she fist-pumped the air. Still tissue-wrapped and perfect. This new bag was comfortably full and could still close! Even her passport and business mobile would have their own pocket. The rest of the bequeathed gifts were packed appropriately.

Racing Combo to the lounge, she caught a glimpse of herself frowning at her reflection. *You. Are. In. Denial.* With dropped shoulders and wet eyes, she had a horrible feeling that Rudy's sordid past would make her presence known eventually. Then wondered if the lads knew about his infidelity. Then all the other questions started. *How old was this older woman? What did she look like? What did the daughter look like? Was it a drug induced orgy? How long ago? Why?*

Combo's bark interrupted the stupid emotional torture. Flicking to the security cameras on the mobile phone, observed the headlights creeping up the driveway, and cried out in fright when it rang.

'Who are you?' she hissed.

'Sergeant Kohli. Apologies for the late visit. May I approach?' he asked sternly.

Yasmin deactivated the audible siren, dashed down the hallway and shut her bedroom door. 'Uh, y-yes, of course.'

Combo, ever the dutiful guard dog except with a wagging tail and happy face, welcomed him. One look at the man's face made Yasmin feel she was about to bear witness to a storm.

'Coffee?'

'Please.'

In an attempt to disguise her nerves, asked him if he knew anything about cameras.

'That was out of the blue!'

'You look perplexed and I bought one today, would you like to see it?' pointing to its box on the counter.

He studied her closely. She knew she gulped loudly. Something kicked in. Yasmin accepted the silent challenge of a stare-down. She flinched at the click of the kettle and he looked away with the slightest smirk.

'It's not even out of the box!'

'I've been busy.' She made a point of looking at her visitor closely. 'Are you okay?'

'What are you hiding?'

They automatically sat at the dining room table with their coffees.

'My hurt. Indignation.'

'I beg to differ.'

'And you look like you're about to explode. Do I need to have an ambulance on standby?'

His hand didn't quite cover his face, but he rubbed it roughly much to the amusement of Combo.

'No.' He removed an envelope from his shirt pocket and placed it on the table.

'Ms Pestel, this is strictly off the record as is my presence here tonight. Pyers and I have known each other for a very long time and although we now work in the same Branch, we do not always work together on every case, nor do we share intel. I have been conducting my own research without anyone's knowledge in the hopes of solving an old mystery.' His eyes were moist, but it was his facial expression that tore at Yasmin's heart. 'I need you to hear me out.'

She nodded encouragingly. 'Talk to me, please.'

He spoke about a former colleague and wife who avoided their deaths in a long-forgotten snow vehicle accident when they took ill the morning of the trip. In the hope of discovering who the actual target was or were, annoyingly the trail had gone cold. That is, until he recently linked Rudy's surname to a young lady who had been killed on the day in question. It had taken a lot of self-imposed detective work to discover the connection between her and an unclaimed laundry bag. Undertaking research on a different case, the same surname appeared on the coinciding switching off of life-support systems two years post-accident date.

'Two and two were put together, and eight years later, the last surviving family member, isn't. I need to know who the initial targets were. And why. I am unsure if I've convinced myself of my original suspicions or if I'm losing the plot. I'm tired, and this burden is making me old before my time.'

He sighed heavily, absentmindedly scratched his chin and got another weight off chest by revealing he carried the file notes with him every day as a reminder of why he does the job he does.

Sergeant Kohli studied her, and said, 'All that aside, I suspect you are going to search for your own answers. I cannot stop you, but what I'm about to tell you must never be repeated. Do I have your promise?'

Yasmin pressed her lips together and nodded.

'The other deceased souls were a couple who had an animal refuge place, and a husband and wife who were celebrating a lucrative contract with their vineyard. Do you know these people?'

She barely breathed. 'No, I don't.'

Again, the big man sighed heavily and pushed the paperwork towards her with his index finger. 'You swear your silence?'

'I swear my silence.'

Quietly regaining self-control, she unfolded the compilation of his research and read them silently.

~~~~~
~~~~~

According to the first responders, police, and coroner reports, the young female seated alongside the male guide (later ID as Emily Craige) died on impact with a broken neck. The older couple directly behind were in a critical condition and stabilised by life-support systems. The two other older couples seated behind them didn't survive their injuries - punctured lungs, heart attacks and metal shrapnel insertions respectively. The guide had to be cut from the vehicle and subsequently lost a leg from his injuries. His left hand had to be broken to pry it from the right of the deceased female. The thumb, index and middle fingers on his right hand had to be broken to release it from the distress beacon. The snow drift slowed the incineration process. Continual snow hampered investigations.

Aside from being mortified, the experienced guide swore on his mother's grave that he was extremely familiar with the scenic track they had traversed. He had ensured it was clear of any rocks, obstacles or fallen trees. Not only had he traversed it two hours prior to the tragedy, but regularly during the unusually long snow season. He was following his earlier tracks. The party stopped to take photos of the scenery. He proposed to his future bride. She said yes.

Int. w.guide in hospital - eight months post acc. - Quote / ad verbatim edited to remove majority of emotional delays:

Of course I remember. I relive the nightmare every time I open or shut my eyes. The picnic table was covered in a gold, white and blue tablecloth with fresh scones, jam and whipped cream, fruit and delicate sandwiches laid out appropriately. There were bottles of sparkling water and fruit juice in the silver ice buckets. A dozen red roses stood in a matching silver vase, three for each lady on the tour. The waiters who were the caterers - there was an unfamiliar one, but with the recent shift change and my recce earlier, I didn't do the usual vetting of the staff. They were very professional. I was very impressed.

The snow-vehicle was parked away so it didn't detract from the scenery. After lunch, everyone agreed to celebrate unconditionally at the wedding rehearsal / fancy dress party. I would move mountains for my beautiful Emily...ahem...now, I wish-I just wish... I noticed footprints in the snow going in the opposite direction of where we all were and the vehicle's position. Wrapped up in the moment, I didn't investigate. Now, I just wish I had. The caterers were left to demobilise and we continued with the tour.

The INCLINE WAS A SMOOTH, gradual winding section NECESSITATING gentle acceleration. As I said, I traversed the track not two hours beforehand. NOR WAS THIS the first time I had taken a relatively full vehicle of VIPs on this tour, on this particular track. It was my preferred, given its CLIMATIC introduction to the spectacular scenery.

The vehicle is safely designed for 12, specifically offered for VIPs, specifically designed for the R.H. drive market. The engineering certificate and additional warranty documents should verify my recollection.

((sic) when asked why only VIPs, the guide explained the exorbitant optional extra was only marketed to the ELITE or soon-to-be famous. On this occasion, he paid for his bride-to-be and her special guests. Aside from them, the other guests were unknown to him. He didn't organise the other bookings.)

As I accelerated, I noticed a pile of foreign debris to the right of us HALFWAY down the slope. It looked out of place and had definitely not been there earlier. Fresh snow-fall disguised tracks of any kind. Suddenly, an awful grinding noise and shaking erupted. The ladies screamed with fright and I called out for everyone to hang on. I grabbed my beloved's hand when the vehicle shuddered uncontrollably.

I had no traction. It was like the brakes were attached to the accelerator. The harder-the harder I put my foot on the brake pedal, the faster we jerked about and continued up the slope. The pedal didn't return. It was like it was jammed on. We sped up. What was worse, the steering seized, and the auto-stop failed. There isn't any resistance on smooth snow. But it was just too fast, too unstable, too much and we-we flipped, tumbled and landed upside down.

I heard a crack. Emily's lifeless body was the last thing I saw, until I fought whoever was trying to put something over my mouth. For the second time in my life, I heard my dead father's voice telling me I was alive and being helped.

((sic) when asked if he could describe the first time, the guide explained he had to be resuscitated after a water polo incident.)
Unquote.

- By the time forensics got to the location, the vehicle had been incinerated.

- Suspicions were high that the batteries were the source.

- Mangled steel indicated possible tampering. Heat source not conducive to fusing of steel, brake and accelerator mechanism or steering manufacture.

- The guide disappeared after the funeral of the parents of the intended bride.

```
. Who was the target? Why?

??????
~~~~~
```

Yasmin returned the paperwork and slid it back across the table, excused herself momentarily, retrieved a box of tissues and stemmed the flow of tears.

'Dear God,' she whispered, 'I had no idea.'

Sergeant Kohli's voice was thick with emotion. 'Imagine my surprise when I learn you're the next of kin of the most recent death, of whom, I believe, never uttered his name during any interview and is taking a road trip while a cremation occurs in your absence.'

They held each other's gaze for a very long time. Neither one flinching, blinking or twitching. Yasmin respectfully broke first.

'I'm innocent. I intend to find a few answers of my own and lay several ghosts to rest, my own way.'

'And?'

Thinking quickly, 'I am no heroine and will not jeopardise Combo's or my safety. And I am not going to dance to anyone else's tune. I feel I've been everybody's fool for too long.'

He looked at her steadily and slowly nodded. Eventually, spoke in a voice that was oddly emotionless. 'For the record, I am not happy about this at all. But you are not under investigation so I cannot prevent you from going. I will ask for your passport.'

She frowned. 'On the condition I get it back along with Rudy's ashes.'

Without flinching, he replied firmly, 'Ms Pestel, we are not negotiating right now.'

'Your visit, and this conversation *is* off the record, so I believe we are.'

Again, they held each other's stern gaze but the hard look in their eyes softened at the same time.

She smirked, leant across the table and squeezed his huge hand with both of hers. 'Sergeant Kohli, you will discover the truth I am confident of that and I will help you in any way I can, but you need to let me do what I need to do.'

They shook hands on their unspoken agreement.

'Please be aware of your surroundings and stay sensible. I strongly recommend you buy a wig and change your appearance. It's not pleasant, but, here ... these may be useful.' He handed her a hard, clear, plastic little box.

'Those are the horrid things from the dentist!'

'Yep, cotton wool rolls. They'll fatten up your face. There's not much we can do with Combo, unless you get him one of those funny costumes! Also, chuck a pebble or two in your sneakers if you're out and about on foot.'

'Why would I do that?'

'Because it changes the way you walk.'

'Oh! Okay, thanks for the advice. Do you usually carry these things around with you?'

'No. But I don't usually deal with someone like you every day neither. When are you leaving?'

'Monday.' Yasmin opened her mouth then swiftly closed it, but it was too late. She kicked herself mentally.

'Yes?' he questioned her diplomatically.

'Why do you think Stu Wilson has gone to ground?'

'Therein lies another investigation I will not discuss with you.'

'Fair enough. Thank you for sharing what you did about the accident, I was not privy to any of the detail.'

An all too familiar sad smile flickered before he nodded slowly. They held out their hands simultaneously and with a firm shake, said, 'Ms Pestel, I will take my leave now. Safe travels.'

'Oh, please take this with you'—handing him the signed A.V.O—'it's all in good order. Thank you, Sergeant Kohli. All the best to you and yours.'

After more sad smiles were exchanged she locked the door behind him.

With the recently gleaned information, delivering mail to Emily's snow man was a very high priority. But first she had a telephone call to make. Waiting for her call to be answered, played with her new mobile phone.

'Oh, so now you ring me, Yasmin from Pestel's Edible Petals! I thought you had shut up shop?'

'And you could have tried harder to contact me, Timmy.'

'Any idea of the time?'

'Yeah, it's late. I'll phone you another time.' She hung up. First. And was ready to answer his returned call. 'Hey, how are you all?'

'You're a smart arse.' Being a good sport too, chuckled. 'Yeah, we're doing well and Bob's getting stronger every day. What's news?'

'Not too much. There's been a glitch at the funeral parlour so all that's been delayed. What can you tell me?'

'Nothing much. When you coming this way?'

'Not for a while yet, tell me your plans?'

'Can't do much without Bob. Anyway, it's late, we'll chat soon, hey?'

'Sure thing, Timmy. Love to you all, good night and—' she disconnected and nodded in self-satisfaction.

Chapter 35

A cold sweat at 05:16am awoke her. Perplexed at the uncanny digits realisation finally dawned. *The keys!* Without hesitating, rummaged through the box and added them into her shoulder bag then keyed in Dean's address on the mapping software and stared in excited anticipation. *Alpine country!* Wide awake; undertook the challenge of deciphering the GPS coordinates. Two coffees later, Yasmin had plotted their trip right down to where they would be camping after meeting the elusive snow man and son. At no stage was she going to let on to the lads where she was going, nor be roped into returning all of the boxes. Devising a plan, she finished packing her suitcase, with the laptop and hardware the last to go in. Standing it beside the box belonging to the Craige family, Yasmin danced a little jig. Then the yawning began!

Combo hadn't budged, until she crawled back into bed. Play time! Breakfast time! With the sun peeping through wispy clouds, she had just finished making the hollandaise sauce when the jangling landline broke the culinary symphony of sizzling bacon. It was 07:38am.

Carl announced himself before she got a word in. 'Ma'am! Good morning, will you be home early afternoon?'

'Morning, young man. Yes. Why?'

'Some people would love to see you and I was hoping you'd be okay if I park up the motorhome, bring Radar too and be back first thing tomorrow?'

'Hmph, the bush telegraph is in large print this time! Yeah, that sounds fine. Tell me, how many am I catering for this afternoon?'

'No, we're bringing that. You're on holidays, Ma'am.' This time his braying donkey laugh had a hiccup.

Yasmin accepted the kind offer and was still chuckling at his quirkiness when they simultaneously disconnected the call. She rubbed away the frown that had gradually grown.

'Super early start tomorrow, Combo!'

The moment she turned around, the pink-stringed lonely box screamed at her. She screamed back at it. Slashing at the string and hacksawing through the layers and layers of clear packing tape with the bluntest of kitchen knives, she paused momentarily thinking she heard a sound. Combo stared from afar. Shaking her head, opened up the box to see volumes of pink tissue paper. *Your game has got on my nerves, buddy.* Not giving into the manipulation, she closed it back up and put it in the cupboard with all the others. Then and only then did she attempt perfectly poached eggs to soften super crispy bacon. The sauce rudely split beyond recovery.

By noon, several bunches of roses with greenery were arranged in more spare vases on the kitchen bench, with handwritten thank you cards attached. Humming along to the strains of her easy-listening jazz playlist while rearranging the additional furniture on the patio, both her and Combo sniffed at the air. There it was again. That delicate scent. They looked at each other quizzically. She grinned. His tail wagged. Dressing in the latest addition to her wardrobe of a cute red and white ruffle dress, Yasmin was ready to party.

Her friends brought a smorgasbord of delightful finger foods and drinks. Nanna, being the natural entertainer with her clever humour, initiated charades which were an absolute hoot. The party was the perfect opportunity to trial her new camera and happily accepted tips and pointers from Helen. Her and Sergeant Kohli had met at a photographer's club in their mid-twenties which led to the long-term friendship of him and Owen. Their combined knowledge was priceless. In a short space of time, Yasmin was taking some rather semi-pro photographs and a heck of a lot of candid ones too, particularly as Combo and Radar were inseparable.

Late afternoon with Carl's motorhome positioned and set up appropriately, he had quite the view. She handed the folder to the young man and explained the contents to all and sundry. As suspected, it didn't take long before everyone was familiar with the projects and whom the contractors were. Carl's demeanour was of confidence and gratitude, but it was his more senior counterparts who beamed with appreciation.

'Yasmin,' Owen, poised with his glass in the air, made a small speech. 'On behalf of everyone here, thank you for getting this young man out of a tight spot. Cheers!'

The resounding celebratory toast filled the air the same time a warm breath gently drifted across Yasmin's right cheek. She responded graciously blinking away happy tears. With all signs of the party cleaned up and the ladies holding their vases tightly, an awkwardness settled over the group.

'Will it be okay if I arrived a little after eight o'clock tomorrow morning, Ma'am?' Carl asked quietly.

'Sure! Only the cottage's internal alarm will be activated. The rest of the property is under your management.'

The men coughed and spluttered. The women rushed over and hugged her tightly, drowning her in questions.

'Friends! I'm only going on a road trip!'

Owen rounded up the mother hens along with an emotional Carl and reluctant Radar. Yasmin happily contributed to Sergeant Kohli's firm handshake. She waved until the vehicles had turned out of the driveway.

'Gawd boy, anybody would think they're worried about me. Or maybe it's you?'

Long after the sun had set, she glowered at the unknown number pestering her business mobile thus breaking her concentration. Why she had bothered to keep it active was a another question she asked herself, then returned to the map covering the table. Moaning at the sixth interruption, stabbed at the answer icon.

'You have five seconds.'

'No, I don't. Listen to me, Yasmin. There are some nasty people in this world, I have done what I can to get away and I suggest you do too.'

'Who is this?'

'Be quiet. Please, it's—'

'*Do not* tell me what to do.'

'Please, Yasmin. I have always liked you so please—'

'Stu? Why the clandestine—'

'Jesus, woman! Your looks drove me crazy but far out, I think your interruptions—'

'You can talk!'

'—would have driven me up the wall.'

'No need to be cruel.' Yasmin disconnected the call and turned off her phone, reached for her personal one and did the same thing. Scoffing harshly, lifted the handpiece off the antique telephone and left it on the table.

***

With a ferocity that surprised himself, Stu put his fist through the acrylic advertising board. Cursing under his breath, shrugged into the jacket and disappeared down the ramp of the underground car park.

It was at that moment in a darkened area beside a seedy nightclub Leigh waved the baggy of tablets in front of the druggo's nose. 'Do you want to make some money or not?'

'Yeah lady, and you know I don't get my hands dirty.'

'Don't care. He's at the funeral parlour, name is Clive. Get rid of him. Then follow the instructions on this note to the letter.'

'Uh ... which one?'

'Huh?'

'The new Clive or the old Clive?'

Leigh scratched her head in confusion. Impulsively, replied, 'I don't care. Just follow the instructions then burn them.'

'Or else?'

'The boogey-man will get you too.'

'Jesus! I grew up terrified of him ... I-I'll do as you say,' he writhed uncomfortably and stepped back into his hiding place.

'Good. Don't ever look for me.'

His trembling voice echoed through the alley. 'Never have, you seem to find me.'

Leaning against the front guard of someone's Lexus, Leigh lit up a smoke and made a phone call. 'Hey Giles, you owe me.'

After disconnecting the call, she removed the SIM and snapped it in two. Keeping her head low, bobbed down and slipped both pieces through the vehicle's front grille. Slinking along the curb, the parked cars provided a good hiding place and an opportunity to watch Callum pocket a wad of cash. *What a good boy.*

***

The stepbrothers sighed in relief when the taillights disappeared in the smoke from the spinning tyres.

Giles covered his vibrating phone by thrusting his hands into his pockets. 'Those women do my head in when they talk at the same time!' he moaned.

'Yeah, and the teeth grinding and you never know who is who! Mega-fugly but!'

'You looked at their butts, Ivan?'

They fell about the place laughing. Their stoned stupor extending the guffaws. The moment he was alone, Giles listened to the message. His high snuffed like a wet wick. He feared his stepbrother, but he was terrified of Leigh's reach.

***

'Girls, we've got a bit of a drive ahead of us and when we get there, I'm going to leave you at the Unit in town, then go and visit Jill for a while. I'll come back for you when I've had enough of her or her dogs. Whichever comes first.'

'Great idea, Travis.'

'We'll be busy getting ready for Moojie Hill anyway. You'll need to buy some paper and printer toner for the information pack, plus get something nice for Sally. I've had a change of heart.'

'We don't want to know,' they sang loudly.

'I'll look after the others.'

'You always do, Uncle Travis!'

Their synchronised snort making him smirk. 'You heard Ivan say he'd meet us at camp a day before Giles arrives with the rest of the supply?'

'Yes, yes we did.' The incessant tooth-grinding falling on deaf ears.

'Excellent.' *Then we'll see who's who in the zoo.*

'Do we get to talk about Stu?'

'Not yet.'

'We don't talk about the boogey-man.'

'No. Never.'

'Poor Sally.'

'We're not going there again.' Travis scoffed quietly. *Poor Sally my arse.*

Chapter 36

An hour after collecting their motorhome, Yasmin's mood competed with the dazzling golden orb climbing skywards. With her business mobile still turned off, she was comfortable with being contactable by the select few who had her personal mobile phone number. Further boosting her newfound freedom; on the noticeboard a pamphlet for a combined art, craft and hippie festival at Moojie Hill. According to Duke, the place was an insignificant bump in the earth with the local population of seven hundred swelling to anywhere upwards of three thousand for ten days. *Synchronicity!* Determined to find the place on a map by herself, they pulled into a rest area where she simply swivelled the front seats, unclipped Combo, walked through to the back together then made herself a coffee. Loving the simplicity of it all, reheated a sausage roll. Sitting beside Combo outside in the shade of the vehicle while swatting away a lot of flies, she plotted their return trip exploring a new part of South Australia.

Suddenly feeling the urge to see a span of water and didn't care if it were a lake or the sea, closed her eyes, circled a pointed finger above the map and let it stop where it wanted. She stared downwards and grinned. Then Timmy phoned.

'Hey!' she answered while getting ready to travel.

'Hey, do you know only Bob had your personal phone number? I've been trying to get hold of you since last night and finally thought to ask the question. What's the go with that?'

'You tell me.'

'Oh.' There was a long pause. 'Where are you?'

'I'm here, where are you?'

'Watching my pilot reposition the chopper. Listen smarty bum, we need to talk.'

'Well, I'm on holiday and my property is out of bounds. Do you hear me, Timmy?'

'Yes, Yasmin.'

'Good. It's a beautiful, cloud-free day and I'll be in Meningie in an hour. Why don't you meet us there for lunch?'

His silence was deafening. When he did eventually speak, his voice was edgy. 'Uh yeah, okay. Suppose we can eat at an airfield!'

'What a great idea. You bring the food, and I'll bring the drinks. It'll be an experience anyway,' she suppressed her chuckle. 'Let's say midday?'

'Uh yeah, okay. It'll be good to see you, Yasmin.'

'You bet, Timmy! I'm looking forward to it too.'

They paused, burst out laughing and disconnected the call at the same time.

Watching the helicopter hover just above the ground, then gently settle, was like watching the dance of an oversized dragonfly. With the aid of the pilot, Timmy and Mike managed to get Bob on his feet long enough to get the wheelchair behind him. Combo sensed Yasmin's excitement yet behaved like he was on duty. His service dog harness fitting snugly around his broad midriff, and he looked so cool wearing his mirrored sunglasses.

'Holy heck, look at you!' Bob said as he rolled through the pedestrian gate. 'Check the pooch!'

Grinning broadly, the group hug was very welcome and they all openly swiped at their own tears. Combo instantly adopted Bob after meeting the lads.

'You in that flashy motorhome, Yasmin?' Timmy challenged.

'Not that one, that's a fifth wheeler you ninny!' she laughed it off. 'Come on, I'm hungry!'

'You're always hungry, Yas,' Mike hugged her again. 'Love your new look by the way!'

Grinning and thanking him for the compliment, they sat around the covered concrete table and chairs under the big tree. The light-hearted jest about her and tablecloths setting the atmosphere perfectly. Chatting amiably while eating the delicatessen style sandwiches and simply celebrating Rudy's life, was an entrée to what would be happening when his ashes were available.

'Yas baby, do you feel as if we've all suddenly grown up?' Bob asked, breaking the light-hearted banter.

Yasmin paused, looked at Combo, silently relived all the recent experiences which lead to her new-found friends and slowly nodded her head. 'Yeah, Bob. I reckon we have.'

Retrieving the mysterious keys from her handbag, she laid them on the pretty cloth. Silence fell.

'Emily indicated there was a cellar in your mother's home which was their hiding place. She loved you guys dearly. These belong to you three now.'

'A cellar?' Timmy barked the question.

The lads scratched their heads and looked at Yasmin for any clues. She reminded them she had never been inside their home, then said, 'To me, scared children would not go into a dark place.'

'I didn't know we had cellar,' Mike mumbled.

Yasmin shrugged, explained she was looking for a specific photo on her phone, then slid it front of them.

'This was sketched onto the ceiling, so look up. Rudy was very cunning and remember he was in the construction business so—'

'Hey?' Bob stared at her. 'Oh, Yas baby.'

She replied categorically, 'Construction! As in building things.'

'Uh, no he wasn't. He never got his hands dirty, Yasmin. Rudy was a project manager in a lot of industries, wherever he wanted to be, self-employed and definitely his own boss.'

Failing to refrain from exploding with questions, her tongue raced ahead of her mind. 'And you all kept me in the dark?'

Looking at their astonished faces, she dismissed another angry retort. There simply wasn't enough daylight to dwell on it.

'Well, that's a conversation for another time. Anyway, he could construct things. Look for a collapsible frame or panels, or a wall that goes inside itself or can be lifted up. Something really extraordinarily precise that you wouldn't believe, but would, knowing Rudy could do it.'

Timmy thumped the table in frustration. 'Like what, Yasmin?'

Pushing herself upwards, stated. 'You knew him better than me. I've given you all the clues and I don't know your home as well as you do. There are the keys. One would presume you will need both of them.'

She walked away to dispose of the lunch wrappers and bottles with Combo trotting happily beside her, firstly to calm her own ire and secondly to give the lads a brief opportunity to talk amongst themselves. Deciding it'd be more appropriate if they received the box before they left, looked across at the helicopter as she approached the table. The lads stopped talking when she sat.

'Hey, there's also a drink for your pilot. But before I meet him, you need to hear some of Rudy's wishes.'

Now that she had their undivided attention, said, 'An account has been opened up in each of your names with the balance to be released to the account holders only, with the documents safely contained. His absolute final wish was to ensure his personal helicopter pilot and dear friend perform a thorough mechanical inspection and pay particular attention to the panel behind the dash.'

The look on their faces was priceless and would be etched in her memory forever. Years of stress dissolved when a faint twinkle in their eyes reignited.

'Oh Yasmin, thank you for being you,' Timmy said quietly, reached across the table and squeezed her hand doing his utmost to bite back a loud sob.

She couldn't stop her own smile and returned the squeeze. 'So, am I going to meet this dude who will have treasured cargo on board?'

'Organising that now,' Bob responded with a wink and picked up his phone.

When he stood, Mike's tender look almost made her cry. Almost.

Combo's tail slapped Yasmin's knee. Their eyes glued on a similar aged man pushing through the gate. His tall, wiry stature and military demeanour exuded a level of control and confidence. Politely removing his sunglasses, his smile lit up captivating green eyes drawing Yasmin's hand towards his.

Holding hers firmly, his gentle voice extinguished any concerns. 'Ma'am, please call me Col. It's an honour to meet you and to be welcomed into this family. As I have sworn before and the same to these three lads, I swear to you that I will protect you and those that enter your life, with my life.'

'Hello Col, those are beautiful words. Thank you,' she said and wiped at a stray tear.

Combo dropped to his haunches. Sniffed the air, then wiggle-waggled closer. For the first time since Yasmin had been responsible for her pooch, she saw him beg to be picked up. Col easily scooped him up and swung him around like a father does with a young child playing aeroplanes. When he pretended to throw and catch, Combo yapped like a puppy. The moment he was sure-pawed on the ground, excitedly zoomed every which way until gluing himself to Col's left knee.

Scratching at her head, Yasmin said, 'Do you normally do that with dogs you've just met?'

'Yeah! Can't explain it,' he replied and accepted the soft drink Timmy handed him.

'We're at the cloth covered table over there, mate.'

Col regaled several amusing stories about Rudy and his antics in the air. The lad was scared of heights until his backside was on the seat, then he was king of the world. He had a nose that could smell gold which took them to some ruggedly remote areas. While describing some of the areas, pulled out a concertina photo album from his flying jacket's inner pocket. The magnificent views took Yasmin's breath away and her travel bug broke free.

They were thoroughly enjoying each other's company, the happier memories of Rudy, and agreed another rendezvous was essential because, alas, time was ticking away too quickly. Col announced he was going to do a pre-start, warmly wrapped his hands around Yasmin's and thanked her again, then knelt in front of Combo. No words were expressed, but the resting of foreheads and simultaneous sigh while Combo's paw rested in Col's hand, gobsmacked Yasmin. She gnawed on the inside of her cheek.

'Something wrong?' Col said when he stood.

'Not sure if it's right or wrong. I'm just amazed at the familiarity.'

Grinning, 'Perhaps we're kindred spirits from a past life! Right chaps, departure in fifteen minutes.' He leant forwards and pecked Yasmin's cheek. 'See you again, Ms Pestel.'

Timmy semi-saluted and clapped his hands like he was commanding his minions to get ready. Automatically, everyone did. Mike took the keys, Bob whipped off the tablecloth with flair and folded it to the best of his ability before passing it to her with a lazy wink. While they made their way towards her motorhome, Yasmin animatedly described how she had donated nearly all her flowers to the hospital and, in typical girly style, the fun she'd had with her new friends.

'Glad to hear you're reconnecting with the living world, Yas baby!' Bob's chuckle was deep and comforting.

'Listen, there's one box you have to take with you. The rest we can sort out much later and I strongly urge you to stay away from my property unless I am present.'

Neither Timmy or Mike commented and walked either side of her amicably. Bob and Combo were playing slightly ahead of them, keeping the atmosphere pleasant.

'We know how much you loved your business, Yasmin.'

'Ah, Timmy, I'm long overdue for a holiday and it's coming into summer here.'

They all shared in a long laugh.

Sliding the box towards the door, Timmy manhandled it easily and slung it on his shoulder like he was carrying a carton of his preferred amber liquid. The one-armed hug around her shoulder was genuine and meaningful.

'Thank you for being you. Please, please stay safe and keep in touch,' he whispered into her ear and kissed her firmly on the cheek before walking away.

Mike hugged her super tightly. 'Yas, thanks for everything. See you soon and drive safe.'

'Thanks Mike, be happy and you owe me a beer!'

Bob held out his arms and she leant into them. 'When I can stand, you are going to get the biggest hug you've ever had, Yas baby! You're a beautiful, mega-tolerant woman with a heart of gold, thank you for being so thoughtful. Take care.'

'Thanks Bob, you get better soon please.'

They caught up to Timmy holding open the gate. On the count of three, the lads blew her a kiss then took turns in shaking Combo's paw. Grinning and waving madly, they yelled their farewells across the airfield's small apron.

Yasmin waited until the helicopter was out of sight before her and Combo raced to the motorhome and tore along the dotted lines. If all went according to plan, they'd be rolling into Horsham, Victoria four hours later. Buoyed with the impromptu catch up and knowing she did the right thing, the weight gradually lifted off her shoulders the closer the sun sunk over the horizon behind her, and the closer she got to their destination. The changing countryside was astonishing, but it was the kaleidoscopic colours of the sky she was driving towards which took her breath away. Wishing it was actually a sightseeing holiday, she pretended Emily was with her to listen to the descriptions. Combo got bored very quickly, searched the sky, sighed noisily and got comfortable on the reclined front seat.

They were still two days away from their ultimate destination, but her mind was made up. She would be contacting Emily's snow man at Sale, their next stop the following night. Settling into the spacious campsite, she enjoyed the sensation of sitting by a fire pit and losing her thoughts into the flames. Combo wasn't sure initially, but felt it his obligation to hang across her lap. Enjoying the two nips of whiskey after devouring the T-Bone, fatigue crept in very quickly.

Chapter 37

Nothing was adding up with the evidence. Yasmin Pestel's innocent question of the location of ground zero had him reviewing bewildering cold cases and tearing out what was left of his hair. The firm rap on the door was a pleasant interruption.

'Excuse me, Sergeant Pyers?' The on-loan communications specialist leant a war-beaten youngish body against the door frame. 'Got an update for you. Our asset's business phone is switched off, but we've traced her personal number to Horsham effective sixty minutes ago. Still no trace of the vet. I heard arson has been confirmed, yet zero skeletal remains were discovered indicating the clinic was void of animals, except for what was a snake.

'Can it be identified?'

'Negative. The general consensus is it was skinned before it was wrapped up and cremated.'

'Your thoughts?'

The man in his early forties smirked. 'I don't do S.W.A.G, Boss.'

'What's that?'

'Stupid Wild Ass Guesses.'

Their mutual loud laugh echoed through the empty Station.

He saluted respectfully and pulled himself to attention. 'Night, Sir. My shift has finished.'

Owen returned the salute, swivelled his chair around and looked at the map on the wall. *Victoria huh?*

Chapter 38

Leigh smiled coldly at the collection of macabre photos. Her thumb gently caressing Stu's forlorn face. On the welcome mat of the apartment they had shared in the very early days of the cult, sat a crate with several paws poking out through the wire. Suddenly, Callum's woeful groan from the downstairs office interrupted her recollection.

'Honey? You okay?'

'N-no, I've just had a phone call, can you come here please?'

Closing the attic door behind her, took the stairs two at a time and found her husband sitting on the floor with his head between his knees.

'Honey?' she sat opposite him.

His voice as weak as his colourless face when he looked up. 'Stu's clinic went up in smoke, so far he's nowhere to be found and Clive has gone missing.'

'Who called you?'

'It was from a public phone box with a squeaky door.'

'He? She?'

'A man! He threatened me. Us. If I didn't say the boogey-man's name, he'd find you, slit your throat, wrap you in plastic and—'

Leigh shivered. 'But you didn't. Did you?'

'I told him to stick it because the boogey-man was dead. So no, I didn't.'

She frowned. 'What's wrong then?'

Callum gathered her into his arms. 'H-he was adamant the boogey-man was alive.'

Wriggling out of his embrace, she sneered, 'Someone's playing games. Get Travis on the phone.'

'No! He can be a dangerous man if crossed.'

'Yeah? So can Ivan. But Travis and whichever twin saw R.J.M. go down. Didn't they? Isn't that what Ivan said? Remember what you told me after Adelaide about being silly? Then you got confirmation from the other lot.'

The pathetic shrug of his shoulders annoyed her instantly. 'You seem to think it was Ivan, but I'm sure it was Travis. Do you know anything else, Callum?'

'No, but look who's freaking out now? Come on, let's go and have a smoke.'

'That'll fix everything, hey?'

Retaliating swiftly, 'Seems to have worked so far.'

She stood and put her hands on her hips. 'Come on sad-sack and turn your bloody phone off.'

Painstakingly, Callum drew himself to his full height and expanded his chest. Standing over her, said, 'That was not nice, Leigh. I could call you some names too. But you need to tell me what has made you so angry?' He held out his arms.

Biting her lip, she lowered her head and pushed him away. 'Sorry. I'm just a bit anxious about Moojie. Like you said, we don't know where Stu is, Giles still has to make the pills and pick and pack the weed, plus we haven't had a rehearsal like we usually do and we'll be leaving soon. I just feel like I'm drowning.'

This time when he gathered her into his arms, she didn't resist. 'It'll be okay, we'll run with the usual programme. We've been doing this long enough to know what we're doing. Trav and Ivan will be okay with that. The girls will follow your lead anyway and Giles will do what Giles does.'

'Thanks Honey,' she mumbled into his upper chest, then seductively pressed her body into his. 'Would you like a smoke with me?'

He responded accordingly. 'Always.'

Chapter 39

Low level cloud and a bleak outlook greeted them when they rolled out just after eight o'clock the following morning. Yasmin dreaded driving through Melbourne's concrete jungle.

'We'll just look for the big green signs,' she reminded herself and patted Combo, who yawned noisily.

Constant drivel on the two-way and prattle on the radio frustrated her no end. The closer they got to the sprawled-out city, the more road-rage she developed. Pulling into a smaller town on the outskirts to stretch the legs, reduce the elevated ire and refuel; noticed several other travellers doing the same. Combo barked enthusiastically when he saw another dog, a large black and tan one and not too dissimilar to The Intimidator, also hanging out their passenger window. They had quite the conversation while their respective owners acknowledged each other politely.

'Good day for it, lassie,' the older ginger-haired man called out over the din.

Yasmin thought Sergeant Kohli was big, but this man looked like one of the ancient giant Vikings missing his horned hat, and bit back a smirk. 'That it is, mister. Not looking forward to the concrete jungle though,' replacing the nozzle.

'Aye, mind if I ask where ye goin?'

Yasmin quite liked the accent, and the dogs hadn't stopped their conversation.

'Aiming for Sale, how about you?'

'Beyon' dat,'

'Oh? Can you show me on the map?' Yasmin asked curiously.

He chuckled heartily. 'Nae, lassie … a bit further on!'

Laughing away her embarrassment, said, 'Whoops! Well, all the best to you!'

'Aye.' He dipped his lid.

Watching him reposition his oversized motorhome to allow the one behind him access to the bowser, followed the trend accordingly. They met at the doorway of the service station with matching broad grins.

'It seems our pooches are content wit' ea' oth' so I be waitin' for ye nearby, lassie.'

Peeling out some cash, she paid for more drinks, a couple of chocolate bars, some plain jerky, an ice cream and the fuel, and accepted the escort back to her vehicle.

'Aye, ye eat, I talk.'

His conversation flowed easily about the best roads to take, which two-way channels to avoid and both shared a good chuckle when they introduced each other.

'Nay be callin' me anyt'ing else bu' Paddy,' he said with a smirk.

'Paddy?' she asked with an eyebrow raised and offered her slightly sticky hand. 'Excuse the bits of melted ice cream!'

They shook hands firmly. His belly-laugh was heartwarming. 'Aye, 'tis a long time since I be seein' someun enjoy one so much! Bu' me story is a longun and I be guessin' ye be known as Kimberly.'

'You can call me that! Pleased to know you, Paddy.'

And just like that, she had a new name! They let their dogs familiarise themselves while the pair studied the map.

Paddy had travelled the roads for many years on his annual sojourn and had discovered several detours avoiding traffic congestion. He freely admitted he didn't like the winter and preferred Australia's southern half during its spring and summer. They exchanged phone numbers and agreed to travel in convoy to Sale. Several interesting conversations were held while they navigated the side roads, but the most entertaining was how Paddy travelled in style with his dog. The Rottweiler called Digby was given to him as a pup when his son tragically died in an accident. Accepting Yasmin's condolences, Paddy described how he had channelled his grief into helping some friends establish their private airline charter catering to the elite and their pets. Over the years, their little enterprise had gotten very popular and were at the stage of either acquiring an additional aircraft and crew to their fleet or upgrading their current Gulfstream. They were leaning towards the latter for simplicity, and probably the latest model.

His description of the aircraft sounded like the most luxurious penthouse suite imaginable. Even mood lighting in the powder rooms! Their base was in Hawaii, purely because he really did not like winter. Strange as it was for an Irish-Scotsman or a Scottish-Irishman—depending on his mood—to not like the cold, it was beachcombing along the powdery-white beaches with his four-legged best mate that suited him best.

She couldn't get enough of his travelling stories and by the time they farewelled each other at Sale, just wanted to fly everywhere with Combo. Then scoffed at the foolhardy thought. Illogically swept up in the emotions of the impromptu party, had slipped her passport into Sergeant Kohli's hand while everyone else cooed over the vases of Queen Elizabeth Roses.

Snapping several amusing photos of Combo wrestling with his toys then of the surrounding area during their walk, Yasmin's nerves became increasingly restless. Settling inside for the night, she took a deep breath, said a prayer for Emily and dialled Dean's number.

'Yes?' A man's cautious voice answered.

'Good evening, this is Yasmin Pestel may I speak with Dean please?'

The silent connection eventually disturbed by his shaky breathing.

'After all these years, why now?'

His abruptness wasn't surprising, and replied gently, 'Our beautiful Emily left quite the treasure map to follow … awfully as it is so delayed, my mail had been compromised until recently,'

The silence returned for several minutes before he asked, 'You're here? In town?'

'No, I'm in Sale for the night.'

'Can I phone you back on this number in fifteen minutes?' his voice choked with emotion.

'I will wait in anticipation, thank you.'

She had to swallow hard to settle her nerves and swiftly brewed a coffee. Her hands shook uncontrollably. Why was she so nervous? All she was doing was carrying out Emily's wishes. Her beautiful and only true human friend. Pouring a shot of whiskey, sipped at it until she could feel it go all the way down. That sensation was what she focussed on and by the time the thimble was empty, a sense of calm had taken place. Mindlessly watching the steam curl above the coffee, nearly jumped out of her skin when the mobile rang. A very punctual man it seemed.

'Good evening.'

'It's Dean. This has caught me completely off guard and I'm not good with that.' He coughed quietly.

'I concur and hoped it was the better decision than just pitching up and knocking on your front door. Emily gave me strict instructions and we both loved her for thoroughness amongst all her other beautiful traits.'

'I recall my bride speaking highly of you too.'

'She was my only true, best friend. Surrogate sister even.'

'Yeah, she said the same. I relive all our conversations. It's like I'm a broken record with a horribly deformed needle in a dank echo chamber. Emily was an amazing woman. Do you know it's been years since I've spoken to another adult about her? It's quite soothing actually. In the beginning, I couldn't even bare to think about having this conversation without sobbing like a madman, now I just sob like a normal man whose grief is never far away from surfacing. You get my drift?'

'Do I ever,' she sniffled quietly. 'The rollercoaster of emotions sure has got some awful drops and curves Dean, we just grip as hard as we like, cry as much as we like, but we need to remind ourselves that Emily lived as well and boy, did she love you guys!'

'Can you be kind to yourself when you're grieving?'

'I'm still learning, and if I can do it so can you.'

Yasmin could hear sizzling in the background and Dean's attempt to speak. Eventually, he managed to ask, 'Have you got kids?'

She exhaled slowly. 'No.'

'That's sad. Who have you got?'

'A service dog.'

'A what?'

'A dog!'

'Pardon me but I have to laugh.' He did, then sniffed loudly. 'I miss her so badly.'

Yasmin nodded dumbly.

'You know he reached out to me for the first time in many years?'

In between sniffles, replied, 'No! When?'

'Earlier in the year. You never knew?'

'No, Dean. No, I didn't.'

'I never blamed the bastard for anything, and I told him so. We both agreed to keep searching the ends of the earth for the culprit. I suspected he wouldn't have given up. I haven't given up, but the trail's gone cold.' He cleared his throat. 'How's he doing?'

After a very pregnant pause, exhaled very slowly and very quietly. 'Resting, but not yet in peace.'

'Oh, no. Oh, I am so sorry for you … when?'

'Last week. It's complicated. Our relationship was estranged, had been for many years. His cremation has been delayed, and my business compromised, so I hit the road with my dog, Combo.' She sniffled and excused herself, then spoke with a bit more pep. 'The twins have left me with strict instructions to deliver some mail to you. It's your call how and where.'

'Combo?'

'Yeah. Combo.' She chuckled softly when he flopped beside her expecting a tummy rub while she described his naming convention.

'Cool name! How long have you had him?'

'About three years now, he adopted me.'

'Herbie's been pestering me for one for ages, good company for both and all, but I'm reluctant. I don't know if I could handle watching it get old and then dying. What say you?'

'I'll be devastated, but a child's understanding of life is a lot simpler without adult stresses. As it should be. And dogs? Well, one will choose you guys. A dog's love is unconditional and that is something they know they have to give, that's why they age the way they do so you can experience their whole life's love.'

She burst into tears and buried the phone under her pillow until she sorted herself out. 'Excuse me, please!'

'I knew you wouldn't be as tough as Emily made you out to be, Yasmin Rose Pestel, but you sure wear your heart on your sleeve.' He sniffled and loudly banged the side of the pot. 'That's how I deal with the stresses of life sometimes, the side of a pot or flattening a chicken breast! Dammit it feels … um … what's the bloody word?'

'Cathartic?'

'Yeah! That's it.'

'I know the feeling.'

'Not in the medical way though!'

'Definitely not!'

They shared a genuine laugh for a long while and sniffed simultaneously.

'There's a rest area combined with a park before you get to Myrtleford, it'll be on your right. How about a picnic in the fresh air?'

'That sounds fantastic! What shall I bring?'

He sighed heavily. 'I don't know. It's Herbie's fifteenth birthday tomorrow and he's down in the dumps. He's a kid, but he's not a kid if you get my drift. And it gets worse each year around his birthday. Any suggestions?'

'Cook him a large breakfast! What's his favourite cake and soft drink, and does he like playing frisbee?'

'Bloody hell! I can almost hear Emily,' he chuckled softly. 'Chocolate cake, ginger beer and yes, but it was a very long time ago.'

'We're going to get along just fine, Dean. You've got nothing to worry about, I'm pretty confident about that. It is essential I hand you what is yours and I'm also going to give you the contact number for the three lads. It's time you all got to know each other. I've got a feeling you're going to need each other as well.'

'I met them and their mum briefly.'

Yasmin cleared her throat gently. 'Therein lies another passing you ought to know of. Their mum died earlier this year.'

'Oh, seems we're all connected by grief.'

'No, we are all connected by loving the same people in very different ways.'

'Profound.' He smacked the side of the pot a few more times. 'Righto. You'll have about a five-hour trip ahead of you, so let's make it for around midday?'

'Done deal. I'm in a motorhome and totally independent Dean, so no pressure, okay?'

'Cool. And you're bringing the cake and drinks?'

'You bet!'

'Well ... it's been a long time coming, see you tomorrow, Yasmin.'

'Yes, I look forward to meeting Emily's snow man and son.'

'Huh?'

'That's how Emily referred to you in her letters. I only discovered your name the other day.'

'See you tomorrow.' Dean murmured and disconnected the call.

Chapter 40

You can run but you can't hide.

A little after midnight, he crept soundlessly through the caravan park. Except when he tripped over the neighbouring caravan's grey water hose and swore under his breath when the tail of the long jacket got hooked on another tap. Relieved the hum of the multitude of air conditioning units would have blocked out the crunch of the gravel underfoot, he clipped the unobtrusive magnetic tracker underneath the spare wheel mount. Keeping to the shadows, snuck away without incident and disappeared into the tree line.

Seated behind the wheel of his hired vehicle, he went to remove the moustache and cursed loudly. Wasting another hour looking for it would put the rest of his plans too far behind schedule. He had to get back over the border before he was missed. With the engine idling, activated the transponder and nodded in satisfaction when it started blinking. *We will meet again, Yasmin Rose Pestel.*

Chapter 41

Trying not to disturb the other campers, Yasmin drove out very slowly into a magnificent sunrise painting the landscape in its radiance, elevating the excitement of their day's adventures. The awe of the grand scenery left her wondering why on earth her family thought they had to go to a different country and hemisphere, when all this was in their own backyard. Never had she been amongst such natural beauty or experienced such a headwind. The coloured foliage looked like a sea of fabric shimmering against the purply-blue hue of the mountains. She finally comprehended why artists described the beautiful fauna as comforting to the eye as grandmother's crochet blanket is to the body.

Driving through a sleepy town, simply loved how the newsagency, bakery and hardware store were right beside each other, and ready for business at the crack of dawn. With the local paper, birthday card and wrapping paper tucked in her handbag, she treated Combo and herself to a great looking Danish pastry for breakfast, and for second course, a freshly baked sausage roll. The sweets baker had just filled the cabinet with the most delectable double layered chocolate cake. Expressing her sheer delight, asked if he could pipe *Happy Birthday* in blue writing while she grabbed some drinks from the refrigerator.

Happily doing as she asked, said, 'You look like a big kid who is all wide-eyed and on an adventure!' His face breaking into a slow grin when he looked up.

Returning it, said excitedly, 'You've nailed it in one!'

After rearranging the inside of the motorhome's fridge, writing in the card and wrapping the brand new frisbee—much to Combo's chagrin—and devouring most of the best sausage roll ever, they made tracks northwards. Their excitement grew the closer they got to the Alpine region. Making good time, she hoped they were in the right park and pulled up underneath a gloriously large tree alongside a concrete table and benches. Ancient branches cast a splendid umbrella of shade. With the tablecloth settled neatly, a white Range Rover Sports burbled into the carpark. Combo's tail wagged and sat on command while Yasmin ducked inside her motorhome to wash her hands.

'Hello, it's Emily's snow man and son,' a pleasantly familiar voice called out.

'Won't be a moment!' she replied happily and retied the belt of her 50s style green and white playsuit.

A dark-haired stranger arm-wrestling a small but strapping young lad on the park bench nearer to their own vehicle, brought tears to her eyes. His small, crippled hand gripped tightly around his dad's and was giving it all his might. The words of encouragement were heart wrenching. Yasmin waited patiently until she caught his eye, and blushed instantly when she had. *Oh Emily, you weren't wrong!*

'Ah, there you are. Hello Yasmin, Combo,' They stood and walked towards them. His prosthetic leg gleaming in the sunshine.

She smiled and approached them ready for a handshake with Combo's tail whacking her legs. 'Hello Dean, you must be Herbie!'

Dean's gnarled handshake was surprisingly firm. They sized each other up and Herbie leant against his dad with his crippled hand extended.

'So, you're Aunt Yasmin! Mummily talked about you and Monet. I miss her, do you?'

'Yes, I miss her very much, more than you probably,' she winked.

'Nope, not possible,' he smiled a little, shook his head and couldn't stop looking downwards. 'Can I play with Combo please?'

Replying gently, 'Let me introduce you guys to him so he knows to protect you too. He's a service dog and needs to be reassured he's not on duty. But he has to be on the leash at all times, okay?'

'Yessy,' he mumbled.

'Combo, sit.'

Her quiet command, instantly obeyed. 'Good boy. Okay, without making any sudden moves, confidently hold the back of your hands towards his nose so he can familiarise himself with your scent.'

'Yeah, I know and smile when we look at him without trying to outstare and never feed someone else's dog unless they say it's okay and not all dogs like their heads patted,' Herbie said with a bit more confidence.

Dean and Yasmin exchanged similar looks of surprise. The males displayed their hands appropriately and Combo wagged his tail enthusiastically.

'Good boy. Shake,' Herbie said firmly.

Combo lifted his right paw and Dean bent down to shake it first with Herbie watching on, then did the same. Their new four-legged friend licked the little crippled hand and nuzzled it gently. Herbie giggled and automatically felt around Combo's head with it and played with his ears.

'One's wonky! But gee, they're so soft!' he giggled again. 'Just love the mini mo-hawk!'

Joining in the laughter, Yasmin encouraged the gentle interaction. 'And he likes that ruffled too!'

They were watching Herbie and Combo play on the grass together when Dean explained his son's diminutive build.

'He was a premature baby with his mother dying during delivery. She was ailing in her last trimester. The poor kid hasn't known one for longer than half of his life … his hand doesn't stop him from behaving like a moody teenager neither. We talk about his three mums regularly. I suppose by doing that we're keeping them alive. But you should see his artwork! Who knows where that talent came from, but I put it down to Emily introducing him to Monet right from the get-go. Actually, she introduced all of us to his art. She was a truly remarkable woman that one.'

Yasmin lowered her head giving Dean the opportunity to wipe his watery eyes.

He cleared his throat politely. 'The downside of Herbie maturing is he's taking people's expressions more and more to heart. Some days it doesn't faze him, but other days it does and that's when he recedes into a shell. It's taking longer and longer to get him out of the mood. After we lost Emily, we made a pact that we would always be in each other's company on our birthdays for a week. And categorically told me he didn't want any more mothers. I think he blames himself for their demise and pray he grows out of that thought pattern. I know it's been eight bloody long years, but it may as well have been yesterday.'

Dean continued to explain the trials and tribulations of them both having disabilities; even he got strange looks with his leg and gnarled hand. He too had weeks when he would resent the reminder of the terrible day but had to hold things together for his boy. Sometimes it just got too hard to go out into the world. He was comfortable with working from home those days, but his heart wasn't into being creative or sociable. He just wanted to disappear into the wilderness. And he didn't care whereabouts.

'To be honest, this is the furthest I've ventured since the parents' funeral. It's our home, but I-I lost myself and fear it's too late to be me again. Emily sort of saved me after Julie's death.'

Searching deeply into her memory banks tried in vain to recall the guests. Failing miserably, rested her hand gently on his arm. 'Dean, it's never too late. I'm hazarding a guess you were the quiet one, but when you spoke people listened; they looked up to you and enjoyed your sense of humour.'

He looked at her like she'd materialised out of a bottle. 'You for real? How would you have known that?'

Shrugging, 'Just a guess. But I can tell you're considerate, kind, thoughtful and a great dad who takes on the world's problems to protect his son. What's your biggest fear?'

'That he takes his own life because of the frustration of his crippled hand.'

His bluntness stunned her, until objective logic kicked in. 'Then do something about it. Granted it's an operation, but they've got these robotic hands that are controlled by the nerves, are somehow attached to the wrist, controlled by the brain and-and they look normal. Come on, Dean! When was the last time you watched a movie and couldn't tell if the actor was real or A.I?'

'Yeah, I'm hearing you. I have done some research on it, but how do I put that to a fifteen-year-old who sometimes has the emotions of a little boy?'

'By being honest with him. It's not a life-threatening operation. Go to Switzerland or Japan, they're doing them regularly.' Yasmin looked at him tenderly and whispered, 'Dean, go through it together.'

'You mean my limbs?'

She shrugged meaningfully. 'Why not? If it's impacting your quality of life, do something about it. Be the inspiration.'

'Geez, I can hear Emily in you! Even Julie!'

'They're probably talking through me,' Yasmin winked. 'Now, how about we have a little birthday celebration, then you can read your mail?'

'You sure you aren't all sisters?' he asked with a grin before calling Herbie over to them.

The two came bounding over and got tangled up with each other, ending up face first in the grass. Yasmin was beside them in a flash helping them both up. Combo shook himself and wagged his tail, Herbie dusted himself off and draped one arm over the pooch.

The other, he extended and asked, 'You don't mind holding this ugly hand do you, Aunt Yasmin?'

'No ways, Herbie. I'd hold your hand if you had one or five. Okay, that'd be a bit awkward! But your hand is part of your body!'

'I hate it sometimes. It's worse when girls look at me weirdly. S-some do.' He smiled coyly and added quietly, 'One doesn't but.'

'That one is a very special girl, you know why?'

They stopped walking. She was a mere two inches taller than him, bent her knees and looked him in the eye as he shook his head and whispered, 'No.'

'Because she sees the good things in everything, and more importantly, in you. When a girl doesn't judge you and accepts you for who you are with all your quirks, treasure that friendship for life. There aren't too many people like that in this world, Herbie.'

He threw his arms around her neck and buried his wet face into her shoulder. She wrapped her arms around him and let him cry it out while Combo leant into him. Herbie pulled back, happily drying his eyes with her belt. He was going to be very handsome and mischievous the older he got. A little smile played around the corner of his lips as Combo nuzzled underneath his arm.

'He's also a special friend, isn't he?' he murmured and toyed with the tuft of hair between Combo's ears.

'Yes, Son, he is. He adopted me, and has all the love in the world to give special people, and he knows who the special people are.'

'Yeah! That's why he chose you. Dogs do that! See, they choose who they want to live with. I did something sneaky at the library and researched everything about dogs I could find when I was nine and still want to learn more.' He shrugged then whispered, 'It's my birthday today, I'm fifteen years old. A little middle teenager!'

Yasmin hugged him tightly and wished him a very happy birthday. He giggled when he saw Combo carrying his leash in his mouth and initiated the race towards his dad. While the males went for a walk, she hummed happily and set the table. Soon afterwards, several happy yaps filled the air and turned to see what it was all about. Dean and Herbie looked like they were trying to have an in-depth conversation while her pooch yapped noisily in between them, when another motorhome drove in. Yasmin recognised it instantly and grinned. She was about to yell, but Herbie swooped on the leash and made Combo sit and stay. Then, when the vehicle parked, he walked him purposely away from it and towards Yasmin, who waved enthusiastically to Paddy.

'Here you are,' the lad said handing her the leash, then squealed delightedly when he saw the table.

Herbie hugged her tightly, hugged his present and asked how she knew the other man with a dog. Explaining their impromptu convoy through the concrete jungle, looked at Dean with wide eyes.

'He too lost someone a while back and I think is seeking closure.'

'Coincidence?' Dean asked lightly.

She pursed her lips. 'There's a fine line between coincidences and things happening for a reason. I believe there's no right, wrong or definitive answer.'

'Deep!' Herbie said ripping the paper apart. 'Oh wow! Dad, we haven't played frisbee for years. Thank you so much, Aunt Yasmin. Can we play after cake?'

He was assured they would, but it was Combo who took it gently out of his hands thus confirming there would definitely be a game!

Herbie then gazed over to where Paddy and Digby were, turned to his dad and said, 'Let's invite the man and his dog to my birthday party. I'll always remember my fifteenth! Two new people and two dogs! Please Dad, please?'

As he turned, Yasmin snapped a couple of cameo shots and kept snapping while father and son had a chat.

'Sure Son, why don't you take Combo over, introduce yourself and invite him?'

'Epic!' His voice-breaking squeal and laugh echoing, running alongside Combo.

'Epic?' Dean and Yasmin spoke at the same time with raised eyebrows.

She handed him the camera.

Emotions flickered across his face. 'Where are you staying tonight?'

'There's a homestead at the foot of the ranges which took my fancy, and the ideal place to practice my photography!'

He grinned. 'And then?'

'Take a different road back into South Aus—'

'How did Rudy die?'

Swallowing hard, she replied quietly. 'Suspiciously and cruelly.'

'Police?'

'Yeah. And a K9 Unit.'

'K9 or canine?' His mouth twitched.

Yasmin chuckled. 'I say K9 ... sounds more manly!'

'Ha!' Dean sobered. 'You're searching for answers, aren't you?'

They held each other's gaze. 'Yes.'

'And then?'

'Lay several ghosts to rest. I hope.'

His quiet grunt of acknowledgement was quickly smothered. 'Do you know what the illustrious family did?'

Blushing, 'I was totally oblivious or blissfully ignorant and believed they were in the construction business.'

'Really? Why?'

'Probably too wrapped in the friendship to pay any attention, but around the dinner table, the conversations always revolved around building things. The men did most of the talking. Don't get me wrong, I remember the trucks, flat-beds, graders and a horrid green concrete truck!'

'And the lads? Their business?'

'Never privy to it, presumed they worked with Rudy who didn't correct me when I asked him about the construction projects, near or far, without any idea of what they were because he didn't like too many questions. It was always the same reply, in the same bossy voice, *"no job is without a hiccup, some good days and some bad, same with clients,"* there was always a pause, then he'd say, *"no more questions, Yasmin"*. Embarrassing, hey?'

'Emily never told you?'

'No, we talked girlie stuff. The lads were the lads, us two had more fun doing gymnastics or dancing, getting our licences together ... eventually. We all loved hiking, orienteering and the like and work talk never came up around the camp-fire. Then as we grew up, Emily did whatever she wanted and as I had been encouraged to be independent from a young age, held down several part-time jobs.'

'But you knew of their phenomenal wealth?'

With eyes like soup plates, her indignation erupted. 'No! I had no idea! The ladies were always impeccably dressed, but they mucked in with all the dirty jobs too. The family didn't behave any differently to what I knew, but after the parents died, then forced to go and see my family overseas, I had five hundred bucks to my name and was under the impression we, as a couple, were broke! So, I busted my butt and only discovered some truths this last week.'

'Bloody hell! Will it change you?'

'Hardly! I only know how to work hard! Besides, I'm about to fulfil Emily's wishes, then I need to—'

The approaching racket interrupted the conversation with Herbie jubilantly making the introductions. The connection was instant. Amid a lot of happy barking and laughter, the Scottish-Irishman and Digby had two new lifelong friends, and the party began. With half the cake remaining, everyone agreed it was time to burn it off. They had a race to kick off their shoes and it didn't long for Herbie and the two dogs to be in the middle and very nimble. The adults having to run, chase and wrestle the frisbee, just to get a throw. It was the most competitive and bonding activity Yasmin had ever had the pleasure of experiencing and was buoyed with the enthusiasm of her counterparts. She was on holiday with active friends in the most beautiful place she had seen in her life so far.

After they caught their breaths, Herbie insisted she teach him everything she knew about dogs. When the four of them were in the middle of the grassy area, the small-boy-young-man tugged at her hand and encouraged her to sit down.

'Do you know why we're really over here? Just us four?' he asked innocently.

'It makes it easier for *you* to tell *me* what *you* really know about dogs, you scallywag!'

His giggle was contagious.

'No and I didn't tell a fib 'cos my fingers were crossed. It's so Dad can talk to another man, even if he is way older. I worry about him sometimes. He puts on his brave face. We ... um ... we let each other see we've been crying, but he's a grown up and I'm not one yet. The ginger man and him seemed to have clicked and dad hasn't got a dad to talk to. I hope the big man will let me call him Grand Papee. I like him. and Digby needs to learn how to share!'

Herbie sighed, laid back with his hands behind his head and stared up at the clouds. Yasmin joined him. The dogs lay either side of them. In a whisper, explained that he had hid in the car at a funeral, but when his father was in hospital, he was allowed to stay with him and got to learn how to take a pulse with fingers and check pupils. He got really good at counting.

'I can see a crocodile!' he suddenly squealed excitedly and pointed out the shape.

He kept talking and how eternally grateful he was to still have a dad, casually rolled onto his side and supported his head with his crippled hand.

'I reckon you're not old enough to be called my aunt. Can you just be my big sister?'

Yasmin smirked. *What a gorgeous kid!* 'What would you call me?'

'Can't call you Sister Yasmin, because you're way too pretty to be a nun, and short.' He grinned and eventually managed to flick his fingers. 'SEEstA ... like with two Es and an A at the end.'

'What? Just seesta?'

'Yeah! But say it like you mean it. Really accentuate the Es and the A.'

Yasmin rehearsed it until they were both laughing wildly.

'You won't ever call me a twisted sister, will you?'

Herbie gasped. 'No way! Dad's favourite rockers, and they were an awesome rock band ... um, not saying you're not awesome, but ...'

'We're not gonna take it?'

His loud guffaw sent a flock of corellas into the sky with both dogs springing to their feet and yapping noisily. He got himself up and rocked out the air guitar.

'Sing it with me SEEstA!' he cried, before leading into the chorus.

She did and jammed noisily towards the men alongside her new brother.

With the shadows lengthening, the party wound up much to everyone's disappointment. After the two men exchanged contact details and everyone making promises of keeping in touch, Paddy and Digby reluctantly continued on with their journey. Sworn to secrecy on all counts, Yasmin and Dean also prepared themselves to take their leave in opposite directions. After sharing Timmy's contact details with him, handed over the two navy blue jewellery boxes.

He gripped her hand tightly. 'Yasmin Rose, I don't know what to say.'

'Nor do I, but these are for you and Herbie as well,' taking the mail out of her handbag.

They all sniffed at the air. Instantly Combo leant into her legs and whimpered.

'Charlie Red,' Dean and Herbie whispered, breathing in the air deeply.

Simultaneously the three of them put their hand to their right cheek and murmured Emily's name. Nobody said anything else. They couldn't. Hugging tearfully before leaving each other's company, they knew they would be forever connected.

Chapter 42

Now a redhead with oversized sunglasses, Yasmin conversed with the woman en route to the homestead who explained there was only one night's accommodation available. Part of that strict condition was the traveller had to be gone by dawn the following morning. The brutal insistence tightened her stomach. The description of the animal refuge property partially froze her blood. Forty minutes later with her abdomen constricted into a knot, dropped the dust at the gates and entered paradise. Words failed her, except for the repetitive *'wow'*. The only other sounds were that of the vast amount of bird life and the distant call of an eagle. A woman with an obvious dimple on her chin and very long plaited grey hair, met her at the designated camping spot flanked by three yapping dogs. With Combo on a shortened leash and on duty, Yasmin smiled politely but could smell the booze from four feet away.

'Hello, I'm Kimberly. My dog is on duty so please don't approach too closely.'

'Hi, I'm Jill, that's fine. We've never had a coppa stay here before. Anyway, these three noisy things are Eeny, Meeny and Moe,' she said with a toothy grin.

Yasmin burst out laughing. Those were the best names ever! While the woman was explaining the dos and don'ts of the campsite, a bearded man appeared out of nowhere. Combo growled softly at the same time Yasmin's icy stomach solidified.

'Miss.' The man looked straight through her. 'You gotta be gone by daylight tomorrow.'

'She knows that,' Jill stated flatly.

He ran his hand through his black, greasy thinning hair and turned away calling out over his shoulder, 'Jill, I'm going to pick up some stuff from town and catch up with the girls. Need anything?'

'Oh, righto. You've only just got back from being away! We've hardly seen each other! Geez! But thanks for asking. No, we don't need anything, Travis. Remember to say hello for me, won't you?' she called out sarcastically.

'I'll be bringing them back so you can tell them yourself,' he fired back.

In a quieter voice, grumbled, 'Righto. If I have to.' Then muttered about how her husband always seemed to disappear in the evening to see either one or both of his twin sisters the night before she went on holidays. Then complained how they always got in late and would party till daybreak making it hard for her to leave on time. 'So annoying!' she continued to mumble.

'Twins! You reckon they'd get into mischief?' Yasmin asked with a fake laugh, burying the urge to vomit.

Jill scoffed noisily. 'Uh, they aren't the prettiest so maybe not, but it's nigh on impossible to tell them apart. Both Trina and Laqueel are the same height, exactly the same features, hell, they even sound the same. I've known the family for fifteen years and I still can't tell 'em apart!' Then abruptly pointed in the direction of the mountains. 'It'll be a mesmerising sunset tonight. I'll join you. Hope you drink wine.'

Yasmin wasn't particularly impressed, but accepted the company provided the dogs did not interact. When dinner was suggested, graciously declined the offer hoping it wasn't said too swiftly.

The panoramic sunset silhouetting the mountains while enjoying a glass of the very nice fruity Moscato, was a feast for the eyes. In fact, the serenity was overwhelming. Even the ice in her stomach started spreading to her veins. Gazing towards the valleys, visualised the shapes depicted on the funeral notices. *Could it be? Surely not. Please, no.* Taking several photos of the mountainous skyline and pretend-sipping her wine, all the while listening to Jill's life story, Yasmin's skin crawled. The woman freely described inheriting the animal refuge property from her parents who died soon after her third marriage, almost nine years ago. Yasmin fumbled her glass of wine, emptying it completely. Jill continued speaking as if nothing happened. The woman's parents had always taken on strays, which was how she met her new extended family and their friends.

'They say the third one is usually the right one, but as time goes on, I have my doubts! You ever been married?'

'No.'

Pouring herself another large glass, Jill talked freely. Being a lover of open spaces, animals and an easy income, she preferred travellers to pay her a wage than getting her hands dirty. Her husband, Travis—a travelling salesman—wasn't an animal lover so the horses, cats and dogs went to homes while she takes her holidays. Sometimes she visited New South Wales, avoided South Australia given a soured family relationship, but mainly went to her birthplace in Tasmania. A drawn-out silence befell them. Above, golden rays reached for the opposite horizon. Tinted, caramel-coloured wispy clouds danced across the sky.

'Do you like hiking?' Jill asked suddenly while opening another bottle.

Yasmin almost bit her wine glass. Composing herself quickly, crossed her fingers and asked with interest, 'Ah, can't really say. Why's that?'

'Travis is putting a tour together. If you're interested, I can find the info for you. There's a great hike through the hills and gullies that border New South Wales and the A.C.T.'

'Is it on your phone?'

'Yeah, want me to text it?'

'Nah, it's playing up. I'll take a photo instead. Hey, have you ever been to Moojie Hill?' She snapped a picture of Jill pointing to the picture.

'Nuh, not my scene. I'm not really into art, weird food or hairy armpitted hippies which suits Trav and his sisters nicely.'

'Oh? Do they all have hairy armpits?' Yasmin couldn't stifle her giggle.

Jill joined in and belched at the same time. 'Dunno 'bout the twins! But I don't get on with their friends, that's why I don't go.'

'Oh. Hey! You said you were Tasmanian ... I've got relations down that way. Wouldn't it be hilarious if we were related? What's your name, Jill?' she faked a silly laugh and hiccup. 'Your last name I mean!'

Slurring quite nicely, said. 'Married name is Wilson, nee Mathews with one T,' then hiccupped, belched again, giggled and took another long swig.

Her throat almost constricted beyond recovery. 'Nope! We're not related.'

Jill laughed loudly. This time, the drawn-out silence was becoming particularly uncomfortable and Combo was decidedly anxious.

'Me folks got killed in a multi-fatality tragedy,' the woman drawled lazily. 'Bloody stupid fools going into the snow. It ain't designed for people! But no, they had to push their adventures to the limit. They same with the sharks at sixty, then went sky-diving at seventy! Unbelievable. Flamin' hell, I miss them but. Wished they could give me a message. Pa was good with horses. Hey, do you know anything about horses, Kimby?' Giggled loudly, 'I mean Kimberly!'

Forcing herself to laugh with her, replied, 'Only that they're magnificent creatures. Why?'

'My Sampson isn't right, and I can't get hold of my usual vet. Even though he's in the Adelaide Hills somewhere these days he happily gives me free advice. Funny thing, we have the same surname but aren't related. Travis thinks it's hilarious!'

Shivering like she'd just been dunked in the Antarctic, said, 'I'm sorry about your horse. What about your local vet?'

'Yeah-nah. Don't trust him with me horses. He freaks me out and has far too much influence over Travis. He's a rare visitor, but I just love his curly moustache!' Jill's voice dropped as she looked over her shoulder. 'I just don't know what to do.'

'Pity you couldn't wait a couple of days to make sure your Sampson and other animals are in a nicer home before you go on holidays, Jill. I hope everything works out, but you're going to have to excuse me. I've had a long drive and I'm exhausted. I probably won't see you in the morning so I'll say thank you now.'

They stood together, folded their chairs and walked back to the homestead with all the dogs silently alongside.

Jill waved her half-full glass in the air. 'I'll take this one with me, nice meeting you Kimberly. If you are going to Moojie keep your pooch on a tight leash. Not too many of the weird-folk like dogs. Happy travels.' She spoke slowly and really concentrated on her words all the while staying upright.

Calling out her thanks, watched Jill's shadowy unsteady swagger dance in the flickering light of the garden flames. As soon as she was out of sight, raced around the back of the motorhome and ferociously lost the contents of her stomach, fuming silently the whole time. *I hate wasting food!*

To appease her busy mind after a little game of chasey with Combo, locked themselves away and compiled all the information into a legible document. The uneasy feeling lessened its grip by flicking through the happier photos of the day and previous evening in Sale. Chuckling at Combo's nonsense, she zoomed into the background. She had captured someone who appeared to be looking in their direction. *Don't feed the wrong wolf.* Frowning because of the pixelation on zoom, flicked back to the day's happy snaps and shared several with Dean.

Combo hopped up on his bed and sighed heavily while Yasmin scrutineered the most recent photos. The pit in her empty stomach cramped. Her breath shook. The photos of the mountain peaks were exactly the same as Rudy's macabre collage. Losing the fight with the tears welling her eyes, the moment she cross-referenced the GPS coordinates for Scaley's Valley and Broken Creek, she choked on her breath. She was one kilometre away as the crow flies.

Chapter 43

It felt like no sooner had she shut her eyes they were open, hands fumbling blindly for the alarm. Combo, happy for the cuddles, did not like being moved nor what was happening in front of him. With the last of her own hair tucked under the wig, donned a pair of blue-framed spectacles and encouraged her pooch to join her outside with a handful of liver treats. Clipping on his leash, promised him they would be having more fun soon. She had just closed up the utilities compartment when a deliberate rustle of the shrubs bordering the path caught them off guard. Hunkering down, flicked her fingers at the growling Combo.

She called out, 'Who goes there?'

A woman stepped into the light thrown from the garden flame. 'Best you and that mutt get going.'

'Yep,' *The side profile of a fleeing mare.*

Yasmin raced Combo back inside the vehicle and locked it. Gasping for air, sat with her head between her knees until she felt capable of driving. When she did look skywards, the twinkling morning star beckoned her to follow its path.

A little over eight hours later with only one pitstop, she sat at crossroads on a desolate intersection before turning southwards and headed for the familiarity of Horsham. Every time she blinked, the hideous image melded with the one from the yellow van and scorched her eyeballs. Dry retching at the revolting thought of Rudy's intimacy, welcomed the fatigue when it crept over her like an icky cobweb.

Hoping the first caravan park they came across would accept a drive-in with a dog, the manager took pity on the petite, red-faced, red-haired maiden and suggested she use the powered site furthest away from the cabins. There was only one other camper also with a dog, but a minimum stay of two extra nights was required. Reluctantly accepting the unplanned delay Yasmin handed cash out the window, thanked him and followed the directions on the mud map. No sooner had Combo spotted the large dog basking in the warm weather under the annex of the motorhome he excitedly wagged his tail and pawed frantically at her thigh. She was relieved she had travelled in jeans. It was useless trying to settle him down. His barking just got noisier and higher pitched. It was also too late to do anything about her appearance when she recognised Paddy investigating the racket. She parked with a concrete picnic setting in between them and tried in vain to control Combo, who was drawn to the fire-pit. Yasmin hissed the *protect* command and instantly he walked beside her.

Paddy's laughter boomed. 'Aye, lassie, I see ye wanna be a Scot?'

She bunged on the best accent she could. 'Aye, laddie, 'tis the company I keep, me thinks! Ye changed vehicles!'

'Aye. Dis one's sides po' ou' jus' like me tum! I'll mind de boys go settle yeself in. Ye look a tad frazzled. When ye done, care to join me for a wee drappy wit' some haggis?'

'Aye for a wee drappy, nay for the haggis, thanks.'

'Ye bring lunch, I'll do tea?'

'You're on!'

Their combined laughter echoed through the majestic river gums bordering the campsites. Forcing the volcanic emotions back down the dark pit, she set about preparing something to eat.

Paddy wasn't joking. Two fingers of scotch in a real glass awaited her atop his tartan tablecloth. Doing her utmost to improve the simmering emotions, placed enough bread, cold meat and salad for them to eat heartily.

'A tigh' lipped smile if e'er d'er was one.'

'Nothing like good food in better company to change that!'

Clinking their glasses together, she savoured the smooth heavenly liquid before swallowing.

'Oh, my! That is a nice drop and very welcome, thank you, Paddy. You be teasing me 'bout your heritage?'

'I cannae be both ye tellin' me?' He looked at her steadily. 'Best be telling me yer story, lassie.'

Accepting the admonishment, broadly described her quest without divulging any names. His look of scepticism was as blunt as a sledgehammer until she mentioned Moojie Hill. He retrieved a newspaper and showed her an advert for a grieving session.

'Care to tell me your story, Paddy?'

He deliberated with tales about flying with dogs, then launched into the importance of attending another memorial service for several youngsters in a different rural South Australian town which revolved around his son's death. The most recent event, northwest of their current location, had been a fizzer as had the one held in further east for the third time in succession. His endless suspicions of the youngsters' deaths and quest to find out why had ostracised him from several of his own family members. Tears streamed down Yasmin's cheeks when he described the farming accident and the all too familiar fatalities. It was his son who had died instantly from a broken neck. For ten consecutive years he had attended the outlying memorials and still none of the victim's families had managed to find peace. That was when she wrapped both her hands around his broad wrist.

'Paddy,' she spoke urgently, 'We may be able to help each other. My next quest is to join the dots between rural accidents and a tragic snowmobile accident. It too had fatalities from very similar injuries, but I'm now beginning to think it was mechanical sabotage. Not only that, there have also been suspicious deaths based around heart attacks. Would you like to work with me on this?'

The large man studied her carefully and sipped his dram. Welling eyes failed to obscure the pained emotions washing over his face. She made another round of sandwiches each, ate in silence and waited, relishing in the fine taste of liquid gold.

'Hmm, 'ow?' he asked quietly.

While cautiously explaining the clues, Paddy ate his sandwich. He was still eating when she described the GPS coordinates and the previous night's accommodation. It was at her next destination that perhaps she could find a sense of closure. Her confidence level of linking the where-and-the-who was highly elevated.

'I'll share everything I learn with you,' she urged.

Staring into his glass, asked with a whisper of a dare, 'What d' ye 'ope to achieve ou' o' all o' dis?'

'Peace. Not only for myself but for several ghosts too. And I need to get to Hawaii.'

'Aye, ye do?' The joyful look on his face didn't quite reach his eyes.

'Yes! Could you tell me about Koala ... oh, sorry, Koloa?'

He patted her hand and smiled tenderly. 'I seen some o' dem! Lassie, Koloa's me 'ome. Bu' tirst, I be needin' t' rest me weary head. Aye, t'anks for lunch, I be lettin' ye know when t' join me for tea. 'ow is Combo wit' fire?

'Seems interested in that pit at the moment! He'll be right. I can build one, you just light it when you're ready!'

'I be likin' dat!' and collected her empty glass.

Digby followed him obediently, leaving Combo and Yasmin with their own company. Building a teepee-shaped campfire and shoving a stack of kindling inside the inverted cone, stood back and squealed silently. It was her best yet!

It was as if she were being watched because no sooner had she stepped foot into their mobile abode, her mobile chimed. Combo decided her bed was more comfortable leaving just enough room for her to read a message from Dean, thanking her profusely, with her head on the pillow. The hum of the air conditioner lulled them to sleep.

Surprised at how awake she felt after a thirty-minute shuteye, left her four-legged hot water bottle to take up even more room. Freshening up and brewing a strong coffee, she was ready to tackle the collage of funeral notices. Almost solving one mystery; her gut told her there had to be a link with the letters of Emily's name. She looked at the dates and discovered the majority were prior to Emily's death. How on earth Rudy would have acquired the clippings was the first riddle that popped into her head. But then her heart began to race. The ages of the poor souls who died were predominantly under forty. In total there were seventy-five funeral notices that had at least one coloured letter. Almost two thirds were in Victoria, and that's when she paid closer attention to the addresses of the funeral notices. They were all rural areas. Same with the ones in South Australia, around grain harvest time. But one in particular stood out.

Almost two years before Emily died, there was a combined funeral for four young male farmhands all of foreign descent. Two Canadians, one Korean and one Irishman. Their working holiday coming to an awfully sad ending. A tragic accident on a farm where the ATV rolled, subsequently killing all passengers, but it was the two Canadians who died at the scene from suspected heart attacks. They were orphans. Yasmin burst into tears.

Searching the Internet for news articles on other farm and snow accidents up to three years prior to Emily's death, revealed a class action had been taken out against an importer and major distributor in New South Wales for causing the death of numerous young adults. It was deemed their all-terrain vehicle had major construction issues. After paying out the court costs and contributing to the funeral expenses of all the victims the company had declared bankruptcy.

Around the same time, a completely different trend had entered the snow market. An open, right-hand-drive snow-limo which was promptly snavelled by several boutique ski resorts. Endless scrolling paid off. A website on the twenty-fifth page of results, despite its copyright date being almost nine years earlier, the subdomain name was oddly still active. Occupying one hand, the knotted rope playing tug-o-war with a playful Combo, the other rolled the mouse wheel through the page's contents. Surprisingly, the importer had declared that a common fault of welds in certain snow vehicles' chassis was prone to cracking. Their R & D team had improved the metal's integrity. A quality assurance certificate accompanied all its sales documentation, and the importer even promoted a seasonal structural integrity clause for an affordable fee. It was all there. In black and white. Even a before-and-after image of the later reinforced perilously thin shaft.

A hyperlink led to the particular engineering business, long since closed, which had done a roaring trade rectifying the weakened structures for three years leading up to the Craige family tragedy. Whoever the blogger was, had annotated an investigative journalist tried in vain to interview the owners, but two months after the tragic deaths in the snow, the business premises had been gutted. A graphic of a newspaper article wasn't able to be enlarged so it was impossible to see who the journalist was. A single sentence gave her the goosebumps.

The names of the deceased have never been released.

Rattled that the paid company extract redacted the names and addresses of the directors, the only information available were the dates of operation which conflicted with the year of the known fatal snow travesty. According to the document, the business had shut its doors six months prior. Cross-referencing the business name with that of the company extract left her scratching her head. They weren't the same. Scrolling through the minimal data, it was as if the website was someone's blog who got bored with it all and just let it go. *But why keep the subdomain active?* With her fingers burning the letters off the keyboard, searched for newspaper articles about the known snow accident and any other. There weren't any. Frowning at the ambiguity of the webpage, her little mind-detective got louder than the little voice in her head. Too angry to cry, compared Emily's letter from the resort with Jill's description of her parents' death. On a whim, phoned Dean and prayed it wasn't inconvenient or inappropriate.

'Hello! Everything okay?' he asked pleasantly.

'Hello to you! Yes thanks. All well.'

He paused for a while, then said, 'That's good! Sounds like you're having a good time.'

'I'm sorry I have to ask this, but can you tell me the surnames of the two other couples, please?'

He groaned then chuckled. 'You did what? That's so cool ... nah, no hot-air balloons for me but hey you'll be the first to know if I change my mind ... yeah, a little busy right now ... thanks, I'll message you. Good to hear from you, Cuz ... yeah, you too, thanks for calling. Ciao.'

'Thank you, take care. Bye.'

Yasmin heard him saying something about a cousin in Canada before the call disconnected. While waiting for either Dean or Paddy to make contact, Yasmin ventured onto an obituary website. After an extensive search, eventually found several related heartfelt sentiments. There weren't many, but of the eleven, a single name appeared eight times: R.J.C.L. Wilsmatson. She nearly choked when she wrote it down. Glancing swiftly at the collage, everywhere she looked, matching letters were traced over in either red or black ink. *You have got to be kidding.* Sighing heavily in exasperation, she was about to brew another coffee when Paddy phoned and gave her ninety minutes to get ready for tea. She was to bring herself and Combo, nothing else. Knowing full well *tea* was not a cuppa, happily accepted the invite. While they were having their conversation, Dean sent through a text message.

Names that will haunt me forever: Sancko/winery. Mathews/elderly couple who constantly bragged about sky-diving to celebrate their 70th. :-(

The goosebumps that covered Yasmin's body were three times the size of normal. Her head was telling her it was the one and the same, her heart was telling her not to forget about Sergeant Kohli's investigation. All her stomach was telling her was get ready for dinner. That was until her phone chimed again. Another message from Dean dwindled her appetite. Briefly.

P.S. I'm off the air for a while. Will make contact with you.

Fresh air. Good company. Sometimes the simple things in life enhance the simplest of meals. Thoroughly enjoying a hearty stew and another drop of liquid heaven, Paddy entertained her with stories of his youth and growing up in several different countries. The son of a mineral ore manager, they ended up in several exotic places as a family. But as the women in the family blossomed it wasn't wise for them to be in the vicinity, so just he and his father worked the operations side of the family business together.

'Aye, lassie, gold is in me blood an' in me bones!' Paddy chuckled softly. 'When ye come to Hawaii, I show ye what I be sayin'.'

'Thanks Paddy, I'd like that very much. Do you do much prospecting?'

'Nae, but next winter I be going to de goldfields t'roughout dis fine country and having meself a proper 'oliday.'

'You best be letting me know when and where you be.' Yasmin laughed softly.

'Aye, as ye best be letting me know when ye be comin' to me Island. Me number 'as global roamin'.'

They smirked and clinked their glasses together. Lost in their own thoughts, an inkling developed into realisation that if she did bring Paddy in on her quest it could defeat his purpose, which would be unfair to him. She would never forgive herself if it eroded her own quest. By asking about the Hawaiian night sky and aqua waters, encouraged him to talk about his home enthusiastically and enough for her to mentally clip herself across the ears with the location of her passport.

'Aye, Kimberly,' Paddy plonked a tin of boot polish between them. 'Paint Combo if ye be goin' in a redhead.'

She blushed.

'I nae be needin' t' know ye name 'til de time is right. Don' be in nae 'urry t' leave. Plenty to see 'round 'ere.'

'Yeah, about that. You see—'

'I nae be needin' t' know, lassie. Can we be settlin' on three nights?'

'I take it we're not sight-seeing together then?'

Paddy took ages to measure out another two fingers. In the firelight, raw emotions danced over his weathered face like shadows on the moon's surface.

'Me lassie, 'tis naught de time for dat, but I be drinkin' to ye 'ealth.'

Yasmin smiled kindly and raised her glass to his. 'Aye, me pal. I be drinkin' to ye.'

Finishing dinner with another wee drappy, Paddy complimented her on the perfect fire then told her he was leaving before sunrise. Their paths would eventually cross, yet all contact ought to be minimised unless he initiated it. Yasmin respected his request, thanked him for the delicious dinner and welcomed the opportunity to be in his company again. With her head full of tropical island images and probably one dram too many of a mighty fine drop, bade each other a good evening. Under the rhinestone filled Milky Way, they waited for Paddy and Digby to walk in the opposite direction.

Combo's elevated shackles matched her goosebumps. 'Best you hurry up and do what you've got to do, my boy.'

Chapter 44

With pulse thumping to the pace of the twitching nerve in his jaw, he zoomed into the digital image. *Preferred you as a blonde.* The annoyance of having to make a phone call to verify his suspicions made the tic worse.

Before the recipient had a chance to speak, in a muffled voice his question hissed. 'Hey, what's news?'

Giles flinched. 'How many bloody phones do you have? Anyway, getting ready for Moojie. Where the hell are you?'

'Doesn't matter. Keep talking.'

'Grumpy arse! It's gonna be a big one this year and all eyes are on the Kraut wagon. We should be right, but rumour has it the pigs are infiltrating the nest. Jill's pissed everyone off but. She let a traveller and her dog stay overnight who put stupid ideas in her head about delaying her departure to look after the bloody horse. So not sure when Travis and the twins will be getting there, but it'll be in time for the thing they do. Anyway, you hear about Leigh and Callum?'

'No?'

'She was threatened if he didn't say the boogey-man's name. Callum refused, Leigh went on a bender and accused Clive of taunting her with the name. Anyway, since then he's gone missing. She's a scary woman that one. Clearly the boogey-man isn't dead. Well, that's what Ivan's reckons.'

'And Yasmin?'

'Not going there, mate.'

'How's your head?'

'Reckon I'm a lucky bloke, so I'm doing as I'm told. Pick the weed and make pills. Everyone's on edge like they're playing off against each other. I don't like any of it. Stu, I want out.'

'Who is Stu?'

The silence was punctuated by ragged breathing.

'Who is Stu?'

'Stop playing the fool, buddy.'

'Are you going to say the boogey-man's name?'

'Hell no. Look, you're being an idiot Stu.'

'You got the wrong person. Watch your back.'

The flapping tails of the jacket coincided with the handpiece landing heavily beside the blue public telephone. *Our paths will cross soon.*

Giles stared so hard at the blank mobile phone screen, he went cross-eyed. When the timer buzzed, he shook his head and continued pressing the last batch of pills. Breaking down the peculiar conversation while doing so, he sealed the final bag and realised he hadn't included the key ingredient.

'Whoops, who's going to know?' he grunted, and tipped the ground cane toad skins down the built-in garbage disposal.

Thumbing through his contacts list, he smirked and dialled Stu's emergency contact number. When it began to ring, he shook his head in disbelief and checked his watch. Eight minutes.

He listened to Stu's subdued greeting and responded, 'Yep, it's me, mate. Are you okay?'

'Why wouldn't I be and what's the emergency?'

'You just phoned me and sounded totally weird.'

'I never phoned you, Giles.'

'Well, someone's got this number, knows the latest about everything and even asked about my head.'

'Ivan playing games again?'

'Nope. He's with Leigh and Callum in the shed. Travis is with the twins. Only you're missing from this party, mate.'

Stu sniggered. 'Listen buddy, you just told me Ivan's in the shed and there's a phone in the shed. Look, I've got things to do. Will find you at Moojie.'

'Yep.' Giles frowned at the sudden disconnected call.

He had just slipped the phone into his back pocket when he heard the door open, and called out, 'Job's done and I'm thirsty,'

'And we're hungry. Just came in to check on you. You can drink while you cook,' Ivan slurred.

Leigh pushed through the door after he walked out and made a beeline for the bench, swiping one of the bags and slipping it down the front of her shirt.

'Hey Giles, how they hanging?' she swooned.

'Uh ... yeah, where they should be.' He made sure it was just them within earshot. 'What did you do?'

'Dealt with Clive.'

'What? Why?'

'Setting Ivan and Travis up for a fall so we can get the flock out of here.'

'We?'

'Not us, well yeah, us, but not us as in you and me. Far out, man! Callum and me. You and Stu. Capiche!'

'What did you do to Stu?'

'Nothing. Besides, you owe me.'

'I owe you nothing.'

'Yeah, you will. One of those blokes is gonna go down for Clive's demise. I know he's been diddling us out of cash and drugs over the years, and I also know there's about $250K missing. Just gotta find it. Any ideas?'

'Nuh. I don't do the money side of things, you know that.'

'Yep. Just keep on keeping your mouth shut.'

Ivan's bellowing demands for food made them both flinch. They watched him through the window and hustled towards the door.

'Keep your mouth shut,' Leigh hissed. 'He's a dangerous bastard.'

'How so?' he replied through gritted teeth.

'Oh good, Callum has reeled him back in. Listen, Ivan and my wayward brother were mates.'

'Your wayward brother? Ivan, a foster child? But-but his ma—'

'A conversation for another time, buddy. We were teenagers when we got split up at the foster home. Was relieved back then.'

'After all these years, you're only telling me this now?'

'Yeah well, I'm tired of seeing you get bullied *after all these years*. And even though mine did the same to me, I'm beginning to miss him. Must be getting soft in me old age! You do know that Ivan also had a wayward childhood, don't you? Can't really blame the foster families but. The government maybe? Dunno.'

For the first time in the twenty years that they'd known each other, Leigh's voluptuous lips quivered.

'Wanna talk about it?' Giles asked tenderly, surprising them both.

She sniffled, 'I just remember a fire and never seeing mum and dad again and I think there was a baby, but it could have been one of my dolls. Dunno, it's all blurry.'

Callum's drunk cooee gave them the hurry-up.

'Coming Honey,' Leigh yelled and beckoned the way with her head. 'We'd best get a move on.'

'Back up a sec. How do you know Callum isn't your brother? I've seen him stand over you a few times like Ivan does to me. Have you ever done a DNA test?'

'You're a sicko!'

'Explain how you two just clicked when you first met then?'

'It happens! Zip it, Giles. I'll collect my dues when it's right.'

'Oh yeah? When will I know?'

'You won't.' Leigh pushed him through the doorway. 'Quick, get your arse over to the barbecue before they go ballistic.'

Giles busied himself with oiling the plate and turned away from the unruly dart competition unfolding behind him.

Chapter 45

Sergeant Pyers eyes flicked between Sergeant Kohli and Yasmin's passport laying atop a bundle of files on his desk. 'I asked you in here to discuss something else and you go and toss that on my desk?'

'Yes, Owen. But I have a question first. Why do you have your comms guy tracing her?'

'Because I'm worried She's young, a pocket-rocket, sassy, good-looking and alone.'

'She is not alone. Combo would kill anybody if they approached her inappropriately ... well do his best anyway. Come on, Boss, what the hell are you playing at?'

Owen held out the passport. 'You can talk! Here, put it somewhere safe.' He went to close the door.

'Is this going to take long?' Sergeant Kohli remained standing. 'I've got the auditors wanting to have a chat before they wrap up, which should be in about ten minutes.'

'Excuse me, I forgot about them. How's it going?'

'Last day, thankfully. They're clinical so don't have a heart in my opinion.'

'What seems to be their bleat?'

'Too many dogs for the size of the playground.' Sergeant Kohli checked his watch. 'Can we reconvene a bit later on?'

'Yep. Your shout for smoko.'

They exchanged a half-hearted grin. 'You're as tight as a fish's butt. It's always my shout.'

'Your budget stretches to catering, Sergeant Kohli.'

'And may I remind you that you are the manager of your own—'

'Blah, blah ... get out of here, and get back as quickly as you can. I'll ring through my order. Perhaps your boys can do a sweep?'

The big man mimicked his colleague and good mate, and pretended to skip away like a dainty secretary with Owen's short laugh following him.

Escorting the droll auditors towards their vehicles, Sergeant Kohli seized the opportunity to demonstrate his Unit's prowess, excused himself momentarily and spoke quietly into his collar mic.

'The boss has requested you guys do a sweep.'

As soon as the rear sliding gate opened, three teams kitted up and on duty, marched towards their designated vehicles. The K9s positioning themselves slightly in front but in between their handlers' legs.

Returning to his guests, spoke loudly. 'Gentlemen, thank you for your time and I look forward to reading your report. If you could make your way to your vehicle, my Unit have some business to attend.'

The stuffy senior auditor reluctantly agreed. 'Righteo, Sergeant Kohli. Mind if we watch how they get ready?'

'Not at all.'

Turning to his Team Lead, a barely noticeable nod was acted upon immediately. In perfect choreography, the K9s sat and waited for the rear doors to raise. Mid-way, they launched and magnetically clipped to securing station.

'What about water?' The auditor's ruddy face seemed to darken as he watched the boot lids close automatically.

'Three litres housed in a bladder within their handlers' backpacks, along with their partners' collapsible bowl. A magnetic stainless bowl is in place in their area in the rear of the vehicle. Sanitised after every task.'

They watched the continued display.

'Well, if synchronised vehicle manoeuvres was an Olympic sport, your team would take out gold!'

Sergeant Kohli smirked, 'I'll pass on your compliments!'

Typically, the senior auditor asked the questions while his staff jotted down the answers. 'Describe the harnesses for us.'

'They're of the tactical design. Fully adjustable with retention loops, reinforced handles for ease of lifting and holding and specifically made to suit the weight range of the canine.'

'Is the vet local?'

'No. I prefer one that cannot get familiar with my crew.'

'That makes sense. Do you have that much crime in this area to warrant the exorbitant quantity and level of canines? I mean you've got a nursery, breeding programme, training programme and the oldest Rotty I've ever seen in my life! Not to mention the largest.' With each statement his hands became more animated.

'Progress is a funny thing. We cover a very large area and sometimes seconded for search missions in the remotest areas of other States. The capital simply isn't an appropriate space for this elite squad or programme.'

'Hmm. Noted. Tell me something else, why are the dogs so quiet?'

'You saw them on duty.'

'Ah. Surprise being the element?'

'Yes.'

'It's obvious you're proud of your team, Sergeant Kohli and your love for the dogs is as clear as the day. Looking to the future, what is something you see that needs improving?'

The big man thought long and hard about his answer, thumbed his broad chin and eye-balled each of the auditors. 'A retirement village for the boys and girls to make it easier for them to transition to the rainbow bridge.'

The surliest of the three let out a loud sob. 'Geez, I didn't expect that! How would you do it?'

'Find a block of land with plenty of grass and large trees, a caretaker's cabin and a separate area for them to be set free.' Sergeant Kohli cleared his throat and extended his hand. 'Gentlemen, please excuse me, but the big boss is expecting me to attend another meeting. Thank you for your time.'

Two of the three auditors actually smiled, shook his hand heartily and stepped away. The ruddy-faced man discretely dabbed at his eyes with a monogrammed starched white hanky.

'Sergeant Kohli, I can honestly say this has been one of the most pleasant audits I have conducted. Where's your partner?'

'Hound dogging!'

'Got to keep those genes happening! Mate, seeing all these dogs have tugged at a long-buried aching heart. I think it's time I got myself another one. Thank you. Congratulations to you, and the two and four-legged team members. We'll be in touch.'

'Thank you. I'll be sure to let them know.' Sergeant Kohli shook the auditor's hand. 'Let the dog choose you. Take care, mate.'

'Hey, pursue that dream, mate. I hope to hear more about it at next year's audit!'

They semi-saluted each other at the unspoken alliance.

'It'd be nice to have a beer with you sometime, Sergeant Kohli. Here's my card. If you're ever off duty and in Adelaide, look me up.'

'Cheers, mate. I will.'

With the entire Station catered for, Sergeant Kohli shut the office door with his foot and put the aromatic paper bags on the cleared space. 'Here you go, Boss.'

'Cheers, Boss!' Owen's eyes widened when he ripped upon the bag. 'Yum! What'd you get?'

'Ms Pestel's special!'

'Yeah!'

They shared a good laugh. In between mouthfuls, Owen explained they were still awaiting the forensics report on the skillet, and that the woman of the hour had asked an innocent question about ground zero.

'She's a switched-on cookie,' Sergeant Kohli admitted.

'Well mate, I haven't been able to get that thought out of my head.'

'Humph. Which explains the jumble of files on your desk and on the floor. All you needed to do was ask for help.' Using his big foot, shuffled a few around. 'Hell man, these go back some ten years!'

'Yep, that's why those ones are on the floor and why you're sitting in my office. I suspect you've been dealing with your own demons.'

'And those bags under your eyes aren't loaded with wisdom. What's going on?'

'Haven't been sleeping well. All that aside, I am positive there is a connection between several rural accidents, some in New South Wales, but the majority in South Australia and Victoria, simply because there are just too many death certificates stating heart attacks for too many young victims.'

Stone faced, Sergeant Kohli asked his question quietly. 'Playing detective, Boss?'

'Going with my gut.'

'Speaking of which—'

'What? My gut?'

'Not likely. This Hillyer bloke.'

Owen grunted. 'What about him?'

'An email request for a telephone hook-up with our petite friend. You right if I give him her number?'

'Her business number isn't active.'

'That's not what I asked.' Sergeant Kohli shook his head slowly at Owen's faux pas.

'You already caught me out on that one!'

'We need to be on the same side.'

'Don't we just? Talking about guts, mine are telling me you're keeping something hidden. So, have *you* heard from the young lady?'

'Nope. What led you to these mysterious deaths anyway, Owen?'

'Initially I thought it had something to do with Yasmin's relationship to the Craige family.'

'But?'

'Putting our egos aside for the time being, I discovered a cult had tried to get established in rural New South Wales about thirteen years ago, but they messed up with the initiation drug and took themselves out. The coroner found traces of alfentanil and snake venom—'

Their awkward conversation was interrupted when the desk telephone rang. Owen frowned and answered brusquely.

'Sergeant Pyers ... put him through, thanks Ruth.'

Owen covered the handpiece. 'Dave. E.R.T. Dave.'

'Put him on speaker if it's not personal,' Sergeant Kohli requested.

Owen hastily scrawled down notes, nodded or shook his head, frowned, mumbled, and after eight minutes, hung up.

'Bloody hell, listen to this, mate! His wanna-be-cop sister is a nurse in E.D. at the Royal in Adelaide. Heard there was a BOLO on our vet, knowing of him and an interest in our region, her ears pricked up. Here's where it gets interesting. Apparently, a John Doe comes in with a head trauma after being discovered in the back of an abandoned white van behind a church. Whoever inserted the cannula in his arm probably saved his life for doing so. Long story short, the patient eventually remembers his name and tells the cops he's Stewart Morgan. That's Stewart with an E.W. The sister's man-friend—'

Sergeant Kohli groaned.

'Not the relationship kind because she's gay ... is mates with a detective.' He ignored his colleague's sigh of relief. 'Anyway, suspicions kicked in, so they ran his name through the database and came up with several close matches. This bloke was flagged, suspected ties to a stolen white BMW, but never convicted. Apparently, it's a surprisingly common naming convention with a multitude of spellings.'

'So, ambiguity cleared him?'

'Not our problem, yet. Get this ... sister phones brother, tells all and asks for a description. Instead, brother cleverly gets sister to describe their patient. He was so bald, his head shone.'

'Bald?'

'Yep.' Frowning, Owen answered his personal mobile. 'Dave? I'm going to put you on speaker, Sergeant Kohli is present. Door's closed.'

'Hey big fella. Thought it best not to discuss this over the landline. Listen, sister jumped at an opportunity to be transferred to our hospital for a three-week stint. Can you guys meet us in your carpark?'

'When?' Both Sergeants asked in unison.

'Uh, now? Apologies for the short notice but we need to have a chat.'

Owen simply replied, 'Meet us around the tree of secrets.'

'Cheers mate.'

Through a discrete arched hedge between the compound and the K9 playground, a gravel path led to a round decorative stone table and curved benches. The shade from the surrounding trees guaranteed a pleasant ambiance encouraging a natural release of pent-up information. Sizing up the slender, middle-aged nurse with her auburn fringe peeping out from her nurse's hat, her facial features resembled Dave's except for the large hazel eyes. Automatically, she stuck out her hand towards Owen.

'Sergeant Pyers, I'm Anita. It's a real pleasure meeting you.'

'Likewise. This is Sergeant Kohli, he's—'

Her eyes flashed in recognition. 'It's been a long-time coming Sarge, and I still love dogs! Any chance?'

He smirked at his cohort's enquiring look, then trained his eyes on the woman in front of him and squeezed her hand politely. 'Nice to see you again, Anita. We'll see what we can arrange.'

'Sis,' Dave interrupted gently, 'These guys have a got a lot going on and you need to be at the hospital in an hour.'

She laid her palm on the cool tabletop and spoke intently. 'I've got a nose for things that aren't right, and should be a cop. Anyway, I conducted my own investigation and discovered the van had a dodgy paint job because the inner door panels were still yellow. I paid a visit to the pastor and had a look through his security tapes, sad that a church even has to have security cameras, anyway, I got a buddy to run the plates. Guess what?'

'They match the BMW?' Sergeant Kohli answered first.

'Yep. But that's not all. A man was captured scarpering from the back of the van, then sticking to underneath the church eaves running his gloved hands along the walls.'

Anita pulled out her phone and replayed the recorded video off the security video. 'It's grainy, but I reckon it's your AWOL vet.'

After several moments of silence, her audience disagreed.

'I get the reluctance, but there's more. My supervisor is in a relationship with the hospital security guard and I'm good friends with them both. I put in for this transfer by the way.'

'Why, Anita?' Sergeant Kohli asked her levelly.

She looked at the big man standing with his arms crossed, and said, 'To be closer to the action of course!'

'What? How?'

Instead of replying, smirked and handed Sergeant Pyers her phone. 'You get to see this first. Believe you and the vet don't see eye-to-eye. Press 'play' on that one!'

Annoyed, Owen shook his head. 'Pardon me, Anita, but all I've seen is two blokes shaking hands at the cab rank. The bald patient gets into one which drives away. The old man enters the amenities. Nothing unusual about that.'

By now, Sergeant Kohli had moved closer.

She took back her phone, fiddled with the screen and handed it back. 'Oops, this is the one,' and gave a running commentary on what they were watching.

'Look! The old man is the only visitor to those particular ablutions in six minutes. Four minutes later, a younger man wearing a long grey jacket and a handle-bar moustache positions the cleaning sign against the door, pulls a cap down over his eyes and strides out of the little boy's room, through the foyer towards a telephone box. Who wears a jacket like that in this weather? Anyway, check this out ... this new dude makes a phone call from the public telephone box. Keep an eye on the nurse, the one with the walking stick and the neon-magenta hair. See! She checks her watch. Then hails a taxi. Cabs aren't that rare at a hospital. Now see who's caught up to her. I reckon they know each other. Anyway, this zoomed-in shot and snazzy facial recog app puts two and two together. Lo and behold, this dude *is* your AWOL vet. The one and only, Stuart Morgan C. Wilson.'

'Bloody hell. He's alive and in Adelaide?' Sergeant Pyers grizzled.

'You know his full name, Anita?' Sergeant Kohli asked.

'Uh, yeah ... well nobody knows what the 'C' stands for. But, woohoo, guilty!' She put her hand straight up in the air, then grinned, 'Can't take all the credit, my man-friend is mates with a P.I.'

'How much does this P.I. know?'

'Not enough to get involved and no more than he needed to. He let me play on his computer while the boys went to the races.' Anita fiddled with her phone. 'Here's another recording from a different angle, but this time pay attention to the taxi.'

They did, and all mumbled when they saw the same taxi pull up at the pedestrian crossing.

'Righto, so Baldy is playing games?' Sergeant Pyers motioned with his finger to the nurse. 'And who is the nurse?'

'Not sure. Couldn't get a clear ID. I can tell you that she's not wearing one of our uniforms. Ours has this bloody annoying pleat at the hips which flare out ungracefully when we sit down.' She demonstrated the annoyance. 'It's fine for the really slender ones, but the larger women really find it off-putting. They know they're not on the catwalk, but still, why should anybody be uncomfortable with an issued uniform?'

'Valid point,' Sergeant Kohli agreed with a smirk and made his shirt buttons strain against the fabric.

The instant laughter encouraged Anita to keep enjoying her moment in the sun. 'Here's a mugshot of the head trauma patient.'

Dave groaned and rubbed his head. 'I've seen this guy before, but for the life of me I cannot remember where.'

Sergeant Kohli scoffed. 'That's Giles. Was the garbo, went for DUI taking a blotto mate home, lost his job and generally gets around making a general nuisance of himself without needing to be arrested. Last I heard he was doing odd jobs for cash and the last time I saw him, had a bit more hair.'

'That's it! That's why he's familiar.' Dave said excitedly. 'Old Sammy's funeral a few months ago! This bloke was helping with the burial plot,'

Sergeant Pyers asked a simple question. 'Anita, can you divulge the nature of a patient's injury without breaking policy?'

'No problems there. The bruising is similar to being hit with something heavy and solid but flat which only knocked him out. If it had been a more forceful collision, he'd have been dead instantly.'

The look of relief that swept over the uniformed men was noticeable, yet neither of their visitors said anything. They made a show of looking at their respective timepieces.

Sergeant Kohli cleared his throat politely. 'Anita, we do appreciate the—'

'Intel?' She volunteered rapidly.

Both policemen smiled and nodded.

Sergeant Kohli spoke first. 'Yes, that's a great word for it. Come with me and I'll give you a quick visit to the nursery. The boys are a bit busy.'

She extended her hand towards Sergeant Pyers. 'Thank you so much for your time. I do hope to meet with you again. All the best, Sir.'

'To you, Anita, and thank you again. Enjoy our town,' Owen replied.

'I do already. Simply love those distant rolling hills!' she hooked her arm through Sergeant Kohli's. 'Let's go, Boss.'

When they were out of earshot, Owen shook his head at Dave. 'Man, you have got to get the notion out of her head!'

'Doing my utmost, believe me. Reckon the old man would reach down from behind the pearly gates and bitch-slap me if she did become a cop!'

After their chuckles subsided, Owen asked, 'Did you find anything of interest from the fire at the vet clinic?'

'Definitely arson. Business neighbours always heard animals, vehicles frequented but they didn't really pay attention to who or what got in or out. Then this autistic kid decides he'd like to learn all about being a fireman, adopts my oldest colleague and they get talking. Because the kid isn't fit for school, he hangs around his mother's coffee van. I quote: *the animals weren't alive. It was a recording. The same cockatoo squawk, the same time every day since forever.*'

'Really?'

'Yep. Explains the lack of carcasses, barring the snake.'

'Did this kid say anything else? Will he?'

'Probably not. Got upset when he saw a customer put rubbish in the wrong bin. He wasn't approachable after that. We respected his mother's warning that the lad was quite a handful when he's unhappy.'

'Fair enough. Best we go and give the dog lovers a hurry up!'

Anita kept wiping at her eyes, being careful not to smudge her makeup. 'Oh, I just want to hide in there forever! Do all the females grow up to breed?'

'Some do, some don't,' Sergeant Kohli replied quietly. 'Come along, you're needed somewhere else.'

'Can I have one? Please?' Anita blushed. 'Heavens, listen to me. I sound like a spoilt brat. Sorry, pal.'

'I get where you're coming from, Anita. I want them all too, that's why I do the job I do. But you must shove all notions of being a policewoman out of your pretty head. You've taken the Hippocratic Oath and you must not break that. Surely you remember me imparting that advice when you first enquired?'

She looked up at the big man and playfully punched him on the shoulder. 'Of course I do! That's why I'm still a nurse. Whoops! Shouldn't have touched you, sorry, Sergeant Kohli.'

He made a show of rubbing the other arm, causing Anita to laugh loudly. As they rounded the corner of the building, she gripped the Sergeant's hand. 'Meow! Who is that bundle of bold beauty?'

Following her pointing finger, Sergeant Kohli noticed the solid, lithe woman jogging across the carpark. Her neon-green hair shining eerily under the sun, while her running gear clung to every nook and cranny. The woman changed directions and raced towards the pair. She smiled broadly at Anita and kept looking at her while speaking rapidly to the big man beside her.

'Sergeant Kohli, I'm Penny. I have to speak with my Boss ... Sergeant Pyers ... please, it's urgent, do you know where I can-can find him?'

'Excuse me, Sarge. Hi, I'm Anita,' and thrust out her hand.

'Hi! That's not our nurse's uniform. Where are you from?' Penny asked happily.

'The city.'

'Oh! How fascinating.'

'Yeah ... but the colour of your hair! It's so bright!' Anita went to touch it then pulled back.

Penny blushed. 'Yep, keeping up with the fundraising trend! Don't ever try bright yellow, I felt like an anaemic sunflower!'

Sergeant Kohli cleared his throat and bit back a smirk. 'Ladies, time's ticking. Penny, here's your Boss now.'

She gripped his and Anita's hands tightly and dragged them with her.

'Boss! Hey, Dave.'

'Penny! You're back early?'

'I'm eloping ... it's a dare. I'll bring him back for you.'

'Congrats! Did you meet him at Moojie Hill?' Owen asked with a wry grin.

'Uh yeah, something like that. Just wanted you to be the first to know. Get ready for a party and a show-down when I get back! Anyways, you're the best boss ever and I'm heading off now, just needed to give you the heads-up ... oh and I needed to grab a dress.'

'A dress? You've never even worn a dress to a Christmas Party!' Dave laughed loudly.

'No, but you have!' she slapped him across his shoulder then pinched his cheek. 'I've got to fly. Really nice meeting you Anita, and I hope to get to know you too. You look so cute in your uniform!'

With a flurry, she pecked everyone on the cheek and sprinted back to her car. Driving a little too erratically for her boss's liking, tooted the horn, indicated left and turned right.

'Is she okay?' Anita asked. The concern for her new friend was pretty obvious.

Dave took the lead swiftly. 'Ah, Sis, we've got to roll. You cannot be late for work.'

Her demeanour changed instantly. With a firm handshake to Sergeant Pyers first, then gripping Sergeant Kohli's hand, she reached up as if she was going to kiss him on the cheek.

Instead, she whispered in his ear, 'I bet you fifty bucks it's the nurse.'

Almost shouting out her thanks, Anita whisked Dave smartly towards their car.

With a twitch of his lips, Sergeant Kohli couldn't resist. 'I suppose your Penny is gay too?'

'Hadn't thought about it, but after witnessing the instant attraction with my own eyes, I'm guessing she is, or bi? Didn't she mention a bloke? Am really curious about this dare but even more how you know Anita?'

'Our paths crossed years ago, besides, who could forget this face?'

The men laughed for a brief moment, before Sergeant Kohli spoke bluntly. 'Reckon your Communications Expert has another number to trace.'

'Appears that way. Have you got anybody you can reach out to? We might need an extra hand or three.'

'Yep. I'll catch you up.'

A little over an hour, they were back in Owen's office where he had used the mobile phone to divide the folders along the length of his desk. 'Can you spare me more of your time?'

'Sure can. My guys have got things to get on with and I believe Helen was collecting Pam and Nanna for a visit to Carl, so I won't be knocking off early.'

'Mother hens!'

'Yep, and we wouldn't have it any other way.'

Owen absentmindedly agreed and rifled through the pile looking for the cold case Dave had mentioned.

Two hours later, Dave swung by the Station. Ruth escorted him into Sergeant Pyers' office and closed the door leaving the men alone.

'Gents, Anita couldn't stop talking about her visit and the K9s or saying thank you! But you need to see this.'

The three stood with their backs to the door. While Dave propped his digital notebook on the desk, he explained the USB was left on his front seat while he was with his sister at the hospital. His cohorts didn't comment, so he pressed play.

Owen spluttered. 'Oh God no.'

'What's she playing at?' Sergeant Kohli scoffed.

They watched in astonishment as the woman transformed herself into a vacant-eyed, Gothic, unrecognisable female.

'Don't know, big fella, but I'm guessing there's more to this dare than we will ever know. Does your reach extend to monitoring any of this, guys? Penny's a top bird!'

Owen said reassuringly, 'Working on it, thanks Dave.'

'Can I do anything?'

Sergeant Kohli put his hand lightly on Dave's shoulder. 'Mate, just keep your sister in check please. Owen will do the same with Penny, won't you?'

'Uh yeah. I had no idea.'

'She's good. I'll give her that much.'

Dave semi saluted his cohorts and opened the door. 'I'm only a phone call away. See ya.'

He was about to walk out when Owen glared at his ringing desk phone. 'Hang five.'

Dave automatically shut the door.

'Sergeant Pyers speaking. Speak up, I cannot hear you.'

'Boss, it's me, Penny. I'm phoning from a public phone box. I'm okay. You need to check out the funeral parlour. Clive's dodgy. I cannot tell you everything but if you get a whack of people in the pens, ask who the boogey-man is.'

'What?'

'Catchya. You're the best boss ever.'

'That's twice ... Penny? She hung up.' Owen sat with the receiver in his hand, looking blankly at Dave and Sergeant Kohli. 'Either of you know anything about a boogey-man?'

Their combined negative answers had them all scratching their heads.

'Well, according to Penny, we'll know when to ask the question. Right now, though, I've got a more pressing matter to attend to. Catch you both later. Please close the door after you leave as well, Boss.'

Sergeant Kohli wasn't used to being dismissed so emphatically and hesitated. Dave turned to answer his phone and waved over his shoulder as he walked away.

'Owen?'

He scratched at his ear lobe. 'I'm late for something and you've got things to organise. Please?'

'Of course.'

Closing the door quietly, Sergeant Kohli stared at the back of Owen's head through the glass panel. *Hmm something's not right.*

Chapter 46

Nagging mental voices and clumsy impatience exacerbated Yasmin ire very nearly on the last day of the forced rest. Indignant that she ignored her own assertion, not even the extraordinary scenery and vastly improved photography provided the pacification she desperately sought. Sighing heavily, they buckled up just as the multicoloured dawn exploded in a messy spectrum.

By mid-morning, her fuse was ready to go off. Combo's annoying yap-and-lunge at every vehicle. One pesky fly. The sheer heat off her face would have easily matched the colour of the wig. They had only stopped for fuel and two necessary breaks, were hungry and desperately needed to burn off the dormant energy. Parking outside the police station in Edenshope, the pair followed the historical trail through the little town, then jogged the five-kilometre track around its lake. Several other people were also enjoying the exercise and frequently stopped to take photos of the abundant birdlife.

Her mood did not entertain being creative. Instead succumbed to the hunger pangs and cooked up two beef patties, three rashers of bacon and two eggs, downed an iced coffee and shared the leftovers with Combo. Afterwards, he rested his head on her knee, looked up at her with large, adoring eyes and wagged his tail lazily. She performed their special ritual which seemed to pacify him enough to warrant jumping back onto his seat and settle in for a sleep. He stretched, looked at her and puppy-sighed loudly. Smiling and yawning was a much-needed facial exercise, so much so, her eyes watered. Then she couldn't stop yawning.

It was Combo's noisy dream that influenced hers and shrieked herself awake when Stu bullied her in the way the high-school jerk did. She stared numbly at the time. *No! Three and a half hours?* It took another half an hour to hit the road.

Long shadows, single lane roads, lack of mobile phone service, roadworks, detours, stressful hours of navigating horridly corrugated dirt roads, getting lost, and miles and miles of farmland heightened the growing anxiety the closer they got to their destination. Twenty minutes out, they bumped off the road onto the rough verge and came to a sudden stop. She gripped the steering wheel tightly. Her breath came in rapid gasps. Combo's concern peaked. He couldn't reach her. His frantic whining elevated to panicked barking. Yasmin burst into tears. Releasing her seatbelt, she wrapped her arms around her beloved pooch and wailed helplessly. He joined her in a mournful howl until he rested his forehead against hers, hushing her instantly.

'Oh Combo, my sedative.'

Morosely, they sat on the sidestep and shared some jerky. Suffocating questions clashed with the dried salty meat. Her throat constricted. Yasmin banged her chest, hit her back as best she could, doubled-over, coughed, spluttered and dry-retched. With tears streaming down her face, stuck her fingers down her throat. Eventually, the offending morsel got flung as far as she could. Panting, sniffling and snuffling, with Combo practically another appendage they walked around the vehicle, checked the connections and listened to the eerie twilight noises. She wiggled the spare wheel and prayed whatever fell off by her feet wasn't important.

Nighttime travelling was not her favourite pastime and joined the snaking taillights of other late arrivals into the small town. A well-lit welcome sign encouraged travellers to tune into the local radio station or Channel 20 on the two-way for all the festival's information. It didn't matter which medium, the compere prattled relentlessly.

'Welcome to Moojie Hill! Respect the locals! Park where you like! Camp wherever you can! Take your rubbish with you! Dogs on leashes at all times! Take their rubbish too! Don't litter! Keep our town tidy! Great food! Great art! Peace, love and happiness!'

With the showground being the nucleus of the festival, everyone naturally fanned out from it. Yasmin had no intention of mixing with anyone, except Paddy. If he was still there. She bristled at the lingering indignation, sighed heavily and did her utmost to dismiss as many negative thoughts as she could. Besides, her throat was raw and she didn't feel like talking. Pulling up behind the closed petrol station on the southern outskirts of town, killed the headlights and reverse parked using the camera. Eerily, they were alone. Angry and emotional, she steamed a paper-thin chicken breast in a blend of lemon, honey and herbs. Combo lay beside her and rested his head on her foot.

'I'm just about done with this game,' she croaked. 'What in the hell was I thinking?'

Chapter 47

Long before daybreak and desperately needing some exercise, Yasmin and Combo sprinted for fifteen minutes, turned around and raced back to the motorhome. Panting more from anxiety than exertion, they caught their breaths and changed their appearances. Combo ended up with a black jagged splotch around his left eye which spread upwards to his ear, and a blackened right paw. The lower half of his tail also ended up being smudged with the boot polish. He was not impressed.

Nor was she. It took forever to get her hands back to normal and even long to blend foundation down her neck onto the natural colouring of where her baggy shirt didn't cover. After a heavy coat of bright blue eyeshadow, on went the fake lashes. With a 'beauty spot' beneath her left eye, light smattering of the pink rouge highlighting her cheeks and eyebrow-pencil freckles across the bridge of her nose, used black ink and drew the only thing she could on her wrist. A love heart. Except this one had an unusual curve given she jumped out of her skin when the mobile phone rang.

After several rings, she cautiously answered the undisclosed number. 'Hello?'

'Ah, Ms Pestel, Detective Hillyer speaking. Apologies for the early call. Have you got a moment?'

'A very early call and only briefly available. You were supposed to contact the police station before contacting me. Just how did you get my number?' she asked quietly.

'I am a detective after all, but rest assured they know I'm phoning you. I wanted to tell you this myself. You'll have to excuse my absence. I was called away on another case and am still stuck in the city. Thought you'd like to know that I sent the woman's blouse away for testing. Unfortunately, there's a backlog and it could take another two weeks before I get anything.'

'Oh, okay. Thank you.'

'Um, this is highly unprofessional, but I haven't been able to get you out of my mind. Could I call on you? Please?'

She felt her face redden. After a long pause finally replied. 'Eventually … perhaps.'

'I would really like that. That constable did remember to give you my card, didn't he?'

'Yes, he did. Thank you. You'll have to excuse me. I have some arrangements to attend to.'

'Of course, please pardon the intrusion. I hope to hear from you soon, Ms Pestel. Wait, before you go,' he chuckled softly, 'How's our jealous furry one?'

She smiled and ruffled Combo's head. 'Still the same. Thanks for asking.'

'Nice. Okay, bye, take care, bye for now.'

'Bye.'

Yasmin stabbed at the disconnect icon and gave herself a stern talking to while stuffing a cotton wool roll into either side of her cheeks. With a fattened face, baggy jeans and oversized pale orange shirt, donned her biggest hat and mirrored fit-overs concealing a pair of in-fashion, tortoise shell framed fake glasses. Looking over her shoulder at the mirror, scoffed at her derriere. It didn't matter what she wore, that part of her anatomy would always draw attention. Combo tolerated the bandana around his collar but flatly refused to wear his sunnies. There was no way she was going to put a pebble in her shoes either.

Astonished at how many dogs went on holidays with their owners, Combo had a fat time partaking in the different scents! Grass was a bit light on, but they all seemed to leave their calling cards wherever they could. He yapped loudly and jumped at her when they saw Paddy and Digby standing at a mobile food van promoting breakfast. She shortened his leash and took another path.

'Not today, boy,' she hissed. 'Heel. Protect.'

He grew in stature. A lot of people took very wide berths, whether they had a dog or not. Very few of his kind looked sideways at him. Standing underneath a tree and observing the varied walks of life, his wagging tail gave away who was walking towards them.

'Mind if we join ye in d' shade, Miss?'

'Not at all. Quite a big turnout I see.'

Paddy grinned and lowered his voice. 'Not sure 'bout de puffy cheeks, ye ain't goin' t' drink 'nough and ye got a big day ahead.'

'Hmm I feel like a fool,' and removed the offensive additions, replenished her gums with saliva then a long drink of water.

'And ye be needin' to eat dis.' He handed her a double bacon and egg burger. 'Den ye 'ave t' be brave.'

They stood beside each other. Their companions in protection mode doing their best not to beg but salivated freely while their owners devoured the welcome breakfast, each sacrificing a rasher of bacon. While they went through the sit-shake-eat routine, Paddy quietly explained that the most recent memorial service had been a repeat of previous years, albeit with less attendees and even sadder because of it. He was about to say something else when an older woman pulling an even older dog in a trolley called out as she approached.

'Hellooo, just taking a breather, me old boy is getting frazzled with the crowds. Do you mind?'

'Let's be gone,' Paddy murmured.

'It's all yours,' Yasmin said politely.

'Thank you so much, he really is grumpy today! Bit like his master who wants the German Wurst, so we'll just wait here! It's probably the busiest food van all the time for years on end! Anyhoo, enjoy. Peace and love to you both and your gorgeous boys.'

'To you too,' Paddy said politely and clasped Yasmin's wrist.

They were silent for a while, until she got the giggles imagining Shrek and Fiona.

'Dat's the long and short of it, aye?' Paddy joined her with a raspy chuckle. Then cleared his throat nervously. 'Me wee lassie, there's a sometin' I need t' do dat be long overdoo. Oi need ye t' mind me boy. Can ye be lookin' at art for t'day?'

She gripped his arm tightly. 'I'm nervous as all hell, doubting my braveness and desperately need to wash my hands! But Paddy, only for you will I look at art.'

'Ye leave ye bravado at the border, lassie?'

He said something to his pooch in a strange dialect, then ruffled Combo's head and slipped Digby's leash onto her wrist.

'Ye wash your hands, while I pour.' Afterwards, looking intently into Yasmin's eyes, he murmured, 'Ye 'ang 'round de art stalls. I be findin' ye.'

She gulped down her nerves and faked a brave smile.

'Dat's me lassie!'

They continued to stroll through the progressively expanding art section and stood in the shade of a large tree beyond the last stall. Watching the construction of its canvas walls with idle interest, drab charcoal smudges mixed with dull green abstract shapes painted on an almost black background seemed odd.

'Aye, t'ere's a darkness in t'ere in no' a hurry t' see d' ligh',' Paddy murmured quietly.

'I thought this section would already be set up by now?'

'From wha' I be seein' o'er de years, de arty-farties always ta'e d'ere own easy time.'

'Who looked after Digby during those times?'

'I dinna do wha' I'm goin' t' do t'day. Fate, wee lassie, tis fate.'

'Have you tried the German Wurst?'

'I b' sayin' nought an' ye cannae d' beer hall.'

During the next hour, five men and four women of varying ages filed past them like strangers in a shopping mall. Paddy simply followed the line. Combo and Digby pulled on their leashes when he disappeared into the darkness of a large old barn. They were about fifteen metres from its entrance when a tall, strong man wearing a sickly yellow suit stepped outside and put his hand up warding them off. His moving scarf shimmered in the dappled sunlight.

'Oi. No mutts allowed here,' he yelled out coldly.

'We are nowhere near you. So much for peace and loving!' She fired back. *You scary freak.*

'You've gone past the last art stall, turn around. No mutts allowed here. Do you hear me?'

She whispered her commands, 'Turn. Heel.'

Amazed that the dogs didn't get tangled up only slightly eased her nerves. When she looked over her shoulder the barn doors were closed. Seating themselves under the large shady tree, she pacified her protectors with liver treats and silently watched the world of strangers amuse themselves.

Melodic chanting drifted through the air. Even the dogs pricked their ears and cocked their heads. She couldn't resist. Stretching as she got up, they made a beeline for the shrubbery that ran alongside the historical structure. Long, gnarled sticks propped up straw windows. Making a show of getting out doggy-do bags on the off-chance someone was watching, she allowed the dogs to lead the way. Their natural instinct kept them in the shadows. The closer they got, the louder the rhythmic chant.

'Choose to stay, choose to leave, it's not too late to choose.'

Goosebumps covered her body. Her protectors growled softly. She crouched between them. The hair at the back of her neck as elevated as the dogs' shackles.

'Soon, soon you will all choose. We have all suffered loss and you don't need to suffer anymore. The highlands will help you choose. You have waited too long.'

Yasmin gasped so hard she nearly passed out. Staggering into the nearby scrub, the distant chant got louder and louder until it filled her head drowning out all ability to comprehend logic. Desperately drinking in oxygen with a dog leaning heavily into each leg, regained control. In a stern, albeit wobbled tone, commanded them to walk away. Forcing the chant out of her head by thinking of her and Emily's silly little ditty, Combo took the lead and led them through the sprawling mixed art and craft stalls. When he sat, Digby followed suit and she paid closer attention to her surrounds. Some stalls had canvas walls, others simple shade structures, and a few open to the elements. Windchimes and dreamcatchers flitted in the gentle breeze while women with hairy armpits tainted it. Yasmin spared a thought for Jill, instantly felt nauseous and swiped at the tears losing both false eyelashes and horribly smudging the glasses in the process. *Why were you so manipulating, Rudy?*

It appeared the menfolk just stood around with their hands on their hips, and nearly everyone shared smokes wearing lazy smiles. Not a lot of the arty folk seemed to want to have anything to do with dogs, yet the majority of show-goers were elderly with their pets either in their arms or in carts. Children were noticeably scarce.

Taking a seat on a grassy mound out of everyone's way, Yasmin couldn't stop staring at a bright, multi-coloured canvas wall being attached to a frame. The happy-go-lucky folk were making a complete mess of it and laughing the entire time. Then she noticed two children noisily rearranging easels and generally getting under the feet of the neighbouring stall holder. Their antics changing the shape of her mouth, but it was obvious patterned clothing and crochet hats were their favourite attire. They changed or swapped outfits three times rattling tambourines on each occasion. At long last, the canvas curtains slid around the frame enclosing the stall on three sides. The artist's name brought on another layer of goosebumps at the exact time a woman walked past carrying a bundle of folded timber easels. Her hideously dense paisley shirt clashed with the baggy tie-dye pants. *Sally White?* Barely breathing, watched her walk into the namesake stall as the two children skipped out, laughing loudly.

Curiosity got the better of Yasmin. Encouraging the dogs to protect, they took the long way around and caught up to the familiar woman and a man bickering, while dragging their old dog in the trolley who seemed to have gotten taller. Combo suddenly stopped, sniffed the air enthusiastically and snapped at Digby who instantly sat. It was only when there was plenty of distance between them did Combo let his party follow at a snail's pace.

Not liking the crowded path ahead of them, Yasmin tugged on their leashes. 'This way,' she said quietly.

Veering between the stalls, inevitably had to give way to a group of rowdy smoke-sharing lads. They ogled her, sneered at the dogs, exhaled in their general direction and moved backwards very quickly when a duo of snarls and growls broke out. When they backed into a tall, heavy-set man twirling one side of his bushy handle-bar moustache, the other on his hips, she bit back a smirk. The mauve and yellow tie-die tunic over black jeans and thongs looked totally ridiculous. More so, the long jacket casually draped over one shoulder. *It's inside out! Hey, is that the cricketer?*

'Either pick on someone your own size or move on.' His nasally voice instantly annoyed her and both dogs cocked their heads.

The group of misfits scurried away without a second glance.

'You okay, miss?' He went to take a step towards her, but changed his mind when the dogs moved.

She bunged on a bogan accent. 'Yeah, mate, grouse. Oi, ya that cricketer? What's-his-name … um … Hughes?'

'I get that a lot, but I couldn't bowl a maiden over let alone wear white!' Both hands settled on his hips. 'Are you okay?'

'Yep! Ta.' She clicked her tongue instantly bringing the dogs back to her knees.

'That's good. Take care.' He smiled politely, turned and walked between two stalls.

Combo and Digby pulled her to where he was last standing and looked around frantically. It was like he simply disappeared but left sweet smoke mingled with a stale spicy scent hanging in the air. Holding her breath, they walked through it, with the last person she wanted to think about was Chas and his alluring aftershave. Backtracking, they eventually stood in front of Sally White's stall. *It IS her!* The woman hadn't changed her dress style since high school and the snake-tattooed index finger hadn't faded one bit. Although the head had disappeared on her non-paintbrush hand.

'You lookin' at something?' the rose-tinted-glasses-wearing-artist sneered at her.

'Your finger actually! You must be talented to paint without a fingertip!'

Sally laughed coldly. 'It's easy. I paint with me other hand!'

'Oh, silly me!' giggling weakly.

'Do you want to come in and have a look around?'

'What about my dogs?'

'Hmm, they don't look the type to run amok, so yeah, let's give it a twirl.'

Oh for the sake of F, she still says that? It's no wonder I don't eat those chocolate bars. Smiling wanly, nodded her thanks.

Bending down to eye level, she looked into each dog's cautious pair of eyes and whispered, 'Heel. Gentle.' A loud gasp escaped when she turned to stand.

'What's wrong with you?' Sally demanded.

'Your easels! It is Silky Oak, isn't it?'

'Yep.'

'Beautiful timber! But the monogrammed stamps? Where does the R.J.M. come into it if you're Sally White?' her mind exploding with a variety of expletives.

'Oh,' the woman's voice softened instantly. 'He sponsored my first exhibition up in Loxton. Do you know where that is?'

Her stomach flopped. Fibbing, 'Not really.'

'Never mind. It was my hometown but we're more gypsies these days,' she said wistfully. 'Anyway, long story short, met a man younger than me who was spruiking the easels from his own timber mill somewhere on the other side of the country. I fell in love with the Silky Oak the same way he loved gold, then we both fell in love with him.'

'I'm confused. We?' fiddling with her phone.

'Yeah. Me daughter and me.' she sniffed and wiped at her eyes from under the glasses with the finger stub. 'Anyway, he donated these to me soon after, but I recently heard he passed away.'

Her eyes filled with an emotional maelstrom and turned away to consciously smooth Combo's and Digby's bristles. A loud commotion outside the tent prevented her from saying anything and both women shrieked when something heavy fell against the sidewall. The dogs barked a warning. Foul language stained the air.

The neighbouring stallholder called out. 'Sorry Sally, that was Ivan's son and his mates. Rascals are all stoned out of their tree.'

The woman wiped at her eyes again and called out, 'Thanks, mate.' Looking back at Yasmin, she sniffed. 'I sincerely hope you don't swear like that.'

'No way! '

'He was so young, so virile and sometimes like he was in another world. Such a shame.'

'You've got his beautiful easels—'

'Yeah, but I missed his funeral. Some friends told me they saw him on the morning of, wandering aimlessly through a paddock,' she snorted noisily.

'Sally, let's stand outside a little—'

'No. If I sit here, I can see him.'

'You can? How?'

'I painted him, you fool!'

Gripping the leashes until her knuckles turned white, replied quietly, 'Yes. Of course. There is no need to be nasty.'

Sally's voice rose shrilly. She didn't even breathe. 'Well, how do you think I feel? I'm talking to a complete stranger about someone I loved, we loved, who fathered my child, my daughter's child and who has recently died.'

They glared at each other until Yasmin looked downwards. 'Sorry for your loss. How did you meet?'

The woman blew her nose noisily. 'Twitching.'

Her head flew up. The look on her face making Sally cackle outrageously. 'It's not some sex thing! It's bird watching. The feathered type! We regularly go to the Victorian highlands ...' Her voice got stuck in her throat. When she removed her glasses, the effects of some mind-altering substance revealed a web of bloodshot, soulless eyes. 'Stay there, I'll bring him to you. It's a bit cramped back here with you mob.'

Instantly recognising the perfect smile, strong jawline, clear skin and dark hair, the large ears and dimple on the chin threw a curveball. Sadly, his wide-set blue eyes were as empty as they were in his later life, death, and on canvas. Her inner voice screamed at her. *That is not Rudy.* She turned towards young children's laughter, who stopped suddenly and stared at the two dogs, clutching each other's hands tightly. The little dark-haired girl with small blue eyes, full ruby lips, a chin dimple and abnormally large ears stood protectively in front of the little boy with very similar features, except for his eyes. They were larger and wider-set.

Sally called out instantly. 'Children, stay there please.' Then to Yasmin, 'These pair are lovers of snakes and terrified of dogs, so if you wouldn't mind?'

'I'll take my leave. Uh, good luck with it all.'

'I'll walk with you.'

With the dogs flanking Yasmin, they stood away from the entrance of the stall and watched the children scamper in.

'I'm Ebony's Mum and me daughter is Junior's mum. He never met the kids. They weren't the healthiest of bubs and were tiny when they were born, but as you can see, they're powering along just fine and are almost ten.'

TEN? The pesky little voice screeched.

'Anyway, he disappeared for ages, eventually I got his crazy stepsister's number from our mutual friends and left messages for him. It might have taken a while for him to phone me back, but this time I never heard back. Now I know why ...' Her voice trailed off at the same speed her eyes closed.

CRAZY stepsister now? Suddenly, Yasmin's head began to pound. The internal argument progressed into a boxing match.

Sally sighed heavily. 'But he was a generous man. Check this out.' She pushed up the sleeve of the hypnotic patterned blouse to reveal a heavy gold arm bracelet curling around her forearm. The head of the snake rested against the inside of her elbow. 'But we are the White family and always will be which is why his name isn't on the kids' birth certificates.'

Ebony White? What sort of sick joke was that? Nothing black and white about that relationship, that was for sure. Or hers for that matter. Yasmin blinked away the rapidly forming tears, begging her own self to keep it together.

'You love snakes too I notice!' she cleared her throat. 'You were saying your friends saw him that morning?'

'Yeah,' the woman caressed the jewellery, covered it up and wiped at her eyes. 'According to them he was walking around with my shirt slung over his shoulder ... he loved that shirt ... they reckon they called him over and offered him a lift which he refused, so they let him be. They were the last ones to see him alive.'

'That must have been awful news for you. How did you hear about it?'

'I don't use mobile phones, don't trust them. I see you're pretty attached to yours but. Anyway, we just catch up when we do. How many times do you catch up with your friends from out of town if you have any?'

Frowning, replied quietly, 'Yeah, good point.'

They both chortled when her mobile chimed.

'Turn it off sometimes, they can track your every move these days!'

The message tone dinged again.

'See what I mean? Anyway, looks like the kids have brought some customers. Thanks for listening, I needed an unbiased pair of ears. Your dogs are very well behaved for their size. You a coppa?'

'Nope. Just someone passing through and thought I'd see what all the fuss was about. Haven't really felt the peace and loving but.'

'Then you won't enjoy a yarn in the barn. This place isn't for the likes of you. Maybe the seaside? Just head south.'

'Great idea. Thanks.'

Sally clasped her wrist, and said, 'I think in another life we could actually become good friends.'

They shared a genuine smile and turned away from each other.

Combo and Digby's shackles lessened the further away they got from the crowds, allowing them a longer leash. Fighting back the tears from the answers she regretfully sought, they stopped under the tree where her and Paddy had breakfast. The first chime - the phone's memory was full and had stopped recording. The other was a message from him asking the whereabouts of her motorhome. She replied accordingly. Crouching in between her two protectors, praised them and ruffled both their heads, then spoke as she stood.

'Sit. Stay. Race. Home.'

She wished she was on roller skates because by the time they could see their motorhome, her legs were burning.

'Slow. Boys! Slow. Stop. Wait. SIT.'

They did, under her command bolted across the road and raced to her motorhome at the same time Paddy swung into the service station. He flashed his lights in recognition. As soon as he opened his door, she released both dogs, opened up her motorhome, stumbled in and burst into tears. No sooner was the door locked behind her, brought up every ounce of food that was left in her already flat stomach. In between racking sobs and eventual dry retching, her heart ripped in several more places. Jealousy, rage, sadness, loss and irrecoverable body clock emotions raced through her body as she curled up into a ball on the floor in the pokey shower cubicle. *Oh, Rudy, how could you? You poor, cruel, confused, controlling, rich bast-basket case.*

Her appearance hadn't changed except for the puffy eyes and red nose. The moment Combo sensed her, he wiggle-waggled over and hugged her, expecting his noisy-pretend kiss and positive reinforcements. Paddy called him back then handed her an aromatically strong black coffee in a travel mug.

'Aye, lassie.'

'Thank you, I need this.'

He nodded his head and averted his eyes. Combo wrestled free and stood beside Digby.

'What's wrong, Paddy?'

'I be takin' me leave soon.'

'And that's not why you're upset. What happened at the yarn in the barn?'

He looked at her through teary eyes. 'Wha' di' ye 'ear?'

'Chanting and some words that confirmed a suspicion.'

He took his hand out of his pocket, clasped her free one and filled it with coated wire, a shirt button, a peculiar pen, and a small green oval tablet nestled against a folded piece of paper in a little releasable bag.

'Nae be needin' 'dis, but if ye a detective, ye will. If y' ain't, 'ope it brings closure. 'Tis a cult dat needs to be stopped me wee, brave lassie.'

Yasmin saw the micro-SD connection. 'You're a legend, Paddy, but—'

'Lassie, another time for ye tale. 'ow you feel 'bout drivin' into d' nigh'?'

'Anything to get away from this horrid place. I need to top up with fuel first.'

'Off ye go. I nae be wantin' to be 'ere. Ye cell phones nae be workin' 'ntil the coast.'

'Suits me fine,' and promptly deactivated both.

Long after darkness enveloped them, Paddy's transmission on the two-way broke her absentminded concentration on his taillights.

'Aye. Ye be doin' okay back there?'

'Aye. You?'

'Gettin' tired and flamin' 'ungry.'

'Aye.'

'Aye. Follow me lead.'

Hypnotised from the right indicator lighting up the solid centre line of the narrow road, their speed dropped considerably after the fourth cattle grid. Paddy suddenly veered across the road. Feeling drunk and disoriented, followed suit. They bumped along a track parallel to a fence line.

'Park to me righ', Paddy suggested.

She did. Killed the engine, the lights and didn't move. Except she did shriek when he rapped on the door.

'Aye lassie, we be visitin' your vehicle.'

No sooner had she opened the side door, Combo dashed out then brought Digby back inside followed by Paddy's question.

'Ye decent?'

'Of course!'

'Aye, promise me ye be lookin' ye normal self when we next meet?'

'Absolutely.'

'Me lassie, let's enjoy d' company, t' good food an' 'ere's t' a wee drappy.'

'Aye Paddy, I be with you on that.'

They shared cold meat sandwiches and several fingers of scotch.

'Dis is where we part ways ... after a good sleep! In the morn, I be gone. D' sea be four hours on dis road', 'tis a long coastline.'

Her bottom lipped trembled. Paddy sniffed.

'Aye lassie, ye be right.'

'How can I thank you?'

'Visit me and Digby on me Island.'

She smiled. 'With Combo.'

'Aye!'

He extended his hand and Yasmin wrapped both hers around his. 'Paddy, it's an absolute privilege knowing you and thank you for entrusting me with this quest. I believe we met for a reason.'

'Aye, as do I, lassie, as do I.' His free hand engulfed hers before ruffing Combo's head.

To be sure, a picture postcard of Hawaii was tucked under her windscreen wiper. A beautiful sight to see in the darkest hour of the morning, made even better with the penlight torch shining on the moon's image. She smiled at Paddy's note: *Aye, ye can trust me crew to get ye 2 to de land o' swayin' palms.* Attached with a paperclip, his business card.

Sighing dejectedly, muttered, 'I really need my passport.'

The glow massaging the sky's palette matched the colour of the fuel symbol flicking on the dash. Yasmin coasted into the service station, refuelled, and with the help of Combo devoured a truckie's breakfast. Taking the coffee back to the motorhome, reactivated her mobile phones. She had just taken the last mouthful. Timmy's jubilant message demanding she got her butt to The Bahamas with Rudy's ashes sent her racing to the sink, coughing and spluttering. On her business phone, the missed call from an unknown caller who didn't leave a message was deleted. Both phones were promptly deactivated.

Smack bang on eleven o'clock, the last bend of the downward winding range took her breath and cast it across the shimmering turquoise sea blending into the horizon.

'Oh Combo! We're finally on holidays!'

Fortunately, they were ahead of the tourist influx and secured the last waterfront powered site furthest away from the path to the beach. With the wig harshly discarded and swimsuit hastily adjusted, they raced each other down to the beachfront and swam in the shallows. Combo's unnatural blotches washing off into the sea, then a dual fresh-water shower resuming their normal appearance. Those precious hours of pure freedom regenerated their energy and fuelled their hunger levels. With the mixed culinary smells of pizza, burgers and seafood tantalising their senses while they walked along the foreshore, they found a lovely picnic table away from the crowd. Yasmin's drool challenged that of her best mate. The aroma of their mixed seafood basket was intoxicatingly delicious, and the flavours were second to none. By the time they returned to the motorhome, their already close bond seemed to have deepened further.

'Just us two, no technology, no contact with the outside world, only sun, surf, seafood, steak and sleep for several days.'

Chapter 48

Typically, the crowds swelled and dwindled during the Moojie Hill festival. Into its last three days, exhaustion and irritability crept in.

'Mummy!' Ebony squealed when Sally tousled both kids' hair as she walked past. 'We finally get to have breakfast together.'

'My Mummy has already eaten and gone off with the fairies,' Junior grumbled.

'She'll come back, bubby. But Mummy, we've been dying to ask about who that lady was? The one you were talking to—'

'There have been quite a few, Ebony. Stop dawdling you two and eat your breakfast please. The show's not over!'

'She looked sad but.'

'We thought maybe she could be a new friend. Who was she?' Junior whined.

Sally shrugged her shoulders at Leigh's raised eyebrow while her and Callum jostled around each other in the small cabin.

Leigh asked, 'What did she look like kiddlywinks?'

'Short! Junior and me will be taller than her when we grow up!'

'Yeah!'

The children giggled naughtily. They didn't see the look Callum gave Sally.

'What?' she challenged him.

'Hope you weren't telling tales out of school, Teach!'

'Hope you're not telling me what to do and who I can and can't talk to, mate. You ain't my keeper.'

And then the two stepbrothers arrived, poked their heads in the door and asked politely for coffees.

'Uncle Ivan, why don't we like dogs?' Junior asked with typical childlike innocence.

'Hey? Where did that come from kiddo?'

The little boy shrugged his shoulders then flinched when his cousin kicked him under the table. 'Nowhere,' he mumbled.

She piped up. 'How come Uncle Stu hasn't visited us yet? He always brings us treats.'

Her cousin's bottom lip trembled. 'Yeah. And Uncle Travis forgot our treats. No fair.'

Leigh frowned at the interaction. 'Come on kids, eat up, the snake charmer will be putting on his show soon.'

'I might even join you,' Giles said quietly.

'Yay!' Ebony and Junior squealed happily and stuffed several egg-dipped soldiers into their mouths.

The moment they were out of sight, Callum and Ivan verbally pounced on Sally demanding she tell them everything about this short woman.

'Hey, back off! It's my art stall, my art, my easels, my customers and you mob can rack off. I even paid for the barn, remember, so go back there and yarn.' Her bloodshot eyes watering up.

'You paid for it with his money.' Callum spat out.

'So? It hasn't bothered you all these years, why now?'

'Yeah well, the boogey-man might reach out if we don't nip this in the bud,' Ivan growled.

Sally looked at him, totally astonished. 'What boogey-man? Nip what in the bud?'

'That flower lady bitch. She knows too much.'

'Who the hell are you talking about?' This time, Sally's voice raised a notch.

The twin sisters appeared and joined the throng. 'Hush up and we'll fill you in. We're waiting for Travis.'

'Well, I've got paintings to sell. Go and entertain yourselves somewhere else,' Sally hissed and shoved past them.

Several hours later, the conversation continued in and around the dynamic art stall of *Sally White*, where they all took it in turns bringing the artist up to speed with the break-in and the curse of the three-named-man.

'My Rupe—'

From behind, Callum's hand covered her mouth. 'Do not ever, ever say his name. We don't know if he really is dead and we don't really care if he is. But we do care that he spilled the beans beforehand and someone is onto us. You know? Like the pigs! You don't want that to happen. Think about the kids.'

Sally wrestled his hand away from her mouth and stomped on his foot. 'I care! You callous bastard. Now get out! Get out, the lot of you!'

No one moved.

'Who was pretty little Ebony talking about, Sally?' Ivan asked, cleaning his fingernails with his pocketknife.

'You stay away from the kids.'

'We always have, but they like snakes—'

'I will kill you myself if you harm any of my kids.'

Laqueel and Trina spoke as one. Their sing-song voices easing the growing tension. 'Help us, Sally. Please help us. We have to protect Ebony and Junior. Help us, Sally.'

'Sally, Sally, Sally,' Travis muscled in and handed her a lit pipe. 'Come now.'

Drawing heavily, her eyes closed wished she was far away in the arms of her beloved. The memory faded too soon. 'She was a short, red-haired piece, heart tattoo on her wrist and two dogs.'

'Describe the mutts.' Leigh spat out the demand.

'Beautifully behaved and big. One black one, one splotchy one.'

'What did you talk about?'

Sally inhaled again, even more deeply then exhaled very slowly. 'She wasn't feeling the peace and love of the festival, so I told her to go to the seaside.' In a flash, her mood and tone changed. 'Now. Get. Out. ALL OF YOU. GET OUT.'

Chapter 49

Callum nudged Ivan. 'Oi, wonder if your sprog saw anything?'

'More than likely. The pervert. Reckon we'll find him near the booze tent. Come on.'

'Flower lady doesn't have red hair so don't get your hopes up.'

Ivan glowered. 'You getting soft in your old age mate? It's flower lady *bitch*. Anyhoo, the kids' behaviour struck me as odd. Even Sally was weird about it.'

'She's always weird. Phone Giles, he needs to be with us, not babysitting.'

'Not babysitting. Not babysitting,' the twins mimicked.

They all shared a laugh and entered the makeshift beer hall. It wasn't hard to find the rowdy bunch of young fellas. The ringleader wasn't the big toughie when his old man cornered him and gave him a grilling after hearing about the interaction.

'What are you doing picking on a woman with two dogs anyway, you idiot?'

'She was hot! I mean red hair hot!' His bravado faltered when he described the man with a stupid moustache.

'Describe the mo. Describe the mo.'

'Like one of those old-fashioned ones. Like Pops had, just hairier and curlier.'

The men swore. The twins cringed.

'Anybody see a bloke wearing a long grey jacket?'

Wide-eyed, all the boys shook their heads. The women sighed with relief. Then the puniest of the lot squared up to Ivan just as Giles joined them with a tray of beers.

'About time.' Ivan took two pints and skulled them one after the other.

'Hey, old man. This mo-fo had his finger hooked through a jacket hangin' over his shoulder. It went down to his knees man.'

'What colour? What colour?' the twins whined.

'Dunno. I'm colourblind.'

Ivan twisted the young fellow's shirt and pulled him off his feet. 'Anybody ever told you to mind your own business?'

'Yep. Right now,' he whimpered.

'Good.' Ivan pushed him away, took a large step forward and firmly patted his son's right cheek. 'Keep your mates in check.'

'But Dad, I don't reckon the black dog was hers!'

'Hey?' all the grown-ups spoke at the same time.

'A huge giant—' he began.

'That Irish bastard at the yarn—'

'I don't know, I'm not allowed in there remember,' and yelped after receiving a loud ear clipping.

'Don't get smart. Best start talking boy.'

He did by over exaggerating the size of the man who left in a motorhome with an enormous black dog hanging out the window. Then got excited about what happened after that.

'Dad, she had the hottest arse I'm telling ya! I reckon they were travelling together, 'cos the blotchy dog was with her. They left together after she took on a tank of juice.'

'Which way did they go?'

'South.'

'Righto, don't make a fool of yerself, boy.'

'Dad, have a drink with us and spin us a yarn, please?'

The twins encouraged the session. 'Yes, yes tell us a story! Tell us a story!'

Giles walked away from the others, circumnavigating the food and drink tents. 'Yes?' he hissed into the mobile phone pressed against his ear.

'Stewart Morgan with an E.W. like we talked about?'

His voice dropped dramatically. 'Who else could it be. Where the hell are you, Stu?'

'Not telling. What's news?'

'It's about to go down. Ivan and Travis are threatening Sally by using the kids. Penny's been drifting around, think she's waiting for you, lover boy! We haven't spoken, but it's her alright. The Goth chick is back! She's hung around the stall, the barn ...'

That's my girl. Stu absentmindedly rubbed his crotch. He was yet to do the deed with the prick teaser and couldn't wait to make an honest woman out of her, even if he did owe her $10K. Then the smile was wiped off his face at Giles' ranting in his ear.

'… you hear me? I said the German Wurst van.'

Stu grunted. 'And?'

'He's shifting mega quantities of powder. And guns. Friggin' commo weapons. I seen him show off to some foreign women. The bastards are still using the oldies and dog trolleys to shift the stuff. Reckon if you wanna get back in the good books with the boys in blue, you should give them the drop.'

'I ain't a rat.'

'Nor am I. Ivan will kill me if he knows I know all this stuff man.'

Stu smirked. 'When last did you see Penny?'

'Not since early yesterday morning. She snuck up behind me while I was taking a whizz. Talk about stage fright! Cheeky wench said to tell you that she will find you again.'

They laughed together.

'I know she will.'

'One more thing before I get sprung talking to you, mate, do you know more than one short woman with a hot arse and a multi-coloured shadow?'

'Nope. What the hell she is doing there?'

'Reckon she's onto the whole thing, which might explain why Ivan's convinced she has evidence that will sink Travis. That's his end game by the way. Was always sus on his belief that the B-man didn't pay his dues.' Giles cleared his throat nervously. 'Um … Leigh's done something plus she warned me too. Some money's missing.'

'You scared?'

'Just a bit! Sh-she's a freaking scary woman. Hey, Ivan's boy has kicked up a stink too. I think I'll forgive the flower lady for knocking me out if we can take down this lot, but she's gotta keep her trap shut. Otherwise—'

'Flower lady? No bitch?'

'Nah not when I'm talking to you, mate. All this isn't her fault.'

'What do you want to do?'

Giles pulled himself up to his full height. 'We should take Penny, get her out of this mess and hit the beach. If that's where the flower lady is, we need to win her over but scare her enough to make sure she doesn't make a peep. Threaten her dog maybe?' His stance slumped again. 'Dunno which beach but.'

Stu breathed noisily. 'Find Penny and be at the southern servo, midnight tomorrow night. You got a bug-out bag?'

'Yep.'

'Cash?'

'Yep.'

'Hey ... this ... uh ... the boogey-man, he is dead, isn't he?'

Giles's sharp intake of breath whistled through his teeth. 'Why ask that?'

'Assurance.'

'Bring insurance then! Gotta go.'

Giles stood in front of the bar watching his cohorts noisily enjoying their beers and flicked the SIM out of his phone. Meandering towards them, put his hands around the thick waist of a buxom waitress as she swayed past, dropping the SIM into her apron. 'How about another round for the lads, honey?'

'Sure, Giles. I'll bring them over. Just get them to smoke outside the tent, will ya?'

***

Meanwhile at the zoo zone, Leigh shivered excitedly when the harmless python embraced the two delighted kids in a figure of eight. Out of the corner of her eye caught a glimpse of a man turning away, and smirked. Thinking it to be Callum getting in a sneaky perve, she slinked out of the enclosure and came to an abrupt halt. A gloved hand gripped her upper arm. Another covered her eyes. Leigh squirmed when an arm wrapped around her neck.

A very soft voice spoke into her ear. 'Hello, it's nearly time you stopped playing with dangerous toys.'

'H-how d-did y-you f-find m-m-me?'

'Aw, you haven't stuttered for a long while. I was never far away. When you wake up, you will only remember this ... Rupert John Matson lives on.'

Chapter 50

During the assessment of the K9s agility regime, Sergeant Kohli looked around and noticed Pyers heading in his direction at the same time his mobile phone buzzed.

Speaking quietly and swiftly. 'Cap'n, how's the fishing?'

'A couple of nibbles, unsure of the legal size.'

'You might need a bigger net.'

'Copy that. Will keep you apprised. Out.'

Scoffing as he pocketed it, walked towards his colleague. 'Any news, Boss?' he asked through the meshed fence.

'Moojie Hill, but that was several days ago. You have anything?'

'Nothing definite.' Sergeant Kohli grizzled and was about to say something else when his colleague's mobile phone rang.

'Listen only ... it'll be on speaker so no noise.'

Frowning, grunted his acknowledgement of the order.

'Forensic Detective Hillyer! Wondered where you'd gotten to.'

'Hey Owen. Yeah, still tied up with the other investigation.'

'Right. Have you got anything for us?'

'No. Still waiting on the lab report. How are you boys doing?'

'Chasing our tails as well.'

'I reached out to Kohli about sitting down with you guys and Ms Pestel, has he mentioned it?'

'Yep.'

'Well, I've heard nothing back from him and she's non-committal. Was hoping you could arrange something.'

'I'll get back to you.'

'I expect you to do it sooner than later, she could be the key to solving this bloody awful long-winded situation. If my suspicions serve me correctly, we could actually close a few cold cases too.'

'What cold cases have you got that could be connected?'

'Lethal opioid combos using snake venom.'

'Do share!'

'You may recall a spate of deaths associated with a cult ... the leaders who got the mix wrong?'

'Yep. You reckon this is a spin-off?'

'Yeah. They weren't city-based. There's something gnawing at my guts, but I just can't put my finger on it.'

'Know the feeling there.'

'Hmm. Anyway, the longer we leave things the harder it's going to get, so let Ms Pestel know that I have talked to you, and I want another interview. By the way, I've gone through my notes ... did you by chance write down the name of the deceased?'

'I'd have to double check. Anything else?'

'I want to catch up within the next two weeks.'

'What's the hurry?'

'For starters it should coincide with the forensic results, secondly, I'm taking personal leave!'

'Righto. I'll be in touch.'

Owen disconnected the call and muttered something undecipherable. Fascinated with the demonstration, he complimented his colleague and walked away, calling over his shoulder. 'They're looking good, Boss. Keep up the great work. If you need me, send a text.'

'Is that it?' Sergeant Kohli called out.

'Yeah. Gotta go!'

Owen's previous visit to the funeral parlour had been a combination of an utter waste of time and an eye-opener, particularly with every gate locked. The folk wanting to be closer to their deceased loved ones had been surprisingly tolerant when the caretaker eventually made his appearance, had kept his distance and eyes downcast, explained that his bosses were particularly unwell.

This time, going on a hunch, Owen took the keys for the 4WD patrol vehicle, put a round in his Glock, a spare magazine in one pocket, sterile gloves in the other and went for a drive. The firebreak made for an indiscernible approach to the back entrance of the oldest part of the graveyard. Several padlocks through the chain confirmed his suspicions. On foot, he joined in the game and cut the link with bolt-cutters, used the grassy clumps as stepping-stones, swung open the gate, and locked it behind him with his own padlock. It was only then that he noticed the different tyre tracks leading to and from an open shed with white paint-splattered heavy plastic sheets set up as a makeshift spray booth. Along the shelving amid a variety of used drug paraphernalia, piles of frog or toad carcasses, snake skins, and scattered green dust, sat a particularly clean spray gun. Behind a tatty old sheet stood an air compressor and a well-loved portable MIG welder. Doing his own bit of detective work, Owen made notes, took photographs and bagged some of the evidence.

Jogging past the warm bricked enclosure towards the rear of the parlour, he slowed down at the sound of the preacher's monotone. He reminded himself that creeping around a godly environment wasn't normal, but when he saw the hearse and the sound of mourners singing the opening lines of Amazing Grace mingled with nose-blowing and wailing, Owen took his leave respectfully.

Chapter 51

Yasmin yawned and stretched lazily, deftly trying to ignore the nagging subconscious reminding her that she couldn't stay in denial forever. Ordinarily the stale mental debate didn't usually get much more attention than that; yet annoyingly, it began to get the better of her as the day wore on. Sighing heavily, dreaded the sounds that would emit from the reactivated laptop and mobile phones. The two missed calls from whoever without messages on her business mobile didn't faze her in the slightest and deactivated it without so much of a blink. Rapid dings on her personal number revealed five missed calls from her local police station and one from Carl, with only three voice mails recorded. These conflicted with her confidence and guilt. All three policemen voiced their concerns and encouraged her to establish contact urgently. Yasmin responded to them with a global text message: *Hi, thanks for caring. We're enjoying the beach and both well. Thank you. YP.* Then completed the noncontactable status. Two of the sixteen emails were worthy of keeping. A progress report on the fencing project from the supplier and settlement statement from the conveyancing firm.

Looking at Paddy's clandestine bugging get-up, she took a deep breath and plugged it in. Filled with dread, Combo whimpered in uncertainty head nuzzled under her wrist, she clicked the play button. The repeated chant in conjunction with the dark interior, lit only by bare bulb desk lamps pointing to the cobwebbed roof throwing shadows everywhere, freaked her out. Two men and three women faced their audience chanting, at the same time the middle woman swayed her upper body and long arms like an uncoiling snake. Their faces glowed orange from a bank of lights at their feet. Shapeless outfits reflected the nonsensical environment.

Yasmin shivered when the tall man with the slithering snake around his neck spoke loudly. 'We are all suffering loss, but we don't all have to suffer forever. Choose to join, choose to leave, choose to stay. It's not too late to choose. The new moon is twelve days away. Join us for a retreat in distant highlands.'

His cohorts chanted rhythmically. 'Choose to stay, choose to leave, it's not too late to choose.'

Bile scorched the back of Yasmin's throat. Two women either side of the seated dancer hadn't blinked since they had sat down. One looked like a weirdly intriguing Goth chick, yet it was the other woman who caused her to dry retch. *Leigh?*

Both men were tall and strong, but the one without the snake was even stronger. Yasmin scrunched up her t-shirt and muffled a strangulated gasp. Another man appeared out of the darkness. His large, crooked nose was the first thing you saw before being sucked into his gaze through broad-rimmed glasses. Somehow the reflected light ignited his cold, penetrating eyes. They were grossly huge. She rewound the video and paused the image. Her blood turned cold. Barely breathing and without taking her eyes off the screen, Yasmin jotted down: Callum, Travis, and a big fat question mark. Then clicked the play button.

Heart-wrenching sobs yanked at her frayed emotions. The dynamics of the addictive chanting was like somebody playing with the volume knob on a stereo. The dancer glided to a man crying loudly. She wrapped her body around his making a show of trailing a piece of paper down his cheek then pressing it into his hand. She movie-style kissed him, then dragged her mouth upwards alternatively covering his ears and rocked him with her body before pecking him on the nose. She caressed his chin. Out of nowhere, produced a little cup and very gently tilted his head backwards pouring something into his open mouth. He eventually stopped sobbing and started chanting. Others had watched the performance. Within the hour, three more men and two women had been consoled in the exact same fashion and joined in the chanting.

She rewound and slowed the video replay. From behind, someone else's hand held out the liquid-filled cup. The fast-forward key was rapidly hit in succession until Paddy caused a bit of consternation when he stood and approached the five leaders. Her and Combo recoiled the closer he got.

'You shall be seated and choose.' Travis spoke firmly and concisely. His hands planted firmly on his hips.

Paddy halted and spoke in the same tone. 'Ye shall tell me more about 'dis new moon meeting before I choose anyt'ing, laddie.'

From the darkness behind the leaders, unified cooing and mimicry could be heard.

Travis, mimicking Paddy's accent, said. 'Ay, laddie, 'ow about me li'l dancer 'ere soothe ye achin' soul?'

'I'd rather watch, ye cheeky prat, now tell me more 'bout the moon. I doth travel from the Shamrock Isle. What do I ha'e t' do t' choose?'

The dancer sidled over to Paddy then suddenly stopped all gracious moves, pirouetted smartly and sauntered back to her peers. They rose, encircled her, before staring blankly at the audience. Callum somehow glided towards Paddy who adjusted his shirt like a boxer pre-fight. Lifeless eyes penetrated the camera lens.

'We all have suffered loss. You don't need to suffer anymore. Come join us on our pilgrimage. We don't like confrontation. This is a loving affair to ease pain. Come join us at the highlands, we can take you there, take you far away, take you to peace, so choose.'

'Choose to stay, choose to leave, it's not too late to choose.'

The hypnotic chant from the women almost escaped Yasmin's lips. Stabbing at the pause button, she raced over to wash her face. In the hope to avoid saying anything bit down on a piece of jerky, before continuing to watch the sordid recording. Combo watched her warily.

'But 'ow, laddie? You ain't told me 'ow. I 'ave t' understand,' Paddy demanded.

Two women stepped out of the shadows from behind the leaders and draped themselves over Travis and Leigh. Their hair pulled into extremely tight ponytails. A mirror reflection of each other.

They appeared to be grinding their teeth, then spoke as one. 'You're not ready to choose. You're asking too many questions. You're not ready to choose.'

Fleeing mares. Yasmin shuddered and tossed the jerky into the sink. Combo didn't move.

This time the dancer waltzed towards Paddy again, and in an eerily husky voice cooed, 'Let me help you see, let me help you feel, let me help you choose.'

'Choose to stay, choose to leave, it's not too late to choose,' the leaders chanted, encouraging the newly converted to join in.

Paddy started swaying to the groove. 'I need to know more, tell me more, show me how. Where de highlands you speak of? I plant me greens by da new moon, I am a child of de moon.'

His voice had softened enough to encourage the dancer even closer. She took his hand. The video was blurred for a long while.

A man's voice could be heard. 'Be seated our fellow sufferer, we welcome you to our pilgrimage. Choose to stay, choose to leave, it's not too late to choose.'

Yasmin blinked rapidly at the sudden focus. Paddy thread his way back through the seated people until he took his original position. The lookalikes morphed into the shadows, where an eerie glow illuminated the unfamiliar man's face. When he opened his mouth to chant, a snake's head appeared. Yasmin dry retched. Combo reared back in fright.

Callum and Travis spoke in unison. 'Soon, soon you will all choose. We all have suffered loss. You don't need to suffer anymore. The highlands will help you choose. You have waited too long.'

Yasmin burst into tears and bit the back of her fist. *No, no, no. Oh Paddy.*

Frozen at the realisation of it all, the video kept playing. The Gothic chick stared straight into Paddy's camera and followed it, even when he stood. The unfamiliar snake-draped man, swathed in smoke, wove in and out of Callum, Leigh, Travis, the female twins and the dancer. He spoke the loudest. His cohorts accompanied in a soft harmony.

'Time. Time to partake. Choose. Choose to partake. Choose to inhale the nature of the highlands. Time to join, time to choose. If not today, we'll reach out in three new moons. Choose to stay, choose to leave, it's not too late to choose.'

The screen went black.

Too stunned to cry, she would never know if the yarn in the barn helped or hurt Paddy, but by the grace of God he had helped nail the miscreants. Incentivised to get the truth out of her head and onto paper; documented her findings. The mystery man on stage gnawed at her. *Clive? Stu? The boogey-man? Who was Rupert? Who IS Rupert?*

Downloading the recorded audio of her conversation with Sally, Yasmin bawled the first time she replayed it. The second and third time, she began to feel sorry for the artist, but by the sixth replay; she was done. Done with the game. Done with being at the beck and call of everyone else. Utterly done with being manipulated.

It was time to go home.

Soon.

Stop procrastinating! She chided herself angrily.

Combo's head on her knee broke her mood. 'Come boy, let's go out for an early dinner. We're going somewhere else tomorrow.'

Chapter 52

BANG! BANG! BANG!

Everyone scattered. In a panic, Leigh cowered behind the sarong rack cringing at the sporadic gunfire. Her mind raced at the same pace as her ragged breath. She blamed Giles for changing the recipe. Everything was blurry. She hadn't seen Callum since their last yarn in the barn, and she still didn't know who the man was who replaced Clive. Nobody else seemed to notice. She hadn't had a smoke since the stranger's voice penetrated her brain. She couldn't think straight at the best of times. And just where was Stu? From her hiding place she had counted three men with handle-bar moustaches and another two with long grey jackets scurry past, ducking in and out of stalls, and also a lot of very agile oldies pulling their dogs in trolleys. The shadows thrown from the towering bank of four-light spotlights terrified her. Spying Sally wrapping her arms protectively around the children near the snake enclosure, dared the bright lights and raced towards them.

'Aunty Leigh,' the little boy squealed, 'Where's my mummy?'

Sally's withering glare caught her by surprise and replied as calmly as she could. 'It's okay, Junior. She's safe.'

'She had better be.' Sally growled. 'What's up with you anyway? You've been really weird lately.'

Repeatedly wringing her hands, murmured, 'I'm trying to quit.'

'Don't lie.'

'Fine. Giles must have changed the recipe.' Her pitch got higher the longer she spoke. 'Stu's gone AWOL and the name of the boogey-man is ringing in my head. It's all I can hear.'

'That again, huh? What about him?'

'What about him?' Leigh screeched. 'He's alive, Sally. He's dangerous. Go via the barn and pick up your other kid, then go away as far as possible. If you leave me the easels, I won't tell on you.'

Sally pushed her face into Leigh's, 'Best you get the hell out of my sight. Forever.'

'But Sal ...'

An explosion erupted near the food trucks. Leigh flung herself into the dirt. The last thing she heard was a man's voice above her.

'You can't hide from the boogey-man.'

Chapter 53

'Got Yasmin's last known location, Boss,' Sergeant Kohli poked his head around Sergeant Pyers' door jamb.

'You look as relieved as I feel! Where?'

'You don't know?'

'Comms guy was seconded by the Feds. All hush-hush. Anyway, tell me what you know.'

'East of Kingston SE.'

'Nice. Take a seat and let me tell you what I found out about Moojie Hill.'

'Righto,' Sergeant Kohli steeled himself the most comfortable chair.

'It's quite the drawcard for locals as well as visitors from across the Victorian border for the ten-day event. The town swells like a blind pimple then goes back to its quiet, hard-working community until the following year. Rinse and repeat. The local blokes describe the annual event as a peace-loving affair with plenty of the following: pot - without breaking the law quantity-wise, hippies, great art and craft, well-travelled dogs and surprisingly all with very little fuss. And the best German Wurst ever!' His stomach growled. 'Oh, boy, what I'd do to have one of those!'

'Ha! Get your Penny to bring one back for you,' Sergeant Kohli chuckled.

'Can't. Her phone is also switched off.'

'She *is* on holidays, Boss!'

'Yeah. Anyway, what have you found out?'

The big man toyed with the leather stitching on the armrest. 'Not much more than that really. Only a few minor incidents. The typical barflies-and-pretty-girls trouble. Should anything major go down, I'm sure the Feds would give us the heads-up given we've got the room and are the logical half-way point.'

Owen looked perplexed.

'You're worried about Penny, aren't you?'

'Yeah. I mean I've known she's been going there for years with her pottery stuff and freely brags about earning almost a month's wages in the six days she's there. The Goth dress-up struck me as most peculiar. Eloping? Something else is still gnawing at my gut and I'm not ready to discuss it, so excuse me if I come across preoccupied.'

'Righto.'

'Anyway, on a clearer note, you right if I sign on behalf of the young widow for the ashes when they're available?'

'Sure thing. Any revelations on your cold cases?'

'Nope ... nothing concrete.'

'Yell out if you need a hand, mate,' Sergeant Kohli said as he opened the door and took a step forward.

Ruth's frantic knocking caught him fair in the middle of his barrel chest.

'Oh! Sir! Please forgive me!'

'Hey, hey ... you practicing CPR?'

Her shrill giggle and wide eyes instantly sobered him up.

'What is it, Ruth?'

'The Feds hit Moojie Hill! My Charlie's out there! The Team Lead will be—'

Sergeant Pyers' desk phone rang.

'Sir, I gave him your direct number.' Her voice trembled equivalent to her shaking body.

'Thanks Ruth ... do you need to sit?'

'Let-let me hear his voice again. Please. There's been a massive drug bust and ...' Her hand flew to her mouth.

Sergeant Kohli ushered the woman out of the office. 'Talk to me, Ruth.'

'Oh, Sir ... Charlie's my son. Joined the Force to prove to his father that he could make it in this world. But then his father got taken out in a hit-and-run and I don't know if I could handle it if I lost my ...' The tears fell.

'He's been well trained, Ruth,' Sergeant Kohli consoled her. 'What else do you know about the situation?'

Squeezing her lips together, she shook her head swiping away the tears at the same time.

'Come on, how can I help you if you don't help me, hmmm? You know I have different connections to your boss. Talk to me.'

'I shouldn't. I did wrong by decoding the file. I need this job, Sergeant Kohli.' Her eyes darted from left to right and pulled him away from the open office door. In a hushed voice, said, 'The Hill is the Op zone for a major bust. But it's not the bikies. It's the oldies! They're threatened with their lives and that of their dogs. Also, there's guns and the runners are dressed as oldies with stolen dogs! It's plain awful.'

'Anything else you can share?'

'Never eat the Wurst sausages. I was there five years ago and was crook for weeks afterwards. Penny will remember. She got me the aerial amb—'

'Ruth?' Sergeant Pyers called out. 'There's a telephone call for you. It's Charlie.'

She rushed in and Owen closed the door behind him. Sergeant Kohli waited expectantly.

Owen brought him up to speed on Penny's intel and the so-called boogey-man, ignoring the thundercloud look explained the German Wurst Van had been identified as a cross-border drug merchant.

'Prepare your K9 Units, as many as possible. Stand by for an influx and long shifts.'

'Yes, Sir.'

'By the way, do you know who died recently?'

The big man shook his head. 'I honestly couldn't tell you. Have you phoned Clive?'

Owen pursed his lips. 'There's something unusual going on out there. When all this blows over you and I need to go for a drive.'

'Righto.' Sergeant Kohli reached for his two-way and strode away barking orders.

Ruth collapsed into Owen's arms with relief when he entered his office. 'Sit, Ruth, I'll go and get you a cuppa.'

Chapter 54

A bleak, blustery morning greeted Yasmin and Combo. It was so miserable the sun hadn't even bothered to get out of bed. Mr Taylor had been on her mind when she woke up in the middle of the night, and had slept fitfully thereon. Playing Eenie-Meenie with the phones, thought of Jill and hoped her horse was okay. Then all the horrible images of Paddy's video bombarded her, along with Sally's story, Rudy's game. Within minutes, her entire outlook was as gloomy as the weather. Combo hated the rainy wind gusts and cowered on his bed staring at the door of the little kitchen cupboard. It wasn't even seven o'clock. With her fingers crossed, she activated her work phone and dialled the dear old man's number. His delightful, comforting voice warming her heart. Even more so when he realised who he was speaking with.

'The lovely Ms Pestel! We were only talking about you last night.'

'You're a dear man, Mr Taylor. But who is we?' Yasmin realised she was on speaker.

'The lads! And I had the privilege of meeting Emily's snow man and son. You sure made a huge impression on both of them. How did you know to phone me so early?'

Yasmin smiled. 'I didn't! You were on my mind when I woke up and it just felt right to phone you now. Sounds like you're firing on all cylinders!'

'Oh, I am. We are! Col is flying us three boys to The Bahamas.'

'What? All that way in that helicopter? Why?'

'No, no, that's only until we get to the hangar. Anyway, we embark on our journey today. The little one is still sleeping, his father has brewed the coffee and insisted on breakfast duties.'

Dean's pleasant voice filled the phone. 'Morning Yasmin Rose, nice to hear from you. How's the holiday?'

'Morning Dean, what a lovely surprise! Yeah, like the rollercoaster, but we've been soaking up the sun until today. It's a grey old day, so I'm cooking up the last of the bacon and will take the day as it comes.'

'Are you okay?' both men asked in unison.

'Sure am, thanks,' she replied as easily as she crossed her fingers.

Mr Taylor cleared his throat and murmured something to Dean. The next thing she heard was the old man's voice in her ear.

'It is only you and I in this conversation. Please listen carefully. I would love to spend time hearing all about your road trip and such, but sorry dear, it will have to be another time. I repeat what I have said before about the dangers of mentioning the primary alias. Someone did and consequently died an awful death. Before you ask, yes, there is proof. I need to tell you some things so you might want to sit down.'

She didn't.

The old man took a deep breath. 'A combined effort discovered the parents and two-year-old sibling died in a house fire when this creature was six years old. From there he got lost in the system until we read an entry about a reunion with an alleged sister. Said creature is particularly dangerous and will strike at the most unexpected time. The sister's trail went cold. Maybe she got married. She may even be dead.' Mr Taylor's exhale sounded like a deflating balloon. 'Be careful, young lady. I want to share at least one meal in your company. Rudy said this creature generally got around with his hands on his hips.'

Yasmin scoffed. 'Gee, that narrows it down! I'm beginning to think it's a South Australian thing!'

'I don't know what to say about that, but he had suite of disguises, a penchant for handlebar moustaches and long grey jackets regardless of the weather.'

The handle of the spatula snapped consequently flicking the bacon out of the pan. Shooing Combo away, she mumbled under her breath. 'Dammit! You're a lucky dog.'

Ignoring the interruption, Mr Taylor's voice dropped considerably. 'There's also proof that the replacement in the lover's triangle was a serial killer, but because his fingerprints weren't on file, Rudy referred to him as a ghost. There is proof.'

Yasmin's voice climbed uncontrollably in pitch. 'Proof? What proof? Where is this proof? Are you convinced I have this proof?'

'I've been churning that over for a long while. You have found the other infidelities, so yes, I am inclined to think you do. My dear girl, you have to be very careful, promise me.'

'I will be, I promise.' She heard Dean calling Herbie for breakfast. 'Better not keep the chef waiting, Mr Taylor!'

'I haven't finished. Rudy may have tried to hide his guilt with inclusivity, but the bond between the brotherhood is impenetrable. Regardless, you and these lads will always be connected, and I am also aware of your part-ownership. My advice to you … use that business head of yours and change the tune. Now I do have to go, dear. CREAM awaits,' he chuckled softly and hung up.

She phoned him straight back. 'CREAM? A yacht with one sail? I suppose that's another lie.'

'Young lady, I can assure you it's the most pleasant of all.'

'Pardon me if I don't share your enthusiasm, Mr Taylor.'

'You aren't a bit curious?'

'Not at all.'

'I have to go now. Please make your way to Great Exuma in the Bahamas soon. We all need a clear path to closure. You look after yourself, Ms Pestel. Like this dangerous name, our conversations must never be repeated.'

'Happy travels, Mr Taylor.'

Yasmin deactivated the phone, watched little bubbles form on the bottom of the pot then slowly build into a rolling boil. The combination of lies and the horridly cruel game blended with the sizzling splashes on the hot plate until half the water had evaporated. Dismissing the thought of breakfast, turned off the gas and let Combo have free reign of the destroyed bacon.

Hugging her knees on the step, she felt the same as the wind-whipped scrubby beachfront. Her heart – the leaves thrashing about. Her mood – the breakers crashing angrily onto the shore. Just when she thought it was all over, the image of the latest cardboard box merged front and centre of her mind's eye. *I hate your game, Rudy.*

Chomping on an apple as loudly as the waves pounding the beach, one-handed rehashed her document into a formal report for the attention of Sergeant Kohli, then as an afterthought included Sergeant Pyers. Making damned sure nothing would link her or Rudy to the evidence, bullet-points became her friend.

Scrawled names captivated her mind. *Leigh, Callum Johns, Mathews, Wilson.* With the half-eaten apple poised near her mouth, she compared the names to the obituaries: R.J.C.L. Wilsmatson.

'It's them! Oh Rudy, you clever, deceptive sod,' she exclaimed enthusiastically.

Instantly her mood improved. Hugging her pooch, she ruffled his mini mo-hawk. 'We've got 'em Combo! If the sun comes out tomorrow, we're having a change of scenery.'

Then the boogey-man's name popped into her head. The jubilation was short lived.

'Who the hell is Rupert then?'

Taking out her frustration on the keyboard, added an appendix with the evidence listed chronologically and formatted the document with a table of contents. Finally, the latest version was saved onto a USB which went into another resealable bag, complete with Paddy's proof, and stuffed at the bottom of her handbag. Now she was really hungry.

Dodging the scuds, they ran to the nearest cafe where she polished off a burger-with-the-lot, shared the yolk-dipped chips with Combo all the while watching a fishing boat bob bravely in the choppy waves just offshore. Ocean, beach, grass, shops was quickly becoming a favourite scene. No cars. No bitumen. No telephone wires or power lines in photographs. She much preferred a calm ocean. Its lullaby soothed her aggrieved soul.

Afterwards, the second-hand bookshop took her fancy. Idly flicking through the raunchy romance novels, blushingly rearranged several titles and hastily moved onto the science-fiction bookshelf.

A slightly older, taller, solid woman with bright purple dyed hair giggled. Combo happily wagged his tail. 'Gorgeous pooch,' she said, and thrust the retrieved novel back into Yasmin's hands, 'Go on! Be a devil.'

An embarrassed chortle escaped her tight-set lips. 'No ways! It's been too long between drinks.'

'All the better. I'll buy it for you and those Tim-Tams you're melting.'

'You don't have to do that!' peering closely. 'Do I know you?'

'Doubt it. I'm a Queenslander, bouncing through to WA.'

'Gosh you look familiar!'

'Yeah, been told I have a double! Bet she's a goodie-two shoes as well.'

She burst out laughing. 'Yeah right! Careful you don't trip over your halo!'

They debated whether or not Yasmin would take the book, with her answer being an adamant *no*.

The stranger grinned. 'How about this then, I'll buy these for you if you buy me something?'

'Like what?' Yasmin replied warily.

'Four double A batteries.'

'Four?'

The combined giggles were without judgement.

'Yep! Four. You go first and leave them on the counter. Wait for me outside on the bench. I'll sit beside you and slip these into your tote bag, then give me five minutes before you go.'

'Uh, yeah, okay but that's a bit weird. Are you hiding from someone?'

'Hell no! No rules, pretty girl. That's what holidays are for!' Penny replied, kept her hands by her side and bent down to eye-level with Combo. 'You're a good boy!' When she stood, she indicated with her head. 'After you!'

***

Sergeant Kohli permitted himself a small smile. 'Yes, Cap'n?'

'One pair of sweet lips.'

'Nice!'

'Purple crown previously spotted with two gropers. Top and tail, or tag only?'

'Tag only.'

'Out.'

***

Secure in their mobile abode with her mind in a whirl, they caught their breath from racing each other. Feeling energised to have shared a good laugh with a stranger who had been kind, albeit naughty and non-judgmental, the packet of Tim-Tams was ripped open.

'Getting too used to these lazy days, my boy!'

Combo yapped happily and stepped up onto the bed.

'Ah, no. Not this time. You can go on your own bed for a while, buddy. Go on. On your bed.'

He barked once and gave her a look of derision, jumped noisily to the floor then bounded onto his seat. His sigh was not a normal puppy sigh.

'It won't be all the time, Combo. Love you boy.'

Chapter 55

Sergeant Kohli's deep voice boomed through the overhead speaker, filling the cells with his elevated impatience. 'I will ask you again. Who is the boogey-man?'

The six K9s snarled angrily at the men and women cowering against the back wall. Their lead handler dragged his baton along the bars, aggravating the boys further. 'Wanna get up and personal?' he challenged.

'Those mutts are gonna get theirs.' Leigh slung at him.

'You'll never get us to say the name. Never.' Callum replied in the same manner.

'Never. Never. Never. Never.' The twins screeched.

The handler glared at the women. 'Which one of you is the leader?'

'We are.' The inmates shouted in harmony.

'Why are we here anyway? We don't do powder, and you never found any pot on us. Are we under arrest? How long are you going to keep us?' Ivan demanded.

'I've got the perfect medicine for those mutts!' Travis jeered.

'You never got us all. Ha ha. Sucks to be you!' Leigh yelled out sarcastically.

'Shut up, Leigh,' Callum hissed.

'Give the pigs something you idiots or shut the hell up! You pathetic bunch of dribbling losers.' The outburst from the cell containing a cross-section of dregs of society initiated an all-in shouting match.

One short, sharp blast of a whistle set the dogs off on a display of teeth-baring aggression. Several long, noisy minutes later the handler clapped his hands once instantly commanding the K9s to be silent and to sit. Sniffles, snuffles and sobbing echoed through the small building.

Stepping out of earshot, he spoke into his collar-microphone. 'They're not talking, Boss. Whoever it is has got them crapping themselves. The other lot are getting restless.'

'Copy that. Make them all sweat.'

'Will need to use the firehose to clean out the pens.'

'Good job. Any wind of something out of the ordinary at the funeral parlour?'

'Not you too! The missus hasn't stopped complaining about the new Clive not being as diligent as the old one.'

'What are you talking about, Constable?'

'Apparently the old Clive went on a holiday, the new guy, also called Clive, is still a trainee who doesn't fill out forms properly.'

'Since when?'

'She's been griping about it for over a month! Didn't know we have that many funerals. Anyway Boss, I'll be handing over to Team Pinscher soon and Sergeant Pyers logged a request that we do a run past the funeral home before end of shift. Coincidence? Pardon, Sir. Do we have your permission?'

'Approved. Try your hand with an extra set of paws for the experience.'

'The Intimidator?'

Both men laughed.

'Hey Boss, did you want me to ask the missus for more information?'

'No. Don't take work home if you can help it. Give me feedback on anything you discover out at Gentle Rest.'

'Copy that ... on all counts. Out.'

***

Owen paged his colleague.

Sergeant Kohli answered gruffly, 'One moment, please.' He acknowledged Team Pinscher taking over from Team Razor, then responded, 'You rang?'

'Yeah, you got anything?'

'Not from this lot. You?'

'A message from Penny.'

'Righto, I'll dial in.'

Shortly afterwards, the two Sergeants listened to the woman's message.

If you have a pair of female twins, one other woman and three men from Moojie who don't like dogs, you've got nearly all of them. Keep asking them the boogey-man question. They're terrified of him. P.S. They don't do powder.

'Boss, we're going to have to trust her.'

Owen shuffled paper around his desk, looked back at the wall map, then answered. 'Always have, Sergeant Kohli.'

'That's very formal, Sergeant Pyers. F.Y.I. your request is approved.'

'Cheers for that. See ya later.' He pinned another marker on his investigation board and stood back. Scratching his head, muttered, 'The Feds should have said something earlier.'

Chapter 56

The evening star twinkled in the clearing twilight. Ever so slowly, Mother Nature calmed down and the noisy grey day disappeared into a beautifully cloudless mild night. Yasmin finished off their seaside holiday with a mountainous seafood basket and a juicy piece of steak on the side, and for the first time in ages an ice-cold beer in a chilled glass stein. Combo's doggy-dish had been licked clean and sat between her feet. The steady glow of a boat's green and red lights danced to the song of the waves.

Smiling and smoothing his funny tuft, murmured, 'As pretty as fairy lights and as comforting as your puppy sighs.'

The publican, who had suggested they sat in the beer garden closest to the path that led along the foreshore, announced his approach with a cough. 'Miss, just coming to offer you another beer and a doggie bag?'

Combo automatically stood in front of her. 'No, thank you. We'll be on our way.'

'You got a good one there.'

'Yep, sure do. We'll wait until you're back inside.' Yasmin made a move to stand.

'Suits me! Enjoy your stay and thanks for the patronage.'

'Thank you! Dinner was delicious.' She didn't hide her grin and patted Combo. 'Let's go, boy.'

Chapter 57

Acting on the rapid-fire phone call from the Team Lead, it didn't take long for the sergeants to arrive at the funeral parlour and take over the inquisition of the graveyard caretaker.

Sergeant Kohli leaned in closer. 'You're telling us Clive left how long ago?'

The evidently drunkard shrugged. 'Dunno. Th-there weren't any funerals so he-he went away, and I know not where. He's the new Clive.'

'What?' Sergeant Pyers demanded.

'The new Clive. The old one just up and went on holidays a long while ago.'

'So where is Giles?'

'Moojie Hill of course! They all go there for f-fun and whatnot.'

Wiggling Zeus' leash, the big man growled another question. 'What about cremations?'

'Only one. I'm trying to remember what he said about it … but your d-dog … he's making me n-nervous … I-I can't think straight.'

Sergeant Kohli rolled his eyes. His angry gait matched by Zeus' as they strode away.

'Now you had better talk. We only let you take this job so we knew where you were at all times.' Pyers tried to talk calmly.

'The big man scares me, you know that.'

'Yet you always blame the dog. Best talk about the cremation before he comes back. But first, talk to me about that shed at the back.'

'I can't. I'm not allowed there.'

'Who died the other day?'

'Nobody. It was another trial run.'

Sergeant Pyers gripped the man's upper arm. 'What?'

'Don't you get it? That's why the gates were all locked when you and the other people were there. Is the new padlock yours?'

'You only pretend to be drunk. Keep talking or I will call the boys over.'

'Okay, okay. The old Clive had a big tidy up. The new Clive organised the people. We did have a real funeral recently. But now both Clive's have gone away!'

'Where is the new Clive now?'

'I don't know! I really don't.'

'Tell me about the cremation,' Sergeant Pyers reminded him sternly.

'The old Clive said to leave the ashes in the incinerator until someone came looking for them.'

'You're joking right?'

The drunkard giggled until he wet his pants. 'Yes-yes, I am! You should see your face! Here'—he dug around in his pockets and withdrew a bunch of keys—'you'll need these.'

'No, you will need them. Lead the way and no more pranks else you'll end up with more than one dog sniffing your crotch.'

The caretaker stuttered and stammered, then shuffled his feet. Sergeant Pyer's whistle caused several dogs to bark in reply.

'Okay, okay, geez no one can take a joke anymore.'

'Clearly.' Owen's cheesy grin held no mirth. 'How come you remember the instructions so clearly?'

'Because I peeked inside the bag. What's really weird is the plaque and you sure as heck don't look like a female.'

En route back to the Station, the Sergeants shared a good laugh about the dogs' antics with the drunk yet were mystified with the information gleaned.

'Did you give them the go ahead for the cremation?'

'The coroner confirmed it was a heart attack. Another bloody heart attack.' Owen rubbed his eyes. 'Nah, I didn't. Can only think that the decision came from higher up. Anyway, drop me off at the hospital if you don't mind.'

'Sure. Are you okay?'

'Yeah. I'll surprise my bride and drive her home tonight.'

'Units Shackles and Fury are on standby overnight if you're needed back at HQ.'

'Yep, cheers. See you then.'

Frowning at Owen's preoccupied demeanour, Sergeant Kohli methodically pondered every detail that lived in his head until the moment he sat at his desk. The duty officer's message stuck to his monitor had him riveted to his chair and Zeus standing guard.

Received an anonymous phone call from a hysterical woman saying some people had threatened her kids while at Moojie Hill. When she described them to the local police, they informed her several had been transferred here and to leave a message with someone in charge. That's you, Boss!

The woman said to ask them about a <u>Rupert John Matson</u> and if they got scared, to tell them he was still alive and would find them all.

Sergeant Kohli, she was adamant about the message and made me repeat it several times, even the spelling (boogey-man is what she said at the end.) The phone number was untraceable. Ten minutes later she phoned again and said that Stu Wilson and his mate Giles left Moojie Hill with a woman at midnight. Again, the phone number was untraceable.

'What the hell is going on?' he wondered aloud.

Chapter 58

S ergeant Kohli grumbled into the phone. 'Fishing so early, Cap'n?'

'Yep. One sweetlip, one doggy mackerel.'
'Get the net ready.'
'Always is. Out.'

***

The pair had crammed as much relaxation, sunshine, sand and ocean into their stay as possible. Being their last morning by the little seaside town they were down in the dumps. Yasmin reluctantly disconnected the utilities and prepped the motorhome for travel before taking their last dose of vitamin sea. The lure of the soft dawn colours kissing the deep blue water and white sand, simply too strong to ignore. They had the beach to themselves, thankfully. Combo's panting mimicked her growing anxiety. And neither of them felt hungry.

With only the vehicle's keys in her shorts pocket, they beachcombed and played in the shallows. She imagined what it would be like doing the same in Hawaii and smiled sadly. The overwhelming sense of loss swept over her like a freak wave. Letting the tears flow into the gentle outgoing tide, a loud attention-grabbing whistle gave them whiplash. A fair distance away, two people jogged towards them. Yasmin squinted, wiped away the excess tears and tried to focus, directing Combo closer to the dunes. She hoped they would give them space. They didn't. The strangers veered towards them instead. They slowed to a walk. Yasmin looked over her shoulder and guessed their mindless stroll had taken them almost a kilometre from the caravan park. Hissing to Combo to sit and protect, he completely disobeyed her and stood his ground. Shortening his leash, she encouraged him to walk slowly backwards. He complied beautifully.

'Not friendly!' she yelled as loudly as she could.

Although they were wearing dark clothing and hoodies, she could tell by their build that they were men. Combo's shackles were as elevated as Yasmin's goosebumps. She casually reached down and unclipped his leash. Estimating the men were about double the fifty-metre distance from the patio to the Jacaranda tree, she looped her hand through Combo's collar and turned him around forcefully, then stood in front of him. With her free hand, pointed behind her. He leant into it and nuzzled it meaningfully. The two men had stopped.

She crouched down. Spoke quietly and clearly. 'Combo. Wait.'

He sat.

'Stay.'

She looked over his head. The men began to walk towards them.

'Stay. Good boy. Stay.' Her voice, low and controlled.

When Combo wagged his tail, she knew he was anticipating the final command. She shoved the motorhome keys into his nose before jamming them back into her pocket. The men sped up.

She spun around on her heels and commanded, 'Race.'

They took off like a shot and hightailed it without looking back. Combo a good ten metres in front and pulling away. There was no way she was going to get left behind. Finding something buried deeply inside her, drew alongside and together bolted towards the caravan park.

'We'll find you,' a threatening voice caught up to them.

'That mutt will die in your arms,' a louder, slightly higher pitched male's voice urged them to run faster.

They both flinched and yelped when something hit the sand either side of them.

'Race, Combo. Race,' she hissed between breaths, both finding an extra spurt of energy.

Ducking and weaving through the windsurfing boards lying up the beach, Combo launched over two canoes at the same time Yasmin dived, tucked and rolled just as a bullet ricocheted off a pylon. They still had almost a hundred metres to the shrubby path. Then the caravan park. Safety.

'Race,' Yasmin urged Combo.

***

'Cap'n?'

'Two groper chasing the bait.'

Sergeant Kohli swore under his breath. 'Any sighting of the other sweetlip?'

'Negative.'

A smattering of expletives echoed. Dead air. Static. Eventually, he heard his mate's animated voice.

'.. lip ... got away ... wait, second ... making an app ...'

'Bloody hell!' the big man was talking to himself. 'Zeus! Here boy!'

***

They flew past the notice board. Combo's ears pinned. He pulled away. Yasmin begged him to wait. As soon as they crested the small sand dune that led onto the pathway, *TWANG!* She screamed and crashed face first into the sand. Dragging herself onto her feet cried out in agony, clutching her hamstring desperately tried to catch up to Combo. The mere thought of traffic spurred her on. Heavy footsteps and loud breathing close behind. Running through the excruciating pain, she had to get Combo. A loud shriek. Squealing brakes. A louder yelp. Her blood turned cold.

She yelled, 'NOOOO!' then screamed.

A hand gripped her upper arm. Pivoting on her sore leg, hopped and drove her hip forward smashing her knee into the assailant's groin. He went down. She rammed her knee into his nose and hobbled backwards away from the moaning man trying to turn away while doubling over.

'Hey, flower lady,' a breathless voice called out harshly.

She looked around to see his mate step out of the shadows waving a gun at her. His hoodie had fallen backwards revealing a polished skull.

She gasped. 'You?' Then looked back at the other man. 'Stu? What the hell?'

Thudding footsteps and panting from behind, Combo whimpered as he barged past her.

'DOWN!'

Combo dove into the ground and rolled onto his side. She flung her body over his at the same time the gun went off. Yasmin gasped inhaling a mouthful of grit. Keeping her head down, gagged, coughed and spluttered.

'Best you leave well alone, flower lady. Consider that your last warning. The others won't be so kind.'

'You did break my nose this time, Yasmin. Dammit woman, learn to mind your own business.'

She lifted her sandy face. 'Stu Morgan C Wilson, how dare you? What the hell is going on?' Glaring at his cohort, scowled, 'And you? Giles, is it? How dare you? Was my skillet not enough?'

'Don't wanna know your backhand, but thanks for the wake-up call!'

'Huh?' She coughed and spat out more sand.

'Dammit, woman. I told you to mind your own business. You know too much,' Stu whined.

'It was you! Wearing that hideous outfit and stupid curly moustache?'

He lost his balance. 'What?'

'Come on, don't deny you weren't at Moojie Hill.'

'No ... no, that wasn't me, I swear,' Stu whined.

Sparks flew out of Yasmin's eyes. 'Well, the least you can do is tell me who the hell is Ru—?'

'No, flower lady, p-please don't!'

Fast-paced footsteps came from behind them.

'Bloody hell you fools! You wanna hope you didn't hurt the pooch.'

The women stared at each other. The solid physique clad in black athletic gear a lighter shade than her wig, and with the straps of the red backpack made her look spider-like. Her arrival spurred on Giles who waved the gun at Yasmin who lowered her head. An argument between Stu and the woman erupted. He regaled the skillet saga then admitted he had always wanted Combo for himself. She threatened to do more than cripple him if he had harmed the dog. Stu's whining admission made Yasmin shiver.

'It was meant to be just a warning, I swear.'

Lifting her head, came face to face with the wrong end of the silencer. Combo's body tensed at the same time as hers.

'Uh-uh, flower lady. Keep your head down and your mouth shut.' Giles waited several seconds, then lifted her chin up with the barrel and looked at her with watery eyes. In a quieter voice, said, 'When you wake up, your dog won't be here, but he will stay alive. There are worse people than us.'

'Oi, what are you saying?' Stu demanded.

'Just passing on a warning, mate. You got that tranq ready to go? This one needs a painkiller. Reckon she blew a hamstring when she hit the dirt, plus her ankle looks busted.'

Yasmin's eyes darted between all three and went to open her mouth, meeting the tip of the barrel.

'You will eat this if you speak.'

Shooting daggers at her assailants, Yasmin flinched when the woman bustled Giles out of the way.

'Clear off, you pair, I'll catch you up. We've been here long enough. GO. I'll bring the dog.'

'But—' Stu whined again.

'No buts, get going. I don't need the gun.'

The woman crouched down, leant forward, pulled out Yasmin's shirt and slipped a piece of paper down its front. After making sure the men weren't around, she made a show of inserting the needle into the clear liquid, withdrawing it and tapping a vein in Yasmin's wrist. In one deft move, Yasmin's hands were pinned down by the woman's knees. They locked eyes, neither giving away their emotions.

Words flew out of Yasmin's mouth like a cobra hiss. 'Only part Gothic today, huh? Who are you? How did you find me?'

In a hurried, hushed voice, the woman replied, 'You're good, I'll give you that much. Trust me. Pooch will be safe. You're going to get sleepy very quickly.'

She gasped, coughed and stared at the needle plunging steadily into her vein. 'P-please ... I need m-my Com—'

***

Gently rolling the sleeping woman onto her side, Penny strapped the hamstring and ankle before pacifying the whimpering Pooch with another tranquiliser and scooped him up. Cursing the men when she saw blood under his harness, laid him back down, cleaned and checked the wound. Deftly applying bandages to stem the bleeding, tightened the harness another notch for added pressure.

'The idiots are lucky it's only a flesh wound. It's okay boy, you're in good hands.'

Hoisting the heavy weight so his head and front paws hung over her shoulder, Penny supported Combo's body, scuffed away footprints with her foot-socks and smiled tenderly down at Yasmin.

'Sleep well, Ms Rose. I love this Pooch more than anything, but we can't hang around. Good luck.'

***

Sergeant Kohli put the buzzing mobile phone up to his ear, 'Cap'n?'

'Stronger trace this time. Two gropers on the run, one with a limp. One sweetlip with doggy mackerel.'

'Which sweetlip?'

'Midnight crown.'

'You got anybody nearby?'

'Negative. Gotta throttle down. Out.'

Sergeant Kohli's massive knees wobbled. There was nothing he could do. He had already overstepped one mark.

***

Walking in between the hobbling Stu and brooding Giles, Penny stopped in her tracks and transferred Combo to her other shoulder.

'Listen up, boys. This is how we're going to play this game from now on. Giles, I'm going to trust you to travel on your own. Is that Ivan's weapon?'

'Dunno, ask Stu.'

'Well, Stu? Whose is it?'

'Mine. Registered to me.'

'You're a bloody idiot. Have you got anything that'll negotiate a deal?' Penny demanded.

'Sure have, but I ain't a rat.' He fell to one knee and reached out with one hand. 'Listen, Penny. I want to marry you. I've loved you forever and a day, this is seriously the wrong time to even consider a proposal, yet here I kneel.'

'You romantic mo-fo! Stu, in another world in another time, maybe. But not in this one.' She handed Combo to Giles with a death stare, dropped to both her knees, wrapped her arms around Stu's neck and kissed him passionately. 'My answer is no.' Then whispered in his ear, 'But if you ever feel the urge to satisfy me again, phone me first.'

He grinned. 'You horny bitch. I need you ... please.'

Giles interrupted them with a loud groan. 'Get a room! I don't want to hold this dog any longer. Get up, Penny. I've been sus on you for a while. You a cop?'

She easily took Combo into her arms then indicated for Giles to help Stu stand. As soon as he was stable, she thrust the sleeping Pooch into his arms. 'Here, hold this.'

Looking at Giles, she said, 'Nah, the German Wurst food van has always been my interest. Anyway, as I was saying, you're going to be driving the ute on your own.'

'Whoa, back up.' Giles trained the gun on Penny.

In a blink of an eye, he was on the ground with his hands high in the air. 'Please don't shoot, Penny. Sorry, Penny, sorry.'

'Get up and don't ever point a gun at me again.'

She unwound the silencer. After emptying the chamber, shoved the bullets and weapon down the front of her one piece. The silencer sat securely through a loop in Combo's harness.

Retaking him, her words could have cut through steel. 'Let's go. We're going home.'

In shocked silence, both men traipsed ahead with their heads hanging low.

Chapter 59

The little boy gobbled down his ice cream and ran excitedly to where the adults were playing cards.

'Mum! Mum, she's waking up.'

Waddling over, his matronly mother wiped her hands on the snug-fitting, well-worn apron and dabbed Yasmin's mouth with a recently sterilised Christmas themed face cloth.

'Here, love, slowly … slowly … I don't have my whole kit with me.'

'Nurse?' Yasmin croaked.

'Farmer's wife.'

With a whisper of a smile, Yasmin swallowed hard. 'I'm in good hands. My dog?'

The woman looked at her quizzically, shook her head and firmly restrained Yasmin's attempt to get up.

'You didn't see a dog?'

'Lady, you must have had a fair bit of sedative and although your ankle is swollen, it's not broken. Some kind person strapped it, and your hamstring which is now wrapped in a compression bandage. No running for you for a while.'

The tears escaped in torrents. Eventually, Yasmin managed to speak. 'What's the time?'

'Just gone midday.'

'My Combo,' she wailed.

The woman's stern voice brought order to Yasmin's mortification. 'Your keys are still in your pocket, but my son picked this up. It fell out of your shirt.' She handed Yasmin a small piece of paper.

The note read: TRUST ME. AA

Yasmin frowned and looked blankly at the woman feeling her pulse.

'Dunno, love, the only other thing I can think of is batteries because you don't look like a recovering alcoholic!'

'It *is* her!' Yasmin's pulse race and struggled to sit up.

'Not yet, heavens you're worse than a ruddy lamb!'

'I have to find my dog. He needs me. There was a screech—'

'Ah! That dog. He met my older son doing tricks on his bike, got a fright when a car slammed on the anchors and hightailed it back down the path. Thanks to Junior, we found you fast asleep but no sign of a dog. That was over four hours ago, not sure how long you'd been lying there but. You're lucky, is all I can say. Not too many creeps around these parts, but you're a pretty one.'

Yasmin's eyes widened. 'I have to get going. I'm—'

'In trouble? Or safe?'

That stumped her. 'Not sure actually, but I mustn't impose on you or your family any longer. Thank you.'

'You'll do a sobriety test before I allow you to drive, young lady.'

She nodded her head and performed the necessary tests.

'Right, you passed but you do need to drink a lot of water.'

'I will, thank you. Nice to meet you, I'm Yasmin and I need to make tracks. My motorhome is the last one with beach views.'

'I'm Marge. Suit yourself, but see if you can put more weight on your ankle. I'll get my boys to escort you.' She hollered out for her sons who eagerly raced into the room.

Wriggling her toes, did some more leg extensions and slowly sat then lifted herself off the makeshift bed. 'So far so good.'

Marge nodded. 'Off you go boys and show the lady the way back here by foot.'

'Yes Mum,' they eagerly replied and animatedly talked the whole way about all the fun they have during their stay at the seaside until after Christmas.

Eventually, Yasmin returned to their site and waved madly at the happy boys who stood either side of their mother. With two bundles of travelling money removed from her purse, she had just folded it in half when Marge opened the driver's door. She stood in the nook with her plump hands clasped underneath her bosom.

'You drink a lot of water, young lady and for heaven's sake, pull over if you're tired.'

She gently pried the woman's hands apart and spoke while pressing the cash into them. 'Yes Marge. Here, it is legal and not nearly enough, but it's the best I can do at this moment. Please accept it graciously. I swear I will find a way to pay you back.'

Large tears traced the outline of her ruddy cheeks. 'You don't have to pay me.'

'I know, but I want to. Thank you for being there. Um, it's early I know but … Merry Christmas?' she smirked and swiped at her own threatening tears.

Marge grinned, 'Merry Christmas!'

Thanking the kind-hearted family again, she returned their energetic waves until they were out of sight. A spare carpark behind the kiosk gave her the opportunity to change her appearance, activate her personal phone then follow an elaborate fifth-wheeler setup onto the highway.

***

Owen's colleagues gave way while he jogged down to the Communications Room.

'Guys, need a priority BOLO on—'

'One woman travelling with two known accomplices and a dog?'

'Yeah! How do you know?'

'The big fella already dialled it through.'

Owen frowned. 'Oh! Needed the run anyway. Thanks, keep us informed.'

'Yes, Sir.'

Taking a detour on the way back to his office, he ventured into the holding cells. Ignoring the jibes and hawked phlegm coming from the yet-to-be-processed scourge, followed the voice booming through the speakers. Zeus' fearsome amplified bark even made his hair stand on end.

On his way out, simply stated, 'Behave yourselves, scum of the earth, or we'll get the boys onto you next.'

'Oi, when are ya gonna process us!' someone yelled out angrily.

'Thanks for the reminder,' Owen waved over his shoulder and kept on walking.

Out of ear shot, made a phone call. 'Hey Kohli, care to share?'

'Could ask you the same question, Pyers.'

The growled reply raised Owen's ire enough for him to clench his fist.

***

The K9 Duty Team Lead continued to interrogate the rambunctious cell mates. 'For the last time, the one that dobbed youse in. What is her name?'

'Who cares?' the twins screeched, their teeth grinding habit mesmerising the staring K9s.

Ivan yelled, 'Shut up! I can hear your bloody teeth from here. Oi, get those bloody dogs away from us and we might consider answering your questions.'

'Yeah, go away! Go away!' the twins screeched again.

'Callum?' Leigh called out over the din.

'What?' he cried out, pushing Travis out of his face.

Leigh whined, 'I'm scared, Call. Just tell them who she is. I want to go home.'

Ivan stepped in where Travis left. 'Who are we talking about here?'

Travis muscled Ivan out of the way and grabbed Callum by the throat, holding him against the wall. Callum allowed himself to be manhandled and grinned sardonically, daring either one to hit him.

Knowing full well they wouldn't, replied smugly. 'Stu's honeypot, has been for years. They only hook up at Moojie. Always liked to watch how she prick-teased him.'

'But she's joined us in the barn for how long?'

'Long enough. She's harmless! She left with him and Giles if you really want to know,' Callum chortled.

The twins shrieked their horror, drowning out the heated exchange developing between the men. When he asked Travis why Stu and Giles had paid a visit to Yasmin Pestel, an almighty all-in brawl erupted.

One flick of the Team Lead's finger set the K9s on a snarling rampage. On command, they fell silent and walked backwards. Their jaws like split liver, twitching and flashing white fangs.

'You happy now?' Leigh screamed, face pressed through the bars.

The Belgium Malinois brothers lunged snapping and snarling.

'Over to you, Boss,' the handler spoke into his collar mic.

Sergeant Kohli shook his head. *Bloody hell.*

Chapter 60

Combo's absence added to the loneliness of the coastal road and exploded out of Yasmin's eyes. Bumping blindly off the verge, the emotional tidal wave ebbed and flowed. She felt as lonely as the skeleton of a lonely tree clinging onto the bank of a lagoon running alongside the highway. Its spindly branches reaching helplessly to the heavens. Pleading silently for some comfort, dialled her local police station. Harried voices took her message, yet neither sergeant would be available for several days. Anxiety levels bordered on palpitation with mobile phone coverage being inconsistent, strong head-winds and a hungry engine. Two and a half hours later, the motorhome coughed and spluttered at the sight of the diesel pump. Doing something highly inappropriate, blasted on the hooter and waved her personal mobile out the window towards the security camera. Nobody came out, so she dialled the advertised number.

'Put that phone away.'

Yasmin poked her head out, looked upwards and blubbered, 'I can't move. I've torn a hamstring. Blown an ankle. I'm out of fuel. Please help me, I can pay cash for a full tank. I've been attacked and-and they stole my dog. P-please—'

Another loud blast on a hooter made her look in the side mirror. A dirty green utility followed closely by a dark grey sedan swerved around a larger motorhome and took up two petrol bowsers. A bald man got out of the utility. Yasmin swiftly pulled her head inside. Wishing the window button would work faster, pressed her herself into the backrest and whispered into the phone.

'Please, please help me. Can you see who is in the grey car?'

'Who do you think it is?'

'A man and a woman who's got gloss black hair.'

'Want me to call the cops?'

'Don't bother.'

'Your funeral.'

'Probably,' she sniffled.

'Say what? I'll send a staff member.'

'Thanks. I'll give him three hundred bucks.'

'Yep. Get off the damn phone.'

A puny lad loped across the driveway ignoring the other customers and stood by the passenger window. With his hands either side of his face, he peered through the passenger window and gave her the thumbs up. Yasmin flipped the lever for the fuel door. For what seemed forever, finally poked the cash through the slightly opened window. He walked away quicker than before, stuffed the money into his trouser pocket and marshalled a departing motorhome consequently preventing anybody else to depart. Yasmin turned the key to the ignition, made herself uncontactable and watched the fuel needle rise to a little over the F.

With her leg and ankle throbbing and her mind in a spin, followed a surge of holidaymakers into a distant town's tourist adventure park. Driving straight into a space that faced the scrub in between a parked large bus and a clapped-out backpacker's bomb, yawned and painfully swivelled her seat. Her heart ached like it was trapped in a cold, steel fist. She tossed three painkillers down her throat, slugged a shot of whiskey and failed to stem the waterfall tumbling down her cheeks.

***

'Sergeant Pyers?'

Owen frowned at the untimely interruption and spoke gruffly into the hand-set. 'Yes?'

'Chas Hillyer speaking. Have you lot discovered anything re the suspicious death at Yasmin Pestel's place?'

'Annoyingly, we have not. You?'

'I'm hanging out for an e-mail from Forensics. A boat load of foreigners ran a sandbank – how the hell they got this far south beats me! There's been another spate of drug ODs. Coroners working overtime. You know how it goes.'

'Yep.'

'How is the pretty little pocket-rocket anyway?'

'How do you think?'

'I haven't read of a funeral notice?'

'Nor will you. It was agreed that it be kept out of the media.'

'Nobody conferred with me.'

'Nobody needed to. Listen I'm in the middle of something here. Did you phone for a reason?'

'Yeah, I'll be out your way next Wednesday, please make the necessary arrangements for another interview with Ms Pestel?'

'I'll do my best as usual.'

'Good. At the Station or her place?'

'The Station. I gotta go.'

'*Capiche*. See you next week.'

***

'Bloody hell, Giles! Why the hell did you pull the trigger?' Penny hissed, threading the needle for Stu.

'They were warning shots. Stu didn't have the balls.'

Stu threw the bloodied tissue into the bin, and spoke like a petulant little boy. 'I wanted Combo ever since I saw him. But he wasn't interested in being my friend.'

'Yeah, could probably smell death,' Giles mumbled.

'Why? And Penny, why do you tease me? Why?'

'A conversation for another day. Hurry up, we need to get the hell out of Dodge.'

'You're always saying that, then you disappear, then you turn up, we have a hot time, then you disappear. Rinse and repeat. Why?'

'For God's sake, Stu!' Penny admonished. 'Stop whining!'

'Yeah man, it's pathetic,' Giles joined in the rebuttal.

***

Combo's yelp had Yasmin on her feet in an instant and just as quickly on the floor groaning in agony. She burst into tears realising she had woken herself up from a dream. Chastising herself for being a cry-baby, strapped a bag of frozen peas behind her thigh with a bungee cord and flung open the door. The backpacker bomb had departed and in its place, a slightly higher budget whizbang. Dinner aromatics filled the air. Reactivating her phone, acknowledged her growling stomach and tossed some bacon into the frying pan. The morning's shockwave transformed into slow-burning rage. Her mood was not receptive to the anonymous caller. Instead, poured herself two fingers and toasted Combo. Biting back the stinging tears, she gulped down a mouthful of the golden liquid, tried to enjoy the bacon sizzle serenade while continual calls from a withheld number incensed her anger.

Eventually, she had enough. 'Yes?'

'Sergeant Kohli calling. You rang, Ms Pestel?' His clipped tone did nothing for her mood.

She swiped at another onset of tears, momentarily relived the attack then changed her tune. 'Yes, I did. Have you got Rudy's ashes?'

'Didn't know you were back in town.'

'I'm not. Nor are three culprits.'

'Anything else?'

'Yes. They stole Combo and one of the bastards had a gun.'

The phone line went dead.

I hate wasting bacon! She screamed into the bunched-up tea towel, tipped out the burnt offerings onto a paper towel, flung herself onto the bed and bawled into her pillow.

***

Riddled with guilt, he thumped his large fist onto the pile of paperwork. Tapping in the code for his contact in charge of highway patrols, Sergeant Kohli paced his office waiting for the call to be answered.

'Hey, big fella! No update on the BOLO.'

He was about to reply when the Comm's Specialist sent a global text.

'Pen plus another vehicle 15km nor-west Murray Bridge. Rose west of same. 90mins apart. Both currently stationary. Different routes. Est. dest = Zulu. Prog: journey intersect 10 clicks south.'

Sergeant Kohli swooped onto his phone call and repeated the location of the primaries. 'Any chance of an overnight delay tactic?'

'You owe me, big time, big fella!'

'Put it on the tab, mate!'

They laughed and disconnected the call simultaneously.

Sergeant Kohli looked out over the compound and sighed noisily. The auditor's words hanging heavily on his shoulders.

'Hey, Boss!' Carl called out, waving as he strolled across the grassed walkway.

'Hey! What are you doing here?'

'The ladies pitched up mid-afternoon and said they'd mind the fort. They had to cut some roses for their upcoming dinner do.'

'Excellent.'

'If you're available, would you like to bring Zeus out and join us for a late dinner? Radar's really missing his mates.'

Sergeant Kohli smiled. 'Great idea, lad. I might just bring a few of the boys.'

The younger policeman grinned broadly and waved like Forrest Gump. 'The more the merrier! You're the best boss ever.'

The big man thumbed his chin. *Hmm, I've heard that before.*

***

Half past ten that night, sitting between the vehicles with a map laid out on the ground, Stu and Giles continued bickering. Their torches flicking upwards and around each time they talked.

'How the hell do we know where she went?' Giles complained again.

'And if you hadn't stuffed around at the servo—'

'Oh, give it up! How'd you know she was even there? Huh?'

They fell silent as an approaching vehicle slowed down, sped up, turned around and cruised past slowly, before turning around again and pulling up ahead of theirs. The brief red and blue lightshow increased the anxiety.

Stu gasped. 'It's the pigs.'

'But how?'

'Pretend you're both asleep. Quick. Giles, cover that shiny bowling ball.' Penny hissed. 'I'll do the talking.'

The men didn't argue. Stu laid down in the foetal position with his back to her. Giles grabbed the map, rolled over onto the grass and covered his head.

'What have we here?' A stern voice called out as he approached.

Flinching at the bright torchlight, Penny stood and leant against the side of the ute.

'Evening, Sir. I'm the sober driver. Glad I found these boys before you had to scrape them up off the road.'

The Road Patrol Officer traced the outline of the bodies on the ground as he spoke. 'My partner is going to check over the vehicles.'

'Sure thing, excuse the mess.' Penny yawned loudly and promptly excused herself.

'Big day?'

'Long day and a bit too much sun.'

'This is a rest area and you're far enough off the road. Are this pair stupid enough to wrestle you for the keys?'

Penny patted her solid thighs. 'They wouldn't dare!'

'Good. Don't get any ideas of leaving before sun up.'

'They'll be right in an hour or so,' Penny said bluntly.

She followed the officer's torchlight shining over her cohorts. Satisfied they weren't looking he lit up his hand and gave her the thumbs up. Speaking sternly, said, 'I have just told you not to drive before dawn. Do you understand?'

She returned the signal. 'Yes-yes.'

'Good. A patrol car will be checking on you several times tonight.'

'Guess I could sleep under the stars for one night. Have you got any spare water? This pair drunk all mine.'

Just then, the officer's sidekick called out, 'There's a dog in the backseat, Sir.'

The senior officer lit up his face and glared at Penny. 'What's with that?'

'Sleeping off a sedation from a procedure earlier today,' she replied casually. 'He's had some water and relieved himself on the towel if you care to investigate closer.'

'Don't get smart young lady. We'll leave you with six bottles.'

'Thanks for checking on us.'

His solid nod dismissed any further conversation.

A long while after they had left, the men sat up.

'Who are you really, Penny?' Stu asked quietly.

'A woman you don't want to mess with.'

'Clearly.' Giles mumbled, handed out a bottle of water each before climbing onto the tray of the ute. 'You two lovers can sleep wherever you like just keep the noise down.'

Penny leant over and whispered in Stu's ear, 'You still owe me ten thousand big ones. Lucky I don't charge you interest.'

Chapter 61

Yasmin screamed herself awake. Several truckies played the air-horn concerto announcing four o'clock in the morning. Utterly disoriented, it took several minutes before she realised where she was, and why she was in a foul mood. Collating her thoughts over a strong black coffee, put Combo's fate in the hands of the double-crossing woman and her mongrel associates. There was absolutely nothing she could do and certainly couldn't go home. *To hell with it all*. She decided a tour of the winery region might be a fruitful idea - rolled her eyes at the tasteless pun and erupted into hiccupping sobs.

***

Sergeant Kohli barely registered who was calling so early.

'Tab's adding up big fella. Primaries are heading your way. Out.'

He rubbed his eyes and sat up. *I need a holiday.*

His mobile beeped with a message from Owen demanding he get to the Station urgently.

***

Fifteen kilometres south of the town under a fiery red dawn, four patrol cars flanked by a pair of tow trucks blocked the highway. On standby, two ambulances. Sergeant Pyers leant against a bonnet eating his way through a breakfast roll.

'You look like Boss Hogg,' Sergeant Kohli's voice crackled through the two-way.

The burst of laughter lightened up everyone's dour mood. Not long afterwards, the call they had all been waiting for came through the secure channel.

'Eight minutes out. Having a drag race. Dark grey sedan. Two occupants, female driver, male passenger. Green utility tailing. Single male occupant. Zero other vehicles for thirty minutes.'

Sergeant Pyers commanded his personnel. 'Right. Get this done and back to the Station without incident, without witnesses.'

***

'What's going to happen between us, Penny?' Stu whined.

'Not much. Not for a while.'

'You know me snake died?'

'Ah hell, Stu. Wanna talk about it?'

'Nope.'

'Okay, tell me this then. What's this crap about a boogey-man?'

He puffed out his chest. 'I reckon it's Travis. Giles refuses to believe it could be Ivan, who is his stepbrother. Could be Clive, he likes to dress up. They got this thing going and I sorta got the low-down on the gang.'

'Ah, that's why you were in Adelaide?' she asked encouragingly.

'Yep. I owed it to Giles to make sure he was okay. He's not a bad lad. You looked so sexy in your nurse's outfit, Penny! That was a nice coincidence.'

'Fancy-dress fund-raising party, remember?'

'No.'

'Back to the gang, Stu.' She rested her hand on his thigh.

He squeezed it and replaced it back on the steering wheel. 'Mmm that's nice, but two hands remember. Yeah, the gang. A bad decision as a teen and have had a loaded gun at my head ever since. Leigh's a callous bitch, can't remember what her other name was, is terrified of someone. And her husband, Callum, is a complete tosser. Reckon there's something sus about that relationship.' He swivelled in his seat and grinned. 'This feels so good telling you, Pen, my beautiful babe.'

'Smoothie!'

'Sally told me she can say the name but. She's known for donkeys. Giles is chicken-liver scared 'cos the story goes that the *boogey-man* will find whoever says his name. When he does, they will end up dead. It's happened—'

'What in God's name?' she feathered the brakes repeatedly until they skidded to a stop. 'Brace yourself, here comes Giles.'

Screeching brakes and a blaring horn shot past. The ute fishtailed, teetered on its side then landed back on its wheels with a loud thud. Penny and Stu flew out of the car, raced over to Giles and helped him out. His face as white as a ghost.

'Are they for us?' he pointed towards the curved line of patrol cars approaching them soundlessly and slowly.

Their flashing lights a psychedelic rolling disco ball. The two centre vehicles sped ahead, then pulled up. Both Sergeants stepped out simultaneously.

'Oh God help me,' Giles muttered. 'That's Sergeant Kohli. I'm a dead man.'

Stu whimpered. 'Not half as dead as I am. That's Sergeant Pyers.'

They lay face down on the ground and put their hands behind their heads.

***

Forensic Detective Hillyer pinned the string systematically joining the mugshots to localities adorning his investigation board. Cross-referencing his notes, he grunted in satisfaction.

'Right under our noses!'

Turning at the lazy knock on his door, his long-term escort swept her lengthy brunette hair up into a loose ponytail. Winking at him, smiled and said, 'I've hidden something for you to find, Chas, follow me.'

'Hmm, I bet you have.' Grinning, he locked the door behind him and removed a bundle of cash from his dressing gown.

***

After ensuring Combo was safe and sound with the K9 crew Penny rode up front with Sergeant Pyers tailing the last tow truck, enjoying a delightfully strong coffee and breakfast roll. She grunted in acknowledgement of Sergeant Kohli's stern speaker conversation, then adjusted the volume when he'd finished his speech.

'He's a good bloke to have on your side, Boss.'

'Yeah. He pulled this all together. More importantly, did you see Ms Pestel?'

'Yes. Her dog took a flesh-wound. Recovered well as you saw, and I got the casing if that helps. We had to take him; it was part of the idiots' plan and I had to play along.'

Her Boss stared at her. 'You've got some explaining to do, young lady.'

'No, I'm still on leave and need to see a certain nurse. But first, I need to get some things out of the ute.'

Penny reached over, flicked the siren once and radioed the driver. 'Dude carrying the ute, pull over please.'

When the truck stopped, Penny clambered up the flat-bed and shimmied under its chassis.

'Oi! What the hell are you doing?'

'Getting what's mine. Won't be long.'

'Sarge? Can she do that?'

Owen replied calmly, 'She's on my watch.'

'You got that right. Don't mean to be rude, but she looks like a freak show!'

'It takes all kinds, mate.'

Wriggling out, Penny flung the backpack to Owen who caught it easily. Both men watched with fascination as the stocky woman nimbly alighted from the elevated platform.

Giving the driver the thumbs-up, said. 'Hey bud, thanks for stopping. Have a nice day!'

Taking the back road towards the hospital, Sergeant Pyers grinned and shook his head while Penny removed the vacant contact lenses. She automatically deposited them into a small vial, slipped that into her pocket and retrieved a pair of gloves from the box on the dash.

'What's so special about the backpack?'

'Several thousand reasons.'

Feeling around the contents, her hand eventually wrapped around a solid bundle at the bottom. *It had better not be powder, Stu.*

Looking at her prize, smiled. 'Ooh, I got a bonus, but dammit, I'm too honest!' Showing off the cash, she said quietly, 'He only owes me ten grand so that's all I'm going to take. This legally is Stu's. Please see he gets it back.'

'He's not being released.'

'Ha! At this point in time you don't have enough to hold him, or Giles. They were threatened by Travis and whoever else you have in the pens, who, are a bonus catch!'

'Humph. With thanks to you. You still have a lot of explaining to do.'

'Oh, I will, but Charlie's got my first interview. Sorry Boss, we've been working on this sting for years.'

'Hey?'

Penny smiled and recounted the childhood friendship she and Charlie shared growing up in the outskirts of Sydney. His father, a very angry man, made for an uncomfortable environment so Charlie sought solitude next door with Penny and her imagined friends. Playing cops and robbers wasn't challenging enough, so they devised crimes for the other to solve. The older they got, the better they got. The pair joined the local drama club which bored them stupid but got clever with disguises and eventually focussed on solving crimes. They both then pursued investigative careers. He, a brilliant strategist. She, a brilliant infiltrator.

'After his old man was killed, I made a vow to Charlie that I would work wherever his mother worked.'

'Why?'

'Just in case there was bad news about Charlie, Ruth and I would have a familiar face for comfort.'

'Very noble of you.'

'Thanks Boss. And no, I cannot divulge the background on this Op.'

'Was your employ here just for this sting?'

'Hell no! I'm here for as long it takes to help bring down the next criminal ring and the next ... and the next.'

'It's taken nine years?'

'This is a baby to the one we're planning. Oh, look! There's the hospital. Nice chat, Boss. See you when I'm back at my desk, where everything goes back to normal.'

'And the boogey-man?'

'Not my story to tell!'

Penny leant over, pecked him on the cheek then peeled off the black wig revealing her neon purple dyed hair. 'See! All for the dare.'

'What about the eloping part?'

She winked. 'Ah, I didn't say who with!' Cheekily blew him a kiss and stepped away from the vehicle. 'Enjoy the next few days, Boss. Make the bastards sing!'

Sergeant Pyers' caught a glimpse of himself in the rearview mirror. A frown and a broad grin was not a good look.

Chapter 62

It was the first time since the phone call with Sergeant Kohli that Yasmin made herself contactable. Lurking on all available lost and found social media pages proved to be futile. Being the third evening of capturing the sunset through her whiskey glass, was calm enough to have a conversation with whoever should phone. The lonely day descended into a burning nightfall when Sergeant Owen Pyers interrupted her reverie.

'Good evening.'

'Ms Pestel, Yasmin. Apologies for the intrusion, I thought it appropriate I check in. How are you?'

Replying cooly, 'I am well, thanks for asking. I hope the ladies, and you and all the guys are too?'

'Yes, thank you. Not a social call I'm afraid. Forensic Detective Hillyer has requested an interview with you at the Station, the day after tomorrow. Are you still in the State?'

Relieved Chas had stopped contacting her directly, contemplated her options before replying quietly. 'I can be. Any update on Rudy's cremation?'

'His ashes will be waiting for you ... excuse me for a sec.' Chamber music filled the airways for several minutes. 'Sorry about that. Sergeant Kohli and I will make ourselves available if necessary.'

Yasmin bit back a retort. 'Oh, it's necessary. What time is this interview scheduled for?'

'Two o'clock.'

'No, that won't work. Let's aim for two-thirty instead.'

'I'll let you know.'

'Thank you. Is that all you have for me?'

His long pause confirmed her suspicions.

Owen replied quietly, 'At this point in time, yes.'

'Fine. Thank you for calling.'

'Thank you, Goodbye.'

She turned off the mobile and automatically clicked her tongue. Sighing heavily, the falsely suppressed grief escaped in salty tears. After a long while, Yasmin looked towards the heavens. *Still trying to get to Hawaii, Emily.* Tidying up the motorhome for the last time, she set the alarm for 3:30am.

*****

Carl was expecting her when she rolled through the gateway shortly before nine o'clock, and greeted her inside the shed by presenting her with a bunch of freshly cut roses. She barely contained her delight, pointed at the panels of the scalloped white fence, albeit an unfinished project, and told him she also loved the combination solid and mesh shed doors.

'Ma'am, I decided the security of the sheds were priority.'

She averted her face. 'Makes sense! Glad my motorhome is out of sight too. And as far as anyone else is concerned, I am not here. No workers today?'

'They're on mandatory time off and will be away for two more days.'

'I'm glad. You're doing a great job, well done,' Yasmin said and got her things together.

'Now that's a shoulder-bag!'

'Yes, it certainly is.'

Deflecting his concerned look when she flinched stepping down, said quietly, 'Combo's not here. Carl.'

The young man's eyes brimmed. He turned on his heel with a hung head and heaving shoulders. Radar familiarised himself, dragged Combo's bed out onto the shed floor and promptly laid in it. That undid Yasmin's resolve causing her to stumble blindly towards her cottage.

A long while later, with Radar remaining guard from his pal's bed, Carl took her for a cruise in the four-wheeler and confirmed there hadn't been any unknown visitors or strange vehicles. They drove in silence afterwards until he repeatedly straightened up his shirt, then ran a hand through his impossibly short hair.

'Thanks for carrying my suitcase, Carl.'

'Well, you shouldn't with your obvious injuries. I'm here if you want to talk—'

'Let's talk about you for a change.'

'Open floodgates! Ma'am, your property would be a great training ground for the pups. If you would consider allowing me to lease the back half and establish a tiny-house, I am eager to pursue my career in dog-handling. The Bosses aren't going to be around forever and the older K9s will need somewhere to retire. But I really would like to follow in Sergeant Kohli's footsteps. Then, when he's ready to retire, maybe he-he ... oh, I think I got a bit ahead of myself.' He slowed to a stop and looked at Yasmin. An embarrassed blush painted his ears red. 'Excuse me, I didn't even ask what you were going to do.'

Yasmin kept her face unreadable. 'Between you, me, and the gate post, you can choose a property either side of this one. You will also need to work out where these amazing creatures will be laid to rest or set free, so best you include that in your proposal. Consider it. Thrash it out silently. Put it together into a business plan and present it with enough time for me to give you an answer by mid-January. Deal?'

He stared at her, an invisible ventriloquist manipulating his jaw. After several attempts, gushed. 'As much as my heart aches and it would be highly inappropriate if I kissed you, Ma'am, I-I-I feel like I've just won the lottery! Deal, thank you! Thank you!'

They shook hands. Their wobbling smiles mirroring each other's. Taking a stroll, she complimented him on his terrific work on their rose garden and agreed that the other pretty flowers were high maintenance.

'The ladies were here the other day helping themselves. They had a dinner do.'

'Fabulous! Whatever makes our lives easier, Carl. I think I'm going to be quite busy next year pursuing another venture, and dogs prefer grass anyway!'

'Sounds exciting, Ma'am. You'll excel at whatever you do.' He straightened up his shirt again and rubbed his head, again.

'What is it you want to say?'

'Um ... whatever makes *our* lives easier?'

He really did blush beautifully. 'Yes. I'm in no hurry for you to leave. Are we running to budget?

'Y-yes! Yes, we most certainly are.'

'Good. Right now, I've got some business to address and to prepare for an interview at the Station tomorrow.'

Carl didn't disguise the look of disappointment. 'Oh. Is he back?'

'Apparently.'

'You know a relationship with him won't work ... um ... you do know that don't you?'

Yasmin stared at him incredulously. 'What? Why? I mean, why would you think there would be one?'

'To be fair, you were grieving! He couldn't take his eyes off you and he is a good-looking rooster. But all that doesn't matter if Combo doesn't accept him. Remember that, Ma'am. As far as your pooch is concerned, *he* is the alpha male! And a jealous one at that!'

Yasmin lightly punched him on the shoulder. 'I pray Combo finds his way home.' She put her hand up to deflect any questions. 'I don't want to talk about it and to be honest, I don't believe I could tolerate the bloke's arrogance, but thanks for the brotherly advice!'

He cast her a look of innocent expectation. 'I appreciate it is short notice, but would you have any objections if Sergeants Pyers and Kohli join us for dinner on your patio? And afterwards, if I brought you all coffee inside your cottage? Tonight? I'll even wear an apron while I'm cooking!'

'Tonight?'

'Yes.'

'I thought I made it clear nobody was to know I was back.'

'Uh, yeah ... about that.' He kicked at the dirt. 'Sorry, Ma'am.'

A million thoughts ran through Yasmin's mind.

'I've got chocolate!' he teased.

She burst out laughing. 'Actually, that will suit me very nicely, thanks Carl. They have several items for me which they can bring too.'

'I'll make it happen. Will 5:30pm be okay for pre-dinner drinks?'

'Perfect! Help yourself to whatever is in the motorhome too.'

By the time Carl messaged her fifteen minutes earlier than expected, her bundle of nerves had tightened into an uncomfortable ball in the pit of her stomach. Reliving the horrid experiences was marginally blurred with the happy photos of Herbie's spontaneous birthday party. Yet nothing seemed to quell the rising anxiety. A quick once-over in her cottage didn't help either. Mostly, she was annoyed with herself for spending so much time on reformatting the known evidence, and not enough on finding Rudy's proof. Everywhere she looked, Combo's fur a reminder that nothing would fill the bottomless hole in her heart. Biting back the tears, donned her white denim skirt and teal blouse. In removing the business card from her purse, Forensic Detective Hillyer's fell out. She blushed, frowned because she was damn sure she'd left it in the laptop case, then got hurried up by Carl's second reminder. Taking a deep breath, dialled the number, ran her finger over the swaying palms, announced herself and asked if she could book a flight to Hawaii per Paddy's recommendation.

'Would your fellow passenger go by the name of Combo, Ma'am?'

'I would love to say yes, but he's gone missing. I hope and pray he comes home before I fly,' she whispered into the phone.

'Oh. Oh, I am so sorry to hear that, I'll join you in that prayer. Given the referral, I'm willing to bet we can most definitely accommodate you, although we are in flight at present. Would ten days be enough notice for you and are you flexible with your itinerary?'

'Absolutely! I ... um ...'

'Wonderful. Was there something else?'

'I will have an urn of ashes,' Yasmin blurted.

'Oh, I am sorry. Do you think your loved one would like to fly up front with us?'

She wiped a tear. 'Yes, I reckon he would.'

'That's settled then. I have your contact number and will send through some details when we land. Thank you for your call. We'll probably lose sig—'

Oh Combo, please find me again. The tears remained unchecked until she caught her reflection in the mirror. Sighing heavily, muttered, 'Add this look to the gallery fellas.'

Venturing outside with her head held high and box of tissues in one hand, failed miserably at walking properly. The greeting was like school buddies at a twenty-five year reunion. Sideway glances, closed emotions, history-forged alliances. Yet the biggest void in attendees were the four-legged companions. Everyone danced around the subject like it was the pox. During dinner the men talked about the expansion plans for the Station and animatedly shared their respective wives' ideas for Christmas. Ever the perfect host, and modest chef, Carl was complimented on a delicious prawn and mango cocktail entrée, followed by a perfectly cooked roast beef, delicious gravy and steamed vegetables, then an award-winning apple crumble with Chantilly cream.

Afterwards, she couldn't contain her disappointment any longer. 'Where's Radar? Zeus?'

Carl answered before the higher echelon could clear their throats. 'It was at my request, Ma'am. I'm a very, very noisy crier and wasn't about to spoil this reunion nor this mammoth dinner venture!'

Acknowledging the sentiment, replied kindly, 'And what a delightful dinner it was. Again, well done and thank you, for everything.'

'Thank you.' He gave her a little smile and offered coffee.

She took her cue. 'Gents, let's adjourn. I would prefer to be inside, plus I need to replenish my tissues.'

Chef turned waiter made a show of stacking the plates. 'I'll just tidy up here a bit, won't be long.'

Around the dining room table, quite the heated discussion erupted when the Sergeants alternatively brought her up to date with the latest news, and admitted they had her tailed. Purely out of concern for her safety, of course.

Yasmin exploded. 'At least that explains the photo-bomber. Carry on.'

The peculiar looks she received replaced her anger with doubt.

Owen continued. 'New evidence had come to light during a different investigation, and we lost sight of you before you even got to Moojie Hill.'

'How did you know I was there?'

'Your phone,' Sergeant Kohli replied quietly.

She sprang to her feet, grimaced, then stared at the men in front of her, totally agog. 'Is that all you can say? You haven't once asked me about Combo. Neither of you! Why?'

At that moment, Carl hooked the door open with this foot, stepped inside balancing a tray of coffees, a box of after-dinner mints, and a bag hanging off his index finger. He looked at her with respectful admiration, pressed his lips together apologetically and quietly nudged Owen with the bag.

'Oh, yes, thanks Carl.'

'Ma'am, please, please sit down. You have to rest that leg.'

With the tray in the centre of the table, everyone reached for the chocolates and snickered at the same time.

'Ha ha! A titter went around the table! That reminds me of a joke,' Yasmin said, wiping her eyes again and sighing heavily. 'But it'll have to wait. I'm not in the mood for laughing.'

Sergeant Kohli did the honours of dealing out the contents.

'Ma'am, I have to take notes, and we're referring to each other formally. I am sorry,' Carl said quietly.

Shaking her head, scoffed loudly. Easing herself down gently, said, 'Let me make myself clear, what is said in this room stays in this room.'

'That's fair. You should know the absence of Combo rips at all our hearts, Ms Pestel.' Sergeant Kohli flattened the chocolate box.

Forcibly widening her eyes, 'Did you ever catch the mongrels who broke into my home?'

Owen nodded. 'The AWOL vet. Giles, he was the bald-headed man you clouted with the skillet and a man named Travis. In our interview with you, you referred to him as the letter T.'

Pleasantly surprised, her light applause didn't quite disguise the sarcasm in her voice. 'Bravo. Suppose it was whoever you had tailing me that got them caught?'

'Not exactly. A woman in Moojie Hill gave us a good lead.'

Yasmin's blush wasn't questioned. 'And? These creatures? What have they told you?'

'Not enough. They're too scared to squeal about a boogey-man,' Sergeant Kohli growled.

Her poker face came to the forefront. 'What do you mean?'

In a rather flat tone, he went on to explain that apparently the last person who uttered a three-worded man's name apparently ended up overdosing, wrapped in plastic, dumped into a coffin and cremated.

'Oh, how tragic! What's all this got to do with me? No. Cancel that. What's all this got to do with Stu and Giles breaking into my home? Hurting Combo? Stealing Combo? You do know it was them, don't you? Where is Combo?'

'We, including Forensic Detective Hillyer, are still trying to work out the connection to the break in, hence the meeting tomorrow,' Sergeant Kohli stated.

'And my Combo?'

'We're waiting for more evidence to come to light, Ms Pestel. We have been assured that Combo is alive.'

The silence was only interrupted with quiet sips, the occasional crunch of mint and the loud clunking minute hand.

Shaking her head in exasperation, said, 'So, it was a heart attack?'

After several silent minutes, Sergeant Pyers spoke. 'Unfortunately, we do not have the evidence to say otherwise. Officially, yes, he died of a heart attack.'

She looked at him directly. 'And unofficially?'

He looked at his colleague with an arched eyebrow.

'I pray you can answer that and—' Sergeant Kohli's pained look stabbed her in the heart.

'And?' Yasmin whispered.

The big man shook his head, returned her direct look and said, 'And we can get on with our lives.'

Yasmin wiped at the sudden onset of tears and slowly nodded. Looking at Carl, he mouthed his apologies and gathered up the cups.

'Feel up to more coffee, gents?' she asked as she stood, grimacing openly.

'If it's not an imposition,' Owen said quietly.

'More like essential. We are not done yet. Feel free to use the kitchen to make the coffees and I suggest you check in with your nearest and dearest, it could be a late night. In my office is a spare monitor. We'll need the necessary cables too and reckon the kitchen bench will be the best place for it. Grab some chairs and line 'em up. Thank you. I shall return with my laptop. Excuse me from the table please.'

While Yasmin was out of the room, Owen put the bag inside the microwave, then checked his phone. Carl automatically unplugged the unit from the wall and went and stood in the void.

'Go for it, Sergeant Pyers, we haven't got much time.'

'Just got an update. The original Clive has turned up. Dead. Was in a coffin inside the morgue. Overdosed. Wrapped in plastic. The drunken bum said only the new Clive wore glasses and was quite strange. Anyway, Gentle Rest has been temporarily closed. The caretaker accommodated elsewhere. The shed behind the funeral home was—'

Carl coughed and indicated his boss should speak faster or be quiet.

Composing herself, did her best to walk properly, and confident there was no incriminating evidence linking back to either Rudy or herself, handed both sergeants a copy of the printed report.

She frowned. 'You could have at least lined up the chairs!'

'Sorry Ma'am, I got sidetracked,' Carl mumbled and hurriedly suggested she made the coffee while he did the heavy lifting.

'Were you talking about me?'

'No, Ma'am.'

'Phew.'

Coffees at the ready, Carl straightened up the chairs while she hooked up the laptop. With guarded faces, the men took their seats.

Paddy's video premiered, next came her audio file, then a slideshow of select photographs during which she gave both evidence bags to Carl to document. Sergeant Kohli didn't move. Owen grabbed the remote, rewound the video to where the cult leaders were clearly visible and froze the playback.

'Boss, do you think Stu and Giles are involved in this?'

Sergeant Kohli quietly suggested they discuss the matter at a different location. A particularly awkward silence settled in the room.

Yasmin asked candidly, 'So, this boogey-man?'

Owen stated, 'What can you tell us?'

'Could be any one of those people. How can anyone trust them anyway?' waving her hand at the monitor.

'Anything else?'

'Yes. What's your take on the photo bomber?'

'Probably one of your worst photos,' Sergeant Kohli grumbled. 'About that video ... where was Combo?'

'Right beside me. And I will take the rest of the details with me to the grave, unless the opportunity presents itself to clear the slate, so to speak. But right now, I do not want to discuss it any further.'

The wall clock's clunk appeared louder than normal and as effective as a dripping tap.

'Where are the ashes?' Yasmin asked bluntly.

'Over to you, Sergeant Pyers,' Sergeant Kohli grumbled.

Owen went into the kitchen and opened the microwave. 'Before I hand it over, Ms Pestel, again, please accept our condolences and our gratitude for your contribution to this case.'

Emotionless, Yasmin took the bag, nodded her thanks and sat it on the dining table, then yawned setting off a chain reaction.

'It's been a big week,' she simply stated and sat. Noticing the envelope, said. 'Thank you very much, Sergeant Kohli. Anything else to discuss?'

'Actually, there is,' Sergeant Pyers said, smothering another yawn. 'Help us understand why you haven't asked the boogey-man's name?'

'You know it?'

'Yes,' both Sergeants replied.

'Because I need to live a long and prosperous life.'

The three men stared at her, then busied themselves with returning their chairs.

'What's on the USB stick, Ma'am?' Carl asked.

'A digital copy of what has been read, seen and heard, of which none shall never be linked to me or my dearly departed.'

'Copy that. You do know you'll still be required to attend Hillyer's interview tomorrow, don't you?' Sergeant Kohli stated flatly.

She returned his gaze. 'Yes. Thank you for the reminder with a time yet to be confirmed, I believe.'

He pointed to the monitor. 'The evidence won't stand up in court, even though it's pretty clear.'

'Irrefutably clear in my opinion. Maybe one of them knows of a pig farm. Then they'll really start to crap.'

'Hey?' Carl asked scratching his head.

'Pigs eat anything.'

After a pregnant pause, Sergeant Kohli said pleasantly, 'We'll take our leave now. Thank you for a delicious dinner, Junior, and you young lady, your company is always a pleasure.'

Yasmin smiled politely. 'We'll talk more tomorrow. Carl, I will see you sometime in the morning. Thank you for your company, gentlemen. Good night.'

Sergeant Pyers clasped her hand gently, 'Good night, Yasmin. Thank you.'

After locking the doors, she glared at the bag like it was the ugliest thing she ever had anywhere near the dining table. Summoning every bit ounce of self-control, pushed it to the very edge furthest away from her usual place.

***

'It's been hours! I'm entitled to one phone call, you bastard,' Stu hissed through the bars. 'I know it's really late. Come on! This lot are all asleep. It's critical I make this call.'

The Watchhouse Attendant tapped his hand lightly with his baton. 'Quit swearing at me, Stu. I mean it, man.'

If anybody could whine in a quiet voice, it was Stu. 'I have to make this phone call. Pleeaase. I'll be your best darn inmate ever!'

'Still can't believe your clinic was a front for such corruption. How could you?'

'Hey, wise-arse, would you refuse to do something if you had a loaded gun pointed at your head for most of your life?'

The two men faced off. 'You better tell Pyers and Kohli what you know. You owe us all that much. But Stu, why did you hurt her dog?'

'That was not intentional, I swear it. He is okay, isn't he?'

'Yeah, flesh wound. You're lucky on that count.'

'Yeah, lucky Pyers doesn't drag me through these bars!'

They shared a very different grin. 'Come with me. Five minutes, no more.'

'I'll tell them myself that I have had my phone call.'

'Yep, you were going to. One way or the other.'

Stu allowed himself to be handcuffed and escorted to the payphone. Reciting the number, the Watchhouse Attendant tucked the receiver under Stu's chin.

Come on, please answer. Yes! 'It's me, please hear me out. I am not the boogey-man. I don't know why Travis set Giles and me up. They've all been in your shed except the twins. They said the place was haunted. Anyway, they were looking for money and gold. Also, I reckon this boogey-man is still alive and you definitely need to register your knee as a dangerous weapon. Travis and Ivan can be very cruel. I'm sure Leigh used to be known as someone else before she married Callum, but I haven't got any proof. Sally—'

'Do not talk about her,' Yasmin hissed.

Stu whispered. 'You know her?'

'Keep talking.'

He gasped. 'That was you! The hot redhead with the two dogs! Did you know?'

'Know what?'

'About the connection?'

'What connection?'

'Listen Yasmin, she can say the boogey-man's name.'

'So can you!'

'No, no, I don't even know it. I only learnt about this crap recently. I thought I could play along to sink the bastards holding the gun to my head, but the prank backfired. Forgive me, please.'

'Where's Combo?' she asked coldly.

'In good hands, I swear.'

'Will I see him again?'

'I'm sure you will. Alive too.'

'And you know all these other—'

'Miscreants? Great word, thank you! Yes, yes, I do and their history.'

'Tell someone who cares then.'

'Hello? Hello?' *Dammit, Yasmin! I had so much more to say to you.*

Chapter 63

*F*ive past nine? Yasmin flew out of bed, pulled up short, and hobbled to meet the day. One hand rubbed the lingering throb of her hamstring, the other her head from the audacious hangover of Stu's phone call. The eye-sore on the dining table didn't help matters. When she opened the patio door, a fruit hamper with an envelope taped to a bottle of bubble bath sat on the welcome mat. The note read: *Yasmin, we are delighted you are home! Believe you have a busy day so don't fuss in calling to thank us straightaway. Please call to discuss Christmas when you can. It's just around the corner. Love, Nanna, Helen and Pam.*

She murmured a prayer of gratitude and met Carl near the shed.

'Ma'am, you will forgive me?'

'You were doing your job. There is nothing to forgive, but if you keep cooking meals like that, I'm going to need a bigger cottage!'

She joined his braying laugh until they were both crying and holding their stomachs.

'Thanks man, I needed that,' Yasmin said wiping her face. 'Hey, has Radar noticed anything unusual or out of place?'

'Not at all. The workers couldn't wait to get out of his company when they did the shed doors.'

'Okay, fine.'

'Good luck today, Ma'am. Pity you couldn't do the interview from here. You really need to rest that leg and elevate your ankle.'

She stared at him in amazement. 'What a brilliant idea! Thanks Carl, I'll catch you later.'

'Roast beef sandwiches for lunch?'

'Sounds great. I'm just going to measure up for an extension!' she gave him the thumbs up.

Standing inside the bare wardrobe looking out at the pile of boxes, two shone under the bedroom light like a pair of beady eyes.

'Last in first out,' she muttered.

Tipped upside down, a key fell out followed by sheets of pink tissue. Landing on top, a side-profile photograph of Rudy looking very dapper in his charcoal grey suit, emerald green bowtie with the longer grey jacket hanging below his knees. His right hand held the handlebar moustache to his mouth. His left, rested on his hip. She was drawn to his warm, welcoming eyes and simply fell into them the way she did when they first met. Flipping over the photo, written in his splendid handwriting: *In my pocket is what you seek. R.J.M.*

The obnoxious wall clock snapped her back into reality. Upon closer inspection of the key, its yellow tone didn't brighten anything up and felt as heavy as her heart. Scoffing at the discomfort of it now sitting in her short's pocket, replaced the pink tissue and glared at the box beside it.

With each utterance, Yasmin clinically sliced through the abundant tape. 'I. Am. Over. It.'

Inside the first manilla folder, on the back side of a photograph written in un-recognisable scrawling writing, five words nearly caused her heart to fail. 'Rupert John Matson, Art Director'. Cautiously turning it over, the painted man in Sally White's stall stood with his arms draped around the artist and a younger version of her. Both heavily pregnant. *The daughter. The snake-dancing woman!* Yasmin let it fall to the floor and in typical Rudy-compartmentalisation flicked open the next folder. A black and white wedding photograph of Leigh and Callum standing under a tree, but oddly the background scenery appeared to be the focus, not the wedding party. Yasmin's brow knotted. The bridal party included Jill sitting on a horse, Giles and Stu were either side of her. Standing awkwardly away from them, the twin fleeing mares in between two men looking away from the camera.

'I've seen this place. Where the hell was it?'

Grabbing the laptop, flicked through her photo gallery, but nothing matched. She looked at the next wedding photo, exactly the same setting with exactly the same people in the exact same positions, except it was a close-up. Deep in concentration, pried apart the furrows pinching her forehead. *Who are you?* One of them looked completely different with short dark hair and held a toupee above his head, like it was a hat, yet still unfamiliar. The other, a younger Travis who favoured greasy hair.

Yasmin shrieked and dropped the bundle when her phone chimed with a message: *Ma'am, if you're hungry, sandwiches are ready. BTW – interview is at 2:30pm.*

The first round of sandwiches was eaten in companionable silence with the mutual racoon look from lack of sleep.

'Oh Carl, I miss my Combo. It's like I've got this lead paw print punched into my heart. Sometimes I feel I can't breathe.'

His noisy sob didn't help, but it brought Radar out from under the motorhome in a flash. He stretched out between them. Tail on her feet, head on his master's, happily played the centre of attention.

'Second sanga was just as good as the first. Thanks heaps.'

'Back to the cottage?'

'No. I have this silly notion to be near the caravan.'

'Do you need company, Ma'am?'

'I'll be right.'

'I know you don't need me to remind you about your appointment this afternoon, but time is ticking away.'

'Yep, thanks Carl.'

Every footfall sent shockwaves through her bones, forcing her to clench her teeth to keep from crying out. Inserting the caravan key angrily and slamming the door open provided little satisfaction. The stuffy warmth reaching for her the moment she stepped inside, incensed her further. Barely containing the building eruption, flung open the wardrobe door and patted down Rudy's long grey coat. The inside pocket contained a tepid gold monogrammed business card holder. When she moved the lapel aside, the suit jacket hung heavily to the left. Forcibly refraining from shaking her head at the culprit, a weighty, narrow gold box with a key slot along its face fitted snugly into her hand. She couldn't bare to hold it any longer and shoved it into her other short's pocket.

Fighting the internal arguments, dared to flick through the pack of business cards. Shocked at the number of different industries he had been involved in, quickly shoved it beside the key. Letting her T-shirt hang over the top of her sagging shorts, locked up the caravan and hobbled towards the cottage.

Carl met her near the steps of the patio. 'Where was your favourite place, Ma'am?'

She studied the younger man. 'Nice try. I didn't think you would try and be a detective though.'

He had the decency to redden. 'Radar would like a pat.'

She was about to reply when her mobile phone rang. Excusing herself, answered the anonymous call with the speaker activated and allowed Carl to help her up the steps.

'Hello?'

'Ms Pestel, Yasmin, it's Chas Hillyer. It's so nice to hear your voice. Um, I'm early and was wondering if I could interest you in joining me for lunch?'

Smiling at Radar and shaking his raised paw, replied quietly, 'Thanks for the offer, but I will have to decline.'

'Oh, have I caught you at a bad a time again?'

'Yes. But we'll be chatting at 2:30pm, is that correct?'

His frustrated sigh may as well have been a shout of annoyance. 'Apparently. Please do not be late. I have another appointment back in the city this evening. Incidentally, forensics couldn't get anything from that shirt, so we're back to square one.'

'Oh, how disappointing,' she stared at Radar, then asked, 'Off the record, what is your opinion?'

'You're a spunky woman who deserves a good holiday! How's that?'

'Smooth. Thanks for calling, I have a few errands to complete. Bye for now.'

'Okay then.'

Yasmin disconnected the call, thanked Carl for lunch, ruffled Radar's ears and grimaced.

'You really need to rest, Ma'am. That's a bad tear.'

'All in good time,' she replied kindly. 'Did you have the other K9s out while I've been away?'

'Yes, Ma'am. They all seem to love it here too!'

'Excellent. Catch you later.' Yasmin hitched up her shorts and stumbled into the cottage. 'I'm okay!'

'I'll always be here for you,' he called out.

Deliberating, she laid the key and box beside the bag on the dining table. It was like her hands moved on their own accord. Several minutes later, caught herself staring forlornly at a stainless-steel box. Its sterile plaque as impersonal as the material. The circular groove on the underside added to the list of riddles. There was no doubt the key would open the contraption, yet her inclination was at its lowest. Everything went back into the bag, a knot tied in the handles and pushed to the edge. Head shaking, tromped angrily into the spare room and continued the arduous task of emptying the carton of ugliness. Kicking lightly at the two folders on the bedroom floor, she begrudgingly picked up the next folder. A typed report covered the all-terrain vehicle debacle in great detail, including the familiar registered domain and subdomain names. Yasmin compared her copy of the death notices with the folded photocopied patchwork stapled to a list of names.

'Humph. I won't be surprised if I find an investigative journalist business card too.' Muttering and shaking her head made it thump like the throbbing ankle. She swiped at wayward tears. 'I hate this game, Rudy.'

Taped to a separate piece of paper, a photocopy of a fancy-dress dinner reservation with the name 'Mathews' circled in red. Sitting down from the sudden dizzy spell, Yasmin gasped for air. Rudy had penned the date of the tragic accident. On the reverse, a certified statutory declaration swearing silence – signed by the owners of the ski resort. In the same folder, yet separated by a sheet of black card, a tear-jerking photo of a much younger Jill hugging a horse with an all too familiar mountain range in the background. Attached to it, the funeral notice for her parents. Confirmation tears flowed down Yasmin's cheeks.

Gently placing the folder on the floor away from the growing pile of revulsion, murmured, 'Your colleague wasn't the target, Sergeant Kohli.'

Warily looking at an overturned piece of paper lying face down by itself without any protection, she took a very deep breath. Her exhalation changed to a painful yodel and raced into the bathroom. Anger combined with disgust escaped in an undignified projectile.

Cleaning herself up with trembling hands, sobbed at the hideous picture of several men and one woman among sacrificial horses and puppies. Livid at losing food, again, her hand covered the obscene images, yet it was impossible to make out the faces of the deplorable bystanders given they were all wearing some form of disguise or masquerade mask. Gut instinct told her it was the wedding party, including the unfamiliar man who was holding something Yasmin had no intention of looking closely at. Covering the obscenity, he was a very strong man wearing ridiculously large glasses and an obviously fake nose. She knew the scarf around his neck wasn't fabric. Dumping the heinous collection onto the floor, Yasmin gawped miserably into the carton. Willing herself to be brave, retrieved a blue manilla folder. In it, a single piece of paper,

The toupee got ripped off and he transformed into a much bigger man after flapping his long, grey jacket. An illusionist's trick. It was after midnight. It seemed

they were doing a deal of some kind. The shorter one said, "You're a dead man, Rupert John Matson." The man in the jacket pulled out a syringe, stabbed it into the other man's eye and said, "You should never have said my name." He laughed when the syringe stood upright from the eyeball, and played with his moustache while making a phone call. Three men arrived in a hearse. They wrapped the victim in plastic, dumped his body in the coffin and left. I spread the rumour. I made them scared to say the name.

Yasmin's hand flew to her mouth. 'The proof! My God, Mr Taylor was right!'

Right there and then, vowed she would never date a man with a moustache, nor one that had a grey suit in his wardrobe. Then reminded herself, that indeed she already had. Repeated the vow and added *'again'*.

Defeated, flicked through the business cards. The deceptive *R.J.M.* sure had been a busy man, yet no indication of being a journalist. Fanning the selection across the top of another box, reached downwards just as her mobile rang.

Jumping in fright, answered quickly. 'Hello?'

'Ms Pestel – uh, Yasmin, are you okay?' Owen asked, concerned.

'No, I've been crying. Can we do this as a telephone conference instead? Please?'

'He's been here for a while and an utter pain.'

She shrugged, swiping at the onslaught of tears. 'You don't really need me to be present, do you?'

'No, I suppose not.'

'My leg is really sore ...' she used its foot to flick open the folder holding the wedding photos. Something wasn't right.

Sergeant Pyers cleared his throat. A drawn-out silence followed.

In a thick voice, he said, 'You once asked me a pertinent question about how many other people have died in the same manner as your estranged boyfriend. I still cannot reveal the answer, however, I have since reviewed the evidence you have inadvertently collected. This boogey-man thing, aside from mentioning his name what else is a discerning feature?'

Yasmin nibbled on her bottom lip. 'Long grey jackets and curly moustaches.'

'We never did discuss the body in the cleared lavender paddock.'

'We did. I said he was shirtless and shoeless.'

'So, it was Rudy?'

She wailed, 'That's so cruel of you to ask me that.'

'Yes, I'm sorry. There are lots of loose ends in this case. Come now, stop crying please. Can you think of anything else that could incriminate the people I have in custody?'

'No.'

'Listen, I am swiftly running out of time. Carl will coordinate the teleconference.'

After a noisy nose-blowing performance, she asked, 'Will Sergeant Kohli be present?'

'Most definitely. The surreptitiously gained evidence will not see the light of day. Think hard.'

'A request or a demand?'

'At this point in time, you can take it any way you like but please don't be late.'

'I won't be. Bye for now.'

'Get some fresh air, Ms Pestel.'

***

Rounding the corner, Sergeant Kohli was surprised to see Penny step out of Owen's office, and looked at her quizzically. She politely nodded her head and stepped away from the doorway.

Waiting until he got closer, she said quietly, 'Sir, nice to see you again.'

'Yeah, you too. What's happening?'

'Just listened to a very interesting conversation. Uh ... I better go.'

Owen called out, 'Penny, you have your instructions and time is ticking. Thank you. Close the door behind you, Sergeant Kohli. Take a seat if you want although I won't take up much of your time.'

'What's with the formalities?'

'Listen up. Yasmin will be dialling in this afternoon. We will be in the Encouragement Room. I want Zeus and The Intimidator to be present with several of the lesser obedient K9s in close proximity. You will be entertaining the city slicker until then, and make yourselves available in the Room at 2:15pm.'

Neither man gave their emotions away.

'What's Penny up to?'

'She's on my staff. I've got things to get on with and so have you. Tick tock.'

'Tick tock?'

'Yep. I heard it the other day and I like it. Time's ticking.'

Again, the dismissal rubbed the big man up the wrong way. The chair scraped noisily as he stood. 'Sergeant Pyers, is there something you need to get off your chest because that's twice you have flicked me off?'

'Just have a lot to do in very little time. Work with me, I'll explain later. Go.'

They exchanged a look of annoyance.

A knock on the door interrupted what Sergeant Kohli wanted to say next. Instead, 'Yes, Boss. I'll open the door now, Boss. Shall I walk out backwards, Boss?'

Owen grumbled, 'Smart arse.'

Waiting to be let in were several members of the Tech Team who automatically saluted the senior officers then instantly retracted. 'It's habit.'

'Right lads, come in and show me how this thing works. See you this afternoon, thanks Sergeant Kohli. Please close the door behind you.'

A million thoughts ran through the big man's head as he strode down the hallway. The sight of the Forensic Detective did not improve his mood.

'Ah, there you are big fella. Where's a good place to go for lunch?' Chas asked, combing his hair with his fingers.

Conceited prat. 'You buying?' Sergeant Kohli growled.

'Yeah, but I'm not much of a talker at the table.'

'Suits me, I know a good restaurant. I'll drive. I don't talk much behind the wheel.'

'What a team!'

There wasn't so much as a grunt in reply.

***

Penny rubbed her hands in glee. She enjoyed tracing phone numbers and triangulating the associated calls. Her enthusiasm was elevated knowing she was about to help her Boss solve several cold cases and help Charlie with his Op. The long-awaited finale was rapidly approaching. She grinned at the thought of participating in the Encouragement Room. But when one particular number kept pinging, she did not want anything to do with Sergeant Pyers' plan.

Chapter 64

In a trance, Yasmin found her way to the Jacaranda tree, leaned against the gnarled old trunk and gazed in the direction of the rolling hills behind the sheds. The shadows of the moving clouds painted a dancing frill along the foothills. She walked towards the boundary and argued with herself the entire way. Tapping the fence to hear it wasn't timber was mildly reassuring and turned to look back at the big old beautiful tree. Her choking sob tore every heart string on its tormented way out. *Oh Rudy, how could you let them get married here?*

Mustering up her fast-failing confidence, limped determinedly back into the bedroom. Feeling numb and utterly appalled after reading three more pages of revelations, fake identities and proof that one man could deceive her and so many others for so long; she hesitated before opening up the last folder. Giving into her procrastinatory habit, admired the etched fleur-de-lis design on the business card holder. Comparing the contact details, nothing changed except for the industry and logo. Scoffing angrily, continued with the task at hand sporadically glancing at the cards hoping for some magical revelation.

Catching herself before rolling her eyes, grumbled loudly. 'Just another level of your horrible game. Because that's who I am, hey Rudy?' She smacked the side of the box. Then again, even harder.

Glued to the outside of the last folder, a black one, a newspaper cutting of a long grey jacket and a picture of a handlebar moustache. Inside contained one photograph. The entire wedding party and extras sat around a barely alight campfire watching a man wearing hippie clothing and a long grey jacket sporting a ridiculously large curly moustache, milk a snake. Only Stu was standing. His stare was so cold, he practically drilled holes into the back of Leigh's head. Only two people stared into the camera lens. Sally and her daughter. Their babies in cradles by their feet. Nobody was smiling. Yasmin stared and stared at the man. When she flipped the picture over, the sight of Rudy's handwriting caused her to shake uncontrollably. *Beware the boogey-man, Rupert John Matson.*

***

'It's unconventional, Pyers is calling the shots, and Ms Pestel will be dialling in, in fifteen minutes,' Sergeant Kohli gritted his teeth.

'That's the most you've spoken to me all bloody afternoon! Anyway, why the hell are we in the same room with these creatures? They're not even in a damn cell!' Hillyer waved his arms around and pushed himself off the wall.

'Careful.'

'Not the dogs, fool.'

'Watch your tone.'

Both Zeus and The Intimidator growled. All eyes were on the perps on the opposite side of the room.

'This mob! No handcuffs, no ankle shackles! What the hell are you country bumpkins playing at?'

'It's not as if they're going to try and escape, is it?' The big man dropped his voice. 'Keep your tone calm, these boys are particularly sensitive to animosity. The people you see are all suspects in the break-in at Pestel's Edible Petals.'

'All of them? Even the women?'

'Apparently. Look, I don't like it either, but Pyers is the Lead in this particular investigation so take it up with him.'

'I really am not comfortable with this.' Forensic Detective Hillyer sighed loudly. 'I'm going to visit Yasmin afterwards.'

'It's Ms Pestel, and you will have company.'

'Not necessary.'

'Yes. It. Is.'

Their angry little tiff was interrupted by Sergeant Pyers striding into the room. Forensic Detective Hillyer's march towards him was abruptly stopped when the two K9s blocked his path. He stood with his hands on his hips.

Sergeant Kohli scoffed. 'What is it with you blokes? Every single one of you! Look around!'

'That's enough,' Sergeant Pyers commanded.

'You and I—'

'Forensic Detective, I can't talk right now, mate. It'll have to wait,' Owen stated flatly and brightened the lights.

'Who are you? Who are you?' the twins chanted.

'You can't keep us any longer,' Leigh screeched.

'Leigh's got a secret, Leigh's got a secret.'

'I have not and stop picking on me.' She shoved both women away from her, then burst into tears. 'Sorry, I'm just so scared.'

The twins chanted softly, 'All you have to do is choose. It's not too late to choose.'

Callum held up his hand, 'Stop it.' He took a step forwards, then a bigger one backwards. 'You haven't charged us with anything. This is illegal.'

Sergeant Pyers made a show of laying out several bagged items on the centre table, including his own mobile phone.

'We haven't charged you with anything … yet. You will recall we took possession of your mobile phones when you arrived. When I call out your name, you will approach and activate your own phone. Do not do anything stupid, this particular pair of K9s are hungry.'

'And sensitive,' Hillyer chortled.

Sergeant Pyers called out the names. Nobody defied his instructions. Even when several phones chimed simultaneously.

'When do we get our phones back?' Leigh asked coldly.

'When I say so. Now, listen closely. To be open and transparent, we will be having another special guest join us. In the meantime, behave yourselves. Be it noted, my mobile phone is also on the table and active.'

'Sir-Sir … excuse me S-Sergeant Pyers,' Stu stammered, whined, 'What—'

'Spit it out,' he demanded.

'What happens if someone is a bit deaf and the Bluetooth answers automatically?'

Shrugging, replied, 'Oh, I'm sure we're all waiting on phone calls, so speak normally! Several of us have hearing aids, don't we Stu?'

Giles nudged him hard in the rib cage and hissed, 'What are you worried about?'

Stu leant into him, covered his mouth and muttered without moving his lips. 'Only you and her have my emergency number! I gave it to her when we first met!'

'You are a total dickhead,' Giles hissed, grabbed Stu and boxed him around the ears.

He retaliated just as Callum and Ivan intervened. When Ivan pulled Giles away, his hand holding Stu's remaining hearing aid got twisted behind his back. He smirked and let the contents fall and ground the tiny receiver into the floor.

'What are you smiling at, you idiot?'

'I'm tired of you bullying me, Ivan!'

The stepbrothers fought hard until the pair of K9s had a barking competition. After the din subsided, Travis growled and pointed across the room. 'What about those two over there? Where are their phones?' He changed his voice to sound like he had a major speech impediment. 'Or are they thpethial?'

The twins parroted the insult in a nail-down-the-blackboard pitch.

Zeus and The Intimidator whined and scratched at the floor until Sergeant Kohli added fuel to the fire. 'Tsst Tsst,'

They erupted ferociously. Lunged. Snarled. Frothed. Snapped at each other and pulled on their leashes.

'Enough!' Pyers bellowed. It took several minutes before he spoke again. 'What's the length of their retractable leashes, Boss?'

'About a metre short.'

'That'll do. Sergeant, Forensic Detective, your mobiles if you please?'

Begrudgingly, they obliged.

Flanked by The Intimidator and Zeus, Sergeant Pyers approached the prisoners. Stu and Giles cowered against the wall behind Ivan and Callum who stared at the floor consciously keeping their hands off their hips. Leigh and the twins huddled in a group a little further away from the men with their heads lowered and hands tightly linked.

Travis stepped forwards and sneered. 'Are you trying to intimidate us, pig? Because I ain't afraid of you or those mutts. What's going on?'

'What's going on? What's going on?' Laqueel and Trina mimicked, momentarily interrupting their teeth grinding.

Clearly annoyed, Forensic Detective Hillyer demanded, 'Do you women have to do that?'

'Yes, yes we do and who are you?'

'Enough!' Sergeant Pyers commanded again. Silence befell the room instantly. 'Sergeant, you can go and get some fresh air, alone. Leave the door open and take five minutes.'

Owen had never seen his cohort so livid. Trying to diffuse the situation, said, 'To pass the time, the Forensic Detective is going to tell me all about Melbourne.'

'I am?' Chas asked, taken aback.

'Yes! I did my first five years there!'

'Pfft, I can tell you there aren't any dinosaurs left!'

'Wise arse. Go and find a wall to lean against.'

The moment Sergeant Kohli walked out the door, everyone sneezed, looked about nervously, muttered the usual sentiments and averted their eyes. Two minutes later, eight additional K9s scrappily entered the room, kitted up to the hilt leading their handlers disguised by their tactical clothing, with enough slack to scare the bejesus out of anyone guilty or otherwise. An all-in scrap broke out, until The Intimidator and Zeus pulled rank.

Sergeant Pyers conducted an audio check and nodded his head in satisfaction. 'Right. Order has been returned. And now we wait.'

Serval long, silent minutes passed. Sergeant Kohli returned giving any of the humans a withering stare if they looked at him for more than a split second.

'Good timing. Close the door and kill the lights. Sergeant Kohli and Forensic Detective Hillyer, you will need to stand very still. The same goes for you lot against the wall.'

The moment the room plunged into darkness, a male voice threatened, 'Now we know your names, you'll get yours.'

'Crew, activate your NVGs,' Owen growled.

He waited until his own optic headset was operational and rearranged the mobile phones on the table.

'Just like a bloody croupier.'

'Shut up!'

'Friggin' hell, it's freezing in here.'

'This is Sergeant Pyers speaking. Welcome to the Encouragement Room.'

Nervous murmurs and shuffling of feet echoed around the bitingly cold room.

***

Yasmin was staring at the stove when Carl knocked on the patio door balancing a tray crammed with a coffee percolator, cups and packets of biscuits.

'Ma'am, Sergeant Pyers did suggest I sit with you and will be expecting your call at exactly two-thirty,' he said gently. Radar strolled in like he owned the place and immediately went to the dining table and sniffed its unconventional decoration.

She smirked. 'Come in ... might as well follow Radar!'

'What can I do for you?' Carl offered while putting the tray down.

'Unplug the telephone please.'

Studying her fingernails, asked for the time and exhaled rather loudly listening to his reply.

'Twenty-three minutes past two.'

She placed both her mobile phones on the table. 'I've just got to make a quick phone call.'

'It will have to be quick. The conference details are preset on my phone. Coffee?'

Nodding absentmindedly, Yasmin thumbed through her contacts and dialled the only number she had for Stu. Strategically positioning the phone against her mug, used her business phone first and put it on speaker as it began to ring. It rang out. She frowned, and redialled. It rang out for the second time.

'Were they expecting your call?' Carl asked quietly.

Sighing in annoyance, she replied, 'Yeah, I got that impression, but of course they mightn't know my business number and thought it was spam. I'll try again then use my personal phone.'

'Please be quick. Sergeant Pyers is on the warpath.'

***

Penny stared at the triangulation and shook her head in disbelief.

Tapping the comm's tech on the shoulder, she simply said, 'We're running out of time. How's it going with the auto-answer manipulation?'

'Set for 1430 hours. Let's sync our watches.'

After nodding their heads in confirmation, wide-eyed, asked. 'What else can we do?'

'Do I have permission to manipulate the Room's built-in speaker so all and sundry can hear the conversation?' he asked with a sly grin.

'You can do that?'

'I can do anything, Pen, you should know that by now. The volume won't be deafening, but it'll be loud enough and mark my words, the quality is crystal clear.'

Nodding her head, she swallowed hard. 'Permission granted.'

***

Even though everyone gasped, nobody moved when the mobile phone lit up the room for the third time.

'This is Sergeant Pyers. Obviously that person isn't deaf. Announce yourself if you are going to speak.'

'Like bloody hell,' a male's voice growled.

Owen smirked, fiddled with his handset and depressed the side button. A hologram of a faceless man except exaggerated illuminated eyes, sporting a handlebar moustache and wearing a long grey jacket materialised at the head of the table. Frightened shrieks, sobs and panicked groans filtered along the back wall. Syncopated low growls amplified the anxiety.

A sardonic laugh rippled through the cold air followed by a bone-chilling voice, 'I dare you to say my name.'

'Nice trick, pig, that's not real. You can't fool us. He's dead. The boogey-man is dead. Ask Travis.'

'Me? Why ask me? I wasn't even there! Ask the twins!'

The twins stopped their teeth grinding to murmur timidly, 'Ask Clive, Clive said it was so.'

'What the hell? What boogey-man, Kohli? I thought we were—'

'Take it up with the Boss.'

'This is Sergeant Pyers. Anybody have anything to add?' he asked with a grin and faded out the hologram.

'This is Forensic Detective Hillyer. Who organised the burglary at Pestel's Petals?'

'Ivan,' two men squealed.

Several solid thumps and winded grunts momentarily filled the room.

'He's mine,' Chas growled. 'Which one is he?'

The K9s started panting and whining.

'Down!' Sergeant Kohli commanded.

'You know my voice by now,' Sergeant Pyers stated. 'It is almost 2:30pm. Our other guest will join us shortly. Stand by.'

*****

Yasmin counted seventy of Carl's nervous finger-tapping, and reached across the table for his phone. She did a double take at the preset digits.

Tapping the dial icon, waited until it was answered on the fourth ring, then tapped the speaker icon.

'Who is this?' An annoyed man's voice echoed in her living room.

Yasmin stood and gazed into Radar's enquiring eyes.

'Hello Rupert John Matson.'

Loud screams, Sergeant Kohli's bellowed command of *ATTACK* and ferocious snarling exploded through the phone. Radar bounded onto the table and replied in full voice.

Carl stared at her aghast. 'The Forensic Detective?'

Chuckling, she grabbed the offending bag and silently left the room.

Chapter 65

Almost twenty-fours after their last conversation around her dining room table, they clinked their beers together. BBQ sauce on the meat-lovers pizza was the popular choice and of course Radar and Zeus hung around like the starving pets they were!

'Dé· jà vu?' Carl offered with a laugh.

'A job well done! Here's cheers!' Tired, Yasmin smirked and took a long drink of her beer.

'Best tell us how you knew, young lady,' Sergeant Kohli said while fighting with a stretchy string of Mozzarella.

Their eyes locked. She made a show of sitting forwards, felt for the bundle in her back pocket and said, 'Only if you tell us why you reacted so quickly.'

'We'll see,' The big man said and devoured the meaty triangle, indicating with his eyes that she should speak.

Chortling, studied the men while contemplating her situation. Radar nuzzled her pocket just as the epiphany hit her like a sledgehammer. *Does a champion of any game reveal their strategy? I think not.*

Patting his head, Zeus joined in for the attention and also nudged her pocket. She removed its contents discretely.

'What have you got that the dogs are so interested in, Ms Pestel?'

'Ah yeah, about that,' she nibbled her bottom lip, shuffled the pack of business cards in front of them and dealt one each to her guests. 'How I came across these will never be disclosed.'

'A chemist?' Carl seethed.

Pyers scoffed, 'Funeral director?'

Sergeant Kohli's comment was the best. 'Forensic detective? My fat arse.'

Realisation of the deceptive, manipulative behaviour suppressed any ongoing hilarity.

'That's arrogance for you. He used the same name,' Carl said in disgust after he compared them.

'And the same phone number,' Sergeant Kohli grumbled, fanning the three cards in front of him.

'Exactly. 75628766 spells RJMatson,' she grinned and took the last piece of pizza, returning Owen's wink.

Sergeant Kohli and Zeus were the last to bid her goodnight. He held his palm upwards. 'Thank you for everything.'

'You don't *know* everything. Yet'—grabbed his hand with both of hers—'Sir, the surname of your colleagues. Was it Mathews with one T?'

He shook his head.

'What about Sancko?'

This time he scratched it. 'No! What game are *you* playing, young lady?'

'No game, Sergeant Kohli. No more games. But what you can do is put your mind at ease for the rest of your life, then start to make up for the years that you have lost stressing over speculation and curiosity. Those surnames? Those were the names of the deceased.' He looked at her blankly. 'In other words, *your* friends weren't the targets!'

'How on earth?'

'All that doesn't matter. What does matter is how you deal with this wonderful news! But I have to know ... did you have your suspicions?'

'Zeus must have had him covered. I didn't even see the signs!'

Yasmin bent over and ruffled Zeus' head. 'You're a good boy. Bet you miss Combo too.'

Upon standing, she caught the wet eyes of Sergeant Kohli and held his gaze appropriately. 'That answers my unasked question. But here's one you should be able to answer. Was I ever under suspicion?'

'There are some things that you will never know. I'm grateful you made it home.'

'Gee, that answered my question really nicely! Where's Combo?'

For the first time, he didn't hold her gaze. 'Couldn't say.'

Gulping down a sob, murmured, 'I don't believe you. But it is getting late.'

'Goodnight, Ms Pestel!'

'I think it's about time you called me Yasmin.'

'No, because I don't want you calling me by my first name.'

'Oh, okay. I get it. What does it begin with?'

'B.' As soon as the letter was out, he bit his bottom lip.

Yasmin's suppressed giggle couldn't be contained. 'It's not Border, is it?'

He chuckled. 'Goodnight, Ms Pestel. We'll be in touch.'

Trying in vain to control her amused splutters and twitching lips, said, 'Good night, Sergeant Kohli. Yes, I expect we will be. Night Zeus!'

***

He hadn't even turned out of the driveway when he collapsed into delirious laughter. *Border? Like Border Kohli? Cheeky wench!* Rolling to a stop beyond the next property, he laughed until he was crying, then laughed-cried-laughed and felt the decades of unbeknownst gradually lift.

Zeus' surprised yap interrupted his private moment. A patrol car pulled alongside with only its interior light on. Silence returned to the night air. What he didn't expect was Combo's head to stick out of the lowered driver's window which encouraged his partner to bark loudly.

'Hey?'

A simple hand command silenced both dogs.

'It's me, K9 Boss!' Penny said with a laugh and pushed her head beside Combo.

The big man couldn't disguise his grin. 'How the hell are you going to get away with this, young lady?'

'Well, Sergeant Pyers isn't going to upset the apple cart. I've always suspected you've had a lot to do with covering my six and I need to return Combo to his owner.'

'Whom should not know who you work for.'

'She won't. Carl's going to meet me down the road and take it from there.'

'There is something I need to know though.'

'I'm hazarding a guess it's about the ashes?'

'Yeah. How in the hell did you—'

'It was part of the negotiated deal.'

'You knew him?'

'Yes.'

Sergeant Kohli shook his head, praised Zeus for being a good boy and they both sighed heavily. 'Ah Penny, I'm sorry. I commend you for your persistence and bravery. I pray we don't break Yasmin's trust. She's been through so much.'

'And did so much for us too.'

'Exactly.'

'Sergeant Pyers will smooth things over. After all, he instigated her involvement.' Penny checked the message on her phone. 'That's my cue. Thanks for everything, Sergeant Kohli, I'll see you round like a fat dog!'

Turning the key in the ignition consequently drowned out his reply.

'I can't hear you,' Penny yelled and waved as she drove in darkness slowly towards Carl's flashlight.

'This is why we're good at what we do! Good boy, Zeus. High Five.' Sergeant Kohli twisted in his seat and rested his large hand against the raised strong paw of his partner.

Penny waited for the rear lights of the vehicle to disappear before she killed the engine and carried Combo out of the patrol car. His gentle sigh coincided with hers. She ruffled his tuft of fur, 'Mission success, thanks to you, my boy! Love you, Pooch.' His wet-nose puppy kiss on her cheek destroyed the self-contained bravado.

From a respectable distance, Carl covered Penny through his NVGs for the agreed fifteen minutes, then approached with Radar on a loose lead.

'Hey Cuz,' he said quietly and sat beside her, letting the two pooches meet and greet in their usual manner.

'Hey Cuz, thanks man.'

'Anytime. Did you want to spend more time with Pooch?'

'I will when he's playing with the other boys ... just let me know hey?'

'Naturally!'

They shared a quiet chuckle.

'He needs to rest a while,' Penny murmured.

'Yep, will make sure of that.'

'You remember what to say?'

Carl nudged his cousin. 'Sure do.'

After a long while of comfortable silence, Penny handed Carl the leash as they stood. She hugged him tightly.

'That's one lot of scum gone,' she whispered.

Carl returned the hug with gusto. 'With thanks to you and Charlie. Take care.'

'Always do.'

As was their custom, they pivoted and walked away without a backward glance.

With Radar by his left knee and Combo in his arms, Carl walked up the driveway with a heavy heart. Ever since he became aware of Pestel's Edible Petals, he had held Yasmin in high regard and after getting to know her on a more personal level, now, even higher. Yet still he deceived her. Asking for forgiveness as he deliberately triggered the sensor lights and alarm, stood facing the camera by the patio door.

'My Combo!' Yasmin's squeal continued, flung open the door and rushed towards them.

Poor puppy was caught up in a hug sandwich smothered in tears of joy.

Eventually, Carl managed to usher them into the lounge. 'Ma'am, I got an anonymous tip—'

'I don't care who, what, why or how.'

'Like you, he also needs to rest.'

Carl fussed around for a while longer before eventually saying goodnight. His words fell on deaf ears and locked the patio door before pulling it shut behind him and Radar. Combo's loud bark stopped them in their tracks. The moment Yasmin had the door open Radar nosed inside, hugged her thigh and permitted Combo to hug Carl. The tears flowed freely and noisily before Carl let himself and Radar out, waited until he heard the click of the lock and walked away.

Much later, he replied to Penny's questioning message.

You were right, Cuz, she didn't want to know anything. Reckon the Pooch's knew!

They always will, Cuz.

***

Yasmin couldn't keep her hands off Combo and groomed him while constantly reassuring him how much he meant to her. It was only when she removed his harness, she discovered a note affixed to the underside.

He's a gorgeous boy and will also have your back, always. Thanks for trusting me. AA

Conflicting emotions flooded Yasmin's trembling body. *Also?*

She didn't have too long to ponder the question before Combo initiated the game of chasey, up and down the hallway, then bounded onto the recliner and promptly made himself comfortable. His loud puppy sigh brought about another round of happy tears. It was when he sat up and looked at her imploringly, did she sob loudly and plant a noisy pretend-kiss atop his head.

***

Sergeant Kohli looked at Stu scathingly. 'You've got some explaining to do.'

'Yeah, I'm the small fry in all this but.'

'Why'd you wear that disguise in Adelaide at the hospital?'

Stu picked at an imaginary sore on his arm. 'Thought I could play the game and sink the miscreants. Yasmin taught me that word you know! But Travis mainly. He should never have brought her into this.'

'And the woman?'

'Which one?'

'Come on, Stu! The nurse that you got in the cab with.'

'Just a share ride. That's not against the law.'

'You're not a good liar.'

'I will take that secret to the grave with me, Sergeant Kohli.'

'Good.' His reply barely audible.

'You showing some leniency?'

'Just write down the rest of your statement.'

'Pyers doesn't know we're having this chat, does he?'

'Not yet.'

'What's going to happen with that bloke the dogs bailed up?'

'Not your concern. Hurry up. Best you keep your mouth shut too.'

'Until the day I die.'

Sergeant Kohli grunted, dialled a number and spoke coldly. 'Yeah, single men's quarters will do just fine.'

Chapter 66

Although Yasmin had fallen in love with the almost completed fence line, she didn't feel like being restricted to her cottage. Deciding on a slow trip to return the motorhome, flicked Carl a text before dawn explaining they would be away for a few days. With just the bare essentials, Combo was as ecstatic as she to be back in the front seat. As the full moon set and the sun lit up their world, the bakery treats were demolished.

With both mobiles switched off, they explored new hinterland roads and oddly enough found themselves back in the Meningie township. Quite liking the tranquillity of lake frontage, stayed overnight. Alas, the yearn for the ocean's lullaby was too strong. Studying the map, Yasmin's eyes fell upon Kangaroo Island.

'Nothing but sun, surf, sand, steak and seafood for us for a while Combo, then we get ready to fly away!'

Her excitable tone encouraged him to wag his tail happily and dip his head in expectation.

***

For days, Sergeant Pyers had waded through reams of statements, denials and sob-stories, and was no closer to presenting anything to his higher echelon. The easiest task he had was preparing the handover of the drug dealers to the Feds. For the first time in his career, he felt very alone.

Ruth knocked gently. 'Excuse me, Sarge, can you take a break for a bit, please?'

'Sure, Ruth. I can't see the wood for the trees anyway.' He closed the folders and put them aside. 'What's up?'

'To tell the truth, I am very worried about you. I've worked for you through some pretty arduous cases. Granted this one must be a record-breaker given most of the cells are still occupied, but you look like you've aged 10 years in a week!' Her mother-hen cluck was distinct. 'You've been burning the candle non-stop since the bust, and that's far too long without a break. You need to talk to somebody. And, I'm going to say it again, you are long overdue for a break. Do you really want to be a blithering idiot at Christmas time?'

He opened his mouth to object. Instead, the woes rolled off his tongue. 'Penny is at a black site assisting Charlie and the Feds, which you probably knew. Carl's still playing caretaker, and Ms Pestel has gone to ground. Again. And I can't reach her.'

'Tell me why that's your problem?'

'She helped solve this case, Ruth! She's out there somewhere.'

'What about Sergeant Kohli? Does he know of her whereabouts?'

Owen's jaw ticked. 'The last I heard before he took off with Zeus on immediate leave, was that he had an off-the-air conversation with one of the prisoners and set up a safe site for two of them. But that's his business. I am more concerned about our Ms Pestel.'

'Come now, Owen. The woman needs to deal with a truckload of things and has been reunited with her protector. She's probably got endless loose ends to tie up and probably isn't accustomed to worry-warts!' Ruth made a show of looking at her watch. 'Now, you don't want to be late to collect your wife and take her out for dinner. Yes, you nothing about the arrangements. You never do! But thank God you pair got married. At least I know you have one night off every year.'

Wide-eyed, he pushed back his chair.

'The roses have already been delivered. Now, sign out, get out and have your-selves a decent night out!'

'You're a lifesaver, Ruth! Again! How do I thank you?'

'By letting me do this for you every year. Tomorrow is Saturday, I'm manning the phones this weekend and I do not want to see you or hear from you until Monday. Go on, scoot. I've got things to do.'

Owen saluted her. 'Yes Ma'am!' Calling out his thanks, he ran to his car counting his blessings.

***

| Coast is clear for the transfer |

Sergeant Kohli deleted the message. With his other hand poised on the emergency stop button by the back-up generator, he dialled the preset number. 'Over to you, Cap'n.'

'Roger. I'll contact you with my new number in a long while.'

'Copy that. Back dock.'

'Any trace?'

'Negative. You have 10 minutes in three, two, one.'

***

Shrieking in fright, Ruth felt around her desk for the piece of pottery. 'Gawd, lucky I made me cuppa when I did.'

Chapter 67

The all-night drive hadn't been without its drama for Cap'n. His shirtless, grease-stained overalls seemed to tighten around his waist the longer he sat. With a bushy beard meshed with his hairy chest, anyone would have thought a gorilla was driving the patina painted old Fairlane. A flat tyre five hours out of town added to the discomfort. Shifting the two unconscious bodies to access the spare in the boot had put more strain on his erratic heartbeat than he realised. Entrails flying off a passing truck which splattered the windscreen had forced him to pull over for a second time, and by then was blinded by perspiration.

Hours later than intended, with the aid of an excavator and an obscene amount of hush-up money, his catch were seated opposite each other on stacked, fuel-soaked pallets in an abandoned mechanic's pit, rapidly coming-to. Cap'n sauntered away from the 44-gallon drum. Its flames licked hungrily at the stringy bark draped over the rusty lip. In between his captives atop a sweet-odorous plywood bench, sat a single roll of duct tape and an open container labelled diethyl ether. He hooked the headcover off the male, sliced through the cable-tie freeing one hand of each, and blew a whistle hard.

'Who the hell are you? What the hell am I doing tied to this ... contraption?' Hillyer exploded. 'You're a dead man.'

'Not I.'

'You look like one walking! Who put you up to this? Giles? Travis? Callum?' He then glared at his opponent scrabbling with its headcover until it sat like a hoodie.

Blinking against the glare, her spittle flew as harshly as the words were flung. 'You? The boogey-man?'

'No! I've been set up!'

'You stole our dead brother's identity which means you have been a pathological liar your whole life, you lousy bastard. Are you really a detective?'

Chase took stock of his harried sister. His mouth twisted into a sly grin. 'I played the role that needed to be played.'

'The art director? Was that you?'

'Bravo! After that you introduced me Sally and her cherub! Ahh those were good times. Cute kids, eh? You even invited me to your wedding! You introduced me to a lifestyle of money which I needed for my taste in expensive whores and hotels.'

Leigh screamed at him. 'You? It was you in Adelaide?'

He looked at her with contempt. 'Thought you were a lot smarter, Cherise Hillyer.'

'I haven't been called that for a very long time. You cunning, manipulative—'

'You mean, clever. Hell, Cherise ... no, Leigh, you're not a Hillyer anymore ... you were so bombed out of your tree you didn't even know it was me who participated in the yarn in the barn! So, yes. I am the clever one. You're the cunning one, playing everybody against each other.'

'You? Clever? Just because you can use disguises? I would have thought you were a lot smarter than letting a flower-growing short-arse with an ugly mutt unravel my whole game. You idiot. I was going to be rich! That place was going to be mine! Callum was going to die just like Clive did.'

'And you dare call me a murderer?'

'I just organised the hit.'

They studied each other pensively.

'You could never be rich, Leigh. You always blew any money that came your way. Who was the Goth chick anyway?'

'Stu's piece of fluff,' she spat and sniffed the air. 'The stepbrother, Rupert? He wasn't the boogey-man then?'

'Stepbrother? You're the idiot. He was her estranged boyfriend! Anyway, that stupid bastard disappeared a long time ago.'

'No, he didn't. Travis and co said they saw him stumbling around clutching Sally's shirt and lugging a backpack.'

'So, you didn't plant the body?'

Leigh glared at him. 'Where's the backpack?'

A floating ember caught her attention. It was only then she noticed they had company. 'Hey! Who the hell are you? Where the hell are we?'

Cap'n painstakingly tore a long strip of tape, submersed it into the container then laid it across the table easily avoiding their flailing arms.

She began to freak out, 'Diethyl ether? Oh God no. Chase? Are we going to die? Here? In a fire?'

The right side of his mouth danced like it was a puppet attached to a nasal hair. Glaring at their captor, growled, 'Tell Yasmin she can run but she can't hide. Tell Pyers to watch his back. Tell Kohli I'll see him in hell.'

'Not likely.'

Leigh screamed, 'Go to hell!'

Rumbling engines shook the ground. The precariously balanced drum teetered and toppled over. A powerful, crude symphony of crunching metal reverberated nearby.

Hands pressed against his chest, Cap'n shuffled towards the rungs leading out of the pit. He turned around and tried to yell, 'There were only two tickets available ... enjoy ... the ... ride.'

Chapter 68

With only one day of sunshine out of seven, Yasmin's tan hadn't improved. Nor had the travel bug's impatience. After giving Duke a generous tip upon collection of her pink van, she paid handsomely for the courier company to deliver the abundant parcels to the seaside caravan park at their earliest opportunity. Their animal fundraising tin was overflowing by the time the transaction was complete.

Nearing their dead-end road, the niggling mystery of Rudy's urn had almost eaten her mind inside out, similar to what the worms had done to her stomach. The wave-like fence quelled the hunger pains and made her smile broadly. *I worked hard for that!* Reality clipped her around the ear. *Okay, the extra money helped.*

Onions frying on a barbecue assaulted their senses halfway up the driveway. Radar ran out to meet them and practically dragged Combo out of the van as soon as he was free. After assurance there was ample food, Carl's interpretation of a hamburger-with-the-lot was devoured with gusto.

'How long are you at home for, Ma'am?'

'All depends on when I get a message. Why do you ask?'

'Just making small talk. I'm concerned about you ... do you need to talk? About anything?'

Yasmin's internal argument almost voiced itself. Instead of replying straight away savoured the last two mouthfuls of the delicious burger. Eventually, wiping at her barbecue sauce covered fingers with a serviette, took a deep breath and lowered her shoulders. Watching Combo win against Radar in their tug-o-war sealed her thoughts.

'I have decided not to discuss anything for fear of getting indigestion!' Her laugh, while genuine, was wobbly. *Do not cry.*

'I am here when you're ready to talk—' his phone rang, 'but please excuse me. I need to take this call. I'll clean up. Hope to see you before you head off this time.'

'Thanks for lunch, Carl! It depends on what time you're awake!'

He stood abruptly, smirked and walked away with the phone glued to his ear.

After trying each dining chair, Yasmin settled for the one without a view and sighed at the same time as Combo when he rested his head on her feet. She fidgeted with the bag and stared at the cold plaque affixed to the colder box.

'Oh, it's for my attention all right. No doubt about that!'

Her muttering incentivised her pooch to see what she was up to.

'My boy, you have no idea how many conversations you missed out on! But believe me I will be so relieved when this game is over.' She showed him the box. 'I mean, check this out. You see this recessed circular groove on the underside? You do? Good. What on earth do you think would fit in there?'

He did his rare Scooby-Do look, stretched and returned to his headrest. Holding the box above her head one handed while trying to find something suitable was getting annoying, so she toyed with the key and the weighty slimline box instead. Excited anticipation bubbled to the surface when the key slid into the slot. A discerning click caught her by surprise and watched in fascination when the inner compartment slid outwards, revealing the most delicate gold chain supporting a gold nugget in the shape of a Y nestled against crushed pink velvet. Underneath, wrapped in emerald-green satin, the family crest cast in gold. Rudy's gold embossed writing on white card was nothing short of flamboyant. The message however, as brooding as its writer.

CREAMY *wasn't going to work. You are a joint owner – but only you could have the Y.*

Only one item will open the containment. Only one thing left to do. Work out the what and the how. Set me free in Emerald Bay then leave me on CREAM. *Game over!*

Her mobile phone chimed with a message: *Can Combo come and play outside with Radar?*

'Outside, Combo?'

He was on his feet and at the door in an instant. Waiting at the bottom of the stairs, Radar with a frisbee and Carl with a box of chocolates.

'Just what I need!' she grinned and caught the flying treats.

Back at the table, a growing pile of chocolate wrappers in front of her, Yasmin had a light-bulb moment and dashed like a zombie into her walk-in robe. Rummaging through her clothes, found the backpack and pulled out their old Quality Streets tin. His gold band!

It made sense, but it just didn't make sense. It was so unlike Rudy to have two vastly different materials so close together. Gold was warm. Mellow even. Stainless-steel; cold, unforgiving. Holding the box above a hand mirror while directing a light at the underside, Yasmin groaned. A distinct darker tinge lined the inner circle. Rolling her eyes in self-annoyance chided herself on not realising the bleeding obvious. There was no way the ring was going to stay in place, even if it were to fit, unless the box was turned upside down. Fluttering her eyelids, looked around shyly and flipped it.

The moment the band slotted into place, three sides fell outwards revealing a Silky Oak, gold inlaid box. Its gold fleur-de-lis shaped hinge flap complimented the masterly crafted vessel.

Yasmin scratched her head. 'That just doesn't look big enough.'

Never in her life had she shaken her head so much in such a short space of time, yet she found herself to be doing it again. The small box of ashes sat atop five gold microscopic screws alongside a gold jewellers screwdriver recessed in an emerald-green felt covered balsawood tray. Meeting the expectation, duly located the discrete screw holes and affixed the splendid crest.

Curiosity did get the better of her, and removed the felt tray. Lying underneath, three chunky gold nuggets cast in the shape of the lads' initials. *That explains the weight.* A cold breeze from nowhere rustled the chocolate wrappers.

Yasmin put her head in her hands. 'No. No. No. This doesn't make sense.'

She phoned Sergeant Pyers' personal number. 'Hi, it's me.'

'Well! Nice to hear from you too. Have you heard from Sergeant Kohli?'

'No.'

'Hmm. Got a lot going on at the moment so can't talk for long.'

'Yeah, that works for me too. Hey, who put together Rudy's keepsake?'

'I don't know.'

'It's quite a small box ... is there any way to prove it is actually him in there?'

'Yasmin! That's bordering on macabre.'

'You don't think any of this is odd?'

'Admittedly we peaked inside the bag and saw the stainless-steel lid marked for—' After a drawn-out silence, he spoke again. 'Listen, I've got a situation that's escalated. You've got your passport, use it.'

Scoffing at the abruptly disconnected call, she returned everything to its original harsh condition and put it back in the bag. 'Yeah, this game isn't over. Not by a long shot.'

Chapter 69

R udy's continued deception paled slightly when a text message advising the location of a private airfield and departure time came through. *A day early!* Her phone chimed again. An undisclosed number had left a blank text. Yasmin shivered, flicked back to the travel message and frowned when she read it properly.

Hope you have your passport ready and can travel light. Paddy has changed the itinerary. Expect an unconventional flight path. Wheels up in three hours.

They had to get ready to leave! Yasmin whistled for Combo. With every intention of travelling light and a serious amount of retail therapy at whichever destination, the bag would travel separately and Rudy's thick gold band would be secured by her watch strap. She whistled for Combo again. Her reply was a lot of playful, happy barking. Smiling bravely at her reflection, bade herself bon voyage and closed her bedroom door. Pausing halfway down the passage, she verbalised a prayer.

'Lord, please keep Combo and I safe while we hop on an aeroplane to somewhere I don't know with people I don't know at all. Amen.'

Waiting for her on the patio, a stocky woman crouched between Combo and Radar. Her face, alive with happiness, admired Yasmin unabashedly.

'Hi. My cousin Carl hoped you wouldn't mind too much?'

His face gave away a combination of guilt and relief.

A flood of emotions swept over Yasmin. 'Well, he is caretaking my property and knows the boundaries. Enjoy your catch up, but we really must fly!' Her excited giggle developing into unapologetic laughter. 'You coming with me, Combo?'

He rested his head upon the woman's shoulder and paw upon her muscly thigh.

With a wry grin, Yasmin asked Carl, 'Your cousin, huh?'

'Yes, Ma'am. I swear on my life.'

'As well as the other souls right here, right now?'

'Absolutely!'

'Okay, Carl's cousin, answer me this. You've worked with Combo and the other K9s before?'

Penny smirked. 'Yes. A long time ago, although my involvement is not common knowledge.'

'Best we keep it that way. Well then, I wish you both well, but I really must go. See ya, Radar. See ya, Combo. Be good boys.' She winked, spun on her heel, set the cottage's internal alarm and strode purposely towards her vehicle. No sooner had she clipped up her seatbelt, Combo bounded over her lap and sat on his seat. She had never seen his look of adoration so deep. With tears welling up, secured his harness, waved and shut her door.

Carl phoned as she raced down the driveway.

'Ma'am? You're speeding! Is everything okay?'

'Yes! I'm fine, thanks Carl. You two have fun!'

'Speed safely!'

'Of course I will. I've got treasured cargo onboard!'

'We need a lot of grass.'

'Get to it then.'

'Can I stay into the New Year?'

'You'll have to! Oh, that reminds me, I need to phone the ladies. Thanks Carl, take care ... hey ... where's Sergeant Kohli?'

'You ... brea ... up, Ma-Ma ...' His braying laugh was drowned out by her fake hilarity, and disconnected the call.

Lighthearted conversation, and the confirmation that a transforming hobby farm would be the venue for Christmas, completed the fast-paced drive to the designated tarmac with the call ending at the last click of the handbrake. Yasmin restrained the crazy-excited Combo and admired the pewter-toned sleek aircraft touching down as she walked away from the lock-up garage. When the plane turned down the taxiway, her laugh was as loud as it was genuine. Its nose cone livery was a very happy dog's face.

'Good timing! That's us, boy. The land o' swayin' palms awaits!' Combo enthusiastically wagged his tail, happily accepted a special treat and watered the lawn.

Several text messages had come through during her telephone conversation, the majority from Timmy. Another from him came through while she was catching up of which was promptly ignored. Dean's jubilation was unmistakable at her acceptance of his invitation for drinks with a date to be confirmed, but she pounced on the surprisingly accurate voice-to-text message from Paddy.

Aye, me lassie. Father and son invited me and Digby onboard a boat?! Let's surprise them.

She grinned and sent off her reply.

Aye, me Paddy, 'tis a grand plan. I be seein' ye.

She clapped her hands excitedly a few moments later.

Aye!

Once again, she relished the sunshine on her bare shoulders with the jersey-knit delicate floral halter-neck dress fluttering above her calves, but couldn't wait to kick off the new blister-forming sandals! The pair of happy travellers were escorted across the airfield's apron by a mature-aged couple wearing stylish turquoise and white uniforms and paw-print ties. Sasha and Tobias took turns in explaining their passion for flying, dogs, and appreciation of Paddy's business acumen; but most of all, treasured his friendship. At the foot of the stairs they chatted honestly about their concerns for expanding the fleet and would rather upgrade to a newer aircraft. They grinned at Yasmin's astonished look and assured her they discuss the matter freely with all their V.I.Ps, then chuckled when Combo found a lonely tuft of grass. All of a sudden, Rudy weighed her down.

'Was that a relieved chuckle?' she smirked and rested the bag on her carry-on.

Sasha giggled. 'Of course! Boy dogs don't usually squat very well on the mess-mat!'

Laughing away her embarrassment at not having to deal with any of the toilet training, asked, 'What if the pooches don't get along if there are more than one?'

'It's not the pooches we worry about ... it's their owners!' A distinguished older man smiled down at Yasmin. His brandy-gold eyes warmed her heart instantly.

'Hello there.' Her sighing smile escaped before she could do anything about it.

'Hello to you! I'm your pilot, Captain Pearson. You will meet wife, who is our co-pilot, once we're at cruising altitude.' He indicated the bag, 'I'll take that off your hands if you like.'

'Yes, please.'

'We thank you for flying with us. Let Combo sniff out his abode for the next long while. The screen will display our adventurous trip with reliable but unique destinations for fuel and obligatory crew rest. We will ensure our passengers have the optimum comfort at all times—'

Ecstatic barking filled the air.

'No!' The tears formed while she semi-stumbled up the stairs. 'Oh, Paddy!' and sobbed into his barrel chest.

'Come, me wee lassie. We be chasing de' sun en route to d' Bahamas wit' plenty o' time to talk.'

'What about Hawaii?'

'Dean be tellin' me o' some overdoo business. Let's be doin' dat first.'

She didn't have an opportunity to argue.

'This precious item will have almost the best seat in the house,' Captain Pearson winked.

No sooner were they at cruising altitude, Sasha handed her human passengers steamed face towels while Tobias poured coffees and positioned a platter of fruit and cheese and biscuits on the polished table between them. Then it was the pooches turn to be fussed over.

'Folks, the mild sedatives are taking effect so these gorgeous boys will be asleep soon,' Sasha said gently, then followed Tobias into the galley.

A tall lady with long ebony hair tied in a perfect French braid made her appearance with an air of calm and grace. When she spoke, her voice as smooth as melted chocolate with a hint of spice.

'Yasmin, we do hope you don't object to this wayward bum changing your itinerary! He was quite insistent.' The woman held out her graceful hand, 'Pleased to meet you, I'm Mrs Pearson.'

Yasmin chuckled and shook her hand. 'I'm delighted to meet you too and no objections at all! Thank you for ensuring the safety of the precious cargo you have onboard and the extra one!'

'On that note, if you'll both excuse me, I best return to my seat!'

She helped herself to a plate of fruit and pecked Paddy on the cheek.

'Aye, be off wit' ye!' he chuckled warmly.

When they were alone, Paddy spoke quietly, 'Yasmin? I be likin' dat name better!'

She nodded her head. 'Kimberly did what she had to do, but she couldn't have done it without you! You solved so many unanswered questions.'

'Me lassie, dat's as much as I be wantin' to know!'

His quizzical look made her smirk. 'But?'

'Best be tellin' me 'bout dis extra cargo?'

'Ashes of my estranged, unfaithful boyfriend. I think.'

'Aye, therein lies another tale for another time!'

They laughed long and hard, both in agreement that she ought to choose her words a bit more carefully should they be in mixed company. Relaxed in the reclining massage chairs, Yasmin broadly described the ownership arrangement of a yacht and her reluctance to be part of something that didn't rightfully include her.

'An' why is dat?'

'It's only got one sail!' The combined belly laughs woke their pooches, briefly. 'Paddy, I was very ignorant to a lot of things, but from what I have recently learnt there is a lot of money at play. And these lads aren't afraid of it either. Hell, they've got themselves a helicopter!'

By now, a rather broad grin creased his face. It was the first time she had noticed the two gold teeth that replaced his molars.

Bursting out laughing, tapped her mouth. 'You've got gold teeth!'

'Aye, lassie, told ye it was in me bones.'

Suppressing her giggle, listened attentively to the lure of a different bug.

Chapter 70

After several hours of chasing the sun, an open bottle of Glenfiddich Single Malt and two crystal glasses between them, they were presented with a mixed selection of hors d'oeuvres.

'Pure class, Paddy. Pure class!'

'Aye, not'in' but de best for de best, me wee lassie. We be doin' two o'vernigh' stays. De ladies be lookin' aft ye and de boys. Ye be doin' nay a t'ing.'

'Our lives are now in your hands!'

He poured two fingers each. 'I got sometin' to discuss wit' ye.'

'I'm all ears.'

In alternating accents explained new laws had been passed which deemed foreign property leases in Hawaii nigh on impossible to be extended, thus giving the locals more of an opportunity to invest in their own islands. Paddy was lucky that he and his father had been adopted by the local family when they employed the menfolk decades earlier, but any leases older than ten years were to be handed back to the local family immediately. Yasmin's crestfallen face caught him by surprise, until she explained about her inherited lease, found the document on her phone and showed him her lease agreement.

'Aye, lassie! That's me penthouse. I ne'er did see dat beautiful young lassie again. Snow White, me name fo' her.'

Yasmin bit back the tears and poured her heart out, only pausing when either Sasha or Tobias swapped out the bottle for water, snacks or coffee.

'T'is no wonder ye were 'appy wit' me evidence! Dean and 'erbie 'er kinfolk den?'

'Aye, Paddy.'

They got lost in their own thoughts for a long while, until she remembered how the conversation started.

Feeling as if a massive weight had been lifted off her shoulders, asked gently, 'What was it you wanted to discuss?'

'Excuse me folks,' Sasha interrupted, 'Paddy, if you would be so kind and assist Tobias with the gear for your stopover please.'

He stood and slid a pair of aviator sunglasses across the table, then swivelled Yasmin's seat towards the window. 'Wee lassie, ye be seein' the setting sun. Relax and enjoy de peace and quiet.'

The moment the dramatic colours dimmed, she was back beside the road all alone staring at a bare tree. Except this time the branches were towering clouds. Owen's question slammed into her thoughts as sudden as the turbulence brought her stomach up to her throat.

'Combo!' She spun around so fast, the rest of her body eventually caught up. Seat-belted in their suspended beds, the sleeping fur buddies were totally oblivious.

Sasha appeared out of nowhere and handed her a pretty seashell-print steamed face towel. 'Like a pothole, except you can't see them up here! How much sleep have you had recently?'

'Not enough.'

'Can I get you anything to help?'

Her head behaved like a rapid pendulum. 'No way. Thanks all the same.'

'Let me know. We overnight in a hangar using its facilities and sleep on board, although us ladies take it in shifts when there are V.I.Ps. It's all very safe.'

'What do the men do?'

She grinned, 'Catch up with their chums and Paddy usually hibernates for most of the second leg. He'll surface before we get to our final destination.'

'Ah, the real reason behind an unconventional flight path!'

'That's the beauty of having your own aircraft and crew.'

Yasmin smirked, 'And time, and money.'

'Interpreted as a compliment, else you two being onboard is from his generosity or history.'

'I like your candour, Sasha. Definitely complimentary. Let's sum it up as kindness.'

'Sounds good to me. It'll be a later start tomorrow and Mrs Pearson will be taking the controls initially. We won't be disembarking at our next layover, but you'll soon discover how comfortable and private these pods can be. I'll show you when we're on the ground.'

'I'm happy to help and learn—'

The seatbelt sign illuminated as subtly as its chime.

'Right. That's our cue. We are on the descent.' She nodded towards the pooches, 'We will all stretch our legs together on the ground, then you and Combo will have your own company for quite a while.

'Thank you.'

'You look relieved, are you okay?

'I will be. Will we have phone reception?'

Sasha smiled shyly. 'Sorry, it was remiss of me not to mention you didn't have any when you boarded. If it is urgent, we can use the satellite ph—.

'No! I'm fine with being uncontactable.'

As soon as she was alone, Yasmin faced the window and drank in the magnificence, murmuring, 'Oh look, I've done it again. Done what I was told to do and this time by Owen!' With a sarcastic sneer, silently mimicked his instructions. *You have a passport, use it.*

Descending through the misty clouds helped blanket the negativity. She closed her eyes. counted to three, opened them and grinned at the pretty lights dotting the landscape. 'Use my passport? Yessiree!'

Chapter 71

The officer tapped his pen in annoyance. 'Her mobile phones are still untraceable, Sergent Pyers, and no, her passport hasn't registered. The location of her van remains unknown. Please don't bog down the comms line. We will contact you with updates, when known, pronto.'

'Bloody hell,' he grunted after slamming down the receiver. Whipped it back up and dialled Carl's mobile.

'Hey Boss! What's up?'

'Is the top dog with you? Have you seen him lately?'

'No and no, Sir. Is everything okay?'

'Where's Ms Pestel?'

'Not here. She didn't have much luggage but I did recognise the bag that contained the ashes. Her and Combo—'

'Do you know where she went?'

'No. Sir?'

'Do you know who took her call the day the body was found?'

'Uh, no ... um, Sir? About Hillyer?'

'What about him?'

'The recollection of this has been making me sick.'

'Of what? Spit it out, lad.'

Carl outlined the day he challenged the forensic detective in the carpark because he had been recording registration plates.

'His attitude rubbed me up the wrong way, but then showed me video evidence of three familiar vehicles acting suspiciously. Two of them had tailed a pink van, the other had been doing burnouts near the vet's joint. I thought I recognised one of the drivers and saw red. We went through all the evidence records trying to find a correlation, without success, but he got excited when he found the data on the white BMW. He cross-referenced it with his findings and categorically stated his joy that they were related to the deceased when the scum took themselves out. He indicated he was one step closer to solving a cold case.'

'So, no bearing on the body out there?'

'None. But he was in our Station. Looking at our evidence. Our files. This is all on me. We even brought him here! He sat with you, and participated in the interview. I let the boogey-man in through the front door! Her front door!'

'Enough, son. Had you had anything to do with Ms Pestel and her dog before this?'

'No. A healthy respect for her business etiquette that's all, and she really does know how to grow nice roses!'

'Righto. I'll swing by one of these days.'

'Can I be useful, Boss?'

'No, Carl. You're on annual leave. Night.'

'Night, Sergeant Pyers.'

Owen gnawed at his bottom lip. While his mind churned over the initial question he asked Yasmin, he thought of another one. *What are you hiding, young lady?*

Chapter 72

Surrounded by clouds, Yasmin was as close to Emily as she was ever going to get. A solitary tear trickled down her cheek. The hours seemed to have flown by and she couldn't care less what the day or actual time was. Her watch had stopped at twelve past seven and didn't recall the last occasion she even looked at it. However, the presence of Rudy's gold band had left one too many indentions on her wrist. She had slept long and hard or short and fitful and twice woke up utterly disoriented. Combo had been there on each occasion and once had Digby nuzzling her foot. Sometimes she felt like she had been awake for days on end, alone with her mind and the enigmas tormenting it, inexplicably returning to Rudy's deception and the boogey-man. The scales just didn't balance.

Combo and Digby's recent aisle races, naughty agility course and tug-o-war had tuckered them out, and were airing themselves in the most undignified manner. Standing and doing some exercises herself, flicked through the aviator magazine laying on the table and forgot what she was doing when she turned to the centre spread. The side profile of a Gulfstream G800 dominating a bank of turbulent clouds took her fancy like nothing before.

'Ahem, wee lassie, 'ow you be?' Paddy's timely arrival buoyed her mood.

Pirouetting, showed him the picture. 'For the first time in my life I have no idea what day it is, and I'm not hungry for food!'

'I be likin' de way ye be t'inking.' He indicated the flight path displayed on the inbuilt screen to her right, 'We be nearin' our destination soon and be seein' Dean and 'erbie. Come, let's be seated, me bones ache.'

Tobias chuckled from the galley, 'It's more like your head, Paddy! You drank the bar dry.'

'Enou' o' ye!' he replied with a booming laugh, 'Ye look aft de pooches, we be landing in a wee while!'

He reminded Yasmin of their conversation before the first overnight stop, slid back the pocket door leading to front section of the aircraft and said, 'I present ye the meeting room. After ye!'

Yasmin did a doubletake and sat at one head of the intimate oval table. 'Now this is an office I could get used to. Can't beat these views through the panoramic oval windows!'

'Hah! Ye been reading! T''is is a good t'ing.' He sat opposite and looked at her levelly. 'I want to discuss livin' in de land of kangaroos. I done me 'omework, 'cept need a base initially. Plus, I jus' dis very minute decided I be needin' a silent business partner.'

'What sort of investment are you thinking of?'

'Hmm, I donnae be knowin' ye business, bu' 'ow 'bout I buy you out ... de yacht ownership, I be meaning? Our secret ... well, ano'er one!'

Contemplating the offer was easy with the birds eye view of the sea sparkling like a carpet of glitter. 'Paddy! You haven't even seen it but where do I sign?'

They shared a good laugh until she spoke again.

'Seriously though, if you think it's going to be a viable business opportunity I'm happy to negotiate. I will be honest with you though, I don't know what to expect at Emerald Bay. My adult life has been loaded with deception.'

'Wha' ha'e ye learn'.'

'Not to get my hopes up!'

'An' aft we see me beautiful island? Wha' den?'

'Invite you to join in the Christmas festivities and use my place as a base for as long you like. There's plenty of room for a motorhome and for Digby to run around in! We can talk serious business when I get back.'

'Ay? Wha' ye be up t'?'

Yasmin described her family and their love for the northern-hemispheric-snowcapped-living over anything else in the world; but she needed to see them.

'So, I'll be hiring your crew and magnificent aircraft for a ten-day trip somewhere in the icebergs. I'm also going to ask you to share Combo's company with my friends from the K9 Unit who you'll meet at Christmas!'

'Can ye make time t' be lookin' at aircraft?' He held out his bear-like hand.

She extended hers and prepared for a shake. 'Aye, 'tis a business trip, me pal!'

Instead, he rotated it and kissed it ever so gently. 'Aye, me wee lassie, ye an eart' angel if e'er d'ere was one.'

She turned to wipe away a stray tear with her shoulder. Her breath caught in her throat. The bird's eye view of the multi-millionaire's playground empowered her decision.

Twisting her hand, said, 'Paddy, let's shake on this silent partner thing right now!'

The twinkle in his eyes was as dazzling as the glint on his gold teeth.

The crew escorted the four very relaxed travellers to their adjoining suites overlooking the marina, then excused themselves.

'Aye, ye do what ye please,' Paddy encouraged them heartedly. 'Lassie, I be seein' ye on the morn. Best ye make de arrangements!'

'For tomorrow night?'

'Aye! Sleep well.'

'Aye, you too.'

The second her feet were free from the sandals, played zoomies with Combo around the suite. It was obscenely spacious, and she had never seen a bed so large, let alone the bathtub. After trying out each pillow she felt rather intimidated with the opulence and sent a message to Paddy.

Are you sure I should be in this suite? It's very flash.

His English reply made her burst out laughing.

Get used to it. I live like a king when I travel, so you should live like a queen when you do. Besides, if we be partners, what's good enough for me ought to be good enough for you. PS. Activate global roaming while we be here.

Accepting the suggestions graciously, took a very deep breath and phoned Dean. 'Hello there!'

'Well, this is a pleasant surprise! I've got company right now though,' he said animatedly.

'That's okay, is tomorrow afternoon too short of a notice?'

'Not at all! I'll send you the details. Thanks for calling. Bye.'

Grinning at their clandestine conversation, she was pretty confident she knew who was in his company. After a long, luxurious soak, communicated with Owen who hastily intimated their small world was now a far better place. She frowned in doubt.

Then Timmy phoned deepening the grooves.

'Hi there! It's been a while,' she said as pleasantly as she could.

'Hallelujah! She answers the phone. Where the hell have you been, Yasmin?' he demanded.

Seriously considering her response, counted to five. Then even slower to ten. 'Here, there and everywhere. And Timmy, change your tune because I will not dance to that number anymore.'

The silence was deafening. Eventually, in quieter voice he said, 'Whoa, I don't know how to respond to that.'

'You'll work it out, and here's what's going to happen tomorrow. I'll end up at Emerald Bay's Marina in the evening and would love to see you guys.'

'That's perfect, Yas! We've been … uh … we'll need to restock. I've got that beer for you.'

'Hey Mike, that's fantastic. Great to hear your voices and I know it'll be a cold ale! How's Bob?'

'Yas baby! I'm ready to give you that hug standing up.'

She squealed with delight. 'Bob! I am so looking forward to that and to seeing you all. Combo will be with—'

'And the ashes? Did you bring the ashes?' Timmy persisted.

'Yes, my friends. Um, can you tell me how this is all going to play out?'

'Uh yeah, about that,' he spoke authoritatively. 'We figured you should stand with Mr Taylor while Dean and Herbie scatter Emily's ashes, and us three and Col scatter the rest of the ashes. Hey … Dean doesn't know about this.'

Yasmin sighed softly and lowered her shoulders. 'Thank you, it'll all work out, I'm sure. Let's do this soon.'

'How about the day after tomorrow, Yasmin? I can call you with the details.'

'Sounds good.' She was busting to hear the lads' explanation and asked innocently, 'Hey, does *Cloud Nine* mean anything to you?'

'Oh Yasmin, we'll tell you all about it sometime. Us lads won't be on that one.'

She smirked. 'Ah, and it'll be safer for you all to be on a little yacht with one sail, will it?'

The explosive snorts and snickers stopped as suddenly as they had started.

'Hmm, okay,' she continued, 'so, when do we discuss the ownership details of CREAM?'

A deathly silence followed.

Timmy eventually spoke. 'Uh, yeah, about that. We need to have a formal meeting.'

'Tell you what, let's leave things as they have been until … hmm …late April early May next year.'

'Us three turn forty in May,' Mike said quietly.

'I know, and by then you'll have a formal agenda ready. Won't you?'

'You have been hiding your negotiation skills! Maybe we'll keep you on!'

'You don't think that should be the other way around?

'Yasmin, we've got another commitment so will have to cut this short.'

'Of course! We'll be together for a special rendezvous which—'

'Oh, that is for sure, Yasmin. We'll keep in touch.'

'Most definitely. I'll wait for your call, Timmy.'

'Race ya!' and the line went dead pretty much the same time.

Combo roused her at the same time Paddy's text came through.

Morn, Lassie. Let Combo in through the interleading door, I be taking dem for a walk. The nice café next door does all day breakfast. Say 30 mins?

Wrapping herself in the fluffiest white dressing gown imaginable, her feet disappeared into cloud-soft slippers. Combo was already waiting at the door yapping as impatiently as Digby on the other side when she opened it.

'Aye, ye be a dream walkin'!' Paddy grinned and the door closed.

Waiting for her nestled amongst a garden of palm trees and hibiscus shrubs, Paddy in a well-loved faded shirt and matching boardies, and a heavenly slice of Bahamian Rum Cake alongside a similar aromatic coffee. Both pooches greeted her warmly and gathered around her feet. The portion sizes were perfect to be savoured and devoured in time for the crew to join them and stay long enough for the women to announce they were taking in some retail therapy while the men dog-sat. Rejoicing in the fun company and falling in love with the tasteful fashion, Yasmin updated her wardrobe with a new outfit, swimsuit, hat, sunglasses and matching strappy sandals for every day of the following week.

'Aye, Paddy!' she cooed into the in-room telephone at half past three that afternoon. 'I'm to meet with Dean for drinks in forty minutes, will you be ready by then?'

'Aye lassie, ye be too cheeky, I leave ye 'ere!'

'Ye couldn't and ye know it.'

She was still giggling when they met in the foyer.

He kissed her hand and bowed graciously.

'Aye, lassie, ye said anytin' 'bout me?' he asked reservedly.

She patted his hand reassuringly and smiled. 'Nay, it'll be a beautiful surprise.'

Mr Taylor met them at the approach to Pier Seven wearing quite the tropical attire. The embrace was comforting and grandfatherly, with their secret agreement set deeply in stone. The two gentlemen hit it off instantly before the pooches led the way down the concrete jetty. Paddy was about to say something when Herbie came racing up towards them, laughing and crying at the same time. The poor lad didn't know who to greet first. Everyone talked at once but fell silent when they stood in awe of Cloud Nine. Her spectacular mother-of-pearl livery and chrome plated railings glistened beautifully under the afternoon sun, enhanced by her handsome captain beaming at the entrance of the Main Deck.

'You scallywag, Yasmin Rose! You are all welcome aboard Cloud Nine. Three decks of magnificence,' Dean said and hugged her tightly when he got down the external spiral staircase.

The greeting he and Paddy shared was tear jerking.

'Aye, me lad, 'tis good to be seeing' ye.'

'You too, Pops.'

Dean swept her into his arms once more and held her tightly, whispering in her ear, 'Thank God for you. I am eternally grateful to you, Yasmin Rose Pestel. Please don't say anything just accept my indebtedness graciously.'

She returned his hug with gusto, craning her neck out from under his arm to stare wide-eyed at how well money could be spent.

Drinks and tapas adorned the mirrored cocktail bar on the Lower Deck amid shared stories, laughter, tears and fears, and more laughter watching the sun sink closer to the horizon. Herbie enthusiastically described how he automatically became a nephew when his father and the lads had reconnected, then excused himself to go and play hide-and-seek with the pooches onboard.

Paddy broadly talked about the death of his son which had the instant testosteronal effect of male bonding. It was at that moment Dean insisted his guests be on Cloud Nine for the spreading of Emily's ashes. He wasn't met with any opposition, only watery smiles.

Smirking at the noisy arrival of his son and dogs, said, 'Listen, Col loves dogs, but the lads don't seem to share his passion, so *if* we are onboard CREAM, which is very much a bachelor pad ...'

Herbie mischievously giggled when he described the calendar girls to Paddy.

Dean smirked, '... I'm willing to bet the pooches won't be the only ones to stay on the Lower Deck. On Cloud Nine, all my guests are free to make themselves at home, even if you're staying afloat!'

Herbie's jubilation encouraged both dogs to yap happily.

'Ah, Dean, that's very kind of you but we're sorted with accommodation, thank you. On a slightly more serious matter, Timmy indicated he would send me the details of where to meet. But either he's forgotten or he's preoccupied.' Yasmin chuckled quietly, 'You see, I told him I don't dance to his tune anymore.'

Mr Taylor's explosive laugh created a domino effect while Dean picked up the inter-vessel intercom.

'Ahoy, Timmy, I have a long-lost friend I want you lads to meet and he's a big eater, and I mean a big eater, plus he's got a dog much to Herbie's delight. So, what time would you like us for dinner tonight and can I bring extra for the table?'

Yasmin smirked and left the men with it. She found her way into the main lounge on the Top Deck and burst into tears.

'Aye, wee lassie, why d' tears?' Paddy called softly from the shadows.

She sniffled, 'Oh Paddy. I haven't paid you for anything yet.'

'Ye nay be payin' me for anyt'in', 'tis I who owes you!'

'But I feel so out of place!'

'Wah? Wit' all t'is love 'round ye? Aye, me petal, Snow White loved ye, accep' dat gift. Ye bes' be wearin' a smile and drink it in like a fine drappy! B'sides, ye be the only one who can allow money to change ye, it cannae be de ot'er way 'round.'

A delicate whiff curled around Yasmin's shoulders. 'Aye,' she said putting her hand against her right cheek.

'Dat's me wee lassie!'

Paddy gallantly offered his forearm and escorted her to the spiral staircase, meeting Mr Taylor halfway up. His look of tenderness almost undoing Yasmin's brave face.

'Come my dear, the lads are waiting. Lighten up, everything is going to be okay. I promise you.'

'We need to have a chat, Mr Taylor.'

'What's been said and done has been said and done, my dear. We're onto the next chapter in our lives now.'

'Me lassie, dis is a wise man!'

Standing on the concrete pier, Dean, Herbie, Combo and Digby waited patiently for the three to turn up.

Soon, Yasmin was alone on the deck and the burdensome bag by her feet. 'I'm not going.'

'Why?' Herbie asked before the men opened their mouths, and jumped back onboard.

She caressed his shocked face and said tenderly, 'Herbie, sometimes some people forget to do something they said they would do. And this time, it is Uncle

Timmy. He knew I was coming, and he said he would send me details so we could meet. Well, he hasn't. So, I am not going.' Then she smirked. 'Do they know I am here? Right here? Right now?'

His youthful face came alive with the murmured negative replies. 'Hey! Let's play a prank. SEEstA. You and Combo hang back out of sight. Dad, yeah, yeah ... Dad, you say something like how nice it would be if this lovely lady were here. Then we make Uncle Timmy feel real baaaaad.' He raised his hands above his head like a monster.

'Aye, me boy! I hereby be ye grand papee!'

'You have been since my fifteenth birthday!' He fist-punched the air with his crippled hand.

Dean's phone rang, interrupting the nonsense. 'We're on our way now, mate ... he'll eat anything ... yeah, Herbie will look after his dog. Yeah, yeah, they'll stay close to the Lower Deck.' He grinned, slipped his phone into his trouser pocket and gave them the thumbs up.

Yasmin and Combo walked several metres behind the group, stopped, watched, and repeated the process until the commencement of Pier Eleven. Under the shrouded orange light cast upon the white-washed pylons and concrete pier, they watched Herbie and Digby circle each other, disappear for a minute then jump down, play chase, then jump up and disappear again. Yasmin took her cue and stood in the shadow two feet away from CREAM's polished stainless-steel duckboard, agog at the floating castle she part owned. Combo nestled in close to her legs and sighed heavily.

'Pssst,' Herbie whispered and giggled. 'Uncle Timmy gasped so hard he almost swallowed his tongue.'

Yasmin grimaced. 'It ain't a pleasant feeling!'

'It was funny but! You should have seen Uncle Mike and Uncle Bob's faces! Priceless, SEEstA! Put your phone on silent and answer it just before it goes to message-bank. He's gonna phone you soon. Answer him loud enough so he can hear you but don't use the phone.'

'What do you mean?'

'You'll see ... shush, look up, it's all planned.'

Shortly afterwards, Yasmin could just make out Timmy's head moving back and forth. He stopped, massaged his back against the railing and ran his hand through his hair. She could hear her own phone ringing. *Of course he's got it on speaker! Of course they have the biggest boat!*

Yasmin counted the buzzes then answered loudly. 'Hi Timmy.'

He spun around, looked downwards, dropped his phone in fright and wailed. Seconds later, Mike and Bob almost fell over the railing when they saw the mischievous cause of the commotion.

The emotional eruption kicked off a very good night. Men on the rear deck of CREAM, woman, child and dogs seated comfortably on the pier.

Much later, Yasmin joined the three lads on scattered cushions overseeing Herbie snoozing with the dogs on a blanket, still on the pier. Uproarious laughter drifted from the upper deck's theatre room. Bob gently explained the décor would need to be adjusted before they gave her a tour.

'Next year will be fine, thanks! I'm comfortable here. Have you guys always been in the boat business?'

Timmy scoffed, 'Luxury mega-yacht business is more like it. Hell, you really were kept in the dark!'

'Appears that way. Nevertheless, here you go.' She handed him the bag.

Making quite the show of removing the contents, Timmy's crestfallen face caught her by surprise.

'What's wrong?'

'He made it for your attention?'

'And?'

Mike interjected carefully. 'He actually made it easier for Yas to collect. You recall how Rudy wanted to be anonymous, Timmy? Bob?'

Grunting their acknowledgement, the three men stared at the cold vessel.

'You playing games with us, Yasmin?'

'Hardly. You're up.'

They coughed and either busied themselves with pouring a drink, adjusting their shirts or combing their hair.

'SEEstA, I'm taking the pooches for a walk!' Herbie's melodic voice, a pleasant interlude.

'Wait for me!'

***

'What the hell game is she playing?' Timmy moaned.

'Rudy's game,' Bob reminded him.

'Nah. He would have given us a clue. How was she ever going to work out how to open this?'

'You reckon she has?'

Mike chuckled. 'Yep. Still reckon we should have brought her into the fold yonks ago. For all we know she can probably weld!'

Timmy held the box to the light and swore loud enough for the other two to tell him to be keep it down.

'There's a bloody hole in the bottom? Do you think she would have drilled it?'

'Come on, Timmy. You've had too much to drink,' Mike scoffed.

***

The three older men took a sleepy Herbie and the pooches back to Cloud Nine. Hearing her full name being yelled, jogged back to CREAM.

'Hey lads, do you mind? This joint doesn't need to know my name!'

'Did you open it?'

'Yes! It was for my attention. The last piece of the puzzle. You ought to know the rules of Rudy's game seeing you were the ones who told me about it.'

'Come on, Yasmin, how the hell did *you* get into that box?'

She joined them on the floor around a chrome coffee table. 'Pay attention.'

They watched in stunned silence when she removed Rudy's thick gold band from her watch strap leaving her wrist bare. Their eyes widened in horror when she spun the jewellery on the tabletop.

'That is not a toy, Yasmin.'

Without responding, she spun it several more times, then let it wobble and rest quietly on its side after the last spin.

'Now that I've shown you what to do, you have to do the same because the ring fits into the groove. Shouldn't be a problem for you guys, you knew Rudy better than me!'

They stared at her aghast.

Giggling as she got up, she blew them each a kiss. 'Send me a photo of where it rests, please.'

'Why, Yas baby?'

'Rudy insisted he be set free at Emerald Bay and to be left on CREAM.' She dusted her hands. 'I have finished this game. Night lads, see you tomorrow.'

Her ringing phone woke her rudely at five past two the following morning. Seeing Dean's name come up, answered it immediately. 'Everything okay?'

'Uh yeah, but the lads are getting really frustrated and really drunk. They even asked for my help to get this bloody ring into the groove.'

Yasmin chuckled in disbelief. 'Really? They've been at it for hours!'

'Yeah, tell me about it! I can't keep up with their thirst. What's the secret?'

'What are they trying to do?'

'Spin it on the table and put the box on it when it falls over, but they keep missing!'

Burying her loud guffaw into the pillow, eventually managed to speak clearly. 'Just tip the box upside down and push it in!'

'You have got to be kidding.'

'It really is that simple!'

'You are nonsense, Yasmin Rose!'

She giggled. 'Again, you're almost calling me by my full name, so I'm almost in trouble! But can you quell your mischievous nature?'

His husky chuckle gave her goosebumps.

'Hey Dean, let me know what you think but don't be sad when it's all about the lads.'

'I wouldn't expect anything else. A million thanks.' he laughed loudly. 'Pardon the shortfall in the pun! See you in the sunshine. Good night.'

The sparkling morning sun's path adorned the splendid Cloud Nine. Her design depicted Emily in every exquisite feature, enchanting Yasmin who eventually found her way back up to the Bridge. There, she cradled her dearest friend's ashes housed in a beautifully tall mother-of-pearl and white gold sealed vase. Biting back a sob when she saw Herbie's impression of Monet's Water Lilies encased in a delicate white-gold frame, she sniffled and snuffled at the Yorkshire Terrier looking at its reflection in the still water.

'It was in the mail you gave us,' Dean said quietly, and squeezed her shoulder in comfort. 'Herbie selected the frame.'

'Great choice! He truly has a remarkable talent. Nurture it.'

'Here, stand in front of the wheel and look downwards ... ahem ... without you, all this would never have happened.'

She accepted his extended hand and did as he suggested. Embossed into the centre of the Mahogany inlaid wheel was the repaired three-strand pearl, five-studded emerald bracelet.

'Oh Dean, it's perfect!'

He had to clear his throat several times, squeezed her hand and reluctantly let it go. 'I had a feeling you'd say that! The lads decided it belonged to Emily and sought my permission. When Cloud Nine is in dry dock, her wheel comes with us.'

'As it should!'

'Uh, they'll be shy of you today. Their egos are massive!'

She covered her mouth in mock surprise. 'No!'

'Uh, his containment ... uh ... keepsake is unusually small.'

'Yes, I thought the same thing.'

They lost themselves in each other's gaze until Herbie's wail shattered the intimacy. Yasmin tore down the stairs to see Col stepping out of an ambulance.

'It's Mr Taylor!' Herbie sobbed as he ran past her. 'Where's my dad?'

'Behind me.' With her hand pressed to her mouth, she raced to catch up to Col. 'What happened?'

'He'd been complaining of indigestion since before we left. I told him it was his heart talking. Stubborn old coot. I'll go with him. The lads don't need me for a few days.'

Yasmin didn't wait for permission and stepped inside. 'Please let me talk to him. I've known him since I was a kid.'

'Be quick.'

She smothered her gasp at his grey complexion, clutched his hands and put her face close to his. 'Mr Taylor, it's me. Yasmin. I love you.'

Tears trickled down his aged face. She wiped at them more gently than her own.

He took her hand and put it on his hip. 'Po-po-ck ...' His eyes closed.

A dreadlocked paramedic spoke firmly. 'Miss. We got to go.'

Yasmin slipped her hand inside the dying old man's pocket and felt a sliver of a note. Leaning over, kissed his forehead gently. 'Go well, Mr Taylor. Thank you for being in my life.'

Col's stern voice cut through the screeching siren. 'Ms Pestel. Time to leave.'

She looked at him desperately. 'Keep in touch, please.'

'You understand it'll be through the lads.'

'Wouldn't expect anything else.'

Chapter 73

A sparkling day marred with pending sadness; only the deep blue of the sea's ombre transition into emerald-coloured waters kissing the pristine white beach brought about a small smile. Yasmin now realised why Paddy's flight crew wore a similar coloured uniform. Even the bathers she wore matched the environment perfectly. If it weren't for her farmer's tan, she'd disappear into it.

Timmy's voice, thick with emotion, burst through Cloud Nine's radio advising the waypoint. The two vessels were to be anchored at a depth of sixteen fathoms and five metres apart.

Instantly Yasmin teared up and murmured with a wisp of a smile, 'Appropriate figures.'

Herbie clutched Paddy's shoulder, did the honours of explaining the relevance to him and continued to talk. 'Grand Papee, I took the liberty of suggesting we have a candle for all our dearly departed. I'm sorry about your son. Dad told me. He would have his wings by now and is going to meet a very kind lady, one I had the privilege of knowing.'

Yasmin wiped at the onset of tears and nodded in silent agreement. No truer words had been spoken.

With the Lower Deck of Cloud Nine comfortably occupied; her and Combo, and Digby and Paddy stood either side and slightly behind Dean and Herbie who eventually got Emily's vase open.

On CREAM, six lit candles flickered on the elevated table behind the lads each holding an urn. Everyone raised a glass of their preferred beverage and sang Amazing Grace. Its strains being sung and hummed while the ashes found their own paths. Afterwards, Paddy's rich, benevolent voice drifted across the gentle translucent waters between the vessels in prayer. Alternating between English and a foreign dialect, heart-wrenching. The moment a unified Amen was murmured, a single dolphin swam between the yachts. Its calming presence leaving not a dry eye.

On the seashore of a small uninhabited island, the newly established, disjointed family sealed its bond with a co-joined celebration of life sharing in happy memories, and prayed for Mr Taylor. Bob discretely showed Yasmin a photo of the pride of place of Rudy's thick gold band. In the centre of their gold-plated wheel. They gulped in unison, wiped at their tears and nodded knowingly.

But it was swimming in the shallows that changed Yasmin's perspective. It confirmed her affirmation that she and Combo would have a beach hut. Somewhere. And could get to it quickly. They were alive and life was for living. Smirking at the realisation of what she could achieve, had to cover her mouth whenever someone looked her way.

Paddy had a similar problem. He spoke quietly while their pooches chased the waves. 'Aye, lassie, I be ha'in' a question for ye,'

'Fire away!' She watched an aircraft fold its wheels, and chuckled. *Yeah, that's the go.*

'Definitely de air?'

Sighing happily, 'Absolutely.'

'Aye, music to me ears!'

'You know something, Paddy ... with your looks and my money, we could go places.'

'Nae, me lassie, wit' *me* money and *your* looks, *we* could go further!'

His booming laugh was contagious.

On the return journey to the marina, Herbie had a rematch of hide-and-seek with Combo and Digby. Yasmin eventually joined Paddy and Dean in the Bridge. Lost in their own thoughts, they were jolted back to reality when Timmy's voice burst through the speakers at the same time Herbie yelled excitedly.

'Dad! Dolphins! They're everywhere.'

'Ahoy, Cloud Nine! Seems as if we're blessed with dolphins today. We are surrounded by the playful things.'

'*Blessed.* That could be the name of Paddy's new aircraft!' Dean replied, high spirited.

'Yeah! The dolphin of the air,' Timmy laughed raucously.

'Best not porpoise at 25,000 feet, Yasmin Rose has just turned green.'

The laughter and conversation continued by way of the captains' mobile phones on speaker, with Paddy noncommittal on the type of aircraft until he had spoken with his silent partner.

Swapping places with Herbie and Digby, she lazed around on the deck chairs with her best friend, relishing in the safety and company of some very special souls. *Made it to Emerald Bay. Next stop, Hawaii. Bless you, Emily.*

She couldn't wipe the grin off her face and slid into the plunge pool. Combo, seeing the small coloured ball bobbing, belly-flopped and yapped at the splashes he continued to make. The ball long forgotten. He dog-paddled over to her and rested his paws on her shoulders. His happy face bringing tears of joy to her eyes. When he lowered his head allowing her to noisily pretend-kiss the tuft of hair between his ears, she received a long overdue puppy sigh.

'Love you too, boy.' Then, she gasped, 'Oh my God! The note.'

Scrambling out of the pool, she ignored the buzzing phones, rummaged around for her shorts, found the piece of paper, and shook uncontrollably.

I lied. Ru alive.

Racing to hang over the rails, she barfed. The wind caught the note. All she could hear were the mobile phones. Buzzing. Chiming. Buzzing. Combo's spraying shake and yap drowned out by the sea in her ears. Her name echoed in her head. Stumbling back to her bag, reached for the phones. Trance-like, sat with her legs dangling over the yacht's side. Phones in hand. Flipped them both screen-side up. The identical unfamiliar mobile number. The identical text message displayed.

R U PERT?   RJM x

A hand gripped her shoulder. She screamed and dropped the phones. In slow motion, they tumbled, clipped the side rail and fell into the sea. Lost. Forever.

Chapter 74

Penny smiled, wiped a tear and switched off the tracking software. Her Pooch was certainly having a well-deserved rest. *Sweet justice.*

With a face like a thunder cloud, Sergeant Kohli's mood reflected in his single knock.

She looked at him steadily. 'Thank God you're back! You know the fake detective and Leigh—'

He put his hand up stopping her mid-sentence. 'I joined the dots with the other names, but Rupert? Where did that come from?'

'Couldn't say. Where did you disappear to?'

'There was an accident at a workplace.'

'What? Like a hit?'

'Couldn't say. Where's Pyers?'

'In Adelaide. An investigation board was discovered at a homicide with pictures of him, you, Carl, some Goth chick and several known suspects linked together like string art, originating from a picture of Ms Pestel talking to a bloke in a paddock.'

'Hey? The body that was taken away?'

'Nobody knows who took that body away.'

'So Hillyer isn't ... wasn't the boogey-man?'

'Who knows now. He's gone missing. But of course you wouldn't know anything about that would you Sergeant Kohli?

'That's right. So where is Rudy Craige?'

'Probably drifting in the wind somewhere.' Penny cleared her throat, wriggled the mouse and said, 'Do you feel up to selecting another K9 for Special Ops?'

'Yeah. In a minute. Where's Ms Pestel and Combo?'

'Lost the trace.'

'And the pilot?'

'Oh, he ended up doing what he always wanted to do and that was flying rich bums around the world!'

They nodded.

Penny tipped her head and rubbed her nose.

'You have another question for me?' he asked her quietly.

She winked. 'Yes. Any idea where I can get a massive bunch of roses from, Sir?'

The big man chuckled, 'Sure do. You can even pick them yourself!'

Nothing more was said about what was, or what was going to be. Like always, they accepted that whatever would be, would be.

Chapter 75

Coming to with a dog either side of her and Herbie's concerned mouth moving like a mute, the text seared Yasmin's mind.

R U PERT? RJM x

'Dad! Grand Papee! She's awake!'

Yasmin sat bolt upright. 'Hell's teeth. What happened?' Both dogs rested a head on each knee.

'Dunno, SEEstA! We heard Combo's crazy barking. Me and Digby found you lying on the deck!'

'Who squeezed my shoulder?'

'Huh? Dunno! Only you and Combo were down here.'

She looked around, noticed her bag was open where she'd left it and bit her lower lip. Dean stepped off the last rung and looked at her with a concerned frown.

'Please pass me my bag.'

'Herbie, go and help Grand Papee stay on course please.' The moment he was out of earshot, Dean said, 'You look like you've seen a ghost!'

'I think I felt one. I may even have heard one! Anyone know how Mr Taylor is? Where's CREAM?'

'Whoa, slow down. Why's your bag open?'

'I-I ...' she ratted through the contents. 'I lost my phones.'

'Back on the island?'

'No. Overboard.'

He helped her stand and led her to a bar stool. 'More shopping for you then! Listen, CREAM's motored on ahead. Col phoned. I'm sorry, but Mr Taylor's gone.'

She sobbed into the back of her hand. 'I would like to drink to him, care to join me?'

'No, I have two inexperienced shipmates steering Cloud Nine back to the marina. Combo and Digby won't be leaving your side any time soon!' He left a bottle of Jameson and two glasses on the countertop. 'What do you want to do?'

'Go to Hawaii.'

She didn't know how long she'd been sitting staring at nothing at all or if Dean had even heard her. Tackling the latest puzzle, mentally opened the dictionary to the word 'PERT' while pouring a couple of fingers. Yasmin knew of several definitions; *bold, chic, small and firm, in good health*. She was all of them. But nothing made sense. And now Mr Taylor, the man with the answers, had died. The first mouthful clawed at the back of her throat and burnt all the way down.

Paddy's quiet whistle interrupted her train of thought. 'Aye, me lassie, sorry for ye loss.'

Nodding and pouring him a dram, 'Here's to the man of the hour. May he rest in peace.' *If only you hadn't lied.*

'Did ye say somet'ing else?'

She let the alcohol numb her mouth before replying, 'I don't want to stay here for much longer, Paddy. Too many li-lives in one place.'

He reached for his phone, spoke in a foreign tongue.

Moments later, said, 'Aye, we farewell these two tonight and be off on the morrow. Do ye nee' t' talk t' d' lads?'

Yasmin's smile was as distant as her gaze, 'Ask me again in April next year.'

'To Hawaii?' he asked gently and raised his glass, breaking her reverie.

They clinked their glasses.

'To Hawaii.'

Also by Lorie Brink

True To Her Word
Insatiable Curiosity
Vehemence – an anthology
Gunnie's Last Round
Operation Incapacitate